WHERE I MUST GO

Peace,
Angela
Jackson

Where I Must Go

A Novel

ANGELA JACKSON

TRIQUARTERLY BOOKS

NORTHWESTERN UNIVERSITY PRESS

EVANSTON, ILLINOIS

TriQuarterly Books
Northwestern University Press
www.nupress.northwestern.edu

All song lyrics reprinted by permission of the Alfred Publishing Company and the Hal Leonard Corporation. Credits to copyright holders on page 385.

Printed in the United States of America

10 9 8 7 6 5 4 3 2 1

This is a work of fiction. Characters, places, and events are the product of the author's imagination or are used fictitiously and do not represent actual people, places, or events.

LIBRARY OF CONGRESS CATALOGING-IN-PUBLICATION DATA

Jackson, Angela, 1951–
    Where I must go / Angela Jackson.
      p. cm.
    A novel.
    ISBN 978-0-8101-5185-7 (trade cloth : alk. paper)
    1. African Americans—Social conditions—1964—1975—Fiction. 2. Civil rights movements—United States—Fiction. I. Title.
    PS3560.A179W47 2009
    811.54—dc22

2009008620

∞ The paper used in this publication meets the minimum requirements of the American National Standard for Information Sciences—Permanence of Paper for Printed Library Materials, ANSI Z39.48-1992.

For

Mama
Angeline Robinson Jackson
1921–

Madaddy
George Jackson Sr.
1921–1993

Mr. Fuller, mentor
Hoyt Williams Fuller
1923–1981
whose graces endow

and for

Debra Anne Jackson
sweet.angel.sister
1958–2008

CONTENTS

ACKNOWLEDGMENTS

I began writing and rewriting *Where I Must Go* in 1969 as part of what would be a trilogy. I have many people to thank, but can thank only a few here.

My thanks to Reginald Gibbons (and Cornelia Spelman), who reaffirmed my fiction in 1984. Reg was a great editor and even greater friend to the final revision of this novel; his insights and knowledge guided me through the delicate task of the last revision.

My thanks to Susan Bradanini Betz, who relentlessly shepherded the manuscript through the process of acceptance at Northwestern University Press.

My thanks to the staff of Northwestern University Press for their excellent attention to my work. Most especially I appreciate the meticulous care and skills of Anne Gendler, Katherine Faydash, Jess Biscamp, Jenny Gavacs, Dino Robinson, Parneshia Jones, Amanda DeMarco, and Mike Levine.

My thanks to Carole A. Parks, who, with Hoyt Fuller, first affirmed the fiction of a young poet.

To D. L. Crockett-Smith (Vivian Cooke-Buckhoy), Eleanor Hamilton, Eliot Anderson, Peter Michelson, Jennifer Moyer, Terry McMillan, Marie D. Brown, Fred Gardaphe, Lerone Bennett Jr., Useni Eugene Perkins, Woodie King Jr., Haki (Safisha) Madhubuti, Pamela Cash, Mari Evans, Toni Morrison, and Gwendolyn Brooks for their belief in my work.

Always, for joy and encouragement and support in so many ways, my siblings: George Jackson (Leslie), Delores Jackson Wolfley, Rosemary Jackson Lawson (William) for singular research, Sharon Jackson Sanders, Betty Jackson Uzzell (Thomas), Margaret Jackson Stewart, and Prentiss Jackson (Cynthia Henderson) for unflagging technical support.

Also, for technical support: Richard Foster, Marcel Dillard, Ricochelle Faulkner, Melissa Smith, and Joanna Johnson.

To Roella Christine Davis, Jacqueline Y. Collins, and Janet Sankey, my college roommates, with whom I shared adventures that are not in these pages.

To sister and brother writers: Janet Pena Davis, DFaye Anderson, Sarah Odishoo, S. Brandi Barnes, Collette Armstead, Soyini Madison, Melvin Lewis, Meta Commerse, Runako Jahi, Ana Castilo, Leslie Adrienne Miller, Gretchen Wahl, Nora Brooks Blakely, Debbie Wood Holton, Patricia Spears Jones, and Joyce Carol Thomas, who believed in this story from its first version.

To guiding lights: Ann Smith, Abena Joan Brown, and Jeff R. Donaldson, visual artist, teacher, and friend.

Thanks and Praise.

Parts of this novel, sometimes in different versions, appeared in *TriQuarterly, First World, StoryQuarterly, Chicago Review, Open Places, Breaking Ice, The Writer in Our World, Chicago Works,* and *New Chicago Stories.*

A portion of the work for *Where I Must Go* was done with the help of a National Endowment for the Arts Creative Writing Fellowship and an Illinois Arts Council Creative Writing Fellowship. I am grateful for their support.

WHERE I MUST GO

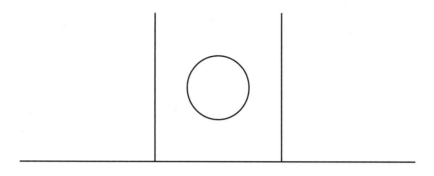

Prologue

Treemont. Treemont Stone. He recalls his name to me. They call him "Tree" or "Stone." I call him in my laughter. My name is Magdalena Grace. He wants to call me Amazing Grace. A man wants to change my name. I tell him I been too long to come by this. He lifts me up in laughter. I am myself. I can see myself.

A body: it is a mosaic made of colors, shapes, designs, textural arrangements, symmetries, studies in contrasts that collide, oils and water that hug like sweat. At last, I am all these forms meshed so fine, so skillfully, that I am feeling. At last, I am so lovely I can touch myself, marvel, be stunned and curious and calm.

I am a portrait that is my mother's twin in the early shadow of decades. I am a clock struck in hands. But more, I am a face that watches time. I am a sculpture made of clay gathered from impoverished resourceful earths of a big womb, with eyes. And heart, organs, and breasts and brain. Inside my skin all these women and men.

At last, he lifts me up; at last, I weigh a fortune in the dull dark gold of my flesh. I weigh a ton of honey. Light enough for him to lift. I look down at him. I look up and around. I pull him into my hands. "Let me." I am tellin him in a voice of so much honey and anchovy (fish and worn salt). What I be sayin is this: You have to know who I am. You have to know. How much I am of you already. There are stories you have to know. There are things I have to tell you.

What I mean to say is this: I am a creature full of caresses. Untidy with eyes of their locked lusts. A sea grinding its own stones for resilient sand and secret bones to salt a spicy weeping. Again, I am a woman unwise with slow aromas, with thighs for aching stalks and hip cradles for arcs. Arms circling in some forgotten geometry of fusion. In answer, I am not all for givings. My ivories are fondled cool with primitive hungers soaked in my mother's broken waters of wishing and polished in her reticence. She and I vagrant in a cloth feminine with masks. I am a creature husky with history, caresses, and mad with aromas.

What I be sayin is myths and fables and lies; rumors of war and physical pain and pestilence; humor and wisdom and love-liness. My imagination and my seven madnesses. The people I come from and for, to him where I go. What me remains is true to them. I be sayin all these women and men, spirituals, rhythm and blues, and jazz.

At long and last I make my arts and biological sciences for him. He eats my flowing mouth and I pour out my eyes for him to drink. I give him my cartilage for jelly.

His skin is tight as stone. His facial bones a dignified study in angles and wood. His free African hair nests out into the air. Moustache moves across the top of his mouth when he speaks. Every now and then his lean leaning body rustles while he listens.

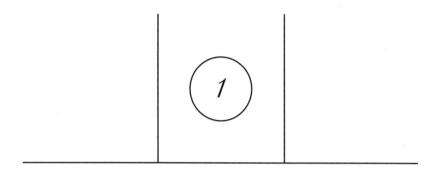

Eden Bound

Now my father picks up the heaviest suitcase and takes it to his car. He is humming under his breath. His eyes distracted with some private dream. I carry the next suitcase and my mother takes the hair dryer and typewriter and places them in the backseat, where I will sit. She is efficient and nervous. Something in her twittering. Checking everything twice. My way is hers, so I take the letter from the Eden University Student Housing Office and read it again, even though I could probably recite it by now. The letter said incoming freshmen (that's me!) must arrive at their residential halls by 9:00 P.M., Sunday, September ——, 1967. The brochure "Your College Room and You" that had come with the summons had thrilled me as I lay across my parents' bed and read it three times back-to-back. It was paradise Eden University promised. There was a bed up there for me and me alone. A dresser and a desk. No more homework on the kitchen or dining room table. No more drawing in the bathroom with a brother or sister banging at the door. No more mile-long treks to the library in the corpse-cold dead of winter. Eden University beckoned warmly, and I scrambled toward it. I do not want to be late for the heaven of home away from home.

Last year my brother Lazarus, who used to be Littleson, got in trouble just by running home at dusk. Two policemen, one White, one Negro, stopped him in his fast gait. They said, "Hey, you," and "Over to the squad car."

After they beat him, they put him in the lockup. He made one phone call. Mama put on her heels and stomped down to the police station. Madaddy left the three-to-eleven shift to get his second son out of jail.

At the station house Lazarus wanted to meet the Negro policeman outside, but Mama said no. When they all got home, a window broke from the inside. No one had laid a hand on it. Screaming pummeled the walls.

"But I wasn't doing nothing," Lazarus hollered till veins big as cobras trembled in his neck and temples.

"What you want me to do?" Lazarus hollered at Mama and Madaddy, who were harsh and upset because he'd gotten into trouble and almost stayed there, beyond the wringing of hands. "You want me to let him beat me to death?" Lazarus's outrage hammered in my chest so hard I could hardly breathe. I wanted to scream with him. "I can't let nobody kill me, Mama. I'm a man." Lazarus is a man.

"I didn't say, 'Let somebody kill you,' Lazarus." Mama fidgeted guiltily and soothed conciliatorily. "Just calm down."

"Shut up," Madaddy hollered at Lazarus. "I had to take off work for this mess."

"Just be quiet now, Lazarus," Mama urged.

"If I'd let that policeman beat on me and keep kicking me I'd be quiet all right."

"If you'd a been on time for work you wouldna been runnin late and you wouldna been running and you never woulda been in trouble." Madaddy heaved the judgment across two rooms. That was it. Lazarus should have known to stay out of trouble. It was all his fault. He should have known. We all should have known. We'd seen trouble coming. Our father tried to tell us with his harsh protection and fierce law that trouble was coming to us the day we were born. Like a fist directed at a dark face, you know it's coming so you damn well better duck.

Every traveler knows that a part of you goes even before the body follows. Some quick, breathless piece of the soul dances down the road before the body starts lumbering liltingly behind, and then, curiously, the same part or its sibling self lingers in the footprints or wheel marks that we leave behind. So my vanguard self is moving away. Moving away from this house of grace and all my noisome and pretty sisters, away from my brothers, away from this street called Arbor after the many, many trees that used to live here before we did and the fewer trees that remain, away from the kitchen smells, and the sirens and the street games and the hopscotch marks on the sidewalk. Away from my mother and father. Away from the Missionary Baptist church next door where we went to youth meetings on Saturdays and the Catholic church and school on the corner where we went every day.

There in grammar school some boys with jokes and tricks up their sleeves refused to be desked beside me—the party pooper who was never in trouble. My one known transgression against goodness—tardiness, chronic and nerve-racking. In first grade I tagged behind the line of the last class to enter the school doors from the playground, behind the seventh and eighth graders, and the seventh- and eighth-grade teacher, Sister Bernard, who wobbled like a fat pigeon on too-short legs beside Sister Callista, the principal, fierce and scatter toothed.

Sister Callista espied me, a little first grader in a red hat with a brim and built-in ear coverings I could hear very well through. Did the vanity that seeped through my Christmas hat into my skull bones make me move slowly? Walking so slow that every tree on Arbor Avenue could see me.

"Get a move on it, Lady Jane." Lady Jane. Susie Q. Miss Whatever-Your-Name-Is. The nuns had the name that announced your most intimate sin. Sister Callista cackled while Sister Bernard twittered like the principal was the wittiest woman she'd ever known. And Sister Bernard, old enough to know better. Hadn't she grown up on those movies from the thirties? Didn't nuns go to movies or stay up for the *Late Show?* Both of them long past fifty and looking it, looking down at me as I scurried through the Bible-thick doors of the school.

"A late Grace," Sister Bernard tittered as she let me scoot by. Then they cornered me in the hall.

Sister Callista bent down toward me. Her face, huge and freckled; her teeth like distant relatives to one another. Spit sprinkling through them. Her face framed unbecomingly in white, the neck choked in white. The rest of her in black like a permanent night of mourning. "We don't tolerate tardiness here, Lady Jane." Sister Callista spit lavishly in my face as she warned me. I touched the brim of my red hat to block the nasty rain that fell from her skinny mouth, to shield my eyes from the too-close sight of her, and to shield from her eyes the nongoodness hot in mine.

She almost broke the brim of my red Christmas hat when she flipped it up to glare at me and wash me with her saliva.

"Oh, Lady, Lady, Lady Jane, what is this insolence? You look at me when I'm talking to you. You look me in the eyes and you listen good, young lady. You will be on time and you will take your correction. Now get to your classroom."

Whereupon I stumbled blind and reprimanded to first grade, where I cried the rest of the day till Lazarus, who was Littleson then, and Pearl came to get me to take me home for lunch. It was being late that had almost undone me once. I don't want to be late. So I get mad when Mama has to go back upstairs to use the bathroom again. Not just because she has a weak bladder from nine babies pressing against it, but because she must delay.

I suck my teeth when Mama gets back out the car and parts the bevy of girls. She looks back into the car at me, apologetic. "I'll be right back." Pain in her face. Shame in her eyes, because her bladder is weak and hurts her and I am annoyed. And Madaddy is too.

"I guess I'll clean up these old windows," he says. So he gets out of the car too and in his good suit picks up the rag and Windex and begins to squirt.

He may as well be squirting tears in my eyes, because they are there. So I close my eyes to shut out the closed door I know will come with tardiness.

I think about first grade some more and how I tossed and turned last night, dream-remembering a day in first grade. The day I acquired an article of vocabulary and knew it.

In first grade of the corner Catholic school, in the front of the room, in the Baby Bear–sized chairs, Black first grade sat, learning words from alphabet. "*U, S,*" said Sister Veronica, who was a colleen not yet come to her majority but just past final vows. Unlike Sisters Callista and Bernard she gave us sweet, encouraging glances, a soft voice, and solicitous inquiries about our homes and health. "*U, S.*" Tiny girl, who was me, heard, and sitting studiously in the Baby Bear–sized chair raised a brown arm and waved a brown hand like a flag.

The kind young nun nodded.

"United States," the brown catholic child proclaimed, proud of her country, proud of her intelligence, of what she's heard on the news on the new TV.

The Irish nun blinked, amazed. "Us," she corrected. "*U* and *S* means *us*."

"Not you" is what her mouth doesn't say, but the unseen leaps into my head and knocks things down. The nun smiles, sweet and startled, flustered. The dark bright girl adds *us* to her vocabulary. Time spreads its arms and holds everything in the moment in unbreakable embrace. The children, the chairs, the nun who is hardly more than a child, a golden lock unraveling from the discipline of her black habit's veil.

Now my eyes fly open from the dream-memory, and Mama is opening the car door and Madaddy is in it already. And my sisters are stepping back from the curb as they've been told to do a thousand times. And the avant-garde piece of spirit is pulling at the rest of me to be off. And my father's car won't go. It only complains when he turns the key in the ignition. So we unload the suitcases and boxes from that car and line them up beside my little sisters on the stoop, after we've listened to the engine whine for longer than any of us can stand. I'm whining now. And fidgeting and fretting my way into minor hysteria. It is four o'clock now. The afternoon sun leans across the sky and the sunlight isn't quite so tall. Time has flown like a white bird in a white sky. Water rises in my eyes and a scared grumble or pathetic whine slides from between my pouting lips. "I'm gone be late. I'm gone be late."

My little sisters, angry at my leaving that has been delayed long enough to grow on them like an irritating itch, act like imps who've lost a soul and sing like the Temptations' record, "I know you wanna leave me, but I refuse to let you go. If I have to beg and plead for your sympathy, I don't mind because you mean that much to me . . ."

They line up before me, mocking me because they want me to hit them, then the excuse to cry noisily and inharmoniously. And beat me until I cry too and they can let me go.

"How come Maggie get to go somewhere?" asks Anne Perpetua, who always wants to be grown because she's the baby and only seven.

"Age has its privileges, my dearest girls," Mama answers teasingly, knowing this will make them madder and more outrageous and funnier too. "One day you'll go to college too." This scares Mama and she looks down, away from those pretty faces that are already lost to her.

"Maggie just seventeen. It's not fair," Ernestine grumbles. She's a few years behind me. This reminds me I am just seventeen and going away from home, even if it is just outside the City.

I'm so nervous now my mind dances hysterically on every surface of time but the present. What Mama said puts me on the train, pulling into Memphis, and my brother Littleson and me stepping out of the coach car, and Littleson, courteous as any well-raised child of Grace, held the door for me and an old Whitelady behind us. The Whitelady kind of pushed me aside gently like she had a right to and I didn't know some hidden rule. She stepped over the door mark and didn't say "thank you" to Littleson or even look grateful. Acted like he was born into this world to hold doors for her and supposed to do it.

Littleson got a funny look on his face. Then he got loud. "Age before beauty," Littleson yelled and held out his hand for me like he was my private coachman. Once I was across and equal on the platform with the Whitelady and she had got her butt off the train and no grown people could hear, including Aint Kit, who was already on the ground looking for our luggage, then Littleson cursed in his own way, kinda like Madaddy. He said that rude Whitewoman was whipped with an ugly stick. And she was so old and ugly she babysit for Adam's shit. That was the first time I heard Littleson curse ever. Because he didn't talk like that around me. Because he didn't talk like that. But that Whitelady made him mad. And Aint Kit made him madder when she caught him cussing and we told her what had happened.

She looked nervous and said real prim, "Age has its privileges." I wasn't sure if that meant grown people were free to curse the way Aint Kit did so extravagantly and vehemently, or if it meant old Whitepeople were free to act ungrateful to others and ignorant too. I wasn't sure.

So I asked. But Aint Kit couldn't say. That's real unusual for her. Not to say or have a quick response.

Now Aint Kit comes quickly in response to Mama's distress call. Cousin Bay comes too and shows the girls on the stoop how to do the booty green. She sashays bony hips from side to side and slaps her behind with one hand, then the other. A fake diamond tinkling on her finger. The booty green is old, but Bay still likes that dance best of all. We've seen it a thousand times. Mama says it's like the black bottom she used to do when she was six and her daddy set her up on the counter of the general store in the country outside Mimosa so she could do the black bottom and the Charleston for the population's delight. The booty green is new and glamorous every time Bay does it like she does it. Because Bay does everything with energy and savoir faire. My little sisters look at her admiringly. They say, "Bay, you know how to do it. Ooh, Bay."

With this encouragement Bay does it better, while Aint Kit, Mama, and Madaddy go upstairs for coffee because Aint Kit lets everybody know again and again that she is tired and she is only here out of the goodness of her heart and her love for me, her niece who is going to Eden. This required courtesy is only time lost to me and another nail in the coffin in which I will arrive late to college. Distraught, I flounce around the sidewalk while the booty green goes on all around me.

Sometimes I think of Bay and she is a hurricane suggesting repose. She slaps her hip now and smiles at me. And it is a smile that must be answered. She slaps another hip and I think of the time she (named Winona, called Bay from Baby Doll) slapped the man who slapped her in front of the family at the Fourth of July (a day so long we called it a place). He ran, stuck his dirty hand in the pitcher of lemonade, grabbed a cold handful of ice cubes, and threw them at her and ran. She caught him by the patch of shirt between his shoulders and punched him clean past the potato salad, spaghetti, and paper plates and cups into the smoking barbecue grill. The orange-hot coals burned his arm in a zigzag Bay swore was an angled *B*.

She said, "Mess with me you so bad looking for trouble, that's my last name. Baby Doll Winona Trouble."

And sometimes Aint Kit would say Trouble was Bay's last name because Kit was Bay's mother by virtue of finders keepers, losers weepers. She found Baby Doll one morning on her kitchen table down in Mimosa, Mississippi. It was the only day in her life Aint Kit missed work. She told her Whitelady Miss Geraldine she'd just had a baby and she'd be in tomorrow. That day she went over to Bellie Johnson's house on Eighth Street to ask Bellie's daughter, Gussie, whose boyfriend got her in trouble, if she was sure she wanted to give up her child. Gussie said she guess so because she heard Kit had money and needed a child and could take care of one. Gussie knew she was a girl and "didn't have nothin'." So she guess she wanted her baby to stay with Kit if Kit let her visit her baby whenever she wanted to.

So Bay grew up calling two women Mama, at least until Kit bent the bargain and moved north to the City, curtailing Gussie's visiting privileges. Bay called Aint Kit's husbands Papa and then their name. She didn't call any man Daddy until she met her boyfriend, Ben, whom she put her brand on. She called him Daddy. We called him Daddy with the *B* on His Arm.

When Bay came home from jail she came by our house. Face heavy with shame and her breath thick with shame, she pulled a baby girl, Anne Perpetua or Frances, onto her lap. She pressed her cheek against baby cheek and looked at Mama with eyes that begged to be innocent. We knew she was in trouble. She had to appear in court, before a judge in a raven-colored robe who intoned sentences in a sleep- or death-inducing drawl. So said Bay. Make you want to die.

Aint Kit was two hours behind Bay. She said if Bay got in trouble one more time she was gone wash her hands of her. Wash her hands. Those hands that pinned on her LPN badge. Those hands that turned the bed-sore patients in the private rooms in the private hospital on the north shore of the lake. Those hands that made the thick ham sandwiches, fried chicken, stirred cake batter and potato salad for the private card parties of railroad men in the early forties just after Aint Kit moved with Bay from Mississippi. Those hands that counted the money. Aint Kit was going to wash those hands of Bay. Because when you were in trouble, people with power in their hands washed their hands of you. You gave one last gulp before you got swallowed and spun like a stale drink down the drain.

I can feel myself spinning down the drain. Sitting on that stoop that juts out from the house of Grace. I know I'm sunk because grown people are still upstairs being social and my sisters are having a good time with Bay and I will be late to Eden and I will be turned away or chastised for what is other people's fault and I won't be the champion of my parents' love.

Bay is Mary Wells now and my sisters are her backup singers. Bay sings:

> *That day*
> *I first saw you-oo-oh-oo-oh*
> *Passing by*
>
> *I wanted*
> *To know your name but I-I-I*
> *Was much too shy.*
> *But I was looking at you so hard*
> *Until you must have had a hunch.*
> *So you came up to me*
> *And asked me my name.*
> *You beat me to the punch*
> *That time.*
> *You beat me to the punch-un-un-un-un-unch.*

Bay's singing is as pretty as she thinks it is. It is like a lullaby upside down and puts frustration to sleep and wakes up longing. I look at her, thin as water and dark as the Brer Rabbit syrup we used to pour over pancakes in Mimosa, smile a smile back at her and my sisters, and rock with the song that used to come on the radio and still does on *Dusty Nights*.

I'll miss those dishwashing songs that fell down into the water from the radio on the shelf above the sink and bubbled back up into the air until I was intoxicated with the promises of romance—seductive, replete, and terror provoking.

One night in the kitchen a song happened to me, "My Baby Loves Me." Hands soapy and head full of erotic bubbles, I crooned along with Martha and the Vandellas about my baby who loves me. New in puberty, then, I knew nothing. And know less now. But then my heart tore out of me, through my throat canal and into the air. I conjured up a love I wanted to put my arms around. To whom "I'll come running on the double!"

The next day, or soon after, blood first jumped out of me. I first saw Malcolm X, lightning coming out of his eyes and mouth, on TV. He wasn't King. He was something else. That's what my daddy said, "He's something else!" Struck by X, the unknown, veritable lightning, I began to bleed unknowingly. When he disappeared, I went to the bathroom. I saw what I saw and called my mother.

"Look," I said, showing her the intimate stain. Like a splash of little broken rubies.

"Oh," she said, and hugged me.

She told me to stay right there. She would be back. I sat on the rim of the bowlegged bathtub while she was gone. Contemplating my foreign body.

She returned with a blue box in a brown paper bag. Then she gave me what I needed. Was it that night I began this dream like a curious new movie in the all-night theater of my mind?

I am stepping down from the train that runs between this city and the one I came from. Only it doesn't stop in Memphis. It goes directly there. I am a woman in a red dress, big gold-hoop earrings in my ears. I float down the steps. The air is so heavy in the dream. The air is clear water. So clear it's disappeared. I swim through the air. Rush toward someone. A smiling man. His handsome phantom face just grinning. Lightning everywhere around him. Blue. Blue lightning and me a woman in a dress blood woven and clinging to breasts and hips that are there in the dream. The train is long and black and smoking. Alive. He walks toward me smiling. About to say my name. This is Love. True and lightning hot.

I've been waiting for him without waiting. Waiting just as right now when I anticipate the heart trouble in Mary Wells's song.

> *Since I loved you*
> *I thought you would be true*
> *And lo-ove me tender*
> *So I let my heart surrender*
> *To you-oo.*
> *Yes I did.*
> *But I found out*
> *Beyond a doubt*
> *One day, boy, you were a playboy*
> *Who would go away*
> *And lea-eeave me blue.*

Now we get to the part I like. My sisters and cousin get ready for it by standing with their feet apart, their hands jabbing the air, their hips swerving around them. (Well, my sisters' imaginary hips swerving around them.) I jump up and get in line. They pull me into the finish just like we do when we play talent show in the living room.

> *So I ain't gonna wait around*
> *For you to put me down.*
> *This time I'm gonna play my hunch*
> *And walk away this very day*
> *And beat you to the punch*
> *This time.*
> *I'll beat you to the pu-un-un-un-un-unch.*

We're all dancing like Cassius Clay–Muhammad Ali, floating like butterflies, voices still stinging and making honey like bees, floating, when Mama, Aint Kit, and Madaddy come down. I turn around, reluctant to leave. So we load Aint Kit's fishtailed Cadillac that she got from her third husband, Herbert Jenkins, who died while eating one of her thick ham sandwiches at a card party. Then the loaded car is ready to swim the avenue toward Eden.

We load ourselves. My sisters wave longingly from the stoop and Aint Kit's dead third husband's car won't start.

It's like déjà vu done over.

Aint Kit nurses the engine, but her car won't start.

"You outta gas," Madaddy tells his sister.

"I ain't outta no gas!" Aint Kit denies. Each word always overpronounced to endlessly held rage and pretentious perfection in defiance of beautiful dark, rich lips. Nose flared and mouth constricted. The upper lip held tight, tense, baring the tips of her teeth.

"Gas gauge says you ain't got no gas," my father says mildly, because it is after all Aint Kit's car. She inherited it. Just like I told my daddy I inherited my smart mouth from him one time when he was holling at me to do something I was already doing. Putting it back on him just made him madder and I cut out the door, flying.

Aint Kit turns around in the driver's seat to scowl at Bay, who is in the backseat with me and Mama and my new hair dryer. "You use up my gas and ain't put none back in my tank?" It's a rhetorical question. A prelude.

"I ain't have no money on me, Muh." Bay looks out the window. Hurt. Gone the superior joy of the singer.

Aint Kit gets out the car and decries the Negro race that has used up all her gas. She opens the trunk and shoves my stuff around and pulls out a gas can.

"This empty too!" she fumes through the window at Bay. Her face in the glass would be funny if it weren't so mean. "You yellow behind——! You used up my extry gas too. I oughta throw you in a basket and drop you in the river. This is a goddamn shame," Aint Kit tells the street and my little sisters on the stoop who will imitate her ridiculous fury this night in the living room without me.

I imagine myself in a quiet room with crisp curtains. My books will be neatly stacked and all my paints, brushes, and pens in perfect pots and containers. There will be no noise. No wild aunt shrieking in the street at a disinterested-acting adopted daughter. No mother and father harassed and worried because they can't engineer my leaving with harmony and order. Even though Pearl got away with no fuss and Lazarus is at a meeting at his university. But it's this moment that goes against their authority.

Aint Kit is still at it. She sticks her head back in the car. "You lazy something. Get your ass outta this car and go get me some gas before I put some knots on your head to match them natural naps."

Cousin Bay says, "What makes you think I got money?"

"You workin!"

"That don't mean nothin'."

"I guess it don't. I have to give you a new dollar bill and clean towels every day. You can't find them towels or that money. A nasty buzzard, you don't want to see a towel."

It is ugly now. And Mama says, "Kit," to keep Aint Kit from embellishing on the embarrassing moment with invented tales of her generosity and hygiene and Bay's poverty and slovenliness. Cruel lie against crueler stymie.

Maybe it is the mute panic that crosses my face at these new delays, maybe it is the dawning belief that my journey is cursed, and if mine be cursed, then all our journeys are cursed. More than likely it is a desire to escape Aint Kit's meticulous tirade that makes Bay take the empty gas can and hike down Arbor, which is now rather softly, almost imperceptibly, shaded in lost sunlight. Aint Kit very dramatically commands, "Here," and thrusts a five-dollar bill at Bay. Bay takes it and tries not to look ashamed. Mama passes Aint Kit a five-dollar bill from Madaddy, which Aint Kit, also known among my brothers and sisters as Fort Knox, quickly pockets.

Then it is after five and Uncle Blackstrap, my mother's brother, Lazarus Dancer, comes down the same street Bay went up. He is walking like he is in the middle of a daydream, spending too much time looking at every tree and bird on Arbor Avenue. That's the way he's been for years now. Ever since he argued with the arrogant policemen. About what I don't know. I know they beat him bloody with billy clubs, nightsticks, *that word–* sticks. He threw up fists from the concrete while his whole body tangled around handcuffs. They took him away. We told one another they kidnapped him. My daddy paid the ransom called bail. He kept telling Mama about it too. Because the whole thing had to be her fault for having a brother who got carted off to jail. But how was it hers? Mama said when any man got taken in. Neighbors wound up in trouble the same way. Mr. Rucker down the street the worst evidence. His daughter, Charlotte, in her own kind of trouble. Even homing pigeons owned by the government pecking in the wrong gutters, alighting on the wrong window-sills, flying in the wrong sky. Even a lightning bug or a butterfly got caught. And sometimes a moth brushed too close to its own territorial love light and burned the ends of its wings. Was there any fault? Where was the blame when a thing was itself and was trapped? Where was the blame when a man acted like a man and minded his own business and wound up in the jailhouse anyway? My father refused to answer that for us.

Suddenly, as if responding to some urge, Madaddy says, "Let me see if I can get my old bird going. Awh-ya-ya-ya." Awh-ya-ya-ya is a sign my daddy gives when he's in a situation that oppresses him. He gets out of Aint Kit's dead third husband's car and goes to his own. Uncle Blackstrap waves to all of us, then he stands at my father's elbow and watches him try to start the old bird. Madaddy is under the hood.

Jeannie, my girlhood friend who got into trouble, comes down the street holding hands with her three-year-old daughter. "Congratulations, Maggie," she sings out at me. Her joy dancing over everybody else's irritation. She waves at me as if I have won a prize. I guess three scholarships is a prize. Then she tells her three-year-old daughter, "She goin to a good school."

Then to me, "You got two brothers and two sisters who go to college or went some for a while at least, don't you, Maggie?"

"Uh-huh," one of my sisters answers for me. Because by now I'm just about catatonic and can only see but can't speak.

"But you going to the best one. And you got a scholarship. That's so wonderful!" Jeannie sounds like one of the women in Star of Bethlehem Missionary Baptist Church we're standing next to. Its doors closed and everybody gone to visit another church. She sounds like one of the women who pray novenas on Tuesday evenings with my mama. She sounds like a little girl being left behind. Jubilant, modest, and forlorn. Tears blurring my pupils, I smile at her. Look at her baby girl and smile some more. She waves at me and keeps on going home.

"You ain't going nowhere, Maggie," my sister says.

"You staying right here, girl," my other sister says.

"You not going to go nowhere to draw some pictures," another sister says.

"Yes, I am," I make myself say against the obstacle of their love and this afternoon of Murphy's law.

I begin to compute how much a taxicab would cost to Eden. It is a town outside the City. Close, but far to me. It would probably cost half of the book money I earned at the job Pearl got for me. I close my eyes and try not to think about trouble. I want to swoon like one of those put-upon heroines in the books Honey, Pearl, and I read and pass on to Ernie, Shir, Frances, and Anne Perpetua, who pulls the covers off everything.

"Let me see up under there, Sam," Uncle Blackstrap asks my father.

My daddy pulls back and draws up to his six feet. His hat pushed back on his Super Groomed hair. He moves over and Uncle Blackstrap bends down reverently into the belly of the car. He touches wires lightly and twists caps tightly. The same things my daddy always did. But it's something else in the touch. And the look on his face is serene instead of hassled. He nods to my daddy, who gets into the car. Sam turns the key and the car comes alive. It is music and loud power then. An answered prayer.

"What you do? Yah-yah." My father purrs along with the engine. My mother won't grin at her brother's success, lest Madaddy take offense. Her eyes light up.

"A little bit of this and that," Uncle Blackstrap replies like a cook who can't or won't divulge her recipe. He's still gazing at that engine like a man in love.

My daddy shrugs. "We better get going in this old baby," Madaddy says to me and Mama and Aint Kit. We are standing beside the working car. Aint Kit starts looking slumped and left out until Mama says, "Come on, Kit." And she knows that's an invitation even though she doesn't have a ticket.

Uncle Blackstrap sets down the hood, gentlelike, and we unload Aint Kit's dead third husband's comatose car and reload our live one. Aint Kit is cocky again, "Tell Bay she bed not take her lil' booty green away from this house in my car," she yells to my sisters, who file into the house for dinner that Mama cooked it seems like two centuries ago. Roast surrounded by potatoes and carrots, string beans, and lettuce salad, fruit punch from a can. Or is it fried chicken, string beans, and rice? The long-lasting smells of that house still lure and my sisters follow them and their own hunger up the stairs. They don't want to see my ship cast off from shore anyway. The horizon is too far away. Aint Kit has reminded them of the booty green and they take the butt slapping up again as they take the steps. First Ernestine Marie, then Leah Shirley, next Frances Samella, and last but not least Anne Perpetua.

I have broken out of that line of daughters and sons on time. I am delirious with relief. I won't be late. My father checks the passengers and cargo and we pull away from Uncle Blackstrap standing on the curb. No room for him on the journey. Or so my father said.

We cruise to the corner and Madaddy stops for the red light. Then we hear the holler. And it's Lazarus, who used to be Littleson, acting like Littleson now he's so excited. He races into the street, dodging the still cars. My mama rolls down the window.

"Hey!" he yells like he's still across the street. His face in the window. The edge of the rolled-down glass at his throat, like a sheer blade.

He finds me with those shiny eyes and says, "Maggie, I brought this for you to put on your wall at school." He passes me a rolled-up poster. He looks at the light—still red. And I look at the light. I look at the scroll and unroll it a little. It's a pen and ink by Kofi X. An African warrior woman with a spear in her hand, her short, light skirt swirling in some invisible whirlwind.

"I almost missed you," he says. His face solemn and happy. His breathing still hard. Our parents wish him away; my mother screws her mouth tight. My father flexes his jaw and checks the gas. They know this is some of his Panther stuff.

"Thanks," I say. The light is red. He runs to the curb. Lazarus my brother standing next to Lazarus my uncle, who has come to the corner to see us some more. The light is green. And my father guns the engine. And I look back at my brother and my uncle and out of the corner of my eye Bay coming down the street with the gas can in her hand and further back I keep looking. Exultant and pleased with myself. I turn in the backseat, bumping against my new accoutrements, and look over my right shoulder at the Grace house. The way I see it, it moves from the inside. Pulsing as if with breath. The house, two stories, of many small rooms and some big rooms, the house itself, so long holding us, living with us, now asleep to me off into the world to put my painting hand into the mouth of the world and take back *that word* from its jaws. That red house of Grace dreaming, storying on its own.

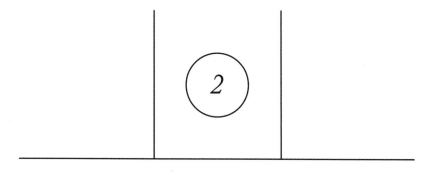

2

Blood Island

There was an island. There is still an island off the west coast of Africa where there stands a large stone structure of sun-beaten tight rooms and yards. Gorée it is called.

The Africans beaten and stolen were counted on that island. In that white mute stone they were stored and numbered bone and teeth. Each room became the white perverse egg of a bird-beast beyond known powers of imagination or prayer. Counted, captured Africans were curled, drawn up for possible attack, in the amniotic fluid of their own sweat and bewilderment. Fluid like bile. They knew with the three-dimensional knowledge of their own bodies that the white cube would crack, and they would hatch into some new form, and they would break open into Death.

Gorée was where the fevered Africans fumblingly assembled their old, complex ideas of God and prayed to that God who folded his hands; they tore their chained hands and burned blood from their wrists until chain met blood then bone; then they waited to die. At Gorée they molded this agony, briny pity, this terror with blood and mucus, bent their heads to the scrape of glistening blood that too soon grimed their necks, and listened for ways to work their lamed fury.

It was from Gorée that they were marched to the faceless sea, through sand, fated and gravid, that held their feet and ankles to home; pulled by chains heavy and unbreakable, coffled together, they walked. A walk halted and harnessed as lightning wrestled by rods. Children, women, men. Their eyes breaking to hold the last look of all that they had ever known, before they were beaten under decks into a betrayed darkness that rocked and wailed and cried out to the slumbering God. Didn't they trouble God's sleep?

The Black Student Union of Eden University christened the university-owned house of white wood and gray stone where we meet and fellowship Gorée, after that African island. This is the official name. Among ourselves we mispronounce it *Gory*, and from there we call it Blood Island. So it is Blood Island to us, like some horror movie site with ghouls as overseers drinking the blood of innocents. The Black Student Union is For Bloods Only. A lopsided joke against the country clubs open to the White offspring of Eden and locked to us unless we come as servants or solitary tokens of equality. It is a joke to us, so it's a sign written above the doorbell: WE ADMIT ALL. Unwritten is: ALL OF THE RACE THAT RODE A THOUSAND SHIPS, EVEN THE LIGHTEST TRACE.

Before last year, Eden had only isolated Blacks who came by ones and twos yearly to the university, a basketball player or a football player, a rare female who need not play a ball. How those lonely onlys must have spent their time cringing inside! Their hearts and kidneys on hold; crimped around the eyes. James Merediths and Charlayne Hunters whose misery went unnoticed by TV cameras.

So the story goes—a lonely-only sister (no one knows her name) was molested, taunted and touched, invaded by some frat boys. She left Eden the next day, leaving only one Blackgirl behind. To quiet the stink the fathers of Eden U. gave the newly formed FBO a clubhouse. But it's more than that. Even if it doesn't look like it.

Once a woman came to the front door of the Grace place and Shir had left the front door open to let herself back in. The woman walked into the house, up the stairs to the second story where we lived, walked into our living room unannounced and took a seat. Shir came back in and said, "Hi!"

The woman said, "Hi!"

Pearl walked through and said, "Hello."

Mama went through the living room, smiled and inquired, "How you feelin?"

"Fine. How you doin?" the woman responded.

I was sitting in the kitchen window drawing a tribe of arrogant trees. My back to the world of the family. They began to discuss the woman in the living room.

"Maggie," Pearl hissed at me. "You so rude. You got company."

"What that woman want with you, Maggie?" Shir asked me, looking at my sketch.

Mama went back to the living room. Curiosity making her assert herself as mother of the house.

"I'm Magdalena's mother. May I help you?"

The woman, whose pleasant trance had been broken, smiled and shook her tangled head. "No. No," she mumbled. "It was nice meeting you all. I was just catching my breath. Just had to catch my breast." She surveyed the room, smiled again, then left our house as quietly as she had entered it, walking in the vacuum of my mother's and our openmouthed astonishment.

I think now that our house must have been a kind of sanctuary for her. Like Blood Island.

After World War II and the Korean War the U.S. Army let loose flocks of carrier pigeons it had used as messengers in enemy zones. It was expensive to feed the well-bred pigeons berries, seeds, and grains, more efficient to give the surplus poultry freedom. Then soldiers let loose the birds. And the homing pigeons took to the air in search of a home, a long way from home. They trembled and shuddered against heaven, lost and needy, propelled by loss, hunger, and bereavement, and guided by whatever insight pigeons are guided by.

They descended on Arbor Avenue and a thousand other neighborhoods. So many that the newspapers wrote about the extravaganza, the mischief of their shit, the pitifulness of their plight, the ubiquity of molted feathers that flew everywhere— the soft feathers into mouths, eyes, and hair, the heavy feathers slammed against the sides of buildings, wedged in corners. What to do with them?

On Arbor Avenue some families made houses for the pigeons on the roofs of garages. The Bridges, down the street, set up a pigeon house atop the doghouse where the evil Calypso lived and barked and slept with his big white head and haunches sticking out, dreaming of the juicy legs of children. When I see him in my head, I see a balloon shoot up out of his head, full of legs of child and bird. Tender. He drools and waits, for dreams come true.

I can hardly believe it. I've left Arbor Avenue behind. Blood Island is waiting for me when I arrive with Mama, Madaddy, and Aint Kit. But we don't notice it.

On the university campus, there is more flat, cultivated grass, there are more obedient trees lined up and bursting with more green, than any place I can remember seeing. What my mother has told me of Mimosa, Mississippi, what I can recall, might match these splendid grounds in colorful abundance, but that profusion is not as precise as Eden's is.

This is some place my blues-dreaming daddy has thought up in a song and sung into being. The newly erected administration building with its glass dome and many stone steps leading to the offices that surround the dome looms in the distance. The stone of it so white it is pearly under moonlight and diamondesque in sunlight, nearly blinding us as we arrive, my father surveying the whole thing from the cracked car window.

He says, "That building over there look like something from Sauuuuudy Arabia."

Car says, "Mmmn-hmm." All very majestic.

The whole world lines up here. Obedient and erect. There is a green peace that spreads out from the administration building for more than a mile: trees, lawns, and stone buildings that squat like minor gray gods in the early autumn dusklight.

The scenery is so beautiful and plush Aint Kit gets worried I won't fit in. "Don't be up here messing up and disgracing us now, Maggie," she admonishes.

My parents get stern in the shoulders. Taking umbrage with the caution; once verbalized it said I needed to be told by an aunt what parents had been appointed to tell.

"Maggie know how to act," my father says. Then he starts to whistle a little like he did when he took the wrong exit off the northbound expressway and drove us too far west. We lost a half hour.

At an intersection where North Campus joins South, and the City flows into suburban town, a Blackman in a business suit stands, under a perfect crew cut, hawking his newspapers that headline DIVINE RETRIBUTION and THE TRIUMPH OF THE BLACK MAN. A younger Blackman hands him a quarter, gives him a grin, and takes the current issue of *Muhammed Speaks* while the Muslim begins his chant about the teachings of the Honorable Elijah Muhammad. The younger man, who is a student, listens politely for a time, perusing the headlines and wrinkling his brow, waiting for the light to change. The hawker presses too vigorously, chiding the young man for not wearing his hair in the scrupulous Muslim cut and shave.

The student looks annoyed, and this is not usual. His name is Stephen Rainey. People say his temperament is sweet and his ways earnest. His revolutionary fervor gives him an edge. The edge is in his voice now as he cautions the hawker of the messenger to "can the hair rap, brother, and let me scan the news before I ask you about Malcolm's untimely demise." The mention of Malcolm X brings a brilliant smile to the Muslim's face. He bows to Steve Rainey and withdraws to the safety of the curb, where cars are known to leave tire tracks. Better to be hit by a car than hit by Rainey. Better a Mack truck than the grievous fury of Malcolm's youthful disciple.

When I think of disciples, I think of Steve Rainey, diligent and unobtrusive, needing little praise, yet eager to give it to the Movement or some hero. Ask Steve when he was born, and he will say the day Malcolm X, burnished and eloquent, furious and cool, first came on TV. Ask Steve, and he was born after World War II and before the Korean War. A year or two before me. He looks older. Do I look older, even though in truth I am being born right now in my father's car in the backseat beside my Aint Kit, my typewriter, and my hair dryer?

His face is rounder than Lazarus's peering in the rolled-down car window. He's on the passenger side so he looks at everybody.

Mama. Aint Kit. Me, a long time. And Madaddy longest. My father names my dorm. The student gives a short nod like he's clicking in the information, processing an answer. Other than "Hey, what's happenin?" twice, he doesn't say anything but directions, which my father repeats wrong and Aint Kit bungles more. Steve Rainey decides to lead the way. He walks in the street a little ahead of the car as he points it to turn.

Curious the grace in his lean lope. How the soft wind crosses itself in the space between his thighs. We can see the soles of his shoes, tan and clean. His jacket, falling back, and his jeans pressing a little against his legs, he half turns and draws his arm up, telling the car to come on. We follow him down a thin street. Shady and one way. Blood Island is on this street. He points it out and tells me I'll go there tomorrow. I believe him. He tells my father to turn and we do.

This street has only one building on it and that is the dormitory. Vine covered and stony.

"I suppose you happy now. We here," my mother says. I don't know why she sounds so resentful.

Steve Rainey gives that clipped nod again as we disembark. My father is telling him thank you and reaching for his wallet in his back pocket. But the standard-bearer says that's cool. "No thank you, sir." He looks at me. "See you," he says. Then he gets gone.

It's dark now and the entrance is not on this street, although a parking place is. My father grumbles because we are lost from our destination. I feel like Little Red Riding Hood carrying my hair dryer shaped like a covered basket. Or is it a skinny Ella Fitzgerald singing "A-tisket, a-tasket, my green and yellow basket" on a crowded bus in a movie I can't call the name of? I don't have much, but it's a lot to me and the people who have to carry it. Aint Kit has a suitcase. And Madaddy has two. Mama

31

has the typewriter. The only thing missing is a shoebox full of fried chicken.

The trees crouch and spin new leaves. Each hedge a row of looms. We find a break in the foliage and then the concrete path. Then we see the arch that leads to an enclosed courtyard, circular and discreet.

The lobby is loud, full of girls' voices saying good-bye. Excitement makes them sound like pulled taffy, sweet and tense. The parents make low sounds, beaten down with letting go, worry, and fear. Fathers straddle trunks and mothers just stand there looking around. Overseeing. It's a lot of Whitepeople. In intimate acts. I've only seen them hug and kiss with tears in their eyes on TV. Good acting. The fathers look down. Which is unusual I know because all the Whitemen I've ever seen have been looking up. Or down on colored people.

Our arrival is an intrusion, and all the Whitepeople act tight and attentive to our movements. The eyes of fathers in sports jackets slide over my father's attire: his Sunday-best suit. But it is not very expensive, and now I see the softest sheen on the pants' bottom as Madaddy goes up the stairs ahead of me. Mothers twitter like scared larks. If they could jump up on one leg and take off they would. They try to now.

This sudden shift in atmosphere hardens Aint Kit's heart, hurts my parents, and hurts my eyes. I squint. The light blares and dims at the same time. I can't make out the features of the faces in the frames along the hall as we go up the marble steps. Aint Kit's face looks like a little hatchet. Her hand fumbles on the suitcase handle. She reasserts her grip. My parents plant apologetic smiles on their faces. Madaddy's a bit jovial. Mama's more restrained.

Then I see the tall Blackgirl and it's like summer. The light haunts her, hangs around infatuated and almost splendid. She is so dark the sight of her causes Aint Kit to cough. My parents relax. Shoulders go up. Unburdened from the solitary confinements of our skin.

This time I am going in, my free hand locked in Aint Kit's free hand. My parents bring up the rear. Another time I was going out of school, dragged along behind Honeybabe and Pearl. They were following Sam Jr. and Lazarus, bringing up the end of the trail that was splashed with rose petals I was dropping whenever I went. I don't know where I got them from. I only know roses and how soft they fell apart like the fingers of an infant, opening. Roses, noiseless and wise to have kept the color of blood. Sam told me to stop doing that. Dropping flowers and humming about the woman who gave me flowers. Who had a scarf she changed to a bouquet of roses. "Stop singing that," he said. But I wouldn't. And they hauled me home from school. An entourage. For peanut butter and jelly I put aside the magic bouquet.

My stomach growls. I don't know whether it's hunger or nerves. Aint Kit is pointing my hand she's squeezing it so tight. I think everybody can hear. And I am ashamed. Perhaps Aint Kit feels me pull back, because she tucks my hand in her armpit now. My arm pinned by her elbow. She shoulda been a wrestler instead of the wife of a prizefighter. I shoulda stayed home. That's what I think. I shoulda stayed away from people with cold eyes who look at us like we snot escaped from dirty noses. It's that humble look on my mama that hurts the most. But Mama fools me.

"Don't break her arm, Kit," my mother warns. Aint Kit lets me out of her armpit. She just holds my hand hostage. Pained hostage.

We wade through luggage and dodge trunks and paraphernalia to the entrance desk, where a white-haired Whitewoman stands guard. The businessman daddies in casualwear make a big production out of acting like we're not there. My father has his back up. Businessmen daddies have backs like surfboards. Their hides are florid and their teeth are polished. Their mouths are thin like roast beef in the restaurant, rare and sliced stingy. They try to look over my daddy, holding their heads real high, but Sam Grace is too tall. He's just too tall to be overlooked. And my mama is too fine to be invisible. The businessman daddies get real nervous.

They open their appointment books and start to fit their daughters in. Their daughters are slim and giggling and skittish. One girl spots my luggage, blinks, then looks at her own. It's the same Sears set. The graduation special. Fathers still rustle on the pages of appointment books, put spit on their thumbs and turn pages, searching for an opening on a Monday or a Wednesday maybe when they have to come to town for a business meeting.

Then the Whitelady in the mauve shirtwaist dress speaks up. "Let's not congregate, ladies and gentlemen. There's too much congestion here. Far too much congestion." She talks like the lobby is a pair of lungs. Madaddy's getting cranky. Quick scowls coming and going. Mama tells me to go to a table where two girls are sitting behind blocks of paper with names on them.

"I'm an incoming freshman . . ."

"Name, please."

"Oh. Magdalena C. Grace."

"Just a minute. Mag-da-le-na."

"Here it is. That's three-one-three."

I've got the keys. I don't know why it's so funny my father starts to laugh. "Oh-hoh."

Aint Kit asks the head lady, "How can we find room three-one-three? This girl, my niece, is beginning her education here."

The Whitelady doesn't look at me. She pauses a little. Her eyes hit Aint Kit's shoes. Open-toed black pumps. Then she deigns to answer. "One of our students will help you. Go through the door to your right." She looks at her watch, nods to somebody else behind the desk, and takes her leave.

That's when we go to the room where I meet Essie Witherspoon and Leona Pryor. Two Black roommates. An accident Mama and Madaddy seem happy with. I kiss my parents and Aint Kit, leave my belongings where they lay as I walk them to the car. Later when I come back in, my roommates and I are careful where we lay our eyes. We lay them down in neat pink cases like contact lenses. That is what it feels like.

"Okay, Magdalena, you choose. Your straw is the longest."

I stand in the center of the dormitory room. It is a larger room than the usual, cut into a third-floor corner of a three-story, ivy-covered building. Three girls will stay in this room. Three girls draw straws for beds and closet space. The Eden administration must have made a mistake. We are three Blackgirls in one room. The other dark girls were matched with Othergirls. We three analyze our situation. Maybe the Eden fathers have plans for us. Maybe they're studying Black students. Maybe they want to observe how we three will turn out. Maybe. Maybe they messed up and we lucked up or out. Depending on how we feel about being a dark trinity.

I pull the longest straw. The tall, plum-black girl, Leona Pryor, pulls the middle stick. And Essie Witherspoon shrugs philosophically and pessimistically when she draws the shortest straw. There is in the room a bunk bed and a single bed that fits under a wide window like a window seat. I try to snare the longing that floats up in me at the sight of the window bed. I have never slept alone and the notion is thrilling. All of my nights have been spent breathing sleep back into the face of some girl who looks like me, and before that a boy named Littleson and I lay like spoon and fork pointing in different directions on the same cot. Always somebody else's breath and limbs to worry about, or suffer the consequences of my own too-eager snuggling or too-fierce kicking and be cast out of the bed by one swift kick onto the floor. Later I watched the ceiling from a top bunk or watched the top bunk from the bottom. I want to sleep alone, sprawled in an elegant solitude, stretched out like a wing.

I want the window seat. But there is such sad hunger in Essie's gaze so carefully averted from the solo bed. And if I of the first luck, for the sake of Essie, don't choose the window bed, will Leona Pryor usurp the bed?

A surge of my mother's kindness seizes me suddenly. I sit on the bottom bunk bed, and in the next instant the long-limbed Leona swings up to the top bunk.

Essie, the small, shy girl, sinks heavily, relieved, onto the window seat. A brilliant gratitude widens her somber eyes. Misgivings are released. I smile. Essie beams. Leona lies back on the bare mattress and greets the ceiling. "We should get along just fine."

We are friends for life.

When it is midnight, after the dorm meeting, we clamber into our beds, each of us. Then we sleep the sleep of the dead. Spent. And joyous. Expanding to fit each circumstance.

Freshman orientation is at nine in the morning. The sun is bright as our eyes. We roommates hurry to the auditorium. We are three black canoes in a flotilla of white. We bob along.

"It sure is a lot of them. More than at my high school," Leona says. She went to a high school with White students.

There are more Whitepeople here than I'd seen downtown when our whole school went to see a religious movie when I was a little girl. I'd thought that was a lot of Whitepeople, coming and going, and in the dark with us looking at the movie screen.

We take our seats in the middle of the packed auditorium. We are welcomed to Eden University, home of the Eden Serpents (or should we say Temptations?). Some laughter. Cheerful school administrators and other students tell us the history and mission of the university, a school so great they don't say *at* Eden; they say *in* Eden usually. They remind us of all the benefits and activities Eden has to offer. The famed drama school and debate team, the Big Ten football, basketball, baseball teams, the fraternities and sororities and clubs devoted to majors.

"We're already sold," Leona opines. Essie smiles. I look around at my fellow students who don't look like me, searching for some other Black faces, finding a few, counting them, savoring the number.

They let us out into sunlight. Leona and Essie want to go back to the dorm to take a nap and digest all the information. They are scheduled for registration in the late afternoon. I am scheduled for early afternoon. Before that I have to go to the Finance Building to pick up a check. I have been awarded another scholarship funded by the family of a woman landscape artist who was famous in her time—A. A. Breton.

"Catch you later on." Leona waves me on. She and Essie seem surprised that I'm getting more money.

I set off on my own. I walk down Eden Road awhile, then turn down Key Street until I run into the Finance Building. Inside there is a bank of teller windows. I go to the first one, where a balding Whiteman is counting cash. Something tells me he is in charge, as he sends a woman to take an early lunch.

"Excuse me," I say. "My name is Magdalena Grace. I'm here to pick up a scholarship check."

He looks at me like he's looking into a crystal ball.

"You got the Breton. *You're* Magdalena Grace. Your hair's not long enough to wipe those feet." He studies my natural.

"What?"

"Just joking."

He hands me the check and my hands tremble as I take it. I sign it and give it back to him. He counts out money.

"That comes with a prize," he says gruffly. "They'll deliver it to your dorm tonight."

This time I say, "Thank you."

It arrives in the evening. It is there at the front desk when I answer my buzzer—a heavy, shiny, tan-colored tripod easel, five feet high.

We are on our way to class. Blond boys in jeans cut around us. Sorority girls with swinging pale hair come out of the stone cluster of houses set behind a circle of willows. They all converge on the walks that cut through the crew-cut grass. Leona makes one stride to my two shorter steps. Confidence is in the sweep of Leona's long, dark limbs. Her skirt rides her thighs like a tiny half-open umbrella.

"What're you gonna do?" she asks as she looks down into my face. An intensity I begin to recognize flashes out like an orange flame in the autumn morning cool.

"What you mean?" I am tempted to feign confusion about the simple question. I am tempted to hide and say, "I'm going to study after class and then . . ." But I know Leona isn't asking about this day. She is asking for a short sketch of my coming autobiography.

"I'm going to make things," I finally say. "Paint. Sculpt. Just make things." I almost add, "I want to know." I have no idea what it is I want to know. Yet the desire quivers on the tip of my tongue.

Leona is still sending flame out onto the road ahead of us. My answer seems to satisfy her. We are running across the street now.

Wind heavy in our hair as it pulls our sculpted round naturals out of shape, tilts our hair in the direction the cool wind blows, then leaves it there. Strange on all our heads. Leona stops a car.

"You better hold it!" she commands.

The driver obeys the tall girl shaped like a stop sign. Everybody stops. Across the street, Steve and the hawker in their usual places wait inside time, watching us. The driver stops on a dime, the fender less than a foot away from us. Leona and I step onto the curb and half run, half walk on the concrete path that winds through grass and light stone buildings. Buildings over one hundred years old.

"You got to take care of yourself. You got to get your education so if some man leaves you, you won't be sitting stupid. You better get a job and a good one at that." Leona lifts her head high and beckons to the world like it is a stupid suitor.

I am silent, awestruck beside Leona with her firm grasp on the future. Such practical matters have never occurred to me. On my college entrance essay I wrote that I wanted to help my people, to be a credit to my race. I wrote that I wanted to be one with the women of the fields who sweated through childbirth and squinted back the sun. I wanted to be Harriet Tubman and Sojourner Truth and the Blackwomen who were artists whose names I never knew. I wrote that I want to paint the world that would be, the world I've seen in my own mother's eyes.

I suck in my full bottom lip. What do I know? I have not written that an education could make me safe. I do not recognize the danger. I have not written that a job will pay my rent. I have always assumed a piece of a house with sufficient sun to see by and room to run through. Why have I assumed this when I haven't seen it that much? Most of my block were renters. I did not write in my reasons for Eden that I will have a husband

and a husband may leave me. I do not really think of husbands. I assume in my vivid daydreams that I will have adventures with a dashing man; he will be a detective or a spy. Taciturn and passionate. Trustworthy. Capable. I assume in my biggest, most exalted daydreams that I will make adventures for myself, bestowing gifts to the world. But Leona has thought of the possibilities. She flicks the bad news out of her orange globe of fire. I scurry to keep up with her.

We left Essie in bed with the clock radio on. She has a class an hour later than mine or Leona's. So she turns over and pulls up the cover and floats in that single bed somewhere between reverie and listening. The news is always on in the morning. On the other side of the world a bastard war is raging. And boys our own ages are dying. And boys we knew could be joining them, but for school, but for the graces of luck and resistance. We are young dreamers trapped like lightning bugs in an empty jar, breaking wings against the glass, shooting our lights against extinction. We go to class and study, or do not; we are in love and dream, because it is the time of our lives for those things. Everything is a question.

Someone is always asking someone else, "What's happening?" Steve Rainey says it twice. "What's happening? What's happening?" So some people call him that, "What's happening? What's happening?"

Someone else is always answering, "Everything is everything." I want to know everything, at least see, so I go to the library. But there's nowhere to go that I don't stop at Blood Island along the way.

A flock of moths circle and circle the lone porch lightbulb. Their feverish wings dipping and glancing in the heat of the light. The light catches us all under it, sets us apart in a vivid detail of bell-bottoms and intricate hair, gathers us together in the shadows of skin and silhouettes of tight coiled energy, and fixes our stances in an arrogant edginess.

Essie falls in love with William Satterfield one night on the steps of Blood Island. She is sitting on the wide railing next to the gray stone porch post when he comes up the steps and into the center of light. One look at his silhouette, the fantastically big Afro, the lean boyish-manly beauty of him, makes her breath hang in her throat. Then water rushes to her eyes and her mouth. She is teary and salivating. She is in love. In love with William Satterfield, who is a junior, who is president of FBO. Who is an avatar sent to stand in a circle of light where moths, entranced and fidgety, dance above his head and sometimes dip into his monumental Afro.

There is an ebullient crispness to the breezes that sweep us up in the dark and stir the air up. A nimbus of innocence we don't know we have surrounds us, flows out of us: Leona leaning against the stone post; Essie sitting upright and prim on the railing; me, Maggie, with my back to the wall of Blood Island. I am one with it all, yet watching. The size of the crowd on the porch ebbs to one or two or swells to a dozen or more. Then the size doesn't matter because the feeling is always there at Blood Island; we feel humungous, twenty-eleven big, like a continent, like one heart muscle beating the same time.

It is William who first calls Essie "Spoon." And what William names stays named. He is like Adam in shades, walking around the garden naming things. When William calls America "an economic vampire draining the vitality from the resources of people of color around the world," we add the name *vampire* to our political vocabularies. It is William who calls Yvonne Christmas founder of HOBM, with Leona and me as her heirs apparent. "HOBM—Hard on Black Men," he chuckles when Leona and I sweep into Blood Island in front of Essie, who trembles in our footsteps while looking shyly up at William. "Hey, spoonful of sugah." William's face turns to a mask, while his tone goes deep and intimate. Essie blushes to the roots of her huge Afro.

"Listen at him, talking a spoon full of nothing." Leona looks all up in the ceiling, over in the corner at the red, black, and green flag hanging unfurled, while her mouth moves innocently. She knows how to talk about people to their faces without them knowing it.

William is eyeing Essie. Essie turns to smiles that spill out of her like sugar from a too-full spoon. "Where's Rhonda?" Leona's voice doesn't bend up at the end of the sentences like somebody who's asking a question. She says this to call up the presence of William's woman, a very middle-class upperclasswoman named Rhonda.

A blowup of a man named Marcus Garvey in a feather head-dress like African regalia covers one wall and my eyes stay on it, dreaming it in red, gold, and black. My head is tilted toward Leona while we gaze around the room smiling, mouthing mean jabs at William hitting on gullible Essie while Rhonda sits certain she's the future Mrs. Satterfield. Neither one of us likes Rhonda, with her snotty way of meeting other women. Rhonda calls us "dear." And kind of coughs to herself behind us, like she just beat us in a contest we were dumb enough not to know about. Leona and I throw out a high hand to be kissed when Rhonda calls us "sister" in that dreadful, insincere style like she's a supporter of drownings for certain girl-babies or would gladly leave us wailing on a cold mountainside. All us other girl-babies.

Fissures run down from the ceiling. The walls the lightest shade of blue, upon which, as if set against a cracked sky, posters preside. The Marcus Garvey. The Malcolm X. A calendar of birthdays of important Blackpeople. Notices of coming events like the green and black grainy sheet with the visage of a youngish man, sunglassed and disdainful, his head lifted in a stern snort. A finger pointing down at us. I stop for that. In a corner of the same sheet the same youngish man. This time without glasses, his eyes available and promissory. A tender smile like light playing across water. I like that. Someone to watch over me.

Us boring Graces, we lived under the gazes of a thousand saints. I am used to living under the doomed gaze of Anglo-Saxon Jesus at his Last Supper in our dining room. In the living room, Our Mary, a full-figured Black Madonna in red, holding a Black, laughing, haloed boy holding a dove washed whiter than snow. Mama got her from a street vendor somewhere, her red robe a central blood-draping surrounded by men and women all deeply colored like her, of many nations, looking at us in anguish, and angles of holiness and glory. These were the first paintings that I saw and loved.

It was William who said our Gorée should have been called Elmina. Our first visit to Blood Island he gave us a tour and told us the history of enslavement. "More than likely we were imported through Elmina in Ghana. Who knows? If we had named it Elmina, we'd be calling this place the El instead of Blood Island."

Somewhere in Blood Island there's always noise. So much so until noise is no longer and hearing fades into discord and the beautiful, solid stomp of footsteps, the whish of skirts, the sudden yelps of laughter. Everyone, everyone, says Essie, has fallen in love. All but me.

In an upper room of Blood Island William and Rhonda would sway and grind in a passion play under the blue lights that replaced the reading lights. Little white cups half filled with 151 rum, Kool-Aid, and pineapple juice would sit forgotten on the rug, while dancing couples, teeth glowing blue as they smiled into each other's faces, would sway woozy with rum against each other, sway into the magnetic heat of sex that flows like legible electricity from their bodies.

The day William names Essie, and Leona and I watch Garvey on the wall and talk about it all, Rhonda sidles by us.

"Wenches," she whispers sibilantly and we know it is not the word she has for us. We live in Wyndam-Allyn, a freshman dorm, and we're subtitled wenches like a subspecies of womanhood. Essie folds in like my high school uniform. Leona fans out like yards of bright, heavy African cloth. I look at Rhonda, then look somewhere else. Leona goes to class. Essie goes upstairs to the library to feign study. She will sit for an hour or two before the open text, scrawling William's name in the margins of her Philosophy 101 text. I sit down in a corner of the communal room because this is where the action is. A weird solitude is here too because I am a freshman and must wait to be invited into what goes on. Essie has asked me to watch William for her. Just like he's a TV.

William consults with graduate students who visit Blood Island. They are men in their twenties and thirties who have married and started families with their college sweethearts, who are never seen by anyone at Eden. Or they are men who have gone to war early and come home before it is too late. Or they are men who have spent their college summers in the South, riding through brown tobacco rivers of spit while faces stretched into masks of hate leered at them; they have marched and organized with SNCC and CORE, and history taught them new songs that sprout fire in their mouths. They are men who ducked bullets on Asian soil or in the American South. Carefully and nonchalantly they've learned to settle their big feet on possible land mines, exploding ground.

At Eden they put their big, broganned feet up on the university-owned coffee tables. They open their army jackets and we see the single chain dripping Africa around their necks. When, in spring or fall, they come in V-necked dashikis, Africa twinkles like a wet star out of the shrubs of hair on their chests. They ruffle their raggedy beards and squint and tell William how to begin to think. Their voices are no longer boyish. The bass makes the walls move back.

In my childhood, Uncles came to push back the walls with their shoulders, to raise the ceiling with smoky laughter and cigar smoke. After waving "hey there" like visiting dignitaries to the audience of nieces and nephews, after laying a kiss on my mother's cheek, they noisily made their way to the kitchen for coffee, ice water, or beer they carried in with them. The kitchen, during the reign of the Uncles, was a place huge with voices lifting and dipping in bravura tales, eloquent lies, and anecdotal amusements. My sister Frances used to run and hide when the Uncles came over. On the way to the bathroom we threaded through the legs of Uncles, stretched like fallen timber across the bruised linoleum. We hung in the doorways like cobweb artists catching smoke and tasty phrases of Uncle-swagger, those gargantuan Graces, that Leviathan Dancer. On the edge of the perilous, prehistoric world of men I'd lean and listen to the tête-à-têtes and sermons, the rumbling footsteps of barber-shops, slaughterhouses, post offices, and factories. I'd absorb the circumstance of their magnificent hurt and randy spirituality and spin these into a web more complex and intricate, an imagination sturdy and awe inspired.

My web interlaced the lines of genealogy: Granddaddy Grace turning back the posse that hounded him into Mimosa, Grand-mama Dancer dying on the road between Mimosa and Letha, Uncle Blackstrap acquiring his name because he said his love was sweet, thick and wholesome as country molasses, Madaddy assuming the status of savior in war-smoldering Germany, saving the world for democracy. They talked about boss men and jail-houses and who was in them and how they couldn't catch them. Blues and land and the money a man could make. The money a man would know what to do with if he could ever lay his hands on it. The love that was never sufficient to cure the insult; the love that was the insult.

In the presence of the graduate students with their wide Uncle shoulders and Big Daddy feet, I am a girl again, no larger than a garden spider hanging on a web, catching as catch can the thick ritual incense of experience, the whimsy and bravado of stories, the private images sustained in cameras of the heart.

They know everything, these graduate students, some of whom are teaching assistants or visiting professors. They see through all manner of Whites and Negro leaders; they call them dull phantoms with jaws flapping in the whirlwind. They carry around history lessons and like story dancers talk out of their hands. They punctuate the air with their index fingers to make their points and fists to make demands. They bandy the names of historical personages as if they were talking about men they've gotten drunk with or women they've wanted for sisters, mothers, or lovers. They talk about the loneliness and impotence of imprisonment in Southern jailhouses.

"When you are in jail, fifty of you in one cell with twenty piss-stained pallets, you are in jail alone. That's a fact."

They talk about King and Malcolm X. Garvey and DuBois. Marx, Lenin, and Mao. They talk about Stokely Carmichael and H. Rap Brown, Harold Cruse and Paul Robeson. Richard Wright and James Baldwin.

Bigger Thomas and John Henry. They talk polygamous experiments and the brother with two wives who came home to find the wives in bed with each other doing God knows what. They look over at me and stop talking about that.

They start in on Fanon and revolutionary art. I draw beards and swinging Africas on my trees. I draw sister-trees in headwraps made of leaves. Rifles and babies cradled in the branches.

At that moment Yvonne Christmas comes in; it is as if I conjured her up. Her coming to Gorée is unusual because Yvonne doesn't hang around much. None of the graduate students do, but her least of all. She is a first; a doctoral candidate in political economics. She is a sister with an attitude: no nonsense. She has a gigantic brown Afro and a mouth to match. That mouth curved under in rueful contemplation of the world has a natural outline, is bordered in dark. When her mouth is closed, the lips lie next to each other like cozy canoes instead of a gunboat. When it is open anything can come out; she almost lifts the male grad students out of their seats when she names them "armchair revolutionaries." Her laugh is wide and deep like the ocean.

She always wears a dozen silver bracelets on her right arm. We can hear her coming. The men put away their bass when she enters the room.

"What you know good?" she salutes the room as she slams seven econ textbooks on the coffee table, just missing a big foot. Levergate inches his brogans to the edge of the table.

"Hey, Christmas!" he says, his eyes half closed as he looks up at her, a half smile softening his mouth. The others grunt as if the presence of this woman chastises them. (Not like my uncles, who received the entrance of my mother with gladness and a thousand reasons to say her name: "Caroline, did I tell you? Ca'line, you remember?" Beside my father's reticence, the Uncles used my mother's name with respect worthy of the coming of the sun.)

Christmas stays for a while. Long enough to argue with the one named Sherman about his not-so-secret liaisons with rich sorority girls. (Talking Black and sleeping White.)

47

Just before she takes her leave, Yvonne Christmas turns and says to the room at large, "Am I so hard on Blackmen or are you hard on me?"

All the brothers (except for Sherman) blushing at the sheer excitement of her, delighted by her audacity, send tributes of raunchy laughter behind her. They slap five over her womanish effrontery. The front door closes and we listen to her quick home going.

Levergate turns on the couch to watch her through the window. "See you, Christmas," he calls after her like a thirsty man talking to water.

The room gives way to a quiet so safe I can hear birds outside making little pinpoints of sound. The graduate students begin a game of chess that lasts two semesters. Now I work more intently, filling in bird wings, careful on the quills like tiny old-fashioned pen tops. The men recline like giants who have drunk rivers.

Sherman chuckles.

"What?" Levergate asks, making his eyes thin as razor blades.

"Just thinkin what I'd like to do."

"Hey," somebody says. Then he jerks his head at me. I look up, making my eyes blank as water.

"What you know, lil' sister?" Sherman asks me, all professional.

"You," I say. "You." Just like that. Like a sullen little girl determined to tell the truth.

The room breaks up and who but Trixia would walk into the wreckage.

Patrixia is her given name. I don't know who gave it. I know she's made up like a little sparrow, soft brown, tiny, full chested like she's got a lot of secrets, narrow legged, and short, feathery haired. Carolinian, she has Southern charm—ingratiating and smooth. She grins most pleasingly at men of consequence. That's who she said she wanted to meet. One night in the dorm meeting. A man of consequence. She could be his helpmate. Just so he ain't too ugly, she said. Then she actually batted her eyes. She really did. I was amazed. I couldn't stop looking at her. She is a girl who bats her eyes. And she sticks out her chest until it looks like a hand is at her back. A pistol pointed behind her heart. Now, march. And she marches too. It's so interesting. She piques my interest when she comes in catching all those men tearing up the room with their scornful abuse of Sherman. I was a big hit with the fellas. A junior Christmas.

She makes a beeline for William, who is all hunched down in a couch. They watch her like a radar blip on a submarine screen. She sits. And there goes that chest. Filling up like she's got a built-in helium pump. She giggles like she's full of helium too. "Hey, you." She only has eyes for William. No telling who the ones in the back of her head belong to.

William gets grown real fast. He pulls in his legs and leans forward like his hair is having an attack of gravity. "Hey, how you doin?"

"I was fine till I went to philosophy class. The professor acts like he didn't know if this was a dream or what." The burden of thought lowers her shoulders.

Ain't I mean? Just to certify my malice I throw this across the room: "Essie's in that class. She likes it."

William asks to see the book. He the TV that can read. I am disgusted. I mess up and go out of my arcs. That's what I get for calling Essie's name in front of Trixia. Her chest is slightly deflated. Her full chest full of aspirations. She's just a braid tied too tight. Pensive. She wrinkles up her face real cute like balled-up laundry. The book is so hard. Is we or ain't we? That's what William says the fundamental question is. He looks around and says it again. "It's like to be or not to be?"

49

He gets glad when Sherman responds, "That's the mother-fuckin question for your ass." The rest act like they don't feel like adding on. So we leave it like that. Trixia is William's student and that seems comforting to him. Someone to pass his knowledge to. What's been given to him this afternoon. Essie should come and watch her own TV. Trixia is in her element: men.

Once I had a friend from school. We used to go places together. To the library and playground to watch the boys dance ball. She must have had a magnet inside her. Boys couldn't help themselves. They hurried to walk beside her. Me? Have I ever existed? Well, sometimes. There was a movie called *The Invisible Woman;* wasn't as good as *The Invisible Man.* She didn't go crazy or want to rule the world. She just wanted to be seen and wear some clothes so she wouldn't be cold. I was like that with my friend from school. Only it wasn't like I was the invisible one. Every other girl was invisible. The formula was a mass hypnotic. My friend was light and willowy. You know the law of electro-magnetics. I walked beside her nibbling between sweet and sour, peppermint stick drilled into a dill pickle from the candy store.

That's where I'm sitting now, between the medicinal sweet and the sour estrangement. And my stomach is growling again.

We line up outside the cafeteria door to be first for food. It's not like that roast beef is going anywhere fast or the mashed potatoes will ever find some connection to potatoes. We're just hungry. White kids let one another in line. Whistling back from the front to their friends in the rear. In grammar school we called that butting. It was a capital offense. You could get your butt kicked.

When Black students butt it's a cause for alarm. Trixia is the cause. She's showing another side to her personality. Gone perplexity. Present officiousness. She beckons to one of her side-kicks, "Come own, girl."

"Just a minute," a Whiteboy says.

"Just a minute what?"

"You can't do that."

Trixia says, "You act like you don't remember what you did yesterday."

"What are you talking about?"

"I was standin right here behind you in this line yesterday when you told yo pale behind friend to get in fronta you, which I must point out is in front of me."

"That was different. We had a meeting to attend."

"How you know what I got. Mind reader. Come on, Maggie, Leona, Essie, Johnnie, you all come stand before me because you got important things to do. It's okay to bogart if you so very important."

The next day the sign in front of the cafeteria reads: KEEP YOUR RIGHTFUL PLACE IN QUEUE.

It's not that big. But it's big enough to bother me. Things add up. And pretty soon your mind is crowded. Like Mama and them used to think Littleson's mind would get crowded from reading so many encyclopedias. I think he practiced traffic control by sending out tidbits of information to me whenever he came across something juicy that made his mouth water and his eyes shine.

"Maggie, do you know Rosetta stone?"

"She our cousin?"

"Naw, stupid, it was the key to language. Scientists could understand about seven languages because they broke down the code. Ain't that unique?"

Unique.

I start with German instead of French and Latin, which I was decent in in high school. Reading facility. German makes my daddy happy since he went to the Fatherland. And saved it. In

German class Miss Harms has skin thin as ale; her body is thick. Her blonde hair in a pageboy. Her skin like onionskin paper, lightly flushed pink. Never a blush.

"Sprechen sie Deutsch?" she asked on the first day. She has no mercy.

"Nein," I say dutifully and honestly, a word I learned from Madaddy. When does excitement put on the coat of dread? The whole class is praying like the people in Egyptland when Moses made a gentle promise.

Each day the words weigh heavier on my tongue. The guttural sounds as I mimic them sear the throat. Ache the chest. I think of my father listening to this. Then I look out the window; my body closed as a tank. Only the head sticking up. Miss Harms looks at me, window gazing. Her look chills. She doesn't anticipate much. Each day, under her flat gaze, the burden of proof gets heavier on my tongue. Sometimes she half smiles at a correct response, but nothing lunges forcefully out of mind. And the clear field of my mind is restricted now by a wall like the one in China, and flowers grow against the wall. And the flowers, petunias and geraniums, do not open. Can a flower grow inside a tank? I sketch the answer. And I transfer to French class. The Louvre, after all, is in Paris. And my father did go through Paris and bought my mother a gold bracelet there.

Where can I go to hide?

I spend a lot of time with Essie or Leona or both, but I feel a big aloneness I've never felt before. There was always somebody at my elbow asking for something, Frances or Anne Perpetua. Always somebody over my head who loved me telling me something. There was always somebody who looked like me who knew my name, who knew my last name even before I did. Who knew my mother was Miss Grace when I only knew she was

Mama or Ca'line or Carrie. Who knew my father was Mr. Grace when I only knew he was Madaddy or Sam.

One time when I went shopping for shoes with Mama and Madaddy, who was "looking into the cost of all this mess," I slipped my foot into a pair of penny loafers, feeling every bit like a princess with my mother and father standing by with money in their pockets and smiles on their faces. A man walked by just as Madaddy was telling the shoe salesman to put my old shoes with the flapping-tongue soles in the box. I would wear the new ones home.

The man passing by said jovially, "Hey, Angelboy!" to my daddy. My daddy nodded his head.

Mama asked Madaddy, "Who that man talking to, Sam?"

"I don't know," my daddy said.

"You spoke back to him," Mama said.

"Didn't cost me nothing, Ca'line," Madaddy snapped.

It didn't cost my daddy to be Angelboy for a moment. But I knew he was Madaddy. I belonged to those two. I was one of their children.

At Eden I live among strangers. Worse than that, I live with Whitepeople. Whitepeople everywhere. What did that poet say, "Water, water, everywhere, and not a drop to drink"? Whitepeople, Whitepeople everywhere; I can feel my poor heart sink. That sign in front of the cafeteria is the white cap of a high wave that gets into your mouth and shoves your body down under it. In class I am usually the only one. There are no other Black art majors. In large general studies lecture classes, we find one another. The dark students huddle together in the back of the class like gathering close will make a fire between us and keep us warm. Yet in Professor I. B. K. Turner's Afro-American history class we sit right up front like we can't get close enough to him.

Some of us sit way in the back. Me, I'm right under his nose, which he wrinkles at me when he says hello. If he were forty years younger I would be in love with I. B. K. Turner, but he is past seventy and I am just seventeen. He is the warmest place on campus, next to Blood Island. He is a raft in an ocean of white.

Have you ever tried to sleep in a bed full of cracker crumbs? It is hard for me to get comfortable in the classes at Eden U. I make everyone nervous. Professors go out of their way to be nice to me. Or they don't see me and act surprised when a voice comes out of blue air. Like Miss Harms, the flat response to talking air.

One time a professor in art history called me "Miss Race."

I said, "Grace."

He said, "I beg your pardon, Miss Grace."

"Magdalena Grace," I reminded him.

"Negro Grace," he said. Then gulped three times, like he couldn't swallow the taste of foot.

I tire soon of other people's discomfort. I am not here.

Being the One, all of my failures are the failures of the race. If I am lazy, late, unprepared, angry, bitter, laughing, cross-eyed, or crazy, I am a whole race of people. Sometimes I don't mind being the race; then I am like Joe Louis who has knocked out Max Schmeling and people are dancing in the streets for me like Mama said they did in Mimosa when the fight was over and the Brown Bomber had vanquished the fairy story of Aryan superiority. People danced so. I mean to ask Mama if they did the Lindy till the dust woke up and wrapped around their ankles like victory anklets. When I'm Joe Louis or Jesse Owens or Wilma Rudolph or anyone heroic, I don't mind being the race. But I am not a hero. I am only seventeen years old and not a martyr who died at twelve for virtue like St. Agnes or thirteen like Maria Goretti. Sometimes I simply cannot concentrate. And the idea of being the race-that-did-not-win looms large over my head. I have taken the whole neighborhood, the whole extended family and lineage, to college with me. All of their dreams pound in my head so hard sometimes it is hard to get out of bed. I have little discipline, or more than I know. I have always easily been smart.

The loneliness, if we bloods didn't have one another, would be unbearable.

Blood Island is a mystery to me. How I find myself there. Sometimes not knowing how I arrived. What route I took. I, who am always looking. There is a hunger. The trees begin to lose and let loose a melancholy I cannot dispel. I long for the concise bitterness of crab apples. The break of berries on my tongue. Most of all I want the tree of heaven in my backyard. But Blood Island is here. And so am I.

Upstairs in the library I find it among the few reference books—photographs of Gorée and Elmina. Slave castles, they call them. I sit on the floor and open my sketchbook and begin to do a pencil drawing of the kidnap castles. The royal slaughterhouses and countinghouses. Out of those minuscule windows cut into stone the dying and stolen could look out on our loss; infinite loss all around. Squalling hostages inside. The ransom was history. And that is what I write under the sketch. The title. I don't know quite what I mean, but I feel what I mean: THE RANSOM IS HISTORY.

Sometimes we fool around on the steps in front of Blood Island. We play games with the White passersby. Harmless, bold games atop genuine intent. We sing in raucous choruses. Making fun of the White quick walkers and saunterers who give us glances full of humor that say they know the rules and underneath the fear that waits for the joyful, life-loving, and "scary Negro" students to break the rules. To do more than grab at them with stanzas that run:

See them Whitefolks
Across the street
Worried about the colored folks
They might meet.
Better run!
Ka-gamma-goochie!

But tonight we're dressed up and too cool for high jinks.

William has a new car, consequently knighthood. After the set, minus his armpiece Rhonda, he pulls up in front of Blood Island. Behind us, on the steps, the lights are gone. The music over for a midnight. It closed down early because this was the first real set of the season and people had places to go and people to meet and FBO doesn't have a permit yet to give parties after the witching hour. There was trouble last year. The bloods got slapped on the wrists. Some row with a fraternity house.

It's rush week. As it was in the beginning and has been so for over a hundred years. All the sorority houses on this end and the boy houses on the other end are well populated and loud. We hear a shriek, and we turn on the steps. But it's laughter. So we look at William, waiting for something to happen. We're dressed up.

"Rise and fly?" he asks as if life were a game of bid whist.

"We're just going around the corner," Essie answers for the three of us because she's the one who only has eyes for him. That was a record Sam Jr. played—"I Only Have Eyes for You"—"I don't know if it's cloudy or bright. I only have eyes fo-o-or you." The Flamingos, who were not pink, or some dark men heavenly and tuxedoed. The moon is big tonight and its light spreads over us. We are caught then between William's bug-eyed headlights and the blue transparency of night.

We look pretty. Stockings and skirts or dresses. High heels that take us closer to the moon like John Glenn. Orbiting. Never landing. Everything spins fast, still in the party. The black light that turned our teeth colors and the strobe light that took our bodies apart and cut into time.

We get in the car, ready for an adventure. No money in our pockets. William directs Leona to sit up front. Her legs require space. Essie and I fold ourselves on the shelf in the rear. Essie doesn't seem bothered. Relaxed. Just happy.

K-a-r-m-a-n-n G-h-i-a. That's the way William spells the name of his preowned car. P-r-e-o-w-n-e-d instead of used. It sounds like a missile. I think about putting my head down and covering my head with my hands like we did in grammar school. Wind rushes in on us because the car has no top. Everything is out in the open and Essie's hair is dancing.

She washed it this morning in the communal washroom. A row of girls lined up, backs bent, washing hair. Me too. All of us Black. Then in came Evelyn Li with the sign around her neck. I wiped the soapy water from my eyes so I could get a good look. My mouth open, I swallowed some water.

"I can't believe you're wearing that," I said. I honestly couldn't.

I MAY BE A CHINK BUT I'M NO FINK. A handcrafted placard slung around her neck like an albatross.

"It's just fun, Magdalena." Evelyn went on about her business, making up her eyes. She put thick bands of liner on each lid. Her hair shone like petroleum.

I said it again. "I can't believe you're wearing that." But by then it was a lie. I could believe it. Sisters brought their heads up and Evelyn zipped her makeup bag. Smiling. Joyous and a trace giddy.

Looking at Essie's hair writhing in the wind's flirtation, I start to tell about Evelyn Li in the washroom, but nobody's listening. The feel of the car is too new. Their faces are turned to the sides in marked disinterest at the sound of my voice all jerked around with indignation. I shut up.

No wonder nobody danced with me at the set until the last two dances after everybody but two others had been chosen. It must be my voice. But I didn't open my mouth, except to ask a boy named Daniel to pass me a glass of punch. That must have given him the idea to dance with me later. I sounded so thirsty. Now my legs are tight. One jammed across the other. The ride is nice. Every frat house light is on. Flags in the windows, every kind, including the Confederate. Beer cans lined up behind them like in a shooting gallery.

"Hey, there's a Black dude in the window."

"I pledged with them."

"You one of them?"

"Do I look like one of them?"

"What do they look like?"

"They don't look like me." This is a dialogue like a circle—Essie and William.

We come to an intersection. The Institute of Technology on one side. A tennis court on the other.

"Which way?" William asks, even though he's made up his mind. I know that.

"That way." West. Leona inclines her head.

"You must smell the money."

He keeps up a commentary that competes with the motor. "They got a roller-skating rink up in Bellfield. It's always crowded. Bowling in Widmark. We went up there around eleven one night, after we couldn't get in the rink. Couldn't beg, bribe, or crash through. I'd never gone bowling before. Those thangs are heavy. You think you're going to break your fingers. Round and hard and black, look like my roommate's head when he first transferred in. He is a Cue. I take it they were named after those funny-looking heads. And they are some crude brothers too."

Weeping willow. Elm. Walnut. Ash. Chestnut. There's an estate circled in Japanese bonsai—midget and economical. Born with or coerced into bound limbs. The skilled persuasion of an immigrant gardener. William says the wooded places remind him of Sherwood Forest. (Rhonda can't be Maid Marian.) If I had a bow. If I had an arrow. I'd send it straight through William's heart with Essie's name on it. Then she'd get this look off her face. Hopeful. The back of his head a superior omen.

We stay in front of the decorated iron gates of the bonsai estate. Engine idling until dashes of light flare up and widen and William slides the car forward again.

I am uneasy on these guarded streets wherein the dark is darkest and the trees have biceps and forceps that facilitate the births of terrors. My thoughts are misshapen now; the sides squeezed and front thrusting out. Leading me to danger. I hum a little. Notice it. Then I stop.

My knees do not yield in their queer angle of placement. My feet are asleep.

"Your feet asleep, Essie?" I whisper across nowhere. Headlights throw light back at us, into Essie's face.

"No. I'm not really uncomfortable." She interrupts the murmur of Leona and William. "What kind of car did you say this is, William?"

He spells it again.

"Is that Italian?" Essie inquires. Her head tilted. Chin up. This gesture is new—rigid and uppity. It demands an answer. He doesn't see.

"Does it sound Italian, Essie?" We all laugh. Essie folds her hands and makes like there's a back window she can really see through.

The path is still hostile and my stomach is jumping when we stop at a juncture. Everybody in the movies knows you don't stop for night animals. Though they scurry nearly soundless away from the bend in the road. Keep going.

We pull into Gemview, a suburb of dollhouses. The main street is whitewashed and picturesque. Hometown, U.S.A. The townspeople have kept their hitching posts. The horses are gone. Bred away for speed, confidence, and thenceforth money. Perhaps the residents leave ten-speed bikes and purebred dogs tied to straight railings.

"This is cute." Essie surrenders to the view. Leona agrees. I don't speak. I rub my knees. William, of course, has seen it before.

A police car. White, not like the city blue, cruises past us. William acts like he doesn't see it. But why are we holding our breath?

A hand comes out of the window of the dark-inside squad car. William cuts the engine off and gets out of the car. He stands next to the white car. Puts his hand in his back pocket and takes out his wallet. I recognize the Eden U. ID card. Somebody in the squad car starts laughing. Then two laugh looking at the ID card. William says, "Hah, hah." He walks away, not waiting for the wave.

We are tourists then. Sightseers. Cousins from the country. How you gonna keep 'em down on the farm after they've seen Paree. That's what my daddy said the troops sang coming home from overseas.

William won't let Essie see his ID card, so we don't talk to each other for a while. Then Essie says, "I'm getting sleepy." She doesn't usually pout.

"Everybody ready to turn in?" William is louder now. Disgruntled. "How about you, quiet Magdalena? You gonna turn in with me?"

"You better go someplace and hide."

"Ah, hah! You got a dirty mind. I didn't say where. I ought to drive through Whitman Junior College. Check me out—William Satterfield almost the third. With three women at my side."

"You could be a driver for the Red Cross." The wind is in Essie's mouth. You can hardly make it out.

"Do you want to let your feet do the walking?"

"Not particularly."

By now I think we're lost. Then William turns off a tree-lined avenue onto a bigger street. The same one that runs like a stream from the City to Eden. We are close to its mouth. William says it ends only a short way further on. Back where we've just been. I don't want to see the mouth. It's too dark.

"What time is it?" William asks, enjoying playing captain.

"A quarter past one." Leona looks at her wristwatch with the tiny moles of diamond on the face. It's her graduation present from her mother.

I look at the back of William's head.

"You still have to sign in?" he asks.

"Mmm-hmm." Leona doesn't mean to sound so urgent, like a scared little girl.

"Sorenson eats Negroes. I saw that old crow devour one, starting with the feet. Shoes and all. All the way to the head. I brought my lady, Rhonda, back tardy one night and Miss S. met us at the head of the stairs with a ball and chain. And she had dark meat on the menu. She does her own cookin in that little apartment on the other side of the desk. Blood soup and Swedish meatballs. She Norwegian, right? I can't figure out what nationality she is, though I. B. K. says the majority of the personnel in Eden's administration are Germanic. The Anglos and the Saxons and the Vandals and the Goths and the Visigoths. Hammler. Weingarten. Ernst Weil. Can you dig that?"

He goes on saying their names. Having a good time with the guttural accent. I feel bad and don't tell William I had to put German down already. I quit. I put my chin on my knees and my lips moosh up.

Essie is looking over Leona's shoulder into where we're going. The headlights so close to the ground make a wider road.

From the backseat you can't really see what's coming, although I catch a glimpse and I know it's big and hollow and flooded at the same time with lights that take your breath away.

An edifice like no one I've ever laid eyes on. "Oooooh," we all say like little children when the birthday cake is carried, bright and becandled, out of the kitchen.

The lights in the hollows are like candle heads, each core a seed always on fire. Wondrous. Like a gathering of suns set into a high cave. Then the dark spot—dark and prohibitory—where bats whiz in and out like living spaceships from the far regions of the galaxy. Crashing and zipping up the darkness behind each passage.

It takes me a while to notice that most of the light doesn't come from the high tower; it comes from the bottom of the temple. At the base the ground itself is sending up light. Like water sprinklers fanning the clearest water, weightless and fine netting, clearest I will ever see.

William is our tour guide, the master of surprise. He says this is the Baha'i Temple. Site of a religion I never heard of on Arbor Avenue, not even on Plenty. There were no temples like this where I come from.

"They believe in universal love." Is it longing that makes his voice so gruff?

It's too much for me. Scary and huge. I wonder how they pray. If there are fountains and crosses and starved geese descending on windows. Dishearteningly, the road too far, far away and I

62

can't tell if there are figured stains on the windows. I can't tell if there are windows you can honestly see through or if the glass is dark from the interior.

We can hear the bats now in sharp recreation and we are ready to go. For what lies before us is Sorenson, in loco parentis. Sorenson. When you get in trouble, Sorenson personally writes letters to your parents, personally. We've been given fair warning.

The next morning I go to Mass in the attic of a rehabilitated sorority house not far from our dorm. It is an extraordinarily hot Sunday and the room is too close. Fans are no help. Somewhere between the Gospel and the Eucharist a Whitegirl from our dorm faints from the heat. She looking all wilted. I don't feel sorry for her because there is too much drama in the fall. She can't just fall down. Hair splashing. I know it's fake. Then I have to wash my heart because the Gospel rebukes my unkindness. And the Eucharist falls on my tongue like a salving slice.

It's a complete service. They got some grape pop and chicken wings. Plus that soggy Wonder Bread that look like limp mold. They're talking about the scheme of things. The graduate students have grown taller; their feet, monstrously large.

They're more somber than the last time I saw them together. The walls are gone. The room a wide-open field of discourse. Today it's Elder who's doing the talking. His heavy voice filling every spot. The short, quiet boy beside me pushes his glasses up on his nose. He rocks a little. His arms wrapped around one leg. The other foot patting to a noiseless music. In the dorm, after the early rushes, the sisters scaled him a two. On campus I've seen the big boys, who walk like muscle is in they crotches, treat him like a batboy. Try to.

Elder says, "Listen, we know these people. Yet we are surprised and horrified like this monster has been sleeping for four hundred years and suddenly awakened. This is his nature. He's a killer with an enormous appetite for flesh. Humanity does not matter to him, especially ours. Morality does not matter to him. It is something to circumvent, to capitalize on when he locates it in other people. Morality is reserved for the poor.

"They packaged whole continents and wrapped them in cellophane with the people in them. Then they sold the people. Like meat. They butchers, man. I'm trying to tell you. Butchers. The pope himself is the main meat man. Pope Innocent VIII. Endorsed slavery, gave cardinals slaves as gifts in the fifteenth century, if memory serves me. They argued over whether we had souls. Another pope said it was okay to enslave us because we can take the heat. Sonofabitch. Ain't that a bitch! The Pope. I was an altar boy so I know whereof I speak. I confessed all my impure thoughts. And I had a lot of them."

"You talk like it's all over now, El," said Sherman.

"I ain't talking about that right now. You always trying to sidetrack somebody into talking about some poontang. Excuse me, little sister, I am heartily sorry to be so indecent. But I'm mad today. The motherfucker try to tell me JFK, may he rest in peace, didn't have money in mind when he laid them technical advisers on Southeast Asia. I was there. I ought to know." He shrugs something off his shoulders. Gulps some grape pop.

Then I notice Yvonne Christmas in another corner and how pretty she looks today. Her hair is undercover. And her eyes don't miss a thing. They smile at me from way across the room. They smile at the brother beside me. He's short and dark and drawn up. He's smart. Among a lot of smart people. He's supersmart. His intellect vibrates beside me. It sounds like a motor. There's something sad in Yvonne's eyes today. I think it's Cletus the Elder. He says he's angry. But he's sad. A hurt on him. He shrugs again. Goes on.

"The thing is: none of this shit belongs to them. You ever hear of the robber barons, lil' sister?"

I don't know who he's talking to, since he ain't looking at nobody.

"Their families are still enjoying the wealth they beat somebody out of. Real respectable people. When the brothers let loose in Watts and Detroit I said more power to them. More property too. That's the way the settlers did it. Pilgrims. You ever heard of more ungrateful dinner guests? Looting and running wild. Our brothers. And at least we got some claim to it: we worked for it, without pay. We the corvée. Around the clock on full employment. So I say right on to the brothers and sisters who take our reparations. Right on and more power and cash to you, cause whatever you take you liberating in the name of the people."

"And they gone take yo ass to jail in the name of the people."

"Then storm the Bastille. And bring out the old chopping block. Heads will roll."

An excited look on his face, my neighbor turns to me. "What's this all about?"

I shrug, imitating Elder because I adore him. Such adoration breeds discontent. Soon I cannot forget the complicity of the pope. My conscience breaks away from its moorings and I search for an anchor. The sign in front of the cafeteria when I go there only aggravates me, runs me further away from the old placement. I want to talk to someone, but there is no one and I don't know what I'd say anyway. Every Communion rots in my mouth because the pope sold me like everyone else. What would I say? I think about calling home, but they would never understand.

The rest of the day is study, adding to my already crowded brain. That night in bed I climbed into the bottom bunk and lay there thinking. I remembered. When I was a lil'-biddy girl, Grandmama Patsy was an old biddy, cumbersome to receive. We were talking about the weather on the phone and I say the winter up here is too cold and too much snow. And Grandmama Patsy gave me a glass of cold water, a chilly reproof.

"Don't get above yourself now." In my face.

Then I don't want to talk to her anymore, because I don't know what I did wrong and I have proof of censure in intimacy. Grown people just grouchy.

It's me and Mama walking down the alley, out of the church by the back door. I am in white organza and lace. The edge of a white mantilla cutting at my neck. First Holy Communion day. I am seven, an age of reason, elevated by the first touch of the Host onto my tongue. How heavy it was! Like a thin stone from heaven that miraculously melts and goes into you and you swell up inside. I am swell.

Hoisted high inside, fairly dancing over the cobblestones, in my new black patent-leather shoes.

Too shy to show how proud I am, I dance and say, "That stuff tasted funny." I go up on one leg.

My mother looks at me, severe and gently reproving. "That's not stuff, Magdalena. That's the Host."

Host she said like a rich relative who always gives the family party, so you'll know how poor you are in comparison. *Host,* I thought once in biology class, *a feeding ground for parasites.*

I'm stung, and poor, and small next to Mama. But the sun lays light on the cobblestones and my shoes have taps on them that make a sharp cadence. Just like Mama's high heels. That moment I was grown up.

Every flat, white wafer I've ever sucked since I was seven is dust in the mouth. And every ash mark ground onto my forehead in the cross shape is a stigma, grotesque and mocking. I sleep with my eyes open, staring at the bottom of the top bunk, watching the bottom-heavy imprint of Leona's body seem to push down through the mattress. Tonight I am sure that the mattress is the sky and it will come crashing down and smother me. The whole bunk bed a frail edifice. My bed not wonderful and solitary tonight. Just lonely. Awesomely, awfully lonely.

Then this funny dream. Like my mama says. A funny dream. Worrisome; a buried bone of a dream you dig up in the morning and gnaw on all day.

We're in this wonderland. And Mrs. Sorenson, the dorm mother, is there. Looking like Alice in Wonderland, but old. Her hair lived-white but in a little-girl style. A pageboy held down by a white band. You can hardly see. It's so white on white. This ancient Alice is at home in the wonderland and knows the power of her magic. She has pills she passes out to all of us in the wonderland. All of us here. Wyndam-Allyn. Wonderland. She has two purse-mouthed boxes on her vanity table with muscular legs like a ballerina. There in the Wonderland, which is winter and summer at the same time. Open landscape and closed parlor in the same space. The purse-mouthed boxes I see. Those are tiny Pandora's boxes, I say. One box—it is oriented like a pearl, now oyster shaped, and the pill inside it says EAT ME and is pearl shaped, so the letters meet themselves on the circumference.

Mrs. Sorenson says kindly, "Take this and eat this," to the White dorm residents. They do, crowds of them, eating pearls and getting big. Bigger and skin pinker like the insides of the nostrils of white rabbits and guinea pigs.

"Oh, that's the Biggifying Pill!" I marvel. This is truly a wonder. Dreadful and delightful to recognize at last.

To the Black dorm residents with all my familiar faces Mrs. Sorenson offers pills from the other purse-mouthed Pandora's box. This box is shaped like a lily, fluted in semibud, almost shut at the top. She opens it and it snaps shut. She takes out a black and yellow pill. This like a bee.

Mrs. Sorenson says kindly, "Take this and eat it," and she gives it to the Black dorm residents. Mesmerized in that dream-obedient way, we each take a pill that is a bee because I know it. This is a bitter pill to swallow and we choke and gag it down. Some of us louder than others. Some of us suffer in silence.

This pill is magic too. And suddenly we dark girls start shrinking down, shrinking down. Like our bodies are fine wool sweaters in hot water.

"This is—" I say as my mouth grows smaller, "this is the Belittling Pill." This too is a marvel, but I fear this. I am afraid and I am afraid. "I am afraid."

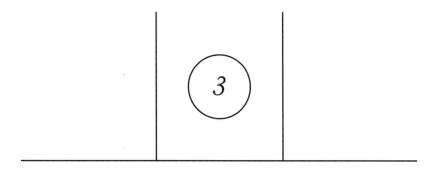

The Ice Babies

At the signal intersection that divides Eden from the City, on the side of Eden there is a cemetery, a garden of pale, porous stone that is studious, implacable, sanguine in the sun or spray that climbs over the jagged rocks surrounding the lake that lives beside the length of the City and Eden.

For generations, the silent Black population of Eden remains at 15 percent of the citizenry. They add to, they subtract from, the population, invisibly.

The Blackboys who hang around the Cave delicatessen and pastry shop assiduously pursue Whitegirls. They are dingy, those dudes, dressed like Sly Stone, in fringed vests and psychedelic pants, hippieish and dingy in the skin. It is hard to explain how they look. Their skin is ashy, as if they've been dipped in flour, or tickled by ghosts, or suffer from a lingering illness. Their hair is not burnished and adored over into acceptable Afros, but dusted by ghosts, grown wild instead like hippie Whiteboys' hair. When they talk there is no music; they sound like Walter

Cronkite giving the news (a deep, sonorous voice, worldwide) but not in it. They spend their lives waiting by the mouth of the Cave, watching the mouths, the hair, the filed-down hips of blondes in granny dresses or swinging bells. They spend their after-high-school, after-college, after-grad-school hours waiting and talking like Walter Cronkite about their luck as Blackmen, about the Black experience. They wait for Susie Coeds to seal the sorrow of the gaping wounds in their psyches—brainy, ambitious, sensitive, young males who want all the wonders the world offers to White males. Oh, to live for only a moment, a fragment of a night, tangled in the moving hair, and to be (in the arms of Whitewomen) Whitemen with all their fortune and privilege. And sometimes, yes, to punish all that White for being White and making you be left out, shunted and shortchanged, to mistreat a Whitegirl. But to marry a Whitegirl and escape at least some of the pain in sanctifying arms, they wait.

They do not look up as a busload of us rides by them on the way to the City.

I look at them for only a moment as the bus slides by. The rest of Eden I don't see at all, until the cemetery. The invisible, the pale, the tomb, the stone of Eden Cemetery by the lake are all perfectly, predictably designed as an Elizabethan garden of English lit. Sometimes, in a rambunctious swoop of sunlight, the stones, the markers, glisten like teeth trapped under glass where Time does not move.

But Time is the father of the malevolent magician whose hand is quicker (or slower) than the eye. The hand has smooched the names, the faces, of many from the markers, so that in Eden so many, the dead, do not know who they are.

We follow the line of water; we follow the burial markers out of Eden and into the City. We, two or three to a seat like kindergartners, are on a yellow school bus. We are bound to know who we are. A rekinkification process. William named it that. The program sponsored by FBO. The name also the goal of our journey back into the City over half of us grew up in. Leona, Essie, and I are City girls, but we are not going to our families' houses or apartments. William says we are going to drink at the ancestral well. That's very poetic. We're really going to EARTH, which sounds even more poetic. Going to EARTH, like we've been on the moon, which sometimes Eden feels like. There isn't much romantic or removed about the mystery of EARTH, which stands for Evolutionary Army Research and Tactical Headquarters. It's a political education center in the heart of what others call the ghetto now and we call home, the hood. After EARTH our bus trip concludes at Great Zimbabwe, a cultural arts center and theater.

Strange how I anticipate these places I might have walked by only six months ago. But six months ago I was a very polite Negro girl with bangs. Six weeks ago. I tell you I am sliding out the birth canal right now. Sliding through the City and seeing it as if for the first time. I look through the window, through my own image, out on sites that are not all that familiar, because this is up around where the other folks live. Before Eden I'd only traveled through this part of the City once that I remember.

The memory is dim and sketchy. All of us in the car with Madaddy and Mama on a Sunday afternoon. Mama would say we had no destiny in mind that day, simply nothing beyond riding and looking at the grand, spacious houses our money would never buy, and if money could, then nobody would sell it to the likes of us. We may or must live in certain spaces, the leftover sections in burdensomely old buildings, one of which my parents have contrived and slaved to own. But dimly I recall the trees and grass so plentiful it seemed squandered, the houses so big a half dozen families could have inhabited a single-family home.

The shiny, mute automobiles that didn't talk back to you as you rode.

I remember most clearly in the heartbreaking spaces, the twilight stop at the ice cream store of an ice cream company owned by a colored lady. How good that ice cream was we spun on cones around our tongues! Mama, brave and dainty, bit into the cold without blinking, placed her hand on her side where the baby kicked.

"This baby likes this ice cream!" she laughed throatily in amazement, ice cream creamy in her throat, making her voice fuzzy. Madaddy jiggled the key in the ignition and talked about one of the new Fords he was going to get him soon, and very soon, because when you see something you want with your heart and can't have you're supposed to talk about acquiring something you can have. Just as Mama's sudden craving for ice cream pulled us out of the affluent tracks of house seeing and back to the side of town we dreamed in.

Essie's eyes keep track of William seated in the front row, his arm draped around Rhonda Selby's shoulders. His shoulders jerk when he turns his head to joke with Steve Rainey; he laughs at Steve's joke. Leona's eyes avoid Steve, who turns his head to catch a look at her. It's all a crazy relay race of fumbled passes; I'm not carrying a torch for anyone, so I just sit and think of what will happen at Great Zimbabwe.

Blinding sunlight splashes through the window. Trixia, who hasn't missed the torture of eyes around the bus, jumps me with a question. "Who you like, Maggie Grace?"

I can't tell her I'm in love with Malcolm X, whose autobiography I just read. He died in 1965 in the Audubon Ballroom. And if I was in love with somebody living, Trixia'd be the last person I'd tell. One thing I've learned, she likes whomever you like or whoever looks at you. She ascertained Essie swooned for

William and she swooned too, although Essie said she didn't and Leona said she did. I saw the concupiscence in her eyes. She knows Steve wants Leona so she gazes soulfully at Steve. Does the girl have an ounce of originality in her passion? Yet, like the armchair revolutionaries who talk bloody change and warfare, Trixia talks sweaty intercourse but gives no action.

Not now. Not now that I know of.

She'd come into our doorway, pulled (she would say) by the heavy chord and discords of James Brown in "Cold Sweat" extending from the box out the door into the hallways. Legs spread, she'd bob from the knees and undulate her hips, making quick slopes with her pelvis.

"Get outta here rolling your belly." Leona'd throw a decorated pillow across the room; it'd hit Trixia's hip like a tambourine. Trixia'd pick up the pillow and grind against it.

"Awhh," she'd say, it hurt so good like she heard it did.

"Girl, you the biggest virgin on campus," Leona'd say, while Essie blanched at such words said aloud. I flinched and Trixia'd get worse.

"I wanna give it up. Give it up, baby," Trixia'd gasp. "But I can't stand still."

Leona'd get up and push Trixia out the door, close the door in her face, while Trixia be screaming on the other side. "Awhh, sistah, why you wanna be so cold? Awhh, sister, why you act so hard?" Sounding like one of the brothers with an unsuccessful rap.

Trixia's clowning makes up for her other sins, at least for a little while, before she hits a nerve. Like now asking me who I like. Just like I'm supposed to unfold the cobwebby corners of my heart on a bus full of bloods leaning this way then that as we roll around potholes. Realizing I have no love life to speak of or not, she gives up on me and looks for intrigue elsewhere. Looking to get in somebody's business. Sexual intrigue is the stuff of life; I'm finding that out. Or maybe it's just sex. Or maybe sex makes us miss the other stuff.

By the time the buildings look like they're falling down while they're standing up, we know we're home.

I can see my mother leaning over the gray banister, or stretching her graceful neck over the brown-trimmed window lattice, singing each of our names, then slamming the window shut in abrupt end to the home-drawing aria: Sam Jr., Honore—O HONey, Katheriiiiiiinne, PEARL, LAZRUS, Littleson! Littleson! MAGGIE—MAGdalena, Ernestine and Shirley, ERNESTINE AND SHIRLEY, Frances, FRANces, Anne? MISS ANNE PERPETUA, you better get in here!

And we would come running, home to that house, home to that woman, that man. Caroline and Sam. The Graces of Arbor Avenue. My brothers scaled the monkey-cigar tree and swore they could see as far as the lake from that tree in our backyard.

How many other houses and families like ours lived in the City then? The City was not the City to me then, but a series of small towns, and we lived in one of them. I was a small-town girl. Other towns set apart from ours by viaducts and boulevards and churches in which people spoke different languages and worshipped a different God and wore skin with the color washed out joined our town at the downtown section. Trains from the towns inside the City looped and connected in the downtown we called the Circle. We rarely went there. And dared not cross the limits into another town. Whitepeople lived there. The same ones who turned dogs and water hoses loose on the colored people on TV. The same Whitepeople with the same expressions. They went to the churches and worshipped the god who didn't love us, or maybe it was like my mother said. The same God as ours told them to love us, but they were disobedient. Incorrigible and disobedient. And surly about it too.

The billy clubs they beat us with on TV, one day God would turn on them and give them a good head whipping. So my sweet mama said.

My father was the one, big as a tree, who could go where the Whitepeople were. On the edge of the Circle, he worked one job; in the center of it, he worked another. One job at the post office where colored men could work; the other at a private charitable organization where wages were meaner than welfare or charity. Or so he said, when he talked about it, which he didn't often do. Because he was tall, we thought he could see above things. Like the monkey-cigar tree that grew so stupendously in our backyard sprouting cigars like an uncle.

I grew up in a neighborhood, a block of time frozen like dry ice from which a heat arises. A drugstore and mailbox stood on one corner. A paper stand on the other. A cluster of churches completed the block, while down the street men and a few women wandered in and out of the Butterfly Inn. We peeked through the dim windows of that place during daylight and saw night, the only constellation a neon sign saying HAMM's. The beer refreshing. Where the big brown bear splashes into a lake of blue (it must be) beer. Hamm's. One time Junior said the drunk man on the block was one of the "children of Hamm's." Mama had to smile but told him don't be so smart.

Everyone had a place on Arbor Avenue. Mr. Rucker, who was the drunk man; Uncle Blackstrap, who was the junkman; Miss Rose, who was Eddie's mother and no one's wife; Mrs. Wilson, who was the head lady; my father, who was the good man you better not mess with his kids; my mother, who was the sun. And a host of women, men, and children.

From the drugstore Mama bought medicine on time. Then everything did not come in a package. And people knew how to open things—like their hearts and conversations with strangers.

Summer nights Mama and Miss Rose brought their kitchen chairs outside to circle the stoop. Passersby could eavesdrop on parental melodies. "Bring me some ice-cold water," "Run upstairs and get me my crochet bag," and "Y'all get off the curb before one of the cars go out of control and come up on the curve on you." Passersby could eavesdrop and ease up on the tension of walking unfamiliar streets because our block sounded like home.

In the absence of elders we children would sing aggressively to the women walkers-by who interrupted our double-Dutch rope tricks, who broke into our Red Rover lines, who zigzagged through our Captain May I, who wore a certain style—tight skirt, skinny heels, and bracelets. Gold-hoop gypsy earrings. We'd sing disapprovingly, gleefully to their posteriors, which were roundly outlined by the skirts fitting like stretch marks.

"Shake it. Don't break it. It took the good lord a long time to make it," we'd taunt the women who were no-one-we-knew's mothers.

"Nine months, baby," a lady would sass back at us. This was a traditional call-and-response. A childish repartee. Harmless and endearing. More than likely it was a memory from the hamlets and towns of the South, something learned and transplanted to the City by the lake. Something carried from Mimosa, Letha, Alligator, Greenwood, Leland, Indianola, Meridian, Monroe, Pine Bluff, Little Rock, Birmingham, Tuskegee, and Tougaloo. In cars loaded down with children, luggage, and survivals, our parents with hard hands and dreamy eyes and mouths thick and heavy with country colloquialisms followed the rivers to the booming factories, yards, and tenements in the North where the dwelling places buffeted back the huge wind that took off from the lake like a plane or a giant bird. The wind called the Hawk that tore the skin off your bones and set the bones to knocking on the street corners while you waited for a bus or a dream to come by.

They settled in the rambling houses on two wide boulevards setting off a park on the South Side, a mile or so from the lake, on the edge of a university and the surrounding posh section inhabited by well-to-do Whites. The Black section, small and contained for fifty years or more, was called Blacksmithville. Blacksmithville, or Smithieville, in its earliest days was the home of the Blacks who served the wealthiest Whites and the factories and yards of industry (especially when the unions struck and owners opened their doors to scabs). It was the home in its earliest days of Black blacksmiths and ironworkers. Sometimes Blackpeople called that place Ironville because artisans lived there who worked in iron crafting fences, grates, gates, and fire escapes, and they called it Ironville because the Blackpeople there were so strong that they had survived the City.

Trains then were the veins and arteries of the nation, not the free-floating circulatory system of the sky, and dapper men of color with quick, quiet tread skimmed the railed ropes to the heart of the country, which was this City by the lake where the Hawk that did not then have a name blew and tore the skin off people and the hordes of farm beasts routed there for dying. The Hawk tore the boweled stink off the cows and pigs and spread the odor over the Irish section, the Jewish section, the Black, and then the Central European sections. They slaughtered the animals there, and people were slaughtered there too. The traveling men who came with the trains made homes in Ironville. Places for quick loving, good food, fast women, and shuffling cards. Out of those places came music that captured the mood and pulse of a people too subdued to chisel a tablet of stone. My daddy told me about that music, while he hummed it under the kitchen sink as water ran down his arms and the stubborn pipes moved under his hard turnings.

My daddy was always fixing things in that house he bought from the widowed Whitewoman who moved to Florida. All the houses on our street obtained from fleeing Whites who scrambled to escape the expansion of Ironville when the post–World War II farmers and laborers came from the unchanging South to the city they had heard about from cousins and kin who came down with stories of plenty and progress. But by then the discarded houses of the European escapees gave off peculiar odors, mice, roaches, and calls for repair. And Madaddy was always answering those calls. The absentee landlords of the tenement that took up half the block turned scarce and the building began to die while the people in it multiplied.

In our house there always seemed a baby and a babysitter. I wonder if my mother found her swollen stomach friendly? When she was round with Anne, Ernestine and Shirley climbed into her high, big bed and drew a big smile and button eyes in red ink across her belly. Mama mostly slept lightly, but not this time. They stroked so softly it was like being tickled. The baby was curved, full and content inside of her. When Mama woke and discovered the drawing she laughed and laughed, until she found it would not wash off so easily. Over a stretch-mark design it stayed a face for more than a week.

I thought that red mouth and those smile-closed eyes were friendly, hilarious. When Mama brought Anne home from the bright Catholic hospital because the colored hospital, ill staffed and broken down, had served her bologna that stuck in her chest when she lay after having given birth to Ernestine and Mama said nobody should be born there until they made it a decent place for human beings, when Mama lifted the soft green blanket from Anne's face, exposed, it seemed to me, was the same face my two sisters had written on the round, outer ceiling of the ancient birth cave. Everybody had a laugh, thinking Ernie and Shir had seen into our mother's womb and translated who and what was hidden in nutritious water. Translated before its time. Or their wish, perception, of such a joyous face was drawn into Anne Perpetua's humors. Anne is the funny one. They molded her into the sister-person of their desire. They founded a friend.

I began in the morning. Katherine Pearl was born around midnight. Sometime around the midnight train going by. Before or after the train whistle blew, she coughed out her birth. Which came first, the whistle or the scream?

Anne Perpetua was born laughing. When the doctor slapped her bottom she looked like a sweet clown or a saint with egg on her face. And she giggled to be here. She was given to appropriate and inappropriate laughter.

Once Ernestine dropped Anne. Anne began to laugh. Sympathy and panic were on my face, stamped in Anne's eyes reflecting me. Anne began to cry. She learned her pain from other people. Just as I did.

Honeybabe said she was retarded. Honey said that I was retarded too. Honeybabe says we all retarded. She is the oldest girl, and disdain is built into hierarchy.

Sometime in my preadolescence the double-Dutchers began to sing a new song about disposable babies born with no certain sex and brutal destinies. They sang and I sang with them a song that came from out of the air:

Fudge, fudge, fudge, boom, boom, boom.
Call the judge, boom, boom, boom.
Mama got a newborn baby,
Not a girl, boom, not a boy, boom,
Just an ordinary baby.

Wrap it up in toilet paper.
Kick it down the elevator.
First floor, Mrs. Carter.
Second floor, Mrs. Carter.

On and on the baby flew, thrown away, sexless, a brown mistake.

This was near the time of the birth of the ice babies. When the weather grew colder after the summery seasons of our early dreaming in the City, expressways cut out memories that ran through the place once known as Ironville until even that name was forgotten, families knocked against one another in the tall housing units thrown up by the City like dams to hold the deluge of Blacks who swelled past the limits of the town inside the City reserved for the darkest children of the American dream. The old Southern gestures mutated and the young men learned new walks that leaned against the Hawk. These young men dipped in their knees. Boys gritted their teeth at an earlier age. Much of the game went out of the flirt, and girls no older than me or my sisters raised their skirts, babies fell out, with gritted teeth and tears of ice.

Packed together in the frozen compartments of the impersonal public housing projects that soared into the cold reaches of the Hawk's nest, children came out like clear, separated cubes of ice—hard and harder. The row of tall buildings that speared the sky sparing no blue space, now (as if under the influence of a comic god) those buildings themselves threw people away as used spare parts.

There was a dog named Calypso. A terrible albino Doberman pinscher dance with long white teeth. Calypso chewed through the fence that caged him and chased children's legs that moved like fascinating pistons just out of reach of his sharp face. Once his tongue licked my calf and the fear made me break the sound barrier. But my scream must have excited Calypso; he pursued with greater zest. He was happy and evil: if he caught a child, he would eat it. He could not catch me.

If you think of cruelty, think of albino haunches, fleet movement, and white fangs. Cruelty is a colorless dance. Malice is a certain kind of motion that chews through wire and chases you and chases. It is not to be explained, and so fascinating that you must look at it. Look at it from over your shoulder, from behind a scream of terror and self-sympathy.

From our father, Sam Grace, Littleson learned to beat wood rats with shovels, then flip the earth and fold them in, furry, fat, and poisoned bodies. Littleson caught roaches and stuck toothpicks up their tails and held them over the front stove burner, watching them crisp and curl while he laughed and I was appalled.

For Littleson these small acts of sadism were practical. I agreed with the intent but hated the style and the delight that Littleson took in the pest penalties. I refused to learn cruelty because I could refuse. Littleson efficiently grabbed the stray cats that lurked over the back stairwell to leap on the least suspecting. He took hold of the spitting, clawing beasts and swung them by their tails, beating them against the back-porch railing, then sent them sailing to the ground below. The cats hit the ground like terrified but instinctual trapeze artists who know how to land on their feet. Centuries before cities had taught them this. Then they gunned across the ground like bullets with Littleson's special notch etched on their sides.

Littleson would dust his palms and stomp down the steps. Fearlessly. Without a swagger, more a glorified practicality. He was, in the moments after the raids on the roaches, the cats, and the rats, heroic. Larger than his still-boy self. He had mastered a degree of cruelty; he had triumphed in the hunt. He could walk in the company of men. He acquired new height.

The other boys, who were mostly the sons of renters, who had no place to protect, no territory to stalk and watch for, turned their cruelties elsewhere. They boiled into manhood. The liquor of them overflowed from their bodies and touched their fiery environment, and their liquor smoked from their bodies into a stench or a lingering musk that drove girls wild. Their aromas arrogant and chokingly alive. Promissory and profane. They could smell themselves.

The Watermelon Days belong to them. They pulled a plug out of summer and tasted their futures. They tapped and knocked a melon and heard the hollow fates. They tore their thirst from sweet red meats and swallowed the black and brown seeds whole. They washed one another's faces in the green and pallid white rinds during the Watermelon Wars. After the battles they piled their flaccid weaponry in a garbage arsenal guarded by flies and went back to the houses cursing one another and wiping the wet from their faces before it syruped in the sun.

They were the sons of men and women who owned nothing or little besides broken promises. They grow up to be dangerously unfettered. They could grow up to be cart men who walked the streets and alleys like refugees from a war-torn landscape. They could be devil-may-care like young Uncle Blackstrap or delirious like older Uncle Blackstrap.

They would always be happiest in summer. Every warm and shining summer day they'd drag their tow-cart lives over the divided avenues, carrying summer ice and variously flavored syrups; a hunk of ice that they scraped, scooped, and stuffed into triangular paper cones, then drenched with fruit tonic.

In winter they would pile rags and refuse (metal, paper, and porcelain toilet stools, face bowls, and kitchen sinks) into the same wooden wheeled stall and wheel it all to a yard to be weighed.

Money things they plucked from garbage cans. Hands that delicately shoveled for wealth among the filthy odds and ends in early fall touched the wet fruit remains of summer and remembered the feel of boyhood.

One summer day Littleson and I were eating a watermelon. Our cheeks rimmed inside crescent watermelon moons. Littleson raised his foot and smashed what he thought was a roach. When he lifted his foot we did not see a roach corpse or milky-white roach guts. There was nothing to despise; in the changing light it had been a trick of the eye. There was only, before us, an adult watermelon seed like a flat, polished worry stone perfect for the palm of a child's hand. Something to fondle the sensitive nerve. Something to touch.

It had been a magic trick of sunlight. Littleson had thought that the innocent seed that came with the sweet fruit was his natural enemy. A common mistake.

"Crawl, nigger. Crawl, worm. Crawl, dog. Got shit in yo pants."

"Want me to put yo nose in shit? Huh, fly? Roach? Worm?"

"Stuff yo mouth with it."

They beat him until they felt the texture of his muscles change. His head slick, syruped over with his blood. His arms and legs limp as rubber tubing. His tongue a strap with no buckle, hanging out the side of his mouth. Mouth unhinged.

In a glistening, gritty pool of his own waste they left him where Uncle Blackstrap found him. Curious, casting a cursory glance in the basement window, a constant eye open for junk and refuse. The sight of the boy made him sick. He took his gloves off. He wiped his mouth with the back of his hand. Erasing the scream before it was born there in the vacant basement. Soothing the vomit reflex. Blackstrap was a man who had traveled in war lands, where it rained shrapnel and stray pieces of human flesh. But World War II before atom bombs and death camps had been a kind of clean war. Hadn't it? That is what they said: a war against evil. In any case what he had seen was nothing like this. A boy who could have been his son. Ruined in this way.

The boy was so flaccid and still that Blackstrap was afraid to stir the rummaged organs. So he stumbled from the basement empty handed, called an ambulance, the police, alarmed the Grace household, and carried something terrible on his tongue to Eddie's mother, Miss Rose.

What happened to Eddie was the first true clue that I had that the worst thing that could happen to a boy or a man was not to be unemployed.

Such cruelty narrowed kitchenette whippings, sister fights over clothes, wars of protection, and hunting to nothing. The hate was too large to go inside us. It lurked, touched us, licked at us. This was the first news heard of the birth of the ice babies in our lives. No one ever knew who hurt Eddie or why. But we knew they belonged to winter, and they were subject to tricks of the eye. They could fall on you like bandits, but they were not bandits. Because they were the ones who had been stolen from. They and Eddie, who did not die in the days after the beating, although all the doctors knew that he would.

Winter yawned in our faces, licked our hands and feet. Caroline would tell us stories of foolhardy boys who went outside without earmuffs, who'd lost their ears to the winter, as if the City were a war. The Hawk a guerilla that ambushed across the boulevard.

Rising before the sun our Littleson pulled a sled loaded with newspapers in the light that the moon sent over its shoulder, the first glance of sunlight.

Eddie was in the hospital all through the winter. We were too young to visit him. Only Miss Rose saw him every day. But once or twice I went, and Littleson went twenty times and stood below Eddie's window so that he could see him. Eddie would look out through the frost-frescoed windows. He appeared to us, a shrunken head on a pointed stick body, smiling like an angel.

In spring when Littleson (who insisted on being called Lazarus more and more) stalked before our eyes, we made new markings on the doorframe to measure his growth. Eddie, out of the hospital, had come back old, walking on wobbly legs. Like a sailor who had been lost at sea too long. His legs folded up unexpectedly under him. Littleson would catch him and hold him tenderly like an autumn leaf that he refused to allow to touch the ground and be gone.

Littleson, now known as Lazarus, who he had always been, would not let Eddie measure his height on our doorframe. He hustled him away and gave him comic books and oatmeal cookies. Eddie soon forgot the notches on the wall; at least I thought he did. But I stood staring at the spot where he had been standing unsteadily. I have an eye for detail. I knew if Eddie had walked and stood against the wall, in that doorway, the top of his head would have come to the same etched line that he had made the year before. He had not grown when everybody else was growing.

This knowledge, which Lazarus protected him from, was known to him. He glanced up from the gaudy pages of the comic book and stared at the doorframe.

I went to the kitchen and took a fresh batch of cookies from the oven. Oatmeal cookies were the only sweet thing that I could make alone. I gave Eddie a whole plateful for his private consumption. Littleson who was Lazarus by then did not complain.

Every two weeks Eddie went to the clinic with his mother. We'd see them walking down the street. Eddie with his pinched body and Miss Rose with her pinched eyes. Miss Rose told Mama that Eddie couldn't hold his water. Mama told us Eddie's clinic visits made her think of her Uncle E. W. and the Keep-You-Sick Clinic.

Later that spring there was so much rain that the eaves were tipsy and the gutters were swollen and drunken, spilling over. Trash tightened the drainage. Yet in places gasoline oil made murals of the gutters, and we, one day, Lazarus, Eddie, and I, would watch our faces shifting in a rainbow when we found one. Such pools could be like the house of mirrors wherein faces would seem huge, gathering comic perspective. We laughed together for a while.

Before the announcement of new watermelon, before the beginning of summer, Eddie died.

Littleson let me hold his hand for two minutes at the funeral in Star of Bethlehem Missionary Baptist Church. This was when Miss Rose rocked from her spine, gathering momentum like a dark, black-breasted bird, stretched out her arms like great sepia wings, sent up one shout that she didn't own, that panicked her, and let grief try to fly above itself, above her body. Her sorrow was magnificent; ours was so quotidian, so humble that we were ashamed and even more afraid that she would pull some of the same overwhelming magnificence out of us. We were Catholic and did not shout in church. Yet our mother and the sisters in white seemed to know exactly what to do for Miss Rose.

Lazarus wiped his eyes and gnawed his bottom lip. Fascinated, I craned my neck to stare one last time at the boy in the coffin in the immutable trance of death.

It was all a mystery to me. We never learned why the ice babies had beaten Eddie. They were never caught, although some people said that a boy who had been in the reform school for stealing a car bragged behind the barbed wire that he was a killer. They said that he had shrugged. It had been something he had had to do. They told us who he was, and we looked for him in the parade named after an imaginary Whiteman that wound its way down three miles of boulevard. He was in the St. Edmund's Drum and Bugle Corps that turned out the annual end-of-the-summer parade. He was a standout musician, in a troupe of gut-grabbing, finger-popping music boys. We all said that you had to respect a bad boy. He could blow a horn with incorrigible style, and his drumbeat was the rhythm that sent a wild freedom through the crowd. We pulsated with the beat they sent out. It was alive.

I remember feeling buoyed up in the crowd. Like someone who cannot drown. This was a mysterious feeling. Lazarus had climbed a tree and was poised like a lookout for a pirate ship. There were policemen all around. They looked displeased with us, as if we were breaking the law by being so happy. Secrets ran through the air. I eavesdropped under the music. Perhaps the boy who killed Eddie was there in the street, making powerful music that jarred our bones and our teeth. Maybe Eddie was listening. Now leaning attentively on a cloud.

Suddenly I wanted to not be sure that the killer boy was blowing a horn. His sound, delicious as it was, could only carry germs. Cold is contagious; soon we could all be frozen in the attitudes of ice, like whole generations playing "Aunt Dinah's Dead." Oh, how did she die? Oh, she died like this. Assuming some bizarre position and freezing there for an endless time. Catching cold and giving it.

✦

EARTH (from outside appearances) is a hole in the wall; inside it is an elaborate array of military maps, weapons, charts, and posters. Brothers in fatigues stand with their feet apart. They look angry and alert. Here I am uneasy about the shady-looking brothers I was taught to avoid. Lazarus my brother and I grew up calling them the ice babies and staying out of their arctic zones. We said they were so cool they were cold and had frozen their own blood. We said hello to them on the street and kept on moving. Lazarus, who was Littleson then, bumped shoulder with a few of them in the alley games of basketball. But ice babies were never his bosom buddies. Their style was too cool.

Girls didn't befriend ice babies. Girls, for the ice babies, were things to use or own. The ice babies had shown us what they were capable of. They had stolen Lazarus's paper route money, tried to steal our trick-or-treat candy, and stolen our friend's life. We were permanently scarred by the scald of their incredible temperatures. We avoided them.

At Eden we come to know our mean attitudes of survival as middle-class notions of self-hatred. The ice babies, who are fighters, fierce and courageous, should lead us. We sit obediently in metal folding chairs as they teach us the cruel, cold facts of social change.

A man with dirty-snow hair and goatee, as old as my father, or "old as black pepper" as our neighbor Miss Rose would say, dressed in the style of our generation, faded jeans and equally well-worn army jacket, introduces himself as Alhamisi and we Edenites sit up attentively. He sounds seedy with age and cigarette smoke; his teeth painted beige with nicotine. He holds his head regally like an eagle in a cage.

The maps and charts dense with the images of rats, buildings, and rifles fill us with foreboding and curiosity. Alhamisi pauses lengthily to let our disquiet sink into awe.

"You come down from that big White university back to the ghetto that spawned you to find something that ain't up there. You really think you're something because you sitting next to some honky in a classroom in his university. *University* got the word *universe* in it (did you see that?) and you ain't in theirs. But you think you got the world on a string. I'm here to tell you and you here to hear, the only use for that string you got is as a fuse for some dynamite to blow that brainwashing bullshit factory up." Alhamisi is like an ice baby in the rapid style and contemptuous undertone of his rap. His mouth is a machine gun, blowing us away.

I'm ashamed for having ever harbored a granule of pride at receiving a scholarship to Eden University. I scratch my ear, watch Essie watch her shoes and Leona observe her perfect cuticles.

"Call that university Eden, don't they? Well, you ain't Adam." He points to Steve Rainey, who jumps at the singling out. "And you ain't Eve." He points to Leona who I expect any minute to say, "Don't point yo finger at me. My mama ain't dead." Just like you'd do automatically when someone pointed a finger at you. Even your mama doesn't know why you say that. You just say it. But Leona is silent, gulping, while Alhamisi jabs the air in front of all of us saying, "You the serpent wrapped around the tree of knowledge. You think they want you there? You the slimy serpent keep putting them up to take a bite out of that apple and live with the knowledge of their terrible crime. You the serpent with the reminder of the strange fruit. Strange fruit. You think they want you there?" His eyes burn into us for a time. Then he goes on. "The government made them take you. All a you. And Watts and them other cities burning made the government make them take you. I don't care how intelligent you think you are. We been intelligent; they ain't taken us before. You think yo intelligence gonna mean something and get you somewhere? It'll get one or two of you specially selected Head Nigger in Charge positions. But you not going to have any power. There he is Negro in charge of grinning and shuffling and talking with a whole lot of er-ahs. Who gone be your boss, potential head Stepin Fetchit, like Lightning and Bojangles? Who?

"One of them mangy, tangle-headed hippies. That's right. One of the beautiful flower children say he don't want no part of this system his daddy waiting to hand over to him. There he is! Freaking off! On the floor! Yo boss! On every drug there is. Doing every kind of freaky unusual sexual activity there ever and never was. Rolling round talking about some flower power sucking on a joint. When play time is over, he gone cash in them flower petals and take his daddy's place, just as nice as you please. And where you educated ass gone be?"

A fatigued dude steps aside and Alhamisi moves to the first chart, which is a detailed diagram of a maze made mesmerizing by the huge illustration of a rat on the border. "Where are you now? You in a maze in a laboratory known as U. S. of A. That's right, you educated out of your minds. You nothing but laboratory specimens. They controlling you like they controlling that fat wig-wearing sister on ADC, like they controlling yo daddies and mamas punching them time clocks every day like good dependable slaves. Look at this illustration here. It shows you how rats trapped in overcrowded mazes grow crazy and turn on each other."

We stare at the illustration of rats multiplying geometrically till in the final frame they are all over one another eating one another alive.

"Did you pass those sixteen-floor projects the government built especially for you? What they look like to you? Huh? WHAT DO THEY LOOK LIKE TO YOU? Mazes."

A mass intake of breath around me—like we've all been blowing up a huge beast-shaped balloon and suddenly it looms before us out of our own breath, large and grotesque.

"That's the plan to pile us up one on top of the other in their government designed mazes we can't get out of. They plan to pile us up till we turn on each other." Dead silence. He looks into our faces one by one, marking the progress of his message. When he begins again his voice is gentle, soft as slow drops of blood. "And we will and we do. Cannibalize each other. Fighting like scavenger rodents among ourselves. Kill each other for nothing. Rip off each other. Rape and disrespect our women. Turn on our own selves. Don't let nobody tell you there ain't no such thing as Black suicide. Suicide is killing yourself. We killing ourselves. Genocide is engineering the death of a race, killing a people. They killing us. Next time you gazing at one of them projects being so glad you ain't living there, think about genocide. Next time you college girls gobbling up them birth control pills, think genocide."

William's girlfriend, Rhonda Selby, in the row behind me, makes a harrumph deep in her throat. I can't tell if she's angry about what Alhamisi's saying or redeemed by it. Essie puts a hand over her mouth, like she's restraining an urge to vomit. I ask her if she's okay. She doesn't answer me. Her eyes glued to Alhamisi.

"Genocide is the order of the day. Genocide is the national agenda. What happens when we wake up and get hipped to the truth? What happens? They'll herd us into concentration camps. They'll round us up—from the projects, from the universe-cities, from the penthouse apartments overlooking the lake, from

Doctor Hill, from row houses, and mud huts, from the American Bantustans—they'll try to run us onto reservations like they ran the Indians, after they broke down and broke their Indian law, and seduced their warriors with firewater and made live-in whores of Indian women. What they gonna do with us after they round us up?"

Dramatically, like a preacher in the spirit, he whirls to a new illustration on the wall: photos of compounds surrounded by barbed wire. Then he lets out a shriek that uncurls our hair and sets it on end, that pries our eyelids open and loosens our mouths in horror and amazement.

"THIS IS WHAT THEY GOT IN STORE FOR YOU. THE SAME CONCEN-TRATION CAMPS THEY USED FOR THE JAPANESE DURING WORLD WAR II. THEY STILL STANDING READY FOR US. WHY THEY STANDING IF NOT FOR YOU? BARBED WIRE FENCES. AIRPLANE HANGARS FOR DORMITORIES. MEN DIVIDED FROM WOMEN. CHILDREN DIVIDED FROM ADULTS. ROBOTIZED. THEY WAITING FOR YOU!"

Our mouths are open and an awful dread gathers around us. We're breathless, looking askance at one another like duly terri-fied children. My head hurts and Alhamisi wants to save my life, wants to save my life, wants to save our lives, keeps going off in my brain.

At the front of the room, Alhamisi chuckles and I am convinced all this concentrated conspiracy has made him crazy. Laughing at a time like this. But he's laughing at us, not with us. "Are we gonna stand still and let them herd us into extinction?" he whispers, then booms. "HELL, NO."

His eyes are bright with a vision he sees somewhere over our heads. The vision causes a hush in his voice and makes him sweat like someone who's just swallowed cooling water after a parching thirst. "When they come for us we'll go for them," he whispers. "We'll head south to the land. Back to the land. Before they round us up, the Black underclass, the masses, will be on the move. We'll *blaze* a path to the South, burning up gas stations, electrical compounds, unchaining nuclear reactors, burning *it all*, leaving total devastation in our wake, heading south, a burning, raging mass of Blackness. The Black underclass will set up in the South to continue to wage our war for freedom, for survival. On the very lands we made holy with our sweat and blood and tears, we'll begin. That farmland will sustain us as we wage our war for freedom.

"How do we move together when the time comes?" He knows we have no answers. So he asks his questions to grind our stupidity in. "We set up a system of order and accountability. We start to live under Freedom Law. Now."

He unfurls a code of commandments printed in boldface on cheap parchment. These are the commandments. Who thought of them I don't know.

1. No Black man, woman, or child shall take the life of another Black man, woman, or child.

2. No Black man, woman, or child shall rip off another Black man, woman, or child.

3. All marriages take place under Freedom Law. A Black man shall take as many wives as he can protect.

4. All Black people must train themselves for survival and war.

5. All Black people must contribute their resources to the survival of the Black Community.

6. All leaders must be accountable in their actions to the Black Community.

7. All Black children, unborn and born, are the responsibility of the entire Black Community.

8. All Black people must be committed to the survival of the Black Community before the survival of any individual.

9. Black businesses that support the Black Community must be supported by the Black Community.

10. No Black man, woman, or child shall betray the community or conspire with its enemies.

We read the commandments in silence. "Come back and see us when you want to get in touch with the reality of war. Come back and see us when you decide to quit bullshitting and be warriors for the Black Nation." Alhamisi dismisses us and we file out in a heavy silence.

The sun is sinking when we come out of EARTH; even so, we blink like once-blind people adjusting to sight. The City looms around us, burdensome and terminal. The storefronts advertise chicken, cleaners, groceries, records, liquor, and God. Everything we might need in a maze. Across the street from EARTH, children in the loud bliss of ignorance enjoy the smell of backyard that coats their skin and call out to one another in the dusk lyrics to a street game:

Last night, night before,
Twenty-four robbers at my door.
I got up, let 'em in.

Hit 'em in the head with a rollin pin.
All hid?

Eavesdropping on the words we grew up singing, some of us giggle because the game has not changed. We giggle giddily too because the children's words harbor a wisdom we need now. It is difficult to articulate in language we learn in Eden. I mull over this while I mull over the Apocalypse according to Alhamisi. Nobody says anything.

We file back onto the yellow school bus bound now for Great Zimbabwe by way of Aisha, the restaurant of the Nation of Islam. We have heard it is a serene oasis on a lazy drive. A quality place to go on a date if someone with some money ever asks you. Christmas smiles at Levergate and I hear her tell him, "It's a good thing we came here first. We need some niceties and music now." We are in our seats and ready to be away.

I avoid the ice-glittery eyes of Alhamisi as he stands in front of EARTH looking into the windows of our bus, watching his long-faced audience retreat.

At last, the bus snorts through the familiarly numbered streets of what used to be an addition to Ironville.

"What the hell," Levergate hollers back to us from the front seat. "Eat, drink, and be merry, for tomorrow we may have to kill somebody." The bus cracks up. We laugh so hard the laughter knocks against our hunger and wakes it up. We head toward the Muslim restaurant where we'll order baked chicken or whiting, salad, rolls, and bean pie.

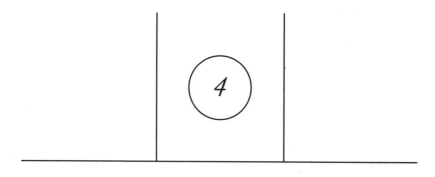

Great Zimbabwe

My daddy told me the story of that block. It was across the street from the end of a mile-long parkway, the parkway's end jutting out like a pier of grass into the concrete. Sometimes the street is so bumpy it feels like it has waves. At one time the block-long building there had housed a thriving catering business that serviced prosperous (need I say) White civic leaders given to having gala festivities. The colored caterer expertly constructed boats of shrimp and ice, frappés, succulent hams, and dishes of freshly slaughtered beef sauced in light butter and spices, the names of which he would not reveal. The civic leaders gorged themselves on his repasts regularly, till they grew most corpulent and the veins in their noses and cheeks swelled to bursting. That chef sent them into epicurean ecstasy. So my daddy said and I don't know who told him these things, because he was still in Mimosa then, or a dream in his daddy's eye in a farm outside Letha. My daddy talked to other men who knew though, in the places where men tell things.

In the same lifetime as the caterer, the huge graystone was also the location of a grand gambling house of silver roulette wheels, loaded dice, and round card tables in small, smoky enclosures. It was an immensely beautiful club—not only because its sporting life clientele dressed in such satin finery. (The pomade-headed men in black and beige polished cloth vests and sleek pants that obediently followed the flow of their sex and limbs and the beige women in overly ruffled pale satin, their kinkless, genetically Caucasian-like hair eschewing the need for the newly devised straightening comb or, before that, the endless need for endless brushing.)

The Ace of Spades, generally regarded as the king of such clubs, was a beautiful place because there beautiful music charged the air. Not the arias of overstuffed or desiccated sopranos, not the mellifluous guitar-striped wail of the Moor-inspired Spaniards, not the chants of the white-robed choirs reading black notes dancing on white sheets to the rapid arm signals of the choir director. Not exactly the hypnotic dust-dancing ritual songs of African cloth makers, reapers and sowers, grain grinders, masked and masqueraded priests and country people binding a nation together with the bloody threads of song. Not exactly that African song, but close. A song divided from the older African ones, divided by guns, bead barterings, war instigators, fearful, duped, or greedy and duplicitous leaders, suicide and oceans and a land where burdens were so heavy and the lash so cruel its cut snaked and churned in the blood and the song laid down too much of memory and picked up new habits.

Still, the Ace of Spades, slightly seedy, of limited opulence and mimicking decadence, was beautiful when the musicians came up the long river and the segregated train and brought the music. The stiff-backed piano opened its black and white mouth and laughed when the velvet-fingered player brushed its teeth.

Saxophones and trumpets at the big lips of round-cheeked horn men became the fabled horns of plenty. A cornucopia of life-fulfilling sound.

Some woman, big bosomed and buttocked, big footed and fine, a shimmy dress fitting tight around the hips, a feather poised in her hair, a river in her throat, would flood the night with blues. Or a slip of a girl would loose all night a stream of pain and wit and sensuality that would work a groove in a heart of granite.

That was in one life.

In another lifetime, after the death of the renowned chef, the shop and club gave rise to a series of ill-financed clubs that opened and promptly failed. In 1939, while Europe flamed, the old Ace of Spades had been gutted by a fire. In 1942, the Colored Bugle Corps opened and closed.

Throughout World War II only rats and Black black marketeers made quick scuffling music in the once regal graystone building. In 1945, two veterans of the Negro Corps of Engineers (chain gangs of college-trained volunteers and draftees who built airstrips in the Pacific theater) came home. They pooled their resources of accumulated army pay and opened the Club Desiree. Negroes, buoyed by the job booms during the War, dressed up and went out at night. The Club Desiree was the place to go. Brown-toned women pressed their hair, curled it, then pinned it into upsweeps that ended in frizzy cliffs over their foreheads.

This is where Mama and Madaddy went when they first moved up from Mimosa. I've seen the one picture of them, seated in a booth behind the curve of a round table. Mama is pretty under a little hat with a black net that crisscrosses finely in front of her shining eyes. Her dress is long sleeved with puffs of air in the shoulders; the neckline swings down to her bosom. She had nursed five babies by then. Looking gorgeous as any woman in love with her husband home and her cotton-picking days over.

Looking relieved as any good mother with her babies safe at home in bed, and another one—Frances Samella—quiet in her belly.

The evening is "a salute to Negro veterans," posthumously honoring Dorie Miller. Dorie Miller, the cook who picked up the rat-a-tat-tat of the machine gun and shot down the enemy planes that swooped down over Pearl Harbor. My father, Sam Grace, bird tail intact in the front of his Negro regulation haircut, has donned his ten- or eleven-year-old army uniform. He is handsome and still hopeful, having found a decent job (two decent jobs), having made steady payments on a house in a neighborhood where Whites were caught as if by a slow-motion camera in midflight, having moved his young yet sizable family up from Mimosa to that street that was Arbor in one spot and Plenty in another. His eyes are dreamy and his mouth is pursed as if he were about to sing.

There is attitude in this photograph of my parents taken I am told by a "cute little" meandering photographer who doubled as a hatcheck girl when somebody called in sick. It is a special occasion. I think the chorus line kicks moon high. This picture in the shadow. Two visitors have arrived from Mimosa, Mississippi, just stepped off the platform from the City of New Orleans. They all lean forward around the curve of the table. My Uncle Lazarus, whom we call Uncle Blackstrap, who is Mama's brother, seated on the edge of the curve beside my father, leans so far across the table the top of a bottle of Scotch seems to pierce his heart. My Aunt Leah-Bethel, my father's sister, sits next to Mama, her elbow propped on the table, a cigarette burning down to her knuckle. She doesn't seem to notice.

My mama told me the singer that night was Mockingbird July. I laughed at the name. I had never heard of her. My daddy didn't look at me but sat in his chair, and half chuckled, half giggled in his deep voice. He rattled his magazine. I felt like saying, "What's so doggone funny?" in just the tone he used on one of us, belligerent, defensive. I rolled my eyes at him and looked again at the picture. Looking at pictures was one of my favorite things to do. Hearing Mama and sometimes Madaddy tell about them was another.

"Mockingbird July sure sang that night," Mama closed the album clumsily and threaded a wisp of hair back into her knot. She shrugged as if she had nothing more of interest to give me and she were less for this. I kissed her on the cheek because this was enough. Is.

My daddy finished telling me the story of that block. I listened without knowing I was listening. The Club Desiree was the place to go for more than fifteen years, until downtown clubs opened up to Negro patrons and the more than three quarters of a century old buildings of Ironville began to fall into extensive, nearly irredeemable disrepair.

My daddy said Mr. Rucker said in the barbershop one time, "Any fifty-year-old man's plumbing fall down, what you expect from a building? Mortar and brick ain't no better than mortal man."

The barber concurred. So the Club Desiree went into gentle decline as Negro entertainers popped up open mouthed and soulful on *Ed Sullivan,* following Nat King Cole and his own show in 1956. "Right in my own living room—Nat King Cole." Mama pretended to faint, acting like Honeybabe and her friend Charlotte would over Smokey Robinson or Sam Cooke at the stage show. Mockingbird July, however, never came on *Ed Sullivan* nor did she grace the downtown clubs. I would have heard of her if she had.

The momentum of the war boom had turned into a cold war. During an especially harsh and frigid winter, pipes burst in the Club Desiree, flooding the basement, warping the dance floor, ruining the walls. After the thaw and survey of the water damage, a mysterious fire swept through the club. In 1960 the Club Desiree shut down.

And that is where my daddy's part of the story ends.

Seven years later my part of the story begins.

We disembark from the yellow school bus in front of what once was the Ace of Spades, king of clubs; briefly, the Colored Bugle Corps; and, finally, the Club Desiree, before this incarnation as Great Zimbabwe (House of Stone), so called after the eleventh-century religious ruins of southeastern Africa. Great Zimbabwe is a mecca for the Black Arts Movement—revolutionary poets who dip and dance like sanctified preachers when they read, saxophonists and flutists who combine the quirky beauty of bebop with the atonal freedom of African ritual music and the lyricism of Ellington, dancers who wide-leg leap to ceilings like spiders on fire under history's inflammatory eye. Artists who carry their paint supplies on their backs in bundles like African women toting newborns washed down the ruined walls of Club Desiree and created a mural documenting Black history from ancient pyramid to urban projects and Southern shotgun shacks. From the magician-warrior Sunni Ali to the murdered Malcolm X. From the Queen of Sheba to Gwendolyn Brooks, poet.

As the final segment of freshman rekinkification ("Guaranteed to put the beautiful, complex curl back in yo mine and on yo haid," says William) we welcome anything after the somber news from EARTH even a quiet dinner at Aisha could not obliterate. A plethora of color and sound greets us. The murals dwarf us. Women and men wrapped in loud prints assail us with warmth.

"It's like going into a new land." Leona says what I am thinking. I am more certain than ever that this long-legged, obsidian-dusted girl with the half-inch Afro, shorter than my daddy's bird tail, is kin to me, like my cousin say. Leona has her own mind. She cut her hair down to express her own style. She's always talking about getting to the root of the matter.

With new, EARTH-sobered eyes, we look around us at the brilliant banners of struggle and ancient glory none of us had really heard about before.

Essie is looking tight in the shoulders, all bunched up. She hugs herself. All three of us are miniskirt wearers by now. It is Leona who stomped back to the dorm one evening, flung open the closets, pulled out our three entire wardrobes (not that much really), cut off hems, and rehemmed for three needle-clenching hours straight. She is a swift, obsessive worker. Her hands fluid and swift like a spider at its craft. I ironed down her handiwork. Essie kept asking, "Should we?"

We march into Great Zimbabwe, an army of miniskirted Afroed girl-women and knit-topped or shirt-and-jacketed boy-men mingling with smiling hordes of cornrow-headed women in colorful long dresses and bearded men in bright dashikis. They stand ready to reclaim our lost consciousness. That is their mission. Blessedly, they don't look nearly as mean as Alhamisi and his crew.

I am hypnotized by a huge poster of a muscular Aunt Jemima arm wrestling with a helmeted policeman. The nightstick in both their hands. Or is it only in his? Her apron whips and tangles. Her neck is stout and knotted in rage. On other posters, a host of haughty African queens, pitch eyed and sloe colored like Leona, glare disdainfully down at us. I want to rise muscular, ox blooded, and haughty. Be "Magnificent Magdalena Grace—isn't she incredible! Her work is so wondrous." My hands itch for the possibility. But what if the prophesied Armageddon the brothers at EARTH promise comes to pass before I do, and it is so terrible I cannot join my destiny with it after all?

Brothers in bright-striped pointed cloth caps sit astraddle big drums. Calloused hands pound and tap into blurs of loud rhythm. We move toward the center of the sound. The drummers make an arc on the stage. We head toward front-row seats. Leona boogaloos down the aisle—both arms raised, fingers popping, shoulders shifting, and hips shaking, stepping forward by gliding from side to side. I follow suit, more subdued but just as glad about the drums and being Black. Essie looks for William to be sure of what she should be. But he doesn't see her so I guess she decides to be invisible. William flings his arm back behind him and Rhonda has his hand and falls into his footsteps.

We sit down and bob in our seats, clapping hands in answer to the drums. A tiny bearded man in a black and purple velvet gown sweeps onto the stage. He gives us a gap-toothed smile, lifts his delicate brown hands, and the drumbeats cease. Our hands stay poised, apart in midair, in unfinished applause. Open mouthed we sit, welcoming the wonders of Great Zimbabwe which tell us our Africaness lives forever. Which is curative, since the EARTH men have told us we'll die tomorrow.

Hazes of incense hang over the purple-draped stage. We inhale deeply, breathing the magic in, imbibing the purple of the little man.

"Who the fuck is he: Tiny Tim?" Oakland is vicious, comparing the purple magician to the stringy-haired flower child who sings "Tiptoe Through the Tulips" in falsetto on the *Tonight Show*. I don't relish sitting next to her through the whole show. I've had my quota of disparagement.

Leona gets away with playing sergeant at arms a lot. The tall have an aura of authority. She reaches the long arm of the law across my lap and taps Oakland on the arm. "This is serious business, sister," she cautions Oakland, who promptly rolls her eyes and tosses her vinegar-rinsed, relaxer-stripped, meticulously curled, instant albeit harshened Afro. Leona makes a soundless "bitch" with her mouth, but only I see this and tell her she ought to be ashamed. We in the temple and all. And she the law.

The tiny priest speaks. "Welcome, my young brothers and sisters, down from the halls of Whiteness into the temple of Blackness. The young brother here, William Satterfield, informs me that you are students at Eden University." He renders a low hum and rumble of a laugh here—wise and dismissive. Whereas my parents levitated with pride at my scholarship to Eden, folks around here act like it's no big deal.

"We know Eden was not the beginning. It's only as far as they choose to record. We speak of the home of the original man—the Blackman—the original man."

"No women in this original land. Right?" Leona whistles renegade and salty.

William and Rhonda, sitting in front of us, turn around. "Sister, why don't you just listen," Rhonda says, like she's an exasperated teacher of sixth graders. William takes this opportunity to stare into Essie's eyes. I can't stand this: Rhonda trying to put Leona down while William's hitting on Essie, keeping her hoping, so I say as loud as I can, "Excuse me, Rhonda, but would you turn your 'fro another way. I can't see." Everybody in earshot, which is everybody from Eden, hoots.

Then Essie comes alive. "You too, William." She yells as loud as I did. William turns red, but he's got the panache to smile. Rhonda just turns around. It's Essie, Leona, and me, vigilante and vindicated, with our eyes on the stage.

The little man in the long gown lifts his arms and horns swell up, the sound pushing the ceiling. The sounds swoop like huge birds with indigo wings. Flutes zigzag through the waves of saxophone and trumpet like moths newly spun out of cocoons. The tiny man's fine-boned hands hold a thumb piano while his thumbs race crazily over the metal slices, leaving heavy throbs in the air.

Then the dancers leap onto the stage, the one male dancer in a ritual costume of straw that covers his face and torso. His bare feet crossing and stampeding, then parting from the floor going high in the air. Each woman dancer is in one piece of cloth tucked at the hips and another crisscrossed upholding breasts. They sway like hot ice is in their hips and livid embers under their feet like the priests of Shango Professor Turner told us about. The Eden brothers look pleased with the rapid intensity of their thighs and pelvises, their legs and ankles.

A girl-dancer's breast breaks out of the cloth and male voices break out in spontaneous pleasure, "Good googa mooga!" and "Good golly, Miss Molly!"

The women die of embarrassment: we imagine our own breasts so unwrapped before the crowd. The dancer dances on, while other men watch the nipple bob like an overripe cherry on a watery surface.

"God gone strike you blind," a cool female voice sails over our heads. And we know it is Christmas with a biblical prophecy for the salacious. At last the sister tucks the disobedient breast back into the fold.

When the dance is over, the priest lectures on African sexuality. There conjugating is not dirty. Secondary sex organs are more functional than obscene or provocative. The women of some people may dance unbound. Puritanism has made us all dirty children in the eye of the nipple. His audience properly chastened, the priest introduces John Olorun, master poet.

"He's so fine," Trixia already in the know about Olorun oozes at the name, as another underfed fine-boned man moves into the lights.

John Olorun wears shades that wrap around his eyes like raccoon's markings, or a Zorro mask. He slips through the crowd of students, the brothers studying his stance and walk, the sisters casting dreams of rescue and romance into the slight mold of his physique. Longing thuds heavily in my chest like a stone tossed into a dry well. I can hear the same desire echoing among sisters gathered here. We've seen pictures of Olorun, minus shades, smiling from a poster Great Zimbabwe sent to Eden, which we unhesitantly posted in Blood Island. Somewhere around Marcus Garvey. A homage achieved in the space of a slim volume of poems, *black acts*.

I wish I could draw in the dark.

We dream of his eyes—a dense brown we imagine losing ourselves in, where we find the lost secrets of cathartic release and serene repose under the gaze of a tender god. The wish stone vibrates inside me. Like an egg cracking into life. He of the hidden eyes has a voice that barely slips out of hiding; it comes out of him husky, covered in innuendo, furtive, quiet as wine. We lean forward, us would-be women, closer to his whisper; we wait for the heady rush of flight, lifting wish stones out of our insides. He knows, doesn't he, his power? He draws images in the air, whispers, and does not look at us with his hidden eyes. All his nuances enchant.

He makes a joke about bloods ripping off sisters, laughs without sound. A twinless dimple flashes in one cheek. A sigh at the sight of the tiny triangle in the cheek ripples through the sisters. Most brothers study him with greater intensity— searching for flaw or scar. The remaining brothers guess what gesture, eccentricity, of Olorun's to cop and incorporate into their caches of coolest mannerism. Always there is one or two or all who listen only to the words.

Ducking his head shyly under the blue glow, John Olorun reads a poem he calls "Promiseland."

> *Race-keeper,*
> *Warm-bringer,*
> *Misunderstood by her man.*
> *I have seen you sisters,*
> *Lovely queens, quiet in your beauty.*

"Talk to me, Black man," Trixia says, lust making her voice old and rusty.

> *Unwrap the brother from the lamppost.*
> *Make him stand*
> *So he can lead you*
> *Into*
> *Tomorrow—a woman.*

"Lead me," Oakland exclaims, like Great Zimbabwe is Great Mount Zion Missionary Baptist Church instead of a remodeled Club Desiree.

> *Angel of destiny,*
> *Queen of horizons,*

John Olorun dips and bends in his knees like a doo-wop crooner pouring out basement music. Smokey Robinson or Sam Cooke, who we still miss even in his heartbreaking death. John Olorun has the moves.

You withstood the ocean.
You withstood the lash.
You without anyone withstood
The cold corners of our
Lost manhoods.
You cried in the night—
The bed empty beside you.

Rise in the morning, sunshine,
Warm-bringer,
Light-keeper,
Sister, mother,
Destiny daughter.

I bring you bloody roses of struggle.
I bring you a tall shadow
To walk inside,

Safe, protected,
Away from evil men's eyes,
Away from mud-mouthed
Usurers,
Pawnbrokers,
And death-pushers.

Unwrapped from the lamppost,
The brother reveres you.
Out of his Cadillac lean,
He stands,
A Blackman.
He will guide you, milk and honey
Woman,
To the only Promised Land.

John Olorun ducks his head in a quick nod to us as all of us rise like pieces of dawn in the darkened theater after he finishes three more poems. (One more to Blackwomen, the others to the Negro man.) Sisters, leaping in place like light racing up and down through blinds, whistle and cry out. He has changed the hint of vinegar to wine, wish stones to iridescent blossoms yawning seductively under his poems. The brothers take his words for the ones they couldn't find. They whistle and pound their palms together. The poet slips from the stage, quick and quiet as the shadow he promises Promised Land women.

We are properly primed now for the segue into LeRoi "Get Down" Clay, the King of Primeval Funk, the Original Toe-Jammer, the Consummate Lover, the Sweet Papa Stopper Doo-Wopper, who steals daughters into righteous frenzy. He does. Even if we're not overcome by him, we act like it, cause it's so much fun. A dynamo of hair, deep dark skin, white perfect teeth, encased in a psychedelic suit—a red that throbs. The color thunders. He lands onstage in a James Brown split, mimicking a hyena with his scream. The spectacle is atavistic wizardry, an answer to an ancestor's prayer, "Do Lord Remember Me."

He steps over the blue horizon of lights and says, "We here. We might as well make it all right."

The Great Zimbabwe Orchestra in the background is too loud to be background. More like a complement. He is Brer Rabbit Foot Clay rising out of a split, thighs trembling and shimmering, fire in his mouth, and visions of the chimera in his hands. Any graceful, muscular animal you can name commanding his body. Each finessed gesture an African survival.

I don't know when it happens but I'm in the aisle with everybody else. Re-Africanized. Jubilant. Dancing in the aisles to the Clay version of "Papa's Got a Brand New Bag."

And we all dance till we can't.

In the lobby of Great Zimbabwe, called the Marketplace, like the selling place of an African town, Levergate and Christmas are standing at a book table, both of them reading one copy of Fanon's *The Wretched of the Earth*. I thought they'd have read that by now. I have. I see Christmas's hand tremble and Levergate reaches out with his other hand to still the quiver in the pages. Then Christmas lets go and reaches for *Why We Can't Wait*, which I know she's read because she marched with King. And Christmas has read everything. Levergate looks at her in a shady way. I drag my feet a little when I turn away, caught in the glance. Magdalena, the Superwoman, guilty as Superman with X-ray vision that sees through propriety and poses.

I walk behind Oakland. She makes flirtatious eyes at a flute player who says he wants to give her lessons. Oakland twirls a stick of incense, lights it, and blows away the fire. She gazes at the man through a twirl of smoke, her lips still puckered from the blow.

"My two wives play flute," the musician says.

"Two who?" Oakland sputters. She recovers real fast. "Great Zimbabwe is so wonderful," she trills. "Goes to show you how African majesty can last forever. I'm never going to straighten my hair again." With a grand gesture she touches the nappy edges at her temple. Does not disturb her kitchen, which I am looking into from behind. The Man with Two Wives smiles wanly, bidding Oakland all praises and telling her anytime she wants to soar, he is here.

The minute he steps away, she turns to me, "Did you hear what that bigamistic baboon said?"

I love to know more than she does. "It's not bigamy in Africa, Oakland. It's polygamy. In many countries it's entirely acceptable."

Oakland, not to be outdone, says, "Everything African ain't wonderful, Maggie. They don't kiss, do they?"

I can't argue with that. Mainly because I don't know if Africans kiss or not. Oakland doesn't care about my comeback anyway. She's off after some new adventure to report at the midnight dorm session.

The man with two wives has found Leona and he's telling her he's looking for a third wife who looks just like her. Tall and dark. His other two wives are yellow and short and red and medium height, respectively. Leona listens politely while she slides away quickly as LeRoi Clay does the James Brown one-foot shuffle.

I feel sorry for the man with two wives. Because two aren't enough for him.

Simba is an artist selling his paintings in the Marketplace. He wants to paint Leona and Essie. Leona introduces me.

"You study art, huh? You gone teach it? Don't know many female artists." His glance sweeps over me like an old broom, passing over, leaving debris. My breath is high in my chest with the vanity-induced hope that he will say he wants to paint me too. But he doesn't. He arranges to meet my two best friends for Saturday sittings at his apartment. I may tag along. My build is heaviest. Size 9. I must be the bodyguard. He might be Bull Connor in a master disguise.

Now Essie is studiously listening to a brother with the biggest gap between his front teeth I've ever seen. It looks like the place the Red Sea came apart and the Israelites ran through. She's concentrating so hard on the brother with the gap, her shoulders are tense, and I guess she misses William and Rhonda at the next table cuddling and being sweet. William's mouth brushing the edges of Rhonda's hair.

Leona is free of Simba, having set the time and place, and she whisks Essie from the gap-toothed wonder. I'm glad because Mama and Miss Rose say that's the sign of the liar. Then again, in Africa I hear it's a beauty sign.

Whichever it is, he's moving on me now and I turn fast to go the other way. To the Queen's Room. Which is a dungeon off to the side of the lobby, led into by many narrow steps.

The Queen's Room is occupied by someone from Eden. "I hope you don't have to use it," she advises, "because it can't be used."

"Beautiful," I say to the toilet that doesn't work. "I didn't have to use it anyway," I say to the girl called Hamla. "I was escaping from a gap-toothed man who tried to swallow me alive."

"Him," Hamla says and goes on working on her hair in the shadowy mirror.

Already she has acquired an African name—Hamla—and Lumumba for the president of Congo who danced the rumba in a silly song. Under the radio, head bowed to a scaly fork, I remember his name announced. He fought for something. I liked him. We are surprised when professors say her slave name, Camille Loomis. She is Hamla Lumumba and she writes poems. On occasion brothers have called me Hamla. "Ain't you the sister who writes?" an upperclassman asked me when I got on the bus going to the City. "Naw, I'm the one who paints." Before that, in one day, three different brothers yelled, "Hey, Hamla, what's happening?" to me. Into the dorm room I had flown to the mirror to engage my true identity. In the mirror we stand together today. And I search out the distinction between us.

Hamla's skin is like polished pecans. So is mine. Hamla's eyes are almond shaped. So are mine. Hamla's eyes are keen with intelligence and soft with imagination. Aren't mine? Hamla's body is ripe and curvaceous, innocently curved in jeans and sweaters or skirts that are modest as minis go. So is my body curved. Hamla's hair is gently sculptured. So is mine, shined with Afro Sheen. Hamla is shy with restrained pride, tender ego. So am I.

In the mirror I am gloomy because I am not spectacularly individual. I search for exemplary deviation—my cheekbones are higher, my face fuller, my hips rounder, my arms thinner, one tooth almost imperceptibly chipped one day when I was seven and drinking water from the kitchen faucet. A piece of tooth, like a large grain of sand, in the palm of my hand. I trace the tiny dent in my tooth, relieved to be set apart by the smallest memory. Hamla leaves me in my minuscule victory. I comb my hair.

When I reenter the Marketplace, Hamla who looks like me is talking to John Olorun, the poet. I recognize the glow around her as she hands him a notebook full of what must be her poems. She bows a little when she talks to him; he looks earnest, ducking his head like a retarded goose like when he performs his poems. I observe him coldly because he's not talking to me. Envy crawls from under my wish stone, slips through me like a snake. I have nothing to show a poet. My right hand lifts to the tear duct in my right eye. I want to ask why my hand paints instead of writes at a time like this, when poets rule hearts and imaginations. And get so much applause and approval in the Marketplace. I scoot near enough to hear John Olorun promise to give Hamla a call after he's read her poems. What's she doing carrying poems around with her anyway? I don't carry an easel. But I sure wish I could.

Everybody but me has found something to treasure in the club known as desire. It feels like that.

Trixia has a craving like she's pregnant all the time. This time she longs for barbecue with mambo sauce. She moans for it so loud and long we start to want some too. Leona swears her daddy's barbecue is the best in the City, but Pryor's BoneYard is too far to go.

"The bus leaves here at eleven-thirty and we're not keeping colored people's time," William warns us in case we're still thinking about trying to make it to Leona's daddy's for free ribs or chicken and back in time for the bus to Eden. Essie knuckles her hunger under William's warning. She gets on the bus obediently, which makes Leona and me more determined to taste the forbidden sauce.

"I heard about a place," Leona declares. Mutinous. "Three blocks from here."

"Who's hungry?" Trixia announces the question to the crowd. And Oakland, Hamla, and two other sisters line up with their tongues hanging out.

Stomachs rumbling, mouths watering, we go in search of mambo sauce and bones to suck on.

"Flesh eaters. Flesh eaters. That pig, cow, and bird will kill you, beautiful sisters." We beautiful sisters now. The man with two wives admonishes us, loud as neon, painting us scarlet. Like the kids sing, "Yo mama got the measles and yo daddy got the pox." Mama laughed one night at the window, crying from that song. "When we was little, pox meant syphilis." Anything evil and contagious. We the ones.

"We gone die smiling," Trixia says, and she trots on down the street behind Leona. Then we follow.

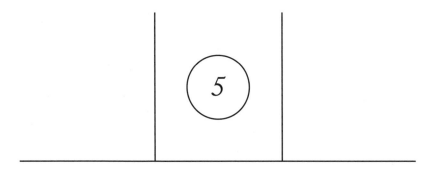

The Blue Rose

We are north of Arbor Avenue and a little to the east, only two miles or so from streets I have known since Mimosa. Leona walks stupid with wonder like that Alice girl, only seeing everyday things as if for the first time. She peers from the sidewalk past the loungers grinning like Cheshire cats at us brave stranger girls; she looks instead at the buildings themselves. What was once grand architecture of splendid lines and enduring construction is now overcrowded brownstones divided into cells of economic mitosis. Sprawling two-story frame houses split in the middle to make five apartments. The buildings have submitted to the crimes of time, neglectful management, and too many inhabitants. They sagged into agedness and disrepair, lost windowpanes like teeth, and shed brick, wood, and paint like hair. They loosened their seams and squatted slovenly behind concrete aprons with bloodstains and raggedy grass splotches. Everyone hates a slattern with a bad reputation, even if she was once a great beauty, abused and ill treated. They revile her and everyone says they are contaminated by her presence. Property values spiral down.

"Why do we always get the leftovers?" Leona's voice comes gently from out of nowhere in the darkness. She is voice for each of us, subdued and sudden. The talk of the day walks with us like Jesus. We cannot shake it off: gloom and glory.

Then from the bowels of the building comes, "Get out! I told you don't bring that shit up in here!" A clutter of footsteps and doors slamming. Then the streets thick with silence like suspended animation.

"Wonder what that's all about?" Hamla lets out the breath she was holding, only to whiff it back in as we pass the reeking urine spot on the corner of a building. Whiskey is next. Another door opens and a man dressed in a security-guard uniform steps out with the hallway smell of burnt beans. He carries a brown-paper-bag lunch in one hand, while the fingers of his other hand caress the curve of his company-issued gun. He eyes us keenly, suspicion coming with the uniform, which has HAPPY'S SECURITY FORCE stitched on the pocket. I can smell the Polish sausage in his paper bag as he brushes past us.

None of these smells is new to me. I have smelled them all on Arbor Avenue, but they strike me as new now that we have left the sublime hallucination of Great Zimbabwe. The majesty was all a mirage, I think, all that lost history, that art, ephemeral and, if not ephemeral, then beside the point. Having glimpsed the radiant shimmer of Great Zimbabwe as fevered desire, how now can I say I want to be an artist? What can I do to change shabby circumstances? What difference can I make?

The Hawk has eaten leaves from the trees that stand between street and doorsteps. And young men stand shivering on corners, their fingers pinching close to the fire on cigarettes, which they pulled from behind their ears. They have to have something between their teeth—I think—to keep them from grinding and gnashing their teeth to bitterest sand. Something (cigarette, toothpick, reefer, wine bottle, whiskey rim, lie) must be there to keep the nuisance chatter of teeth muted in the awesome chill that is more than something on the wind. It is early autumn and should not be this cold. We college girls pull our sweaters and jackets around our breasts. My nipples turn hard and I am nervous.

We giggle and make small jokes as we saunter through the dark, nodding congenially but quickly at the doorway loungers and the judges of the stoop who pass judgment on us. But the tactic of swift politeness does not work. A lounger slides from his position and matches steps with me. Why me?

"Hey, mama, what can I do for you?"

I can't think of one thing.

Trixia, who likes whoever likes you, says, "Hey, brother." She is just the right casual. "Ain't this the way to the best barbecue in the City?"

"BoneYard the best. But Roscoe's will do." He is very serious about food. "You hongry, baby?" he breathes in my ear, determined to make me in his family. His mama or his child.

"I'm looking for some barbecue." I don't turn my head cause I don't want to look in his nose. He's that close.

"I got a bone for you. The mambo sauce inside."

"That's too nasty," I sputter.

Leona joins in. "You ought to be shame."

Then Hamla recruits him, "Why don't you respect Black women and walk us to the place. Instead of talking that old talk?"

So he walks with us. He tells us his name is Berry, spelled *B-E-R-R-Y* as in the blacker the sweeter. He promises me he's sweet. His last name he says is Loomis. Hamla, who used to be Camille Loomis, observes him closely in the dark. "I don't suppose we related."

"What's your daddy's name?" Berry asks with interest.

"George."

"And your mama's named Beatrice? And your daddy's got a older brother named Abraham?" Berry is gleeful and talking really quickly now a genealogy of names nobody would or could make up out of the blue. "And the oldest brother Abraham had a son named Edward and Edward have a son name Berry and that's me."

"I think you my cousin." Hamla whistles.

"Gimme a kiss," Berry says angelically.

"I ain't that happy to know you." Hamla pushes him away. Her hand pressed against his chest. But he looks so sad, so she brushes his cheek with her lips.

Now we break past the shadow of trees lining the sidewalk, and moon finds us. Leona says, "Anybody know the man on the moon's mama's name? I bet you he colored and she from Mississippi or Alabama."

We are happy to be Black again, gliding through the nearly midnight streets. By now I'm sure we're not going to be back to Great Zimbabwe in time for the bus back to Eden, but that doesn't matter. We can glide back with grease around our mouths. The night's like that. Even Mrs. Sorenson, the dorm mother who will put us freshwomen under house arrest when we come in late from the City, doesn't faze us. Trixia will cry and lie for us about how we went just around the corner for something to eat and we didn't hear the last call and we got left and we were all alone in the terrible city. And it will be all right.

Roscoe's is next door to the Blue Nile, a basement blues club giving notice to the densely quiet street with a blue neon rose positioned on an iron banister that leads to the cellar. When I see the notorious electrified rose blazing blue from roots coming out of the iron railing, I point it out to my friends from Eden and begin to tell the story of the Blue Nile.

I don't know who told me or told someone else I eavesdropped on, but the Blue Nile is the place for authentic blues. The owner, who was called Blue Nile before the club was, is a big, buxom, double-barreled woman who's a cordial hostess who sets you up once you come to her club the second time. She's a smart businesswoman, honest as glass, and a connoisseur of the blues in its many shapes, especially the form that evolves along the Big River and shadows that river, then jumps a train to the City by the Great Lake.

Sometimes people don't read the words and read instead the bright neon symbol that smokes when you get up close to it. Then they call it the Blue Rose instead of the Blue Nile. I don't know which name I like best: Blue Nile because it is ancient and I exult in the smallest survival and like anything that's African, or Blue Rose because I've never seen blue roses and their existence here is improbable and evidence of miracles.

Sometimes, too, Miss Rose's boyfriend called her Blue Rose down at the garage when she sold fried chicken dinners (fried chicken, potato salad, spaghetti, green beans, salad, homemade pound cake, and two slices of white bread still smelling freshly baked from the bakery around the corner; on the side, a personal mayonnaise glass of lemonade costing extra), which we delivered for her church's charity drive. "The poor giving to the poor," Mr. Boyfriend said as he tipped me and Littleson and Eddie before Eddie died. The mechanics, drenched in grease, would wipe their hands or not, poise the paper plates on their laps daintily like well-schooled princes, and praise Miss Rose, who they called Blue Rose or Miss Blue Rose, while blues rolled from the grease-smudged jukebox in the corner that only played Jimmy Reed,

Little Milton, B. B. King, Bobby Blue Bland, Dinah Washington, Joe Williams, a girl named Aretha Franklin, Billie Holiday, and a woman named Mockingbird July singing a song I didn't know. Now that Mama and Madaddy had told me about her, her name was everywhere.

The greasy mechanics lit into the church food, stuffing their mouths with crusty pieces of meat, slippery spaghetti, and buttery pound cake that left a film on their hands that blended into the film of oil already there. They licked butter and the blood of cars from their fingers while we watched them like acolytes permitted the vision of gods at supper. It was supernaturally romantic to hear Mr. Boyfriend call my mother's friend Blue Rose; I knew then that wonders were possible.

Maybe it was at Mr. Boyfriend's garage that I first heard about the Blue Nile, also called the Blue Rose, or maybe before then from the mouths of loud-talking and mumbling uncles, or women who tell stories with the lift of an eyebrow and the purse of a mouth, or maybe I heard about the Blue Nile through my skin anywhere on Arbor Avenue or around there, simply through osmosis.

No one's listening to my story of the club in the basement where pipes sweat, washroom floors rot, and walls break in waves like the Mississippi River. Not to mention the percentage of customers who are low down and lecherous. Leona, Hamla, Berry, Trixia, et al. are absorbed in the street noises and characters who surround us and may mean serious business. Each is poised for the sound or shifting shadow that will come around the corner and say, "Run." It's rough around the corner from the Blue Nile, which is where Roscoe's is.

The Blue Nile, the only bright spot on an essentially residential street, is joined to another building in which Roscoe's is located. Thick hickory smoke billows out onto the avenue from a faulty chimney. Leona says you could get drunk off the smell of her daddy's mambo sauce and this smoke is not the real McCoy. But Trixia says it'll do.

We are on the edge of the corner now, caught between the smoke from Roscoe's and the sound that opens up behind us as the door to the Blue Nile opens up, sending blue light and blues people and the sound of Jimmy Reed ambling about a woman who had him going every whicha way, with mysterious power over him.

"Listen at that crying music," Hamla's lost-and-found cousin says of the sounds that come over our shoulders.

Everybody else just listens. I don't say anything. Do they remember what I do?

The blues I remember from sounds spilled across the kitchen floor, pouring out the doors of the tenement on our street, seeping through the walls of Mrs. Wilson's Beauty Salon, next door to Mr. Boyfriend's place. Those blues singers I never saw (except on posters) like torn cats licking their wounds, healing on their tongues. But Berry, and I know William and some of the authoritative grad students, would call that careful cleansing: the vanity of injury, the seductive canonization of the bruise, the dirty, defeated Negro slave music. Jazz is music (though few buy it) that is cool, cerebral, self-possessed, and assassinating. Rhythm and blues our heartbeat. Blues is crime. Like a parent you're ashamed of and won't be seen in public with.

Jimmy Reed ends as we keep moving away from the Blue Nile. I want to know the rest of the song that slips up behind us in a different voice with lyrics like footsteps walking, "Jailhouse, crazy house, outhouse." The words keep tapping me on the shoulder. I want to turn around, turn back and go down those steps, touch the black railing and the outline of a blue rose, and walk inside the light and smoke that roll out of the Blue Nile like fog around a river. But I keep going away and turn into Roscoe's with the rest of the ravenous crowd.

I miss the waiters at Aisha, the Muslim restaurant, moving like quick air, while the maître d' curved his back in brief elegance as he greeted the flock of us just flown down from Eden by way of EARTH. As we clustered in the lobby, I strained over someone's shoulder to see into the dining room, a section of which was reserved for us, the tables covered in crisp white cloth brightened with red flowers and glasses of cold water served with a stream of courtesy. All of this was waiting for us to follow the maître d' who bobbed as he bowed and fired out "Yes, sir," "Yes, ma'am" in answer to our queries like we were all on film and he was playing in fast-forward and the rest of us in slow motion. The maître d' ahead of our time; we watched the blur of his bow like a character in a Superman comic book.

On the other hand, the folks behind the tile counter at Roscoe's got no time to be pretty. So they act real ugly and look that way too. Mouths all tooted out in attitudes, rolling their eyes when the door opens and the bell tinkles our arrival. More customers. They're squinting and bumping into one another because spicy smoke backed up from the chimney is in their eyes. The little runty man with the prongs, and the woman with the spoon stirring sauce, and the boy shivering the basket of fries. I guess they think they're moving fast, but the motion here is desultory, like they're doing customers a big favor. We should know it's hot, with the grease flying up from the bubbling baskets of fries, and the glass pit that encases the ribs is hell to juke the long prong into to spear the right rib tip or slabs to slather with the sauce that'll do if you're desperate like we are and can't walk to the BoneYard. We should know working at Roscoe's ain't easy, and just in case we don't know, they show us by being grouchy and bored. This is a bad night, I figure.

The chef-waitress leans on her side of the tiled counter and doesn't look at us through the window, which she can't see out of anyway because of the smoke.

"Uh-hmmm," she says to any one of us like she's finishing up an unpleasant conversation she began with us a while back, and she knows anything we've got to say is aggravating.

Trixia orders a double order of rib tips with the hottest mambo sauce, fries with sauce, and a strawberry pop. She and the woman dialogue real well. Trixia is turned sideways too, looking jubilantly at the piles of pork. The rest of us order the same way, turned kitty-corner to the woman. Leona and I ask for chicken, thinking we'll appease the virtuous of the Aisha and Great Zimbabwe, where pork is the embodiment of all racial evil, a slave sandwich.

Does it ever smell good. Knocking at our taste buds.

It has begun to rain. No one anticipated rain. My mother and aunts would have preknown the coming of the waters. The knowledge garnered in the loud ache of joints and bones. Our bodies are young and don't prophesy or remember much.

"When did it start to rain?" Leona asks with a little bit of awe, making her voice go up like a little girl's. Nobody answers that, instead we talk about what the rain means. It is a harsh rain that looks like it's here to stay. Getting back to Eden, now that we've missed the bus, will be difficult. Perilous and slow, now that it's raining and past midnight too. We are not undaunted. So we give up the talk of our predicament and wait for the ribs and chicken.

The Blue Nile has separated me from my friends. I'm hungry like Leona and susceptible to the smell of pork; I'm wary like Berry who keeps looking at the door. I'm loud like everybody for a while. But the rain lends metaphor and atmosphere to my mood: melancholic and grumpy because I was not brave enough to walk into the Blue Nile unescorted. It goes on without me as a witness, the thing that makes a man or a woman go crazy or want to fight or make love all night and I have missed it again. I am always amiss.

The day feels century long. We came down from Eden in a covered wagon maybe, or more likely, we sailed down in a customized slave ship.

I have found a nook in the libraries of Eden, a Gothic terrible place looking like *Dark Shadows*, the daytime soap-opera domain of Barnabas the vampire, Angelique the witch, and sundry other monsters. We watched in high school when we got home from school early. I'm safe from TV monsters and Eden monsters in the cranny where Africana is stored. Eden is endowed with academic rights to West Africa and its Diaspora, which means it has a department devoted to the study of Africans, and Africans from the continent and White students from here and abroad make up the department. It's mostly White students. Most of the Africans (graduate students who have come to study engineering or political science) look sad or mad when I see them on campus. Steve, who's in the technological institute, runs sometimes with the Africans. The rest of us are too young for the Africans to bother with. Only one or two are in For Bloods Only, but the grad students of Blood Island from here are in the All African Alliance of Graduate Students of Eden University. Africa to the Third Power.

The African section in Dark Shadows is the place I love. Statues, with mouths, breasts, and behinds that toot out like mine, stand guard around the two rooms, poised, some of them, with bent knees like little girls about to jump between the curves of the moving double-Dutch ropes. One statue has penis and breasts like the picture of the hermaphrodite in the anatomy book, but not so gross.

On one wall, just above my favorite seat, is a large photograph of a Benin mask, a queen, with wide eyes and mouth, wearing a crown of Portuguese soldiers carved into her head. Like Excedrin Headache No. 99. The original mask is in London. I have read this a thousand times, inscribed beneath the photograph. The original in London.

Underneath the hostage queen, I fell in love with Joseph Cinque. Cinque was an African prince captured and on his way to America aboard a slave ship. It was he who led the war of the Africans aboard a ship called *Amistad;* who seized the vessel, subdued the barbarian kidnappers carrying Bibles and guns, and turned the *Amistad* back toward the shores of Africa.

My newest acquisition from the Africana section of the library of Eden is this love for Joseph Cinque—another incendiary angel for a daydream.

Water races across concrete and slides over the curb, stops at the blocked sewers, and grows large around the curb, swelling over and spilling back onto the sidewalk. Who could navigate through this? I look at us college girls. Are we the cargo or crew, bound for home or for someplace ugly and new?

Then the ice babies come. They burst through the door and bring the cold rain in with them. They spin the water off their fake leather jackets, shake it out of their hair. One unwinds a red silkish scarf from around his do; it is soggy with rain. His hair sparkles. He wipes his dripping nose. He eyes us, shivers in the shoulders a bit, then leans toward us. We scrupulously avoid direct eye contact. The open door has let in a chill, so we wrap our arms around ourselves more tightly. We shift in our tracks.

Time is doing tricks again. The seconds accelerate and I know things are happening faster than I can make sense of them. But the dudes who just arrived follow the slow-motion lead of the one with the red scarf. In decelerated time he drops the scarf at Berry's feet, like a kid playing Lost My Handkerchief Yesterday. We used to play that, a circle of us holding hands singing, "Lost my handkerchief yesterday, found it again today. And then I threw it away." One of us, circling the circle, skipping behind us as we sang, would be holding a handkerchief that she dropped behind whoever, who in turn became It. And whoever who'd become It would spin around and chase and chase the one who dropped the handkerchief. The dropper would be safe from It with the handkerchief only if she made it back to It's place in the circle before she was tagged with the handkerchief, which was the reason for all this squealing.

For one microsecond I think Berry will pick up the scarf this dude has dropped in front of him and chase the dude all around Roscoe's. Jump over the counter and dance between the popping grease and the smell of ribs. So he can tag the dude with the scarf and be out of the game. But it doesn't go that way.

Berry is It. All the wet boys jump on him and start hitting him in the face and stuff. They shove him back into a corner away from the counter and the door and us and pummel him. The leader, spitting through clinched teeth: "Told you don't bring yo mug around here." He averages one strike per every two words. I'm counting because this is slow motion and my brain is careening along with the screaming and pleading we're all doing for somebody to help Berry, Hamla's long-lost, soon-to-be-dead cousin. The woman behind the counter comes around and pushes us girls back, because we're making crazy moves to plunge in.

"Don't you get in this mess. That's all this is. Nothing but mess."

Then she yells above the patter of fists and the splatter of skin, "Get offa that boy. Double-teaming that boy. Stop it, I say. Somebody call the police."

Berry is crunched up like a fetus being sucked out the womb. He slings a fist out and twists out a kick into the groin. One of the dudes pulls away, doubled over, holding his self. His face jumbled up, yowling.

"Do you wanna burn?" comes a voice behind us, quiet as rice steaming. And it's the wizened looking man who's been turning ribs. He's gripping the handles of a huge kettle full of mambo sauce that bubbles with heat, steaming so fierce he blinks against the blindness.

"Whoever ain't offa him in two seconds flat and outta here in one, gonna be licking mambo sauce off they behinds in the burn unit. So get yo ignorant asses outta here with that shit. My name is Roscoe. This ain't none of nobody's territory but mine, cause I got the business here."

"Naw, brother," the dude who drops scarves for a living says. "You must understand. This little mawofuh knew his time was up. Maniac Apostles run this. Taking what we come for." They turn to grab Berry, whose head is tangled between his legs.

"You ain't taking nothing but that nasty rag you dropped on my floor," the man with the sauce says. Then with no further warning, he flings the kettle red at them like a woman emptying wash water. We girls cringe further into our corner, using our loudest screams as talismans against the scalding liquid. The Maniac Apostles streak past us shrieking like demons shuttled back to hell. The sauce breathing equally evil on the cold of their jackets. The rain slaps inside and sprinkles us with grains of water that have turned hard in the new cold.

"Maggie, it couldn't hurt to call."

"Go on and call him, girl."

We are in a world of trouble with no safe way back to Eden. Leona calls Blood Island from the emergency room; the yellow school bus would have dropped everyone there before the tribes scattered and fled to their dorms. We think Essie the Cautious might be sitting near the phone on the reception desk waiting to hear from us. We are too wise to try to get through to the desk at Wyndam-Allyn. Mrs. Sorenson is on the lookout for lost Negresses, which is what Trixia heard her refer to us as one day to one of the residence counselors. Nobody answers the phone at Blood Island, so us Negresses are consigned to sit rescueless amid the smell of squandered blood, bowel movements, and disinfectant in a hospital my mother refused to give birth in and Eddie refused to die in. It's a quarter to three ante meridiem. Berry the reclaimed cousin, saved and anointed by the murderously hot mambo sauce, sits bandaged and mildly sedated. He's checking in. Even though his burns aren't that serious and his bruises and taped-up ribs will heal, he says he wants to cool out some, eat the nutritious, delicious hospital food, and dream about the ribs from Roscoe's we never none of us got. Leona promises a rib-tip special from the BoneYard. She just has to ask her daddy and it is done.

Berry groans when Hamla hugs him for old times' sake, touching his multiple bruises. "Sorry it had to be this way, little cousin," Berry apologizes. "I knew I was outta my hood over round Blue Nile and Roscoe's but I had to escort you pretty young ladies through Maniac territory. Specially when I found out you was blood. Couldn't let you go round there alone. I should have called my friend earlier to give you a ride." His friend long ago disappeared after dropping us off.

"Ain't nobody beat us up," I remind him more drily than I intend. He was only being nice. He tries to purse his lips in disgust at my ungrateful remark, but his lips are too swollen. Like humungous blueberries. I tell him we appreciated his company anyway. He didn't have to be the cavalry. "I might," Berry says, "be the cavalry, or with this barbecue sauce on me be grade-A government-inspected meat. I am 1A. If the streets don't get me the jungle will." He scares us good with his draft status.

Trixia, who has to be the last word and have it too, flings her skinny arms around his braced thick neck and offers him a fervent good-bye that pops his eyes with pain at her embrace. She invites him to come visit us at Eden. "Just don't bring the Black KKK." Patience thins after midnight and no sleep, so Hamla snatches one of Trixia's arms and yanks her off the cousin in the wheelchair. Trixia is so into her scene she looks discombobulated. She curls up her hand real cute in a good-bye sign. The orderly wheels Berry away.

I wish somebody was riding me home safely to my own bed. Bring me in out of the rain and the smell of blood and mambo sauce dabs that splashed up on my clothes.

Leona's daddy would kill her if he knew she almost got scalded to death at Roscoe's; not because she was in an imperiling situation, but because she was at Roscoe's, his chief rival's. So we can't call Daddy Pryor for a ride to the dorm. Nobody in Hamla's family has a car because they live right next to the El. Needless to say, nobody else knows a way. So they say "Maggie, why don't you call your daddy?" When I say no, they whine, "Maggie, why won't you call your daddy?"

It's hard to explain without telling a piece of a story from my life as a child in that house on Arbor Avenue, where I wish I was right now, asleep and not smelling anything that should be locked up in a whole human body.

It was already after eight. If Pearl didn't hurry she would be late. It was okay to be tardy in grammar school—that was right around the corner anyhow and the nuns didn't mind it so much. They took it as the way about our family. With all of us kids, how was we all supposed to get out the house on time?

Anyway, it didn't take Pearl so long to dress because she was in high school. She went to school with Whitegirls on the Eastside, and they wore whiteblouses and greenplaidskirts and plaingreenblazers and big ole blackandwhite shoes you could use horseshoes for taps. Like I tole you it didn't take Pearl long to dress. But she was always late and this morning too. She couldn't get up enough nerve to do what she had to do before she could catch the bus.

She was goin to be late and we all knew (me and Ernestine and Shirley) what would happen before. Even the two little-bitty babies knew. Running aroun' the house up behine Mama or Pearl. Pullin on anybody's arm. Spoiled. Junior and Honeybabe was already gone. Honeybabe begged Mama out of her money to buy a special book. Here come Littleson fast through the back door like somebody knocked him into the kitchen just like they knocked that melon-sized hickey up on his head. Mama didn't even ask him what happen to him. We all knew he got hit and robbed again on his paper route. Somebody backed him up in a hallway and beat his head. We all knew Mama would go help him collect tomorrow morning. We all knew what Pearl betta be doin before she was so late the sisters made her stay after school in detention.

Me and Ernestine and Shirley and Littleson saw Pearl start to whimper up behine Mama with her grown self like she was two or four like Anne and Frances. Pearl was goin, "Please, Mama, please . . . Mama don't you have justa little bit . . . please, Mama." And Mama was shakin her head tellin her she knew she didn't have none. Didn't she see her give Honeybabe her last few dollars for that book? Today was Friday; she just had her own carfare to

132

work. Pearl didn't whimper now. She was hollin. And Mama was pushin her out the big door tellin her to go on. She knew what she had to do and she better stop this foolishness and get herself out of here and go on to school. She didn't want Sister Mary Agnes calling her up and writin them letters with outstanding number of tardy days and all a that . . . so Mama shoved Pearl up to that door with Pearl pullin back and holdin on to Mama's waist. Goin "Mama, please, Mama, please cain't you give it to me. Mama, I don't want to. I *cain't* Mama . . ." we heard Mama spin Pearl through that door and the door creak wide open.

Me and Ernestine and Shirley and Anne and Frances and Littleson got realquiet with oatmeal in our mouths didn't even chew. We was listenin so hard.

We could hear Pearl step over the side of the big king bed that filled the room and the man fillin half the bed. We could hear Pearl go whimperwhisper, begging, "Madaddy . . . Madaddy . . . Mama said would you give me some money for carfare." Once she said it. And Mama came back in the kitchen combin Shirley's hair but everybody listenin. And Pearl's voice gettin loud and skinny scared. We heard her again, "Madaddy, Mama . . ."

It happened again so bad we all wanta jump through the back door. Saw it in my head. Madaddy's long musclebody jerkin stiff up from the bed like a corpse sittin up in a quickfit, sittin up hollerin, "Girl . . . didn't I tell you I ain't got no chainnngggeee! . . ." I saw Pearl draw back on the wall and doin nothin' but shakin shakin like everything and the corpse was still hollerin. And Pearl was moanin and wailin into the wall. And I wanted to cry but I didn't cause the last time I cried for somebody else was at Ernestine's whippin for being wasteful and catchin rainwater in a baggy in the backyard and messin up that grocery money. And I got a whippin for cryin at Ernestine's whippin. So I let Pearl-girl suffer alone. And the sugar oatmeal taste nasty in our mouths. And the corpse was shoutin up enough wind to shake the whole block. In our house the walls trembled and trembled and the roaches ran and hid and we couldn't. And the corpse kept on, "Y'all cain't stand for me to have no change in my pocket . . . always gimme this and gimme gimme. I feed you. Buy yo clothes. I ain't got no money. I ain't got no chaiiiiiiiiiiiiiiinge." Then Pearl was just screaming pitiful. Ran up into the kitchen into Mama's arms. That ole corpse steady 'splodin called her right back. And Mama pushed her just a little bit gentle smilin to herself.

We heard the dollar slap Pearl's palm. And he was sayin, "You betta bring me my change . . . spend it and ahma beat yo tail blacker. Close that do' and get outta here. I know yo ole evil mama sent you up in here with her crazy self just study evil cain't stand to see money in my pocket. Close that door . . . I gotta get my sleep get up and go to work. I said . . . 'Close that door.'" Pearl close the big door and we heard him push hisself into the bed.

Mama hugged crybaby Pearl and said, "That wasn't so bad now was it?" Just like them other days.

We could hear Pearl runnin down the front steps. Just when the tardy bell rang at our school aroun' the corner. And Mama was shakin her head. She do declare we never be on time.

We was halfway to school. Runnin. When I heard Ernestine tell Shirley, "When I get big I'm gone walk to high school." And we came on the playground laughin till one ole nun gave us the evil eye and tole us all to get in the late line.

"So he just hollered a little bit when somebody asked him for carfare," says sanguine Leona, whose father is her personal angel.

"I just don't know him well enough to ask," I mumble.

"You don't know your own daddy well enough to ask him to pick you up at the hospital and take you back to school!" incredulous Leona yells. Vested interest making her lose her cool.

"And it's raining Doberman pinschers and Siamese cats!" Trixia hyperbolizes. It's not raining that hard.

"I didn't suggest this safari, Trixia," I cut.

"Your stomach followed the trail, Miss Grace," she comes back quick with guilt.

I go and stand by the glass exit door; with wet heat all in my eyes I roll them up to knock off the film of moisture and fix my mouth in a determined hurt. "My father doesn't know me well enough," I say to Leona when she comes and stands behind me. "He doesn't even know my name." Now why I want to drag that up? I wonder. All my armor in the closet cause I'm hungry, sleepy, and just been last-worded by Trixia, whom I can't stand.

My father thinks my name is Maggie Lena, after the Penny Savings Bank founder woman, founder of the Independent Order of St. Luke. She did a lot for colored people. Money smart and powerful. Neither of which I am. No matter how many times I tell him I was named for a saint with long, feet-wiping hair (which I don't have) and a shady past (which I don't have either), he talks about the woman with money and power who did something. Who I was named for.

"Maggie, it would not hurt you to ask him," Leona says simply, dispirited by my stubbornness.

I look at her and reach for the dime.

Anne Perpetua, my baby sister, never said her first word; she sang it. An entire song: Mary had a baby. Anne was given to singing. I was given to images. Then Anne started learning words one by one the regular way, beginning with Mama. She belonged to music before she belonged to her own mother. I belonged to colors and shapes before I belonged to anyone. Tonight I still see the bright blue rose on an iron railing, and mambo sauce like broken branches of blood ominous on the walls of Roscoe's. I see the house I grew up in instead of the urine and water the orderly is wiping from the emergency room floor, instead of the gun on the hip of the police guard.

One summer when Anne was still tiny she and Katherine Pearl went away and stayed with a "nice White family" in a church program. Anne Perpetua came back singing but singing different. We kept telling Anne to say "Kathy." Kaaaaathy, Kaaathy—her *a* flat as the bleat of a black lamb. A flat American Midwest *a* learned out of Whitepeople's mouths we loved to laugh at.

Anne Perpetua answers the phone sleepily with no trace of the unending plain in her singsong voice. I struggle to keep the little-girl lostness out of my sound. "Madaddy there?" I say in a heavy hurry like I'm very important instead of saying hello.

"Yeah, he here. What's wrong with you, Maggie? Calling here in the middle of the night."

"We got left."

"Left where?" Her inquiry gives me impetus to be adult; she is after all the baby sister. I must preserve the hegemony of birthing order.

"Listen, J. Edgar Hoover, would you put Madaddy on the phone?" I dismiss her.

She doesn't say good-bye, just as I hadn't said hello. Her parting shot is, "You know there's a curfew. And you ain't eighteen."

"You ain't eight good, so what you doing up now?"

"I had to pee." I listen to her softly calling our father's name in the house I know is dark as the center of a dark rose, secure beneath many petals. The streetlight I know is raining light and blurry rain on the side of the house where I slept first with a brother, then a sister, my immediately older sister, Pearl.

I could see Pearl coming down the long street with a rise in its center. She was riding the top of the street and the street was full of wind. Wind sucking her greenplaidskirt tight around her wine-bottle thighs. Her legs were big and fine; Junior still called me Bird Legs. In the wind my hair traveled like weeds. My dull green uniform crumpled in the wind. I was always lost, Mama said, about to take flight. Pearl was a gift to the earth. I was the last grain of sand. She was a high school senior. I was a freshman. It was soft spring. The day was heavy with wind.

Our father was painting against the wind. Smoothing the face of the house a warm red, eye-catching to passersby and drivers-by. The wind tangled him in his ladder. He persisted, breathing heavily from the work and the wind. I could see his chest reach and recede. That night he would suffer; his muscles would ache and tighten. He would worry Mama and her words would sound like annoyance and charity.

That night he would enter the living room full of his children like a hostile tribe. He would cough from his gut once or twice, then hum a little bit to himself. That hum. He would look around at us, nod his head, then go to his room. After a while we would hear the sound of his harmonica drifting under the door like Junior's forbidden cigarette smoke sliding then swirling up from under the bathroom door. When he left the room, and we were all sure that he had gone, Lazarus (who was then acting as Littleson) would stand in the middle of the room, standing among us like him, and Lazarus would do a soundless imitation of his fierce cough, then contort his face and shake saliva out of an imaginary harmonica. He'd feign playing a tune a little, then his wrath would rise for no reason. He'd turn on us like our father did. At the top of his lungs. We would giggle and roar with mischief.

Sam Grace would return and be seated in his chair. We'd all sit in silence till he'd address a question to one of us. A shrug would be our answer. He did not seem to notice.

But this was the windy day before that night. I could see the cars switching lanes approaching the wide intersection. Pearl and I were walking against the flow of traffic, parallel to it. And our father was painting the house. His back moving from side to side. His muscular arms pulled back and I sensed the physical power of him. It struck a memory in me: I remember a man squatting in our backyard. His pants down. We rushed through the gangway, then just little-biddy kids. We were big eyed at the sight. Man. Pants down. Doing business in our backyard. We yelled the atrocity at the top of our voices. Our father appeared like a wrathful god or a chief emissary of one. Sam became legend as Moses descending from the mountaintop bearing the law and his wrath on a whip. Driving evil away. Jesus in the Temple flogging the merchant of manure.

Our father beat the Pants-Down Man up and down and around the alley. Our father's mighty chain wrapped around and around his booty-behind. "Man is you crazy? You a fool? Nigger!"

When I saw my father slapping paint across the slats of the house, I thought of supreme wrath, restrained rage. I had waited obediently for Pearl because Pearl was beautiful and older than me. Artists at some time in their lives genuflect, even kneel all day long to a physical notion of beauty. This is before they learn to see in light, and absences of light, in variations of light that is color. This is before they learn to see inside the wonderful blackness of space itself. I don't even know that now and didn't then.

But that day I was worshipping Pearl and she was deigning to match steps with me. Our father was painting and watching our adolescent approach. Wind circling our legs like ribbons. Cars on the busy street switching lanes before coming to the intersection. I had thrown back my head to shout or laugh. (Pearl no longer shouted or laughed except with her friends.) A car was losing control. Suddenly, the wheels turned one way toward the sidewalk, toward us. The driver's hands went another way, away from us. My father was poised in the middle of a stroke. As the car slanted and slid toward us. My eyes were on his eyes, his entire face a mask of hopeless terror. His mouth began to open, to call back everything he loved so fiercely that he was about to lose, surely, about to lose.

But the car knocked against the curb. And stayed in the street. Pearl let loose my arm that she had grabbed. My scream turned to a giggle. The wind dried the fear from our eyes. My father lowered his arm, relaxed on the ladder. He trembled. The wind is strongest when one is so high up.

I can hear my daddy coming around the rim of daybreak. The old station wagon grunts along the avenue. This car is a chronic complainer, a noisy nag, beat up and dull, but I feel thrilled at the sight of it breaking through the darkness. My father thrills at the sight of it always and permits no one the right to sit at its wheel. In the days, last year, after I completed driver's education he answered my thousand requests to take a spin with a hundred nos. And not one yes. Always his no. One morning he tore out of his room after I had been in there to get money Mama put aside to send away to Eden. He tore through the house up toward the front and peeked out the front window, after yanking up the shade. I guess his heart rested easy when he found his car still there and me too. I'd followed up behind him because I was just that mad that he'd think I'd take his stinky old car. "You find what you lookin for?" I said real sassy.

"You better not a taken my car, Maggie Lena," he chuckled in his long johns and barefooted back to his room to say his morning prayers. Probably praying for that car.

"Hi, Mr. Grace. Thank you so very much for saving us from this terrible place. We got left by the school bus, they wouldn't wait for us, then we ran into trouble and Hamla's cousin got hurt and we brought him here but we didn't have a way back to school." My friends babble on as they hurriedly climb into the car. My father acts as if he doesn't hear any of their excuses. He yells, "Hey there!" real jovially like when he walks into a room with a lot of folks from Mississippi and he lifts his hand a little bit in that country salute he and my uncles are good for.

I'm the last one in and I feel like It, a rotten egg, or an old dead dog, the one that got left. I'm the only one who knows the temper of this Grace in the raggedy car.

"Thank you for coming to pick us up, Madaddy," I say without a hint of gratitude. My heart's beating faster because I don't know how he's going to greet me. In what way the embarrassment will come. Through quick rebuke or rambling tale of childhood peculiarities.

"Your daddy's so nice," Trixia says all satisfied to be riding. "My daddy never would have gotten out of his bed to pick me up somewhere. He'd a tole me to stay my a— behind where I was." The car is crowded with giggles. The girls go into rough imitations of their fathers who are not redemptive like mine. They are loud and entertaining and they win my father's approval. He smiles and chuckles behind the wheel.

Then they start to tell him about our day. Before I can stop them. They begin at the beginning with the Cave brothers who sleep with blondes of Eden, who will not be seen with beautiful Black girls like us, even if we wanted them to, then they take him to EARTH and the terrible Alhamisi, whom we have decided by now is a known thug, a little simple in the head and full of malice to boot. They do imitations of his warning us about the hippies who will turn in their hair and wind up as our bosses. Even though we agreed with Alhamisi about a lot of things, his style was so pompous and belligerent we give him no credibility. If he had worn a three-piece suit and spoken softly with multisyllabic words we would have spoken of him with awe. As it is, he wore dirty jeans and looked unkempt and uncouth and had a nasty attitude, so Leona goes after him for handing out the commandments of Freedom Law.

"He thought he was Moses, Mr. Grace, coming down from the mountain with the two tablets," Leona says. "I wish they'd a been some aspirin cause he gave me a real headache. He wanted us to give up our educations and be farmers down south."

My father says, "Back where I come from. Ah-hah-hah-hah-hah. Wooooh," he gives a little song that is his delighted and ironic laugh. Leona is a real hit with Madaddy. Miss Charm.

Then she and Trixia and Hamla fill him in on the fine cuisine at the Muslim restaurant and the music at Great Zimbabwe. I clear my throat but everyone ignores me. I try to talk about the grayness rising over the lake, to steer their talk away, but it's too late.

My father snarls, "You been over there eating that ignorant Muslim food. All them slick head zombies, goose-stepping like Prussian soldiers I saw over there in Germany. Where they oughta be. Pack of crazy fools. Ain't good for nothing but eating stanky sardine sammiches and selling newspapers. Bunch of grown men ain't nothing but paperboys. Littleson and June did that when they was twelve." He takes his eyes from the road long enough to do a full spotlight sweep of the car. "I hope none of you were taken in by any of that nonsense. That old nutty talk about a mad scientist inventing White people. If anybody but

God invented White people it was the devil, and the Negroes was right behind 'em in the lineup."

My father fumes silently like a furnace. Then he pops, "Your mama's brother got caught up in that old mess." He is talking about my Uncle Blackstrap. What is unsaid now but said loudly at home in the kitchen is, "But a Dancer ain't never had good sense. Your mama included."

My friends make placating talk now about how the food at Aisha was so insubstantial they had to have some barbecued ribs to tide them over till breakfast, which right now isn't that far away.

My father is appeased. "Maggie Lena always did like to suck on them barbecue bones." This is a lie, but I don't set it straight. It was some other daughter or son, but he wants it to be me so he can launch into a long, humiliating story from my humiliating childhood. Which he does. He's telling the story of me and best friend Jeannie who liked to fight and one time fought me over the right to suck my chicken bone. Jeannie is married now. I don't guess she likes to fight so much. I don't guess. Or maybe she does. That's why she married a minor amateur prizefighter.

Feverishly I tune out the dumb tale from my youth. I look instead at the way we came, which is even more startling as the way back. After all we have seen.

Now Leona tells my father about the Man with Two Wives and LeRoi "Get Down" Clay, who is a poor man's James Brown. She is an amusing anecdotist and soon has my father laughing. The car is crowded with laughter. It bumps against me. Sam Grace tells us he had been by Great Zimbabwe. He peeked inside and smelled the incense that rushed through an open window to meet him. He tells us Great Zimbabwe is not nearly as fine as Club Desiree was that night he took Mama, Aunt Leah-Bethel, and Uncle Blackstrap to hear Mockingbird July sing. It wasn't the same magic place now, so he didn't go in.

When my daddy finishes the story I tell him we passed the Blue Nile and I wished we had gone in. His face is quietly happy and he makes no comment. Then he clears his throat. "Hey, you ever hear this song, Maggie Lena?" And he sings this song soft and raggedy while I look at the light on the dark road and listen. It is a song about a city by a river, which I do not remember well. Mimosa. It is a song about a place where cotton grows, and figs, pecans, persimmons (the *per* is silent: *'simmons*), and blues. About crackers and cotton gins, trees, boss men, floods, and fine women. All that will send you to jailhouse, crazy house, outhouse. It's the heart house.

Jailhouse, crazy house, outhouse. I don't ask Madaddy if he'd heard that song I eavesdropped a snatch of as we passed the opening door of the Blue Nile. He thinks all his little songs are original. So I don't mention I've heard that line once tonight. It is a pretty song, rough and sad like a painting by Charles White. It is witty too like that man at the Sixty-third Street bus stop who wears a rooster on his head. The man sings and blows into his harmonica and the rooster dances on his hat and my daddy's song is like that. Sweet and magical.

We enter the outer limits of Eden and the cemetery is on the left side of my daddy's voice. I imagine those Blackpeople buried there would rise up and walk into the Great Lake like that lake is the Mississippi River or the Niger. And some woman ghost who came up at the turn of the century and started to talk keener and forget her grandmother who talked to animals would do a sassy, butt-swaying, foot-sliding dance on the jagged rocks around the lake and look out over the water with her hand curved across her eyebrows and smile.

I smile and fall into the safest sleep (a gentle sleep so soft my eyelids feel like the inside of a rose), even though we are only a few minutes from our beds in the dorm rooms of Wyndam-Allyn. Those solitary, noncommunal beds. My own like a boat or a private plane I love to float in. It is still novelty. Once a week we strip those beds and leave the linen in a pillowcase on the floor by the door. A woman, brown as we are, only five years or so older than we are, who lives in Eden a distance from the water, will pick up our bags of dirty laundry and leave freshly ironed linen on our beds. She will scrub the toilets and telephones at the ends of the hall, suck up the debris from the carpet with her noisy vacuum, then go home to a life like my own at home. Home. To a mother like my own, maybe, to a father who makes blues songs a lullaby like my own, maybe. To a chaos of kids and good things cooking: skin and bones covered in red sauce called mambo.

Life is good now for me and I stir in my sleep, catnapping on the edge of memory. Eyelids trembling, I wonder in the fog-soft edges of my contentment if this soft song would sweeten the rage of Alhamisi and the EARTH men, and melt the atmosphere of the Maniac Apostles who beat up on Berry who was family but who maybe was just like them with a different gang name. I sigh and burrow more deeply into the worn cushions of my father's car. This old car he prays for daily.

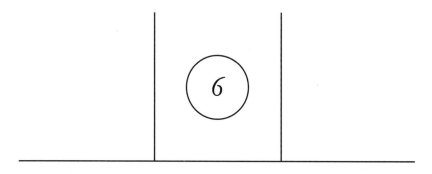

Wyndam-Allyn

Wyndam-Allyn was named after a rich woman who tried to stop poor immigrants from drinking and her husband who tried to stop himself from drinking once or twice. He did nothing; she did something; and they had a lot of money. Their namesake building is seventy years old and sixty-nine-year-old ivy swarms over its gray stone skin, creeps across the wood and glass of the window frames and windows like tiny balconies. Sometimes a well-read girl with a romantic heart and unrealistic turn of mind must have pushed out the miniature balcony window, greeted the wind swirling softly up from the lake, and recited Juliet's balcony speech to Romeo. "Romeo, Romeo, wherefore art thou Romeo?" The spiders in the ivy must have loved it, trembled in sympathetic ecstasy and woven gossamer valentines in the recesses of the thick leaves of ivy. Alas, methinks, the only Romeos who've stood under these old windows came in hordes like pre-Shakespearean barbarians to demand funky panties instead of virginal kisses.

Penelope Hanes, the hippie who lives down the hall from us, sits down and tries to help the girls on our corridor see this foolishness in revolutionary terms. Everybody wants to know what's hip, so we listen to Penny talk about the importance of being serious about ourselves and not participating in frivolous activities. Most of us think it's just gross, but Penny's got a point, so we listen and say, "Yeah, yeah." We ain't in it.

Oakland is Penny's roommate and sometimes they talk the same language. I guess. Penny is a Whitegirl. She has swinging, uneven, healthy hair that swishes against her shoulders as she lopes down the hall in her blue jeans and antique coat or sweater. In winter a fur, in warmer times a crocheted long sweater made in three-inch-wide squares like windowpane stockings.

She has traveled and can cuss in four languages: English, French, German, and Dutch. She says *fuck* in English like a magician yanking an endless multicolored scarf out of his mouth. She is rich and her daddy does something with oil. Not like Leona's daddy who is colored rich and does fried chicken in Crisco oil. Her daddy's into crude and refined. We think Leona's daddy's rib and chicken restaurant is the height of venture capitalism, but it's just a joint, albeit a nice one, a ligament of a luxurious beast of conspicuous and ravenous consumption. Penelope's daddy does things for the Pentagon.

Penelope asked her roommate, Oakland, if she could use half of her closet because one closet was insufficient for her wardrobe. Everything matches like uniforms—minis, tops, tights, shoes, purses and coats and jackets and sweaters. We know because Oakland wears whatever she likes out of Penelope's closet. Penelope has a lot of things, but she doesn't really care about them. She drops her clothes on her floor and walks on them. She leaves her panties in puddles. She wears one pair of jeans over and over again and if any water has hit them it's because it fell on them.

Everybody thinks Penelope is crazy because she hates her father and shrieks at her mother over the phone. Her "MOTHER" riding the tight hallway air a little longer than her "FUCK." She yells *fuck* into the phone right after she yells *mother*.

"She talking to her mother?" Leona whispers as we pass Penelope's wide-open door. "Valerie Pryor would send her arm through the phone after me. Knock my eyeballs out of my head and shoot 'em like marbles back into the sockets."

"Caroline just kill me quick," I nod. " 'I brought you in this world and I'll take you out.' " My mama never had to say it but I know she would just like Miss Rose would tell Eddie before the ice babies beat her to it. Miss Rose never meant it. That's the way we talk. In gross hyperbole. Penelope means it.

Leona and I imitate our mothers simultaneously and knock on wood, which happens to be somebody's door. A California girl surfer from Laguna Beach pulls the door open and pushes back her bottle-streaked hair at the same time.

"Did you want something?" she snaps and turns up her nose before we can answer. "I get so tired of you people." Then she's closing the door and closing out Leona's mouth, which is wide open now hollering, "You people" over and over again. Leona's shoving her shoulder onto the door stopping it from closing. "Tell me what you people means and I'll tell you what bitch means, bitch."

I try to pull Leona away. Surfer girl gives a big whoop and a mighty shove and the door snaps shut. There's a scratchy fumbling for the lock. The lock clicks.

Talking fast, I comfort Leona saying it isn't worth it to beat up the California girl and go up before Sorenson's dorm disciplinary committee. Leona stops dead in the center of the hall. Chest heaving and nostrils enlarged, she looks at me coldly.

"That's the only thing about you I can't stand, Maggie. You so damn passive with your well-mannered, middle-class Catholic ass."

My breath flies back into my face, making my cheeks turn cold. I can't talk behind this, but my mind is busy and telling me Leona's letting me have what she couldn't give the face that sank a thousand surfboards. "That's not true!" I finally yelp like a just-kicked puppy, denying passivity. Again, in my head, thinking, *You're the one who's middle class, Leona Rib Tips Pryor.*

"Well, when is it ever worth it to fight? When is it worth it, Miss Grace?" Her tone is softer now, but this hurts more because I cannot hide the hurt behind anger. I walk away from Leona, and Penelope yells *fuck* for the fourteenth time in half as many minutes.

Leona has hurt me. So I move away from her some place inside and take back the space I had reserved for her and give it to myself. I lie across the bottom bunk and pretend that I am reading a book so that Leona and Essie will not try to talk to me. Actually, I am not studying art history but myself. Because I don't know how not to listen to myself when she is crying and needs me so. I am seventeen years old. Remember?

Sometimes when I am not taking a thought and simply passing a looking glass, a mirror, or a window, I will happen to look up suddenly, come up too fast like a scuba diver breaking the surface too quickly, and be thrown into a time warp. I will expect to see etched sweetly and vibrantly in the glass my face as I was as a little girl. Round faced, richly brown, with the straightened hair pulled and twisted into three braids, my impudent edges turning back. My body gently round and long of limb. The eyes busily hiding who I was but witnessing all that I was and would be. The mouth turned up and quick or quiet as the case might be. The hands momentarily landed in my lap folded like birds between extended flights.

Even today as an almost woman I am surprised to find that I am not the little girl. Her presence is in me indelibly. Her voice talks in my head.

Cain't have no privacy. Tip in the bathroom wid my own bloody nose. Look in mirror at everything swellin. Lip fat. Nose big. Not wide like Mama say from diggin but big on top. Face hurt when I touch. I'm touchin anyway because this is my face hurt. I halfway cain't believe. So I'm comfortin myself, pattin myself off wid a cold towel. Water droppin over the bathroom floor. Here come Littleson wid his nosey self. Don't knock on the door just walk on in. I mighta been doin somethin' important steada standin in the mirror. He come all up in my face. Lookin at me. Talkin 'bout:

"Oooo-wwweeee, who got you?"

My eyes be wet and I starta blinkin. He bringin the shame down front.

"None a yo business, monkey face."

"Bet you didn't talk that bad to whoever beat yo head."

"I did too." I push him out the way between me and the sink. Wettin my towel again.

"Who you fight wid?"

"Ole bald-head Jean." I'm back in the mirror pattin my face. Littleson looking over my shoulder.

"Wha'chall fight for?"

"Stop breathin on my neck." I jerk myself so he move back. He move up again.

"Wha'chall fight about, Maggie?"

"She cheat."

"Everybody know that. What y'all fight about today?"

"I told you she cheat." I'm tired a his nosey self. He know it. He just sit and look at me. Quiet. Then he say, "Who won?"

I don't say nothin'. Then he say again tryin ta get in my business, "Who won, Maggie?"

"Didn't nobody win."

"Oh."

He watch me watch myself some more and I'm watchin him out the corner a my eye.

"You wanna fix Jeannie so she don't mess wid yo no more?"

I don't say nothin'.

"I said you wanta kick Jeannie's butt?"

I fold my towel. And lay it on the radiator. I'm cool. "I might be interested."

Then I say, "What I gotta do?"

And Littleson say, "It's my own scientific invention. Don't I win alla my fights? Lemme teach you advanced technology."

I say, "How much this gonna cost me?"

"Maggie, you my sister. Besides . . . you ruinin the family reputation on the block."

In the book they say when the man drown he go down three times. And his life keep passin before him every time. Same wid fights.

In the backyard me and Jeannie apart for the second time. She been whippin my tail. Eddie push us apart the first time. I say, "Uh-uh. Now you goin git it . . . lemme at her." I say to nobody, in the backa my heart wishin somebody would not let me at her. (Who like to hum anyway?) Anyway that first time and we apart and the ground in my mouth and my hair cryin at the roots in the wind it been pulled so hard and me breathin the jerks in my body lookin at Jeannie and seein her like a twenty-leben times and fights and she half kill me. And I never remember how the fights begin but know they happen all on top my head. The first time we come apart like a crazy machine comin apart for a second or so and I just look at her and don't know her except as a piece-a-me machine. And then we come up on each other again botha my arms swingin everyway through the air and Jeannie and her claws tearin every any place she want and her bite and pull and stuff bein hot stingy marks on me. We apart the second time. Is where we at and I'm shakin my eyes clear in my head clearin my lesson rememberin my science gonna whip some advanced technology on this . . . heifer. And I think I got Littleson's voice in my ear sayin okay Maggie this called the power punch, okay Maggie make a fist make a good tight fist Maggie loose yo body okay Maggie think all yo strength in yo super hand swing Maggie swing Maggie go girl swing oooweee Maggie. And Jeannie lookin at me funny then her stomach goin soft around my fist and she double over screamin and I step back lookin at what I done don't believe and Jeannie rise up with double hate and slobbin a little at the mouth her eyes dark and watery like never cause I never hurt her before and Jeannie rise and kickin me and scratchin and spittin and cussin and everything and I don't believe it that this is worse than the first comin apart. And the ground in the mouth and spinnin seesaw in my eye and Littleson standin by the jumpin tree for real and all I can hear him say is, "Awh, Maggie, goddog." While he and Eddie pull us apart.

I never learned to fight with any kind of style, unlike my brother who is a black belt in karate. Lazarus the Warrior. Yet I am amazed at my early definition. My surefooted stance in the world in the face of certain defeat. How I wandered wild and protected in the embrace of family. But I cannot be one moment always. More sooner than later womanhood knocked me from the perfect gravity of childhood. And dragged me off by new hair and curving handles that I could not keep from coming.

I was off balance and learning new walks. The world itself would not be still. It was wound up in its own motion. I was caught in the motion of life itself, and I was not alone.

Ernestine spent entire summer afternoons underneath our mother and father's bed, tearing apart whole blue boxes of sanitary napkins. Thinking that within those rectangles of cotton and gauze and blue lines would be found the secret of womanhood. The central mystery of breasts and bras and black or beige silk panties. The busy hands of rosaries, fans, cigarettes, and picture-less books. After she tired of Kotex and Modess she turned to baby bottles, sucking the man-made nipple and picking in her hair underneath the bed in which she had been conceived, and under which the water surrounding her still curled and unborn had run out. She would experiment with the sensations of objects of womanhood and babyhood until the afternoon wore out and her interest. Then she would sleep amid the dust and echoes of our footsteps not far from her face. Until she was tired of being alone and not an infant and not a woman.

At this moment I am in love with the way Daniel Moody (like a slim, insouciant Santa Claus) carries his books in a duffle bag slung over his shoulders. By virtue of his infatuation, I am in the club of swooners and piners. Membership temporary but intense. Essie's a founding member. And Leona's emeritus. She says she is for the moment. When Essie suggests a late walk for tea and grilled cheese, I'm ready. This gives us a reason to slow walk under a radiant and ponderously full moon, which feels like it has dropped down inside me. But Essie says that feeling is just because my period is on its way. I'm at high tide so to speak. A red-moon high between my legs about to unravel. My breasts like two moons. I try to think of a planet that has three moons, but astronomy is not my thing. We're into astrology. Essie brings the star books with her and I bring the birth dates and times of the heroes of our hearts. A young woman in love is a zealot detective, an assiduous gatherer of data, cross-references, and minutiae.

The Saturday dance is over and no one's asked us to the after set at Blood Island. It's a secret rendezvous closed to singles, open mainly to the royal couples, cuddling consorts and the like. Leona has gone with Steve, because she loves to dance with him. Dancing is what they do. Slow drag, walk, hesitation, bop, Watusi, funky Broadway, jerk, and African twist. They do them all as if they were twins with complementary moves and style. William and Rhonda and the other couples do other things in corners, on the couches, in the closets of hot Blood Island. We, Essie and I, imagine what they do. We don't really know. Later Leona will tell us enough of what William and Rhonda did to send Essie to bed sick and insomniac.

I feel unearthly and untimely—as if I'm looking back on myself—as we walk the downtown streets of Eden on our way to the quiet greasy spoon where we can spread our *American Astrology, Horoscope,* and *Heaven Knows,* and papers over the table, while we nibble grilled cheese sandwiches and share a large order of salty, greasy fries, sip cherry-flavored Coca-Cola, and chart the courses of true love through the heavens. Essie has plaited her hair and tied it with a scarf, so she looks tinier, more vulnerable, than usual. She carries no terrible thundercloud of hair to protect us from the night terrors that scurry and scramble past midnight, lunatic and howling like frat boys who've drunk too much beer.

Stores hawking records, books, jeans and other fashions, ice cream, drugs and notions and fast snacks line the neat streets, which seem less narrow under the moonlight. As if night gives life here width and breadth. All other eateries, pizzerias and hamburger joints, are crowded or closed except the one we're heading for. Few people are about. And the world howls with such loneliness I feel heroic walking beside Essie. Together but somehow separate as we go.

Everything is spooky; pale mannequins in store windows lunge toward us like they want to tell us something heavy or do us in. Shadows lead us. Yet Essie says tonight is a time for lovers, and why can't William be hers and here with her now? They are meant for each other. She's checked the stars. Too bad she can't do the higher math of it, with all the exact degrees and minutes. Maybe then she could plot the inevitable time of their eternal and everlasting union. Her eyes blur with faith like some ancient mystic. She talks about the love match unceasingly like somebody hypnotized her and said the chief topic of her life should be William Satterfield. The acuity of her feeling infects me too and I try to stay with her by rhapsodizing about Daniel Moody, who totes his duffle in such a romantic way. But my evidence is insufficient beside the masses of information Essie has accumulated over weeks. Hers is the love of a lifetime. She and William have actual conversations. He caressed her as they sat on the manmade bluff that juts over the lake. Stroked her back and fit her petite breast into the palm of his hand, his tongue wiggled in her ear, sliding deep in her mouth over her tongue, but he's never done it to her. That would be too dirty. To sleep with both Essie and Rhonda. I guess.

Our game is guessing the identity of Fred (who we've never seen) of Fred's All-Night Restaurant. Fred Flintstone, Fred

Mertz, Freddie the Freeloader. We reel off a list of every round-faced, jovial Whiteman named Fred we ever knew from TV. Essie says Fred Weinberg, and I've never heard of him. He's the man who owns the building her mother cleans, she tells me.

Fredonia Witherspoon is the glamorous one of a crew of Black and Polish women who work the same hours as roaches. Sunset until clean, Fredonia scrubs like a queen, her iridescent red wig glowing in the vacated offices under the fluorescent lights. "My mama working nights now," Essie ends.

"My mama do days," I say like we've never talked about any of this before. I launch into the tale of my stolen hair dryer Mama bought with her daywork money a day before I came to Eden. We go over again who might have stolen my hair dryer bought with my mama's red hands. Essie thinks it was the maid who got fired who stole it out of my closet. I think it was Trixia or Oakland who did it for kicks, because in the early days I was quiet and was tight only with Leona and Essie. They called me "boojie." Me. Because I wore tiny pearl earrings and was always polite enough to say "please," "thank you," "excuse me." And I wasn't free enough to say "shit," "bitch," "motherfucker," "bastard," and "niggah," which I can almost if I ever open my mouth to do so reel off rather deliciously by now. But it always happens. Whenever Essie, Leona, and I talk about the work of our mothers, I think of the stolen hair dryer and I want to hunt down the person who stole it and with it my mother's sweat. I hope it is a Whitegirl who's stolen from me, but that's unlikely. Someone would have seen her. A Whitegirl going in three Blackgirls' room. Even a friendly Whitegirl.

As usual, Fred is nowhere for our eyes and I am more certain than ever that he doesn't exist outside the booths, the sizzling grill, and the little square tables with the Formica tops. He's only a figment of the sleepy waitress's imagination. She looks up at us grouchily as if she'd rather not. Only her paycheck is real. If we disappeared back into the dark she'd happily keep leaning on the counter dreaming of new shoes, compassionate kisses, shiny golden hair where the brunette roots don't show as they do now. She snaps her jaws and gives the gum one last crack, then she shoots the wad into a napkin as she moves toward us.

"Where's Fred?" Essie asks facetiously, imitating the bravery of Leona as she does when Leona's not around. Maybe it's her own bravery that only comes out when she's the bravest one here. I giggle at the audacity of extending the joke of Fred's identity to someone who may know him. "Tell me the truth," Essie keeps on good-naturedly, "Is there really a Fred?"

"Is there really a God?" I whisper over the salt shaker.

The waitress, BEV in white letters on the black name tag, does not give us a smile. She asks us what we want and we look up and giggle and order grilled cheeses and cherry Cokes and an order of fries between us. This is the ritual meal we eat as we pour over astrology's wisdom. We are severe as we thank the waitress who toots out her mouth and screws her lips like she's holding something nasty like liver or cold cooked carrots. She goes to wake the napping chef.

"Why do Whitepeople always shorten their names? Bev instead of Beverly. Sandy for Sandra. Jenny for Jennifer. Ellie for Eleanor. Like they're so friendly. When they are so unfriendly." All this we whisper across the table as we spread out our paraphernalia like mapmakers of divine destiny. In the earliest dorm meetings which everyone in Wyndam-Allyn went to in every kind of pajama and gown, the perky Whitegirls called Essie, Essie, and I was Mag until I set things straight—Magdalena please, only my old friends called me Maggie. And Leona was Lee for a day. Penelope, who is Greek, begs us to call her Penny.

We call Bev, the waitress, Miss when we ask for water. She brings it with no ice in the glasses but plenty in her eyes. Water sloshes over the table. Bev sits down at the counter watching the Black chef in the head scarf shake the basket of crispening fries. Too much tolerance in her watchful waiting. Too much insistence and too many directions as she tells him how to do his job. Too much silence on his part tells us he doesn't relish her instructions.

Bev acts all happy when the bell tinkles the arrival of a blond lanky dude and his crinkly headed date. They slide into a booth near the door, and grinning Bev is taking their orders before their buttocks hit the seat good. They act like they don't know her.

Essie and I avoid each other's eyes because we don't want to see the difference in her treatment of them and us. If somebody else sees you seeing something wrong, then you have to speak and get loud. Then you have to do something. And Essie and I want our girlish evening of romantic meanderings; we want to tell each other the birth date and times and places of the men we love. So we do that. Instead of breaking Bev the witch-waitress's face.

Essie opens the book and begins to read about William born on the cusp between two signs. I draw the symbols for the placement of his signs. If our breath is high in our throats, it is the excitement of love and not the tension of ignoring being ignored.

The waitress saunters to the phone in the corner. She hangs on to the receiver, leans against the wall as if she were weariness watching herself, and listens. After a while she slams the receiver down. Essie and I look at each other to make sure we've both witnessed this business in the corner. We pretend to peruse our astrology charts spread out like ancient sea charts that end in cliffs into the abyss.

157

Bev, the waitress, picks up the phone again; money makes a lot of noise when the machine swallows it. Bev swallows, drums her long fingernails on the phone, then yells into the mouthpiece.

"Oh, you think you're so goddamn smart. You're a stinking son of a bitch, Freddie."

There is a Fred and Bev is on his case. And Bev is about to cry. Essie and I giggle and whisper.

Bev lowers her volume, but we can hear anyway because intensity carries and we listen attentively to it. "Don't screw me like this, Freddie. I told you two weeks ago I need the time off. You may not have to go to your sister's wedding, Freddie, but my family is a family. I'm a bridesmaid."

Bev has won our sympathy now. She's got to dye her dress shoes a funny shade and look happy while her sister gets married and she works at a diner in the middle of the night. She looks like the type I've heard Penelope talk about—"Always a bridesmaid, never a bride." I'd never heard that saying before Penelope said it. It's something no one ever said at the Grace house on Arbor. Maybe I didn't hear. It sounds sad, "never a bride." Bev acts like she would cry if she weren't at work. She hangs up the phone again. She flips her eyelashes and passes over her wet nose with her index finger.

"I hope she washes her hands before she touches somebody's food," Essie says.

She doesn't. Bev's back at the counter. She pushes the bread down more firmly atop the Reuben sandwich and carries it to a truck-driver-looking man across the room.

"Now you know that's nasty. Rubbing snot on that man's sandwich." Essie pushes her plate away and sips the Coke to wash away the nasty taste of unsanitary thoughts.

"Fred better give her some time off before the health department close this place down," I say, just so Essie will choke on her Coke. She chokes. And coughs it all over the table.

Bev looks at our mess out the corner of her eye and I know being Black doesn't pay when a poor Whitegirl's in pain. In a hassle with her boss. Bev walks over to us with a rag in her hand and an ugly look on her face like a squirrel in a trap.

The door opens and I hear it out the corner of my mind but none of us looks that way while Bev slams ketchup and plates around the table knocking our star books on the floor.

"Excuse me," I say as a reprimand.

Bev grunts like she's accepting an apology and is still mad about it.

"She's not the one apologizing," Essie says. "Miss, you messin with our property."

Bev says, "So sorry, big spenders." Then she walks away talking about how she hates to wait on us people because we don't tip from shit.

"I'm going to tip her upside the head," Essie promises, and glares so hard at the woman's back I'm nervous she is going to jump on the woman's back and ride her like an addiction. Essie is usually less violent than this. All her injuries that she spends her time on are internal; Whitepeople's belligerence goes right past her usually. She lets the racism slide. Not like some of us who ready to jump to anybody White's chest when we having a bad day and somebody White cross that fine line. Somebody like Trixia would kick a Whitegirl's behind on g.p.

Trixia says, "Hey, now" from a table behind us. And Essie and I turn to salute them, her and three other sisters. It is they who've just arrived, whose entry we hadn't taken time to note. We don't try to mix company. They can tell I guess that we're in a slow mood, and they are still busy and boisterous from the after set they went to and we didn't. We pick up pieces of their talk about how the after set wasn't all that much fun. Couples cuddled up and boredom.

By the time Bev, who is busier now, makes a move to Trixia's table, Trixia is long past ready to eat. Everybody's starving.

Bev says, "Are you ready to order?"

They had a name for girls like me. They called us smart girls. They had other names for girls who went to all-girl Catholic high schools, who walked on the cutting edge of nun's habits. They called us whores, nymphomaniacs, and lesbians. They called us stuck up. Sometimes they called us good. I wanted to be good like one of the girl saints, brave enough to look into the mouths of lions without flinching. Being gobbled up singing.

One year when I was thirteen I kept a little spiral notebook, a diary I addressed to Jesus.

Dear Jesus, (I wrote)

The Freedom Riders were on TV. They are brave and holy.
I want to be one of them. They ride buses into the jaws of
death. People spit on them and they keep coming. They
are more like you than the apostles who turned their backs
on you. Remember Peter said he didn't know you and lied
about it three times. I bet the Freedom Riders wouldn't lie.
They'd just go on singing and walking through the spit. The
White people pour ketchup over their clean white shirts. On
television it looks like blood.

Some of them shed blood for the cause of our people. Like
you they were crucified. And their bodies thrown away.

Those four little girls in that church in Birmingham I
know they're in heaven with you like the Holy Innocents. I
know they are angels with you.

Dear, dear Jesus, I want to be good and brave like the
Negro people down south. I was born there, remember, in
Mimosa, Mississippi. My Aunt Leah-Bethel whom we call

Silence is with them and she was never brave before. But now
she is. "She used to be crazy, but now she's courageous," Sam
Jr. said yesterday in the living room when we were watching
the news. Mama didn't say anything. She smiled. One day
I'll walk to school and won't ride the bus because the bus
drivers are so mean to us. Some of them are colored. One day
when you are with me I'll go to the Catholic church across
the viaduct, right where the Polish and Irish lions stay. They
call themselves Christians. But we know, you and I, don't we,
Jesus? The priest over there wouldn't give one of our boys
who went to late Mass over there Holy Communion. He was
wearing his army uniform too.

Excuse my penmanship, you know I can write better than
this. I am real good with my hands. Aren't I? But it's late and
I have to finish reading *The Bridge of San Luis Rey* for school
tomorrow. I'd rather read what I want to read, but it's a good
book. I just didn't choose it. I'll try to do better. Honest, I will.

In true friendship,
Maggie

I'm still seduced by the spiritual romance of the images of
nonviolence, the radiance of bloody submission and transcen-
dence, the neat collegians in white shirts with ketchup splattered over them like blood. I like being good. There's a kind of
supremacy in turning the other cheek.

Mama the Roman Catholic and Miss Rose the Missionary
Baptist taught me. We are not like Whitepeople. We are better
than them. No matter what ugly thing they do to you. They
are less for it. We are the holy ones. We've held on to that for
decades, centuries even. Maybe because it's true.

"Nobody needs as much water as you," Bev says after refilling
Trixia's water glass for the fourth time and setting the pitcher

on the table so they can serve themselves. Slamming the check down beside it. "You should take some of that water and wash that black off," she mumbles more to herself than anyone else. She's just fed up because she can't go to that wedding. But what she want to say that for?

Trixia picks up the check, so wet from splashing water the ink runs, and they can't read the money numbers due for the hamburgers that were served cold. The chili that came with no crackers and they had to ask for them. The pop with no ice.

Trixia leads the line to the counter and Essie and me bring up the rear. Bev yanks her body to the cash register. Is it fear that slices through the sullen anger in her eyes? Trixia slams her money on the counter and then she hawks and spits in the waitress's eye. And then comes Oakland and Letitia and Ramona, one by one hawking and spitting in the woman's face. Paying the money and not waiting for the change, because they know the price and have counted it out to the penny. They open the door and stand in it. The place is still in the first moment when Trixia first hawked and spit and it is Essie's turn and mine and I just put the money on the counter and look away and Essie spits on the money and we walk outside. Bev's eyes are squeezed shut, her mouth wide open. Nothing coming out.

Trixia and Letitia and Oakland and Ramona look at me but don't speak. We are walking down the street when the truck-driver-looking man comes and stands in the doorway and calls after us, "You sonufa-bitching Black bitches." And Letitia hollers back, "Come and get us. You so bad, blue-collar motherfucker. It's a ass-kicking moon out tonight and I want yo ass." He gives us the finger and goes back inside.

On the street Trixia and them keep repeating what happened. Stroking the nuances and accelerating the rage every time it slows down. They disturb the peace. One by one they applaud one another—how loud Trixia was when she yanked the phlegm out of her throat and threw it at the Whitegirl, how strict the set of Oakland's neck when she fired, how perfect Letitia's aim and Ramona's scowl. They talked about Essie's imagination to think of spitting on the money, so the bitch had to pick it up.

When we get to the doors of Wyndam-Allyn they look at me quietly and there is no praise.

We come to Letitia's room first on the corridor and she opens the door for all to fall in for a victory celebration, a recounting of the battle for the rest of the sisters.

"Come on in, Essie," Trixia says without looking at me who is next to Essie now, on my way back to the room. Essie looks at me sheepishly and follows them in.

"Tell Leona to come on down, Maggie," Oakland says with a casual fling of her scarf onto the bed.

The hall is quiet except for the noise escaping from Letitia's room. Everything is empty. And I am hollow inside except for the sloshing of like a gallon of water in my stomach and chest and I wish, I wish, that I could spit.

Leona, Essie, and I walk through the huge oak doors of Wyndam-Allyn. Nearly paralyzed by the frost-forming wind that rushed under our navy pea jackets and wide-legged jeans, we slap the cold out of our clothes and head for the mailboxes beside the switchboard in the lobby. The switchboard is off behind a large oak counter where the dorm mother stands like a state trooper. We come back from the little black mailboxes with golden knobs, still excited from our survival of the cold, and excited too about some pieces of mail from home! Mama writing in her pret-tily formed alphabet sending me the address of a good Negro hairdresser in Eden "not too far from where you are." It hasn't occurred to Mama that when Honeybabe washed my hair and lifted and scissored the liberated kinks into an Afro and sent me forth to strut and shine in my remembered beauty that I would stay nappy and happy about it forever.

We crack up over Mama's urgent (but ever-kindly) directive. "That hairdresser farther away than the home your kitchen is at now." Leona squints at the stubbornly curly hair in the back of my head that looks just like her own. I squint at the newspaper clipping from the colored daily about the opening of her father's third barbecue house. Leona flourishes the paper with haughty pleasure. "Why he send me this shit insteada some chicken in mambo sauce?"

Essie saunters away from us, looking sad over a letter on notebook paper from her sister LaVette. We linger for a minute in the lobby beside the cute little treasure-chest mailboxes. Trixia passes by and waves. Her eagle eyes checking out who got mail and who looks happy about it and who doesn't. Mostly we chat, Leona and I, sheepishly trying to pull Essie out of the aura of the trouble at home before she goes into a three-day depression.

Mrs. Sorenson, all hardened strawberry Jell-O under marshmallow-swirl hair, in a severe beige suit, folds her hands on the counter and issues orders sweetly like somebody's fairy godmother.

"Girls," the word is eternal, coming out from paper-thin sliced lips. "Let's not congregate in the lobby. Let's not congregate." Any time more than two Black students stand in the lobby, under the darkly oil portraits of the benefactors for whom this dorm is named, Mrs. Sorenson gets nervous. She twitters like a dizzy blonde character actress from the thirties. On pins and needles because she thinks we're like rabbits or roaches and will multiply before she can blink her blue eyes. She acts like we're about to riot or hold church—sanctified. "Let's not congregate."

"I think Whitepeople go to school where they teach them how to act White and how to treat Blackpeople," I suggest to Leona. But Leona says no; they learned all that stuff as a rationale for slavery and they been practicing ever since.

Essie doesn't say a mumbling word; she folds up her letter from home, sweaty and wrinkled by now.

"Why do you people do this repeatedly? I have asked you not to congregate." Mrs. Sorenson is so exasperated.

Leona and I look at each other. "You people?" we shout uproariously into the dark of each other's faces, so loud White-girls turn to stare at us and even Essie wakes up from the bad glow of her letter from home.

"Let's do a scientific study on this issue," Leona says. "Do Negroes as a rule congregate more than Caucasians? Or do they only appear to do so to Caucasians? How many Negroes constitute a congregation?" We are walking down the hall now past the broom closet.

"Whenever two or more of you are gathered in my name, then I am here." A woman in a blue uniform backs out of the broom closet, butt first, a vacuum cleaner in her hand. She's been working in this dorm so long, she has a son named Allyn. He's in Vietnam.

I hate to go to work in the early afternoon. I hate to stack the beakers and test tubes neatly in their racks. I hate to turn the private key in the service elevator. Hate to wheel the noisy wobbling cargo of glass in the cart over the bump and onto the manually run elevator. I hate to run the elevator when I could be alone somewhere drawing. I pull the lever and see images inside me. I check the cart to be sure I stashed my sketch pad between two beakers, like I always do.

One afternoon later than usual, in a post-surprise-French-quiz fog, I pulled the elevator down past the basement to a subbasement. I didn't even notice the differences. The air thick with disinfectant, the furry smell of animal and animal waste. I didn't notice anything beyond the alarmingly noisy rattle of the cart full of glass as I pulled it over the basement floor to the room where I'd stack the glass instruments into a washer and watch the germ-killing hot water absorb the harsh soap and bubble up so completely I couldn't see into the round window of the washer. After the beaker and test tubes were obscured by the soapy mist, I began to look around me. Oh, it was a dish room with the same appliances; it was a dish room, but not the dish room basement level.

The flat windows didn't reveal the bottoms of the bushes as on the basement level. There were no windows. Tables and counters didn't shine from frequent use and cleaning in this room. The overhead bulbs didn't beam down light in a glow that brought well-being. There was no sun to augment poor wattage. The place was foreboding and quiet. The loudest thing there the smell.

Because it is like nothing I've ever smelled, I have to see where the odor comes from. Mama says none of us would have made good Germans in World War II; the trucks and trains overloaded with children, women, and men would not have gotten by us without the wildest and most vocal conjecturing. A thousand terrible explanations would have abounded—eventually someone would have had to verify his tale. That's part of our role in history: spies in the Big House, blank-faced eavesdroppers in the field.

"Negroes are the nosiest people on the earth," Mama said after Littleson went through the garbage cans on Christmas Eve.

"That's why them noses built so wide: to get all that information inside. So half of it can get to the brain and half can come right on out the mouth," Miss Rose said as she shook the thermometer down and slid it between my baby sister Anne's naked cheeks. Miss Rose jiggled her knee and Anne bobbed up and down. My brother'd broken our thermometer and Miss Rose came running through the snow with hers because Anne felt so hot and Mama was so worried. It was Christmas Eve.

"This baby girl's normal," Miss Rose decreed after she held the thermometer up to the light and squinted at the mercury. I had to read the mysterious little wand and crowded close to Miss Rose's elbow.

"Nosy," Mama said to me.

"Curious." Miss Rose defended me and pulled me into the crook of her elbow. She taught me then how to read the skinny line of mercury. "She's a smart little lady," Miss Rose further decreed. Mama tried not to look too pleased by compliments, lest our Christian humility be stunted and we grow up arrogant. It was, however, okay to be smart and interested in the methods of science and medicine. Better to be smart than artistic. From that evening on I gave voice to a curiosity about things scientific while remaining curious about everything. Especially light, color, and shape and motion and the burst of beauty that throbbed in my chest when I made a painting with the brushes Mama and Madaddy gave me at Christmas.

So it is that in Eden I was assigned as a helper in a lab in the Lichtenstein Biological Sciences Building, known as Old Science, next door to the Institute of Technology. Both buildings connected underground by a vast system of tunnels. An underground maze.

Now I discover the maze beneath the basement maze—a subbasement. The elevator, I was told, would not open on that floor marked *S* without a special key. Someone has made a mistake, and I another. Perhaps I am making a third as I travel the ancient halls behind the shadow of that smell that gains substance as I get closer.

After turning many corners, I stand before the last door on a short corridor. The odor is so palpable that I stifle a gag and turn the knob at the same time. Only a quick look.

It's enough. Enough to see the cages of half-flying, half-fumbling pigeons ceaselessly flapping against the ceilings that have no outlets; pigeons tiptoeing over old newspapers, twitching like junkies. My eyes are fine instruments defining every detail. I begin to heave even as I turn to run. Protective instinct pushing me through the maze of the subbasement, up a stairwell I've never seen before, and out a fire door that screams and gives way when I slam my body against it.

I leave the beakers and the test tubes in the steaming rinse water. I leave the pigeons sick and enthralled, breathing, defecating, eating, defecating, and dying. I leave my sketch pad. Go pounding away from the nightmare.

The next day the girl at the front desk buzzes me, two buzzes because I have a visitor. The visitor is my sketch pad and my coat. One week later a check from work study comes for me, and no one contacts me from the lab.

When I told Essie and Leona what I'd seen, neither one of them acted surprised.

Essie said, "I ain't got a tear for dumb animals."

"If you'd only seen them," I said.

I wrote a letter to the *Eden Daily* about that room in the subbasement, but it was never printed. I wrote a column in *BloodLines,* the new mimeo of FBO, but no one mentions it but Steve Rainey, who says, "I thought you knew they do war research over there. It all leads to war. In the early part of the century they did tests on Negroes there to see if we cried real tears. Do Negroes cry real tears? Forty lashes, then they collected the tears in tiny test tubes and analyzed them. They went to the county and to charity wards of hospitals and collected the tears of poor Whitewomen in childbirth to compare. They didn't use the tears of Blackwomen because they said that they were fake." He peers at me out of clear eyes. "Nothing about that place surprises me, Maggie. Don't worry about the pigeons. Worry about us. They know everything about us. Me? They know I'm a motherless child and a fatherless son. They know our pasts and they've projected our futures. They've predicted who will succeed and who will fail. They've even calculated our GPAs at graduation. I've seen the data, happened on it at Tech. Admissions officer was there. Didn't know I saw it. Old Science is the granddaddy of studies on Negroes. I know and I'm telling you. That makes me a stool pigeon." He laughs, throatily. "In Old Science they dissected and displayed like cuts in a butcher shop the bodies of recently dead Blackpeople if their families did not claim them within twenty-four hours. In other words, if your family didn't take you home, you were not only dead but desecrated. That's what they did in Old Science. I don't have a family." He lapses into a melancholy moment. I touch his hand tentatively.

I incorporate the image of pigeons in cages into my dream vocabulary. Sometimes, when I am afraid, I dream that scene. I am in it.

One day the woman from Student Employment calls and tells me I have a job—a people job—more to my liking than the lab I won't go back to. She assigns me to the switchboard at Wyndam-Allyn during dinner, on Mondays, Wednesdays, and Fridays from 4 to 7 P.M., and every other Saturday from 7 A.M. until noon.

I have a short, sculpted Afro, a neat natural that curves on my head. My hair is not so long and free that it rides atop my head like a thundercloud. My hair is quiet, I guess. Mrs. Sorenson, the dorm mother, sees something safe in me. I guess. My voice, Leona says, is demure. "You're *quiet*, Maggie." I never knew. Perhaps that is why Mrs. Sorenson has singled me out and gets more than she bargained for.

I am standing in the lobby with Leona and the other girls, waiting for Essie to come clambering down the two steps from the dorms proper into the lobby, when Mrs. Sorenson steps out of her office beside the front desk. She appears from around the little rows of black mailboxes with a stack of letters in her hand.

"Miss Grace," she says preemptively. "Magdalena, you have a new work-study job." I already knew.

Everybody starts cracking up. "Cleaning toilets," Leona whispers in my ear.

"Come with me," Mrs. Sorenson commands. "Follow me."

I wear a headset like an airline pilot. (Is God really my copilot?) I sit at the switchboard. The brothers in FBO, who come to visit other Blackgirls, call me Lieutenant Uhura. Actually, I heard one White, big-shouldered guy ask another (with a kind of sneer in his voice), "Who's behind the desk? Lieutenant Uhura?" He didn't know I heard him, until I said, "You're not Captain Kirk and you're definitely not Mr. Spock." He turned red, splotches in his cheeks.

I answer the phone and announce visitors. I buzz the girls once if they have a phone call. They can answer at one of the phones at the end of the hall on each floor. In a little phone booth with a seat inside. I buzz the girls twice if they have a caller at the front desk. A flag goes up on a board full of room numbers when I buzz; it goes down when the girl answers. They come running breathlessly. Soon some of the Whitegirls learn my name, if they think to. "Thanks, Maggie," they say if they're picking up a package. "I've been waiting for this." As if I sent it. Sometimes I sort the mail, putting it into the boxes of the little treasure-chest mailboxes.

I am taught to do my job by a girl named Maureen, a Whitegirl from a neighborhood I cannot walk through. But she is cool, in a world of her own in Eden. She is waiting for her first date, who is coming in an hour. She is happy I am relieving her. She whispers conspiratorially like ours is a conspiracy of virgins, which it is. "My prince awaits!" She is ecstatic. We talk about going to all-girl Catholic high schools. We see boys every day now and what is there to say to them all the time? "I'm going to throw myself at him." Maureen is very determined. "He's the first prince who asked."

"Even thinking about it is a mortal sin."

"I'm mortal," she says.

We all are.

She leaves me alone behind the desk.

Leona blows through the front door like a wind, both playful and ill. She leans her lean frame across the oak counter.

"Now I call that high visibility, Miss Grace," she opens. "New *j-o-b?* Ain't no monkey here, but there's a big albino baboon hangs around these parts." If Sorenson could hear Leona now she wouldn't be so reassuring about her future. A while ago when Leona was doing an independent investigation, asking questions about the housekeeping staff's employment conditions, work-load, pay scale, retirement, Sorenson had found out about it. One day she called Leona to her parlor office. (Come into my parlor said the spider to the fly. We are flies in the buttermilk.) In that little tête-à-tête Sorenson had assured Leona that she had nothing to worry about. "You're an Edenite now. Your future is iridescent. Let the help help themselves." When Leona began to protest, Sorenson simply said coldly, "You may leave now." Leona left.

The switchboard lights up and sings at the same time. I take command.

"Don't you look just like Lieutenant Uhura!" Leona bats her eyes at me. Lieutenant Uhura I don't mind. Not really. She is the regular Black face on *Star Trek*. She wears a micromini that cuts across watermelon thighs. She has a shape like a Coca-Cola bottle. The compact bottles they sell Coke in down in Mimosa, Mississippi. You can't get them like that up north.

"Good evening. Wyndam-Allyn. One moment, please, I'll see if she's in." I say all this with a smile modulating my voice so that it sounds just right over a phone line. Leona is reading everything on the oak desk. I interrupt her nosy perusal.

"Let's get this straight. This may be a strange new world, but this ain't Starship Enterprise. This ain't *Star Trek*. And you ain't on TV. I, however, am Lieutenant Uhura, your communications officer. Pick up the line on the hall phone. It's yo mama."

Leona's off, cursing me for fooling around while her mama waited on the phone.

Soon Mrs. Sorenson comes by to find a million things to do behind the front counter. I know she's checking up on me. When I'm free for a minute, she compliments me on my lovely speaking voice, my manners, blah blah blah. And my grammar so correct. I don't tell her Blackpeople have to speak and understand a thousand tongues, especially forked ones.

That's how I get to work the switchboard at Wyndam-Allyn. That's how I know who calls who. And if I weren't so ethical I'd know why.

Leona, five foot ten barefoot, walks into Vanity Stares, the new store for coeds, and is offered a modeling job on the spot. Naomi Sims, a very long drink of well water, is splashed across the pages of *Vogue* as exotic elegance personified. Sims is dark, thin and supple, tall and fine-tuned. A classy somebody who is the darkest girl we grew up with, grown up, dressed up, pampered, and praised. Instead of being called Tar Baby and Blackie. Wonderful names like that. Finally *Vogue* has admitted in its pages what it's imitated all along. Black must be beautiful. What *Vogue* says goes. Naomi. Leona. Of course, it helps to be tall.

Leona won't slick her hair back into the severe bun that Naomi wears as a trademark, but Leona's natural is close cropped and meticulously pruned. Like a tight skullcap. The owner of Vanity Stares says Leona has only to pretend she's a tree—stand still in the middle of the store or sway as the mood like lightning strikes her. "So I sway once a day, cause lightning don't strike the same place twice a day." She doesn't need the money. This is something to do.

One day the mood strikes Leona to be a little wild. She wears psychedelic colors and dances the funky Broadway to her personal transistor music that bangs in her close-cropped head. The speaker like a hearing aid in her ear. Her mother has told her a thousand times that she'll need a hearing aid when she gets through playing that loud Motown music in her ear all day long. Leona doesn't give up the beat. She has such a good time Saturday afternoon at Vanity Stares that she takes her transistor to work with her all the time after this.

Leona loves to go to work to dance off the strains of study. Her face acquires a glow like a woman in love. She is even more beautiful now and the owner of Vanity Stares gives her a raise and tells her to keep on dancing. "My dear, I'm bringing in a new line to highlight around your beauty. Black is beautiful," the owner sings as she rings the cash register.

Leona stays tuned in in the center aisle of Vanity Stares doing every dance she knows and loves: funky Broadway, boogaloo,

African twist, the monkey, and the bird. She doesn't remember the booty green, when I tell her about that. Her favorite dancing record is "Dancing in the Streets." She gets down. Sales increase and Whitegirls get the toughest clothes and dance lessons for free.

Pretty soon the owner brings a seven-foot-high, three-foot-wide cage with psychedelic lights around it for Leona to dance inside. Like a go-go girl on *Hullabaloo* or *Shindig* doing the swim or the mashed potatoes way behind the time we did them. Leona comes in all exhilarated from the cold and the idea of being on her feet all day, takes one look at the mind-boggling electric cage, and turns right around. She doesn't even take off her coat. So she doesn't have to put it back on to face the wind that is so high it talks.

Without saying one word to the owner of Vanity Stares who stands in the doorway staring and catching the voices in the wind, the owner calling Leona's name over and over again, Leona walks down Main Street and through the tree-lined path that runs between Wyndam-Allyn and the sorority houses. A girl comes out of one of the houses and calls to Leona about her free dance lessons, but Leona acts like she doesn't hear.

"I didn't see you come in," I tell Leona when she suddenly appears beside me in our room. Leona doesn't say anything.

It's clear that she's not into conversation tonight, dinner or otherwise. She's not into dinner either. She throws off her coat.

I put mine on. "Can I bring you a grilled cheese or something from 'cross the street?" She gets up onto her top bunk. I don't say a word. Just stand in the middle of the room with my coat on. Burning up. I wait.

She doesn't answer my invitation, but at last she looks at me with incredible eyes that make me say in exclamation points: "What's wrong?"

"I'm the biggest phony—"

"Not you."

"Yes, I am." She sounds angry because I won't let her say this. "I wasn't outraged with Sorenson about no racism or sisters and brothers trapped in this mire passing for life. It was about me all along." The last is a revelation. "No one is immune from the bullshit, Maggie."

She gets up on her top bunk. I don't say a thing. Just stand in the middle of the room with my coat on. Sweating. I wait.

"They wanted me to dance inside a cage." She describes it for me. So carefully it rattles in my head.

"It was a good time when I was just dancing and being a tree. It was that cage. And that hurt me, Maggie. That I can blow my cool over some simple nonsense like that, but I can stay calm over the sorrow of all these wasted, unappreciated, undignified lives." She swings down from the top bunk and goes to the mirror. She points to herself like a victim-ghost might point out her murderess. "There she is. Miss Pryor. Leona the fake." She digs her index finger into her breasts so fiercely I fear she'll puncture herself.

"You're not a fake, Leona."

"Yes, I am. If I can name it in somebody else, I can name it in me."

"Don't misname it then." She can't talk about my best friend like this. One of my best friends. "Everybody should be able to have a little pride."

"Maybe I have too much," Leona offers.

"That's for you to know."

"Thanks a lot."

I help her as she shrugs back into her coat.

She flings a scarf across her neck and is trying to be Leona again. "Besides," she says, pretending like it is an afterthought, "Leona doesn't dance for pennies. She dances for millions."

It is Homecoming time and bands of students swing banners across the wide avenue that divides the campus. The front of each dorm is decorated with streamers saying WELCOME HOME. All these signs that say WELCOME HOME are not for us. We know that. The brothers at EARTH don't have to tell us that. We are outsiders. FBO is holding a Black Homecoming dance. Something just for us. We will not stand around like orphans with our noses pressed to the department store glass. But no one has asked me to go. Which is no surprise to me.

I am nearly deafened by the loud ecstasies of frat boys running in front of ribbons, collecting beer and wine for the post–Homecoming game parties for a football team that never wins. (Early on we went to a football game to support the brothers on the team. The cheerleaders, rose cheeked and corn headed to a woman, frolicked out of step and sang off-key, "Give 'em hell, Eden U., give 'em hell." And Daniel Moody, who I say is a wit and Leona says is a nitwit, yelled at the top of his voice, "Eden U. ain't give nobody hell but the niggers."

Of course, the Serpents of Eden slithered off the field in defeat, and the rest of the student body was in a particularly foul mood that they sure enough tried to rub off on us. Fights broke out and we seethed at each other across the races. The student body is serious about nothing if not football. Even in this age of flower children, they love the brute force of victory. Which is about the only way those Serpents would win. They are not especially cunning or skillful, as their losing streak attests. Everyone will want to drown his or her sorrows this weekend; sorrow and giddy nostalgia for (in the case of the alumni) what has passed and for (in the case of students now) what has never been. Eden is a dry town, but this weekend the spirits will flow through its thoroughfares and in its houses.

One night before sets and after sets are starting under blue lights, William is walking Essie and me from Blood Island. We come upon one of the football players in the path. He won't budge, blocking our way.

"If it isn't the Supremes," the boulder boy slurs. William doesn't say a word. He glances beside him as he pushes Essie and me to the rear.

"Okay, Diana, why don't you and the backup bitches get out of my way." That is it. William swings. Somebody's calling a Blackwoman out of her name. Somebody's calling *Essie* out of her name. *His* Essie. He can't love her publicly, but he can protect her (and me). William swings again. The Whiteboy topples like Goliath.

William straddles him and pummels him, panting. "Now say 'Miss Essie, Miss Maggie, Miss Diana Ross,'" he punctuates each name with a fist on the Whiteboy's face. "'Miss Mary Wilson, Miss Florence Ballard.' Don't you ever disrespect a Blackwoman again. You hear me. My name is William. Say it. 'Satterfield.' Say it. 'William' . . ." Blood is in the night air.

I am yelling, "William, quit it. William, that's enough."

Essie follows. "William, they'll blame you."

Campus police has pulled up. One of them is out of the black and white car. Pistol drawn. Voice gruff. "Freeze. That's enough now. Get off of him slowly."

Goliath lies on the ground moaning and groaning. I can see the cartoon bubble with ARRRRGGGHH and GRRRRRR coming out of his bloody, swollen mouth. The campus policeman comforts him. "Lay still, son. We'll get you some help." He goes back to his car and radios for an ambulance. He says he's bringing in a Negro boy, the assailant, and needs another squad car for two Negro girls. He doesn't ask to see our IDs. He acts like we are just intruders from the City. Come to make trouble. To put innocent Whiteboys in the hospital.

More policemen and an ambulance arrive. The Whiteboy is babbling now, "He tried to kill me. He jumped me for no reason. I was just walking by." His mouth is so swollen the words sound like monster talk or prehistoric man.

After Essie and I tell the same true story to the chief of campus police, he is disgusted with us and waves us away with his hand that holds the cigarette like a pencil. He has a tight, tanned face like the star of a Western movie. His mouth is tight now. "We'll get to the bottom of this," he promises ominously, like he's going to make a bottom if he doesn't find one he likes.

They don't give us a ride back to Wyndam-Allyn. They give William a swift ride to Eden Town Jail. We see him looking bleak and angry in the backseat of the squad car as we slow walk across campus in the dead of night under a semiobscured moon. Essie is crying softly. The wind drying her tears. I am dry eyed. The trees on the other side of the street seem stern, look down on us; they are shadowy and wise. When they lose their warm leaves nothing will be left but bone. I will call Eden the Bone Yard then, and I will not mean Leona's father's establishments.

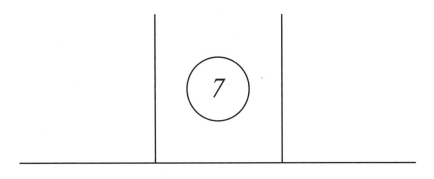

Homecoming

When it is Homecoming time, I feel like going home instead. All the way to Mimosa, Mississippi. Even if it takes me a week to do it. Aint Kit asked me to go with her to see about Bay, who is in jail, and I can say no to Eden classes and I don't want to say no to Aint Kit. "She done gone down there and got in trouble," Aint Kit told Mama, who told me, "Bay in trouble again." Because I am good and a student at Eden University, Aint Kit wants me to go with her to Mimosa. She has enough shame and worry to travel with; I am her escort of goodness and success. If she only knew. I can say forget you to Eden classes, but I don't want to forget Aint Kit.

I've been south before. Both times with Aint Kit. When I was four or five I went down with Aint Kit on the City of New Orleans. A milk-chocolate bar of a girl no bigger than a Hershey's Kiss with a silvery bow propped in a braid upside my head. I've seen her in a photo a friend of Aint Kit took. One of her husbands I think. At the end of my hand in that picture is a woman in a pair of white gloves, black silk stockings, and a flamboyant dark hat that dips over her eye. She wears a dark skirt and suit jacket with no blouse underneath. The jacket buttons up the front in single file. It must be blue. Deep blue. This suit that rolls across her bust and hips like rich night sky. She hugs her big pocketbook tighter than she hugs me. She is not my mother. She is Aint Kit and I am the kid.

We stand next to the train. Like fishermen showing off a gigantic fish they've yanked along on a line, we show off that train, the City of New Orleans.

No photos as perfect as this one remind me of my second journey to the birthplace. That summer after Eddie died, Littleson and I went south to hide from the hauntings in all our playing places. In the center of that Mississippi summer we grew through grief like flowers absorbing sunlight and water. I imagine we gave away a bare-stalked beauty that ended in a burst of wild-headed color. I imagine.

But I remember stories. Stories out of synch with transistor radios; they don't come in over them. Stories planted too deep in the brain cells to bloom on television screens. They can only be outlined. Stories that I tell no one now.

My grandmama, Sarah Mahalia Dancer, walks down Old Letha Road with her head in her hand. With insouciant grace she totes her braided head with its crying mouth and seasick eyes, tucked in the curve of her akimbo arm. Poised there, her lovely face with its wet, wet eyes running tears, and its heavy, tremulant mouth, stares and cries. Even now Mahalia is walking and crying, walking and crying. She has been crying and walking with her head in her hand since World War II.

Sometimes she places her head on her shoulders, balanced on the graceful stem of her neck, connected at the place where it was severed. She poises it there like a village woman carrying home a clay pot filled with vital river water. Gracefully she sails underneath her reconnected head, connected again where it was severed during World War II by the draft dodger in the red roadster who, drowsy under the influence, sent his car climbing into the side of the truck my grandmama rode to the cotton fields outside Mimosa to pick cotton for the War. Blackwomen and Blackchildren at the seam of dawn, sleep still tucked over their tear ducts, yawns still thick in their mouths, on the way to the fields where beautiful cotton waited to eat the skin off their hands.

Mahalia Dancer raises her blossom-scarred hands to wave to me. She blows me a kiss from her trembling lips. Then she lifts her wobbly head from her shoulders and tucks it under her arm again as a mother tucks a worrisome child. She walks and walks till Old Letha Road rises, and I watch her take the top of the slope. Light sweeps past her shoulders, the wind fans her washed, plain blue overalls out so that she seems to have collected stone or cloud next to herself in the pockets. Then the full-faced moon meets her and sits on the broken stem of her neck.

This is how I will paint her when I paint her.

It is dark when Aint Kit and I land in Mimosa-Letha Airport. We climb into a freelance cab, just a car with a driver who is probably a farmer too. He wears brown wool pants and a blue plaid sports coat, a blue button-down shirt with the throat left open. He wears a hat that looks like a cat played and peed in and on it. He lifts the hat to greet Aint Kit and his hair looks so ratty I can't wait for him to put it back on. Naturals have arrived, but Afro picks and big-toothed combs are too far behind.

It was crisply cold in Eden in obedience to the laws of northern Novembers. There are different laws here and the weather is warm, about sixty-five degrees.

The driver half whistles, half hums, while he swings our bags into the trunk of his car.

"How y'all been?" the freelance driver asks, once we've settled in the backseat. I am sitting on a taped-over rip in the upholstery. The tape is bunched and pinches into my tailbone.

"We doing very well. Thank you," Aint Kit replies. More grand than usual because she's feeling disgraced.

"Your face look kind of familiar to me. You been to Mimose before?" Natives of Mimosa let the *a* go silent.

"I was born right outside the city limits," Aint Kit tells the man. Her face says "Who are you to be asking me that?" Kit puts great stock in having Indian ancestors, so she figures she's known this land forever.

"I knowed you looked familiar. You used to live over there on Charles Street."

"Naw, we stay on Chinaman's Store."

"Oh, yeah!" the driver exclaims. "I got you now. You Miz Grace, Bay's mother."

"I wouldn't say that," Aint Kit sniffs and bats her eyelashes, which are still wet with the dramatic tears she's shed on the plane for my entertainment. She cried and bad-mouthed Bay awhile until I gave in and patted her on the back of her hand and swore to her everything would be all right.

The man is dense underneath that hat the cat has peed on. Maybe it's soaked into his brain. He doesn't read the signs of Aint Kit's tight posture and frozen face that tell him not to say, "How is old Bay? I heard she was back in town." Aint Kit acts just like she doesn't hear him. So when she interrupts, it doesn't sound like an interruption. Just two trains on different tracks.

"This is my niece," Aint Kit touches my shoulder and pushes me a little like a chaperone pairing two reluctant dancers. "Magdalena attends Eden University. It's a beautiful school, just fabulous. Like nothing you will ever see. It's one of the best colleges in the country. She is going into internal medicine."

My mouth drops open. Aint Kit punches me in a rib; my mouth closes. Aint Kit has to make things more to her liking. She tells the stories she would tell if things were just as she would have them. Madaddy says his sister is a born liar. When he is so angry at her he could curse, he calls her a "greasy-mouth, gap-tooth lie." Not to her face. To her face he simply thunders, "That's a lie and you ought to stop telling it, Kit."

But the lie has accomplished her purpose. The freelance driver is impressed. He looks at me. He chuckles. "I never met a doctor who was sick or poor."

That was Aint Kit's thinking too.

"Who you telling?" Aint Kit says.

The man has forgotten Bay.

I turn my face to the wind rushing through the open window taking my breath away. The air smells like sweet Mississippi nothings. I know the water in my grandmother's house will taste as if a strange honey ran alongside it in the pipes.

The water will be sweet there, in that house, but my grand-mother won't be there. She lives out in the country now with Aunt Charity. Aunt Leah-Bethel is staying in Grandmama's house now, because her house was burned down. The sheriff tried to say she burned it down herself smoking cigarettes in bed. Aunt Leah-Bethel used to have a problem and the sheriff said maybe her mind just tripped over itself for a minute and a lit cigarette fell onto the mattress. Aunt Leah-Bethel said her mind was upright and full and she wasn't in the house when it burned down. A voice called her up and told her to go see about her mama. She went. The house burned down. The sheriff didn't investigate the empty gas can in the vegetable garden. He took the can for tests; then he said he lost it somewhere. Aunt Leah-Bethel moved into Grandmama's house and Grandmama went to the country to stay with Aunt Charity because Leah-Bethel was too busy to care for her. Aunt Leah-Bethel is still working with voter registration. Nothing can turn her around. I love Aunt Leah-Bethel even though I've never been around her as much as I've been around Aint Kit. Once, Aunt Leah-Bethel and my mother were best friends. I know those stories.

I lean forward in my seat to look through the sweep of the headlights for the sign that says Chinaman's Store, which I always thought was a peculiar name for a street. But there are and have been for a long time many Chinese people in Mimosa and most of them own corner stores. Littleson and I used to wonder where the Chinaman and his wife who has a store on the corner of Chinaman's Store came from. When I first asked Littleson, he said, "China you fool." But that didn't explain enough for me. So I asked the Chinaman on the corner, reading his paper in the store, how they got there. And he said, "The same way you did." That is why for the longest time I believed the Chinese had been brought to America on slave ships. "They did it to them too," I told Littleson. He said, "When we get home, you read the encyclopedia, dummy."

The names of the streets are written on thin, white stone markers, like skinny headstones on the corners. We pass River Road, Indian Mound, Kirkwood, Cadoree, then Old Letha Road, which makes me jump in my seat a little.

The driver points the sign out to me, while Aint Kit fluffs her dewy eyelashes in her compact mirror. We turn on the next street, because Old Letha Road makes strange twists.

"You from the North, young lady. You don't know about haints. We got a lot of that still goin on down here. There's a ghost that walk down Old Letha Road." Mystery is in his voice, and he studies my face in his rearview mirror.

Aint Kit snaps her compact shut. "She know about that ghost. And she know who it is." Aint Kit has to be the sole custodian of drama. "Sarah Mahalia Lincoln Dancer." She says my grandmother's name like she wants her to hear and come walking alongside this beat-up car.

"You kidding!" The man is astounded, then suspicion that my aunt pretends to know more than she knows rolls across his face. He only knows folk who say they've seen the ghost; he doesn't know anybody who acts like they know her. I put in a word.

"She was killed during World War II." I add to Aint Kit's story. "She's been walking a long, long time."

He looks at me in the rearview mirror, like he's afraid I may detach my head from my body. I know about these things.

I am talking more to myself now than either of them.

"When Aint Kit brought me to Mimosa when I was a little girl, I used to worry about what kept Mahalia Dancer walking. Why she kept walking." The night is soft, outside the car. Soft and dense.

"I remember you asking me about that." Aint Kit beams softly on me, happy remembering my inquisitiveness as a child. Especially when my questions weren't questioning her stories. I am her voluntary ally even after she's made up that story about me studying internal medicine.

This time I know there will be pictures to take back to Eden with me. Images so wonderful, Essie's account of the Homecoming won't leave me feeling left out. I will be one who has what no one else has. Because I've gone looking for it, for something more.

185

We turn onto Chinaman's Store. And the house is there at the intersection of Old Letha Road and Chinaman's Store.

It is a magic house. Big trees populate the yard like robust children. Squatting shadows in the dark. A crepe myrtle tree does a backbend over the front walk. We get out of the freelance cab and just stand there and look at the way things are.

The last time I was here, I stood before this same walk beside Littleson, until a tornado built up in my throat, then I walked into my grandmother's waiting arms and burst into a torrent of tears. Where had that feeling of immeasurable loss come from? It eludes me now as I grab things in the dark with my eyes. The fig trees, crepe myrtle, the further-away pecan and pear trees that almost spread halfway across the intersection of Old Letha Road and Chinaman's Store.

We pay the man and he carries our luggage up to the front porch. Aint Kit gets out her key. Time stops. And in the distance I can hear the footsteps of the man and the ignition catching and the engine coming alive. Then wheels grinding gravel and dust as he pulls away. A wind goes by and Aint Kit unlocks the door.

My grandmother's bed is big in the small bedroom in the small house. The bedposts rise more than halfway to the ceiling. I have to climb to conquer the height of feather mattresses piled on top of one another on the "Princess and the Pea" bed. This house was made for little people by an even littler man, my grandfather, Malachi Grace. My father doesn't fit easily into this house. His height of six feet two so much that the top of his head skims the ceiling, and he stoops to get through the boxy doorways. He has to wrestle his way from room to room.

Aint Kit fits right into this house. She is small anywhere. At her house in the Northern city she slides between the fake French provincial furniture pieces without rattling their plastic covers.

She leaves no footprints in the deep pink carpet of her living room. All taken out, the contents of her freezer would dwarf her. She's not much bigger than the broom Mama and them say she used to use on Bay.

Littleson who is Lazarus now says that's why Bay's so crazy. She been gone upside the head with a broom handle too much. He says that's why Bay likes to fight. She got all those licks she couldn't give back to Aint Kit stored up inside of her. Aint Kit would work with her slaughtering broomstick for the easiest reason: Bay ate more than one egg for breakfast. Too much milk was drunk in too short a time. Too little polish was used on the furniture. Too little elbow grease used to make the tabletops smile back at her when she smiled at her furniture. Bay took money from her purse.

Sound is enlarged in this small house. I can hear Aint Kit in the next room. She's on the telephone talking to Aunt Charity.

"That's no reason to break somebody's nose. Cause they say you always thought you was cute and you still think you cute. That's no reason to wind up in the jailhouse." She says this with the same exasperated incredulity Mama used to say, "That's no reason to flog a child with a broom handle." As if there were someplace a reason sufficient for the brutal fervor of tavern fights and kitchenette whippings.

Aint Kit hangs up the phone, then comes into the bedroom with her mouth turned down in pure disgust. Her suit jacket and blouse hang open and she pulls on the lace of her longline bra. She looks at me.

"Well," she says. "You know they found a knife on her." Just like I knew. "Good thing she didn't use it this time. They pressing charges." She's sitting near me on the side of the bed now, having climbed up with alacrity, incongruous in her elegant suit. Her back is to me and she unsnaps her garters. The rubbing sound of the stocking tops coming out of the hooks fills the room already outlined by her disappointment, shame, and frustrated rage at Bay. "I took that girl in out of the goodness of my heart," Aint Kit announces. I don't say a word.

The most important thing Aunt Leah-Bethel says she learned in the hospital is how to move without making sound. She learned other things, but she will not tell them. She just told Lazarus who was still Littleson then and me how in a hospital you never knew who you might disturb by your movements. By paying attention to not making a sound, she focused her self on silence inside and around her and healed herself. Silence and the spiritual waters she drinks from a free, naturally blessed spring.

Littleson and I started calling her Silence then. It was our name for her. When we wanted more of the fresh okra, tomato, corn, and onion she stirred up in the skillet and the hot-water cornbread that went with it and everything else, we begged, "Silence, please." And she'd give it to us. Because she liked that name. It suited her.

Suddenly, Silence is in the bedroom with us. I don't know what makes her so large because she's only my mother's size. Not too much bigger than Aint Kit. Her presence, however, is gigantic; she causes time and Aint Kit to stop. Silence's hair is white and fans out all over her head. She looks like someone who has seen a ghost and gotten used to it. The first shock refined into a bravery.

Aint Kit keeps her back to Aunt Silence. "You knew we was coming. You could have at least had the common decency to meet us."

"I was at a meeting, Kit," Aunt Silence says mildly to Aint Kit, but her eyes are on me. "You have a key." We both grin.

"Maggie, you know who that is with her hair standing all over her head just like yours?" Aint Kit asks me unkindly.

"Aunt Leah-Bethel," I reply, excitement bubbling in my voice. I scurry down from the bed and stand shyly next to it, till Aunt Silence throws wide her arms for me like the doors to a church of deep peace and urgent compassion. Silence enfolds me in her arms, while Aint Kit goes on about Leah-Bethel never knew family came first. "Never knew it and don't know it now."

Aunt Silence whispers down into my ear, "How your mama, Magdalena?" I am mouthing "Fine" as she turns those eyes on my face again, tracing the parts of my mother, the parts of my father who is her brother, and the parts of me.

"Pretty girl. Pretty girl," she murmurs approvingly, and that affirmation eases the wounds of all of Eden. I look at this woman who is my blood relation and spiritual beacon and I only smile.

Aint Kit begins to cry. She wails she is just that worried about Bay and nobody knows or cares what she's feeling.

Aunt Leah-Bethel sits beside her and takes Kit into her arms, affectionately. "We know you upset," Aunt Silence croons while she rocks Kit from side to side like Aint Kit is a little lost boat and she is a big river. Aunt Leah-Bethel winks at me over Kit's shaking shoulder. In the drop and lift of an eyelid is the speech of wit and understanding. Aint Kit was feeling left out and she had to bring the center of the drama back to herself. That's the way she is and has always been as long as anybody's known her, including her mama.

Silence is sorry for her; she comforts her but is not in her thrall. In this way Silence is like my mother who is wise to Kit but loves her with full knowledge. After all these years Silence and Caroline, my mother, are still best friends. In the same manner, they wink at the foolishness of small and troubled hearts. They use their power to protect us against the minuscule heart of a world that has no room for us, crowds us, and shoves us over the edges into the mouths of demons. I wish I could use their abilities to overlook the dramas of Eden. Left out of White Homecoming and alone for Black Homecoming. Essie had a date with William, who is estranged from Rhonda for some reason, and Leona is dancing platonically with Steve Rainey. I left as soon as Aint Kit asked me. Aint Kit, my unfair godmother, who lifts me up.

Now I sit in my nightgown, having changed my clothes in the bathroom my father built in this house when the idea of the outhouse proved unbearable to him. I am sitting at the heavy, antique dining room table with Aint Kit and Aunt Silence. My sketch pad is open before them.

"There are so many trees on campus. Big, tall, thick trees. Here. See." I show them a scene from Eden in my sketchbook. They ooh and ahh, surveying my work serenely, taken to that serene-looking place.

"Oak," Aunt Silence points to a tree.

"They ain't got no pecan trees up there," Aint Kit sniffs.

"This is the fountain where we make wishes. I wish I make good grades," I say because I know this is what they want to hear. Good grades.

"Oh, Maggie, you sure can draw." My Aunt Silence affirms me, praises in a way my mother never does. Directly.

"It's beautiful. Like a fairyland. Make a wish and you got it, girl. You got it made. It's fabulous. I knew it when we took you up there." Aint Kit is rapturous and she gets a chance to dig at Aunt Leah-Bethel.

My Aunt Silence touches the back of my hand, holds my fingers gently. "You can learn so much there. The door is open."

"Lee-Bet tellin the truth. Doors were closed to us or there weren't any. Now this fabulous school has opened the door to equality for Negro students. I wish I could have gone to a school like that. I had to make my way the hard way."

Aunt Silence looks at my face and studies my silence. Then she says, "Every way's a hard way sometimes."

"So you say," Aint Kit snaps. "They ain't cleaning toilets. Or picking cotton in the roasting sun."

We three women crowd into the one big bed, and Aint Kit tells stories all night long. This keeps her mind off Bay. Her accounts are as near to truth as possible, because Silence always reminds her when her memory fails. I add to their telling all my mother has told me privately. They tell me the story of my mother, because they know I like to hear about her and my father, who is their brother. I like to hear about the way things used to be.

Leah-Bethel knew my mother long before my father did. Leah-Bethel was Sam's sister, but she was always like Caroline's sister. Caroline and Leah-Bethel went all through school together at the Catholic mission school, Jesus of the Resurrection or simply Resurrection. My father went to Mississippi Trade School for Colored, where he was taught carpentry and other skills, while he yearned for the more abstract knowledge his brain easily mastered. He never forgave my mother her success in high school, her presence in high school. ("Just like it was her fault," Aint Kit says bitterly.) This was, after all, the South of the thirties and forties. Post-Depression and Pre–World War II.

Once Sam discovered that gorgeous, red-skinned sister of Lazarus Dancer who was so smart in school, he courted her furiously. In the evenings, bringing by candy and sweets, big talk about what and who he was going to be and what and who she could be, the romance of his promises thrilled Caroline. After all, she and Leah-Bethel had for years gone downtown on Saturdays to sit in the segregated balcony of the River Road Theatre to imbibe the glorious illusion of swift-talking Whitepeople spun out like gossamer from the belly of the projector. Women with names like Bette with an *e,* Katherine not pronounced Kathereen, Greta, Rosalind, Norma, Myrna, and Paulette. Men named Cary, Clark, and Tyrone.

They cried until they laughed at Stepin Fetchit and Lightning moving so snail like and impossibly stupid on the screen, turning white with fright. The few "race movies" they saw at the club they loved. Everybody colored like them and smart and swift talking and solving crimes and being in love.

How they loved the romance of it. And Kit, who had by then married, told them all the glowing romance was true. Love was a real son of a gun, but Kit loved best of all the furniture, the clothes, the hairdos, the cars. And yes, she enjoyed the kisses—in those luxurious settings. Men in tuxedos and women in gold lamé dresses that shimmied and would have whistled in the air if the fabric could have made such a sound.

Sam spun dreams and one day brought over a borrowed and beat-up guitar. He and Caroline sat on her front porch and Sam sang a song about a girl with fire in her hair and sunset on her skin. That night Caroline agreed to be his bride. They married and babies followed, then the War and the Occupation Forces my daddy served in. After the service my father went north for a time to scout the lay of the land.

After scouting, my daddy, Sam, came back from the North to witness the birth of a baby girl and to contribute the middle name Pearl to Katherine Pearl. He worked land for the widow of my mama's Uncle E.W., who had died in the Keep-You-Sick Clinic. My daddy, Sam, got the land ready for planting. He worked for several seasons, while babies grew and the palms of his hands itched for the ebb and flow of money. He took Caroline to visit Leah-Bethel in the hospital in a little piece of car he bought with the money he'd made soldiering and that Caroline had saved for him. He sat in the car while Caroline visited his sister. He sat thinking about the North and what he'd seen there. The smoking factory stacks, steel mills, post office, the millions of people, the millions of jobs to do.

He dreamed of the North while he planted in the South—two more babies in three years, Lazarus, named after Caroline's brother, and Magdalena, named by Caroline. By herself for herself. Sam pretended he didn't know his daughter's name wasn't Maggie Lena. That's what he called me. Three months after my birth, Leah-Bethel came home from the hospital for the last time, but she was older than she should have been and largely disinterested in everything except the green penile shafts of okra that grew prickly in the garden outside her back door, the voluptuous tomatoes, and the children who ran between the vegetable rows. She loved especially the babe, Magdalena.

"And to this day I love me some Maggie," Aunt Silence says.

"I love this girl too." Aint Kit shoves aside her rival sibling and sends me to her overnight case to fetch her cold cream.

I do her bidding readily enough. I want the story to go on into day. Aunt Leah-Bethel says it is time to sleep. I ask them about something I've always wanted to know—what my grandmother ghost said to my mother when she visited her once, standing at the foot of her four-poster bed. Mama had awakened in the middle of the night to find her dead mother shining there.

"You haven't told me the word my grandmother told my mama," I remind them.

They look blank, then uncomfortable. Aint Kit covers her face with cold cream, like grease can hide something.

"What's the word?" I ask the two of them. "What's the word?"

"Thunderbird," Aunt Leah-Bethel replies absurdly and then she laughs so hard her shoulders shake. She has a coughing fit. By the time she quits, she's asleep.

Aint Kit wipes the cold cream from her face, gets grouchy, and tells me to turn out the light. She's got to face the law in the morning.

When I sleep at last I dream of my grandmother Sarah Mahalia Lincoln Dancer. Only she is not walking down Old Letha Road. She is standing in a harsh, heavy light at the crossroads of my life—that place where Eden meets the City. She is mouthing words I cannot decipher, even though I look and listen in the dream. Then comes fire. Then a scream. And she is gone.

Jail is not a pretty place. Even if it's just a little cell on a small cellblock in a relatively small Southern city and like Bay you've been in it so much the jailers know you by name and address, jail cannot be pretty. You cannot come and go as you please. There are no short runs to the store for a pack of cigarettes or to the ice cream store and back before the cone melts. You can't do the booty green in the jailhouse, slapping your hips and swinging what you got. You'd have to be good and drunk to do the booty green in the Mimosa jail; then one of those times when you slapped your own butt, you might wake up from the drunk and know where you are. What could you do but cry?

No one brings flowers to the jailhouse, as they do to the hospital or the funeral parlor. No one brings fruit and nuts. People who love you just try to get you out. Unless you are irredeemable and have murdered someone with forethought and confessed to it with a sense of impunity. Or stolen or maimed with no afterthought. Aint Kit says Bay is beyond redemption, yet here she is with a pocketbook full of money to get Bay out of jail. My mama says Bay has a good heart; her crimes are always self-defenses, protections of her life or limb or dignity.

In this case a man she went to high school with (Aint Kit sent her to Mimosa for high school because Kit said public schools in the North were too undisciplined, plus Aint Kit was married to Mr. Git-Been-Got then, and he was a little too nice to Bay and Aint Kit didn't want to have to hurt nobody; she was in love with all that money he made prizefighting, but the ring knocked all the sense out his head, so he didn't know better not to turn over his money to a woman so much in love with it she dreamed about silver dollars hopping over fences instead of sheep) had called Bay stuck up and bad, and his girlfriend shoved Bay in the chest so Bay jumped to her chest, blacked the woman's eyes, and bloodied her nose. Then Bay broke the man's nose, knocked him down, and stepped in his groin.

Aint Kit is so embarrassed to be in the jailhouse fetching her daughter. She is not as haughty as I've seen her, wheeling and dealing among her Black brethren. She is drawn up erect and severely in her seat before the sheriff's desk, but the edge in her voice is filed down and she looks at the floor more. She doesn't study the floor, but she's not nearly as direct with this Whiteman in charge. I want to pinch Aunt Leah-Bethel so she can witness with me this change in her sister, but Aunt Silence wouldn't come with us. She's working for voter registration and is unpopular with the law. She doesn't want her unpopularity to rub off on Bay.

The sheriff says Bay's name affectionately as if she were a member of his household—a maid or a frisky pet—with whom he must be stern.

His kindness is tainted with condescension; my teeth are on edge. I want to get loud and ugly like we do at Eden. But Bay is in jail and I'm not free to be righteously rude in her name. I acquiesce by being silent and seeing every detail in the room. The bars on the windows. The scratches on the desks. The papers unfiled.

The guns in the holsters—one on Sheriff Columbine's hip, the other swinging from a coatrack.

Sheriff Columbine is chastising Aint Kit because she hasn't trained Bay better. I cannot bear to look at my aunt who must suffer through a homily about how you must not put too much salt and pepper in a girl; a girl needs plenty of sugar. Her fingers tremble as she counts out Bay's bail money. Her voice thickens as she tries to say the numbers. She grows feebler with each second's passing. When she is like a vase teetering on the edge of a high table I count the money for her quickly because I will not let Aint Kit fall before this Whiteman who acts like the weary benevolence of God Almighty.

This is the same sheriff who dispersed the lynch mob from the door of the Chinaman's store on the evening of the attack on Pearl Harbor. It's twenty-seven or so years later and the law down to its physical representation is unchanged. It, like the man, has only grown more benign looking, solemnly white. The well-fed gut pushing against the leather belt and the holster.

This is the same sheriff Aunt Silence says people called to come get that colored woman with her head in her hand from off Old Letha Road. This is the sheriff who braved the dead and living of night to arrest whatever and whoever it was that was disturbing the peace by walking against the laws of nature and Mimosa city statutes.

The same one who came back to his office, unstrapped his holster and hung it from the coatrack, opened his desk drawer and pulled out the bottle of whiskey, poured himself with unsteady hand a shot glass full of the amber, and tossed it down straight. Then he stuck his arms straight out in front of himself chest-high like a sleepwalker in a movie and waited for the trembling to quiet. About that call to Old Letha Road in the winter of 1951 he wrote in his sheriff's logbook, "Let the dead bury the dead. I ain't dead yet." The next morning when he read what he'd written, he felt pretty silly, but it had all made sense to him the night before after he'd seen what he had seen.

He set about convincing himself that morning that he hadn't seen what he'd seen after all. Nobody had set its head back on its shoulders as nice as you please and said one mumbling word to him. Not one word.

Except that somebody had.

And he told an inmate about it, and the inmate passed it on, and the story keeps going through the cells.

That was in 1951. It is 1967.

Sheriff Columbine reflects for a moment. His head nods forward and his blue eyes stare at me while I'm handing him the bail money. He's looking at me as if he was seeing a ghost. What looks to me like horror seeping along the edges of his smile.

"Do I know you, young lady?" the sheriff asks. His whole face is wilted now, as if energy had fled and left the skin limp. He squints at me in the morning light.

"I come from up north." I aim to put as much distance between me and Southern justice as I can.

The sheriff keeps looking at my face while he takes the wad of money. "I hope you have some idea of what a waste of money this is. You'da done just as well burying this money, then forgetting where you put it."

"It's my money, Sheriff," Aint Kit's teeth are clenched. Her whole face is clenched. But she can't be quiet anymore.

"You should start respecting money." Sheriff Columbine jangles the keys as he goes out the office door. That shows what a poor judge of character he is. Anyone with eyes can see how much respect Aint Kit has for money. A beady-eyed fox was sprawled across her shoulders before Aunt Silence suggested she leave the fur on the bed. "You wouldn't want the sheriff to up the bail, just because you looking like a million dollars." Aint Kit left behind her diamond rings and diamond ear studs in favor of pearl ones. She wore a geometrically designed dress and short jacket and a pair of go-go boots. Mama would have died to see the go-go boots: "Kit know she too old for go-go boots. Goodness gracious."

Aint Kit begins to lie compulsively about Bay being her secret sister, Grandmama Patsy Grace's secret last child. Aint Kit says Grandmama was so old the family was afraid the authorities would find out she was fifty-five and still bearing children, and the same doctors at the Keep-You-Sick Clinic who wrote notes over my mama's Uncle E.W. while he was drawing his last wet breath would stand over Grandmama Grace's open legs and look all up in her coochie day in and day out to find the secret of everlasting Negro fertility, the population boom.

Aint Kit says she didn't want those people upsetting her mother like that, so she just claimed Bay was left on her kitchen table in a basket when the real truth was Bay was born at the kitchen table because that's where Grandmama Patsy, miraculously way past menopause and without benefit of sexual intercourse for twenty years, dropped her. Just like the goose that laid the golden egg.

After a while Aint Kit's voice is big and brazen with the lie, growing steadier as her tale grows more fabulous. Mama and my sister Pearl get aggravated at the way I listen to Aint Kit's fabrications, silent as any conspirator. "It's just imagining," I've told them time after time. "She's just making things up like Littleson used to tell me hero war stories in the bed at night in the dark." The dark was like no one I knew and trusted then; it spoke a language of cries—floorboard creaking, bedsprings bobbing, trees fighting the wind and themselves. Monsters grew out of the mysteries of that untranslatable language of night— and Littleson's stories kept us safe. Same with Aint Kit.

She is nervous and scared Bay will wind up dead or living behind bars till the end of her days, so she's telling a lie to buoy herself up, like a tired swimmer humming ecstatically.

I wouldn't stop her lie now to save myself. Besides, it's so outrageous I have to remember it, so I can tell Mama, Littleson, Pearl, Honeybabe, and them. I wouldn't dare tell my daddy or my friends at Eden. They wouldn't understand. I can imagine Leona's sarcasm and Essie's wide eyes.

Aint Kit's eyes have a precious luster like Mama looking up at the thin white cookie framed in gold the priest hoists high while bells ring out roundly, strict and awesome. It is the same look too that Essie casts up at William like she had just sent a flock of birds once caged in her heart out to him. My Aint Kit loves lies; they are her personal lullabies. Her eyes caress the lie in the air between us. Her lie decorates the spare impersonality of the office, gives reason and order to the clutter on the sheriff's desk. Files and files. Bay's name on one of them: Winona Grace.

The story now is how she'd sneak the foundling Bay over to Grandmama Grace, who was the real but ancient mother. Milk welled up in my grandmama's breasts like water in Buckingham Fountain. Aint Kit says she had to resort to milking her own mother and squirting the milk into those little Coca-Cola bottles they sell in Mimosa but not up north. I can picture my grandmother's wizened nipple squeezed into the mouth of a Coke bottle.

I say, "I'm surprised she didn't get stuck."

Aint Kit likes the idea so much she says it happened. "It did! One time!" she exclaims with delight because making a good story is a joyful and time-soothing thing. "Girl, we had a time getting that titty out of that bottle."

"You would have had to break the bottle," I begin.

"We did!" Aint Kit exclaims. "I took off my spiky heels and I struck that skinny heel just at the rim of the bottle. The rim broke in two like a wedding band. But the bottle shattered clean to pieces. Ooooooh, and Mama got cut all up on her breasts. Blood and milk was ev-e-ry-where."

I am picturing blood and milk and broken glass when Bay comes in with Sheriff Columbine.

Bay's not talking. She just hangs in the doorway like a broken spiderweb. Aint Kit waves her to the side and struts out the doorway, leaving everybody else behind.

Bay still doesn't open her lips, but her chest heaves rhythmically. The rhythm accelerates. Her body is swollen with humiliation, as if her physical self tries to expand to hold in humiliation and anger. Her body vibrates when I hug her and she clings to me. I smell the old Dixie Peach in Bay's hair; it is mixed with sweat and perfume, stale and inexpensive.

There's another smell that hangs around her. I think Bay is like a struck tuning fork heaving, resonating so wide you can see the arc of the tremor. I hold her, but she doesn't cry out. She snatches her body from mine, squeezes my hand, and follows Aint Kit and Sheriff Columbine. I walk behind them. Like the little girl that I am, picking up the pieces of this history.

When we walk onto the sunny street, leaving the sheriff at the jailhouse door, I am still shadowing them. They are so real to me now, this mother, this daughter. Real as spilled milk, running blood, snot slung and wiped, sweat and pee and toothache. Real as everything I cannot stop and cannot help but be.

We walk on the sunny side of the cracked concrete walk. Bay keeps planting her feet on the cracks, and I will not follow in those footsteps. I make my own.

The sun, at this time of day, at this longitude and latitude, is omniscient. I can feel the scoop outlines of perspiration under my arms, melting and gliding uneasily under my blouse. Aint Kit is too mean now to sweat. And Bay does nothing but—the swollen rage bursting out in sweat and staining her whole body. She looks like she's been dunked, and she stinks like jail. That is the other smell. The odor reeking with a concrete mustiness, a piss-stain glow, an anonymous hollowed-out aura—I can't describe it. Bay steps on a crack and gags on her own smell at the same time. She stumbles over the curb, squats, and dry heaves over the edge.

"You want to get arrested again, Bay?" Aint Kit spins around and spits at the emptily vomiting Bay. "I don't have any more money to get you out of jail. I got plenty more money, but I don't have none to get your black tail out of jail again."

Bay, who has vomited without throwing anything up, speaks now without saying a word. Her mouth moves. "Mama," she would've said if she had made a sound. "Mama!" I get into the backseat of Aunt Silence's car that Aint Kit borrowed. The sun ricochets across the windshield. A bird with a razor in its throat usurps the air. Then Bay begins to howl and get in the car at the same time.

"Jesusjesusjesusjesusjesusjesusjesus. My God. Mama!" she shrieks and taps her head against the dashboard all the while.

"Shut up." Aint Kit turns the key in the ignition, and the car's growl almost drowns out Bay's excruciating wailing. I stretch out my arm and touch Bay on her back. It is taut and full of tremors. I cannot sit by and listen to her crying without trying to comfort her. I can't listen to her crying without crying either, so I cry too, not daring, however, to add to the noise, lest Aint Kit turn on me.

Aint Kit puts her hands at ten and two, then she sighs with cruel exasperation, turns, and glares at Bay. "You ought to cry. Cause this ain't nothing but some old two-cent discount store mess that I had to pay good money for. You better cry. Cause I'm gone get my money back, or your ass is going back to jail."

I wonder if Bay knows this speech means Aint Kit is glad she's safe and out of jail, and she was worried about her, and would have moved heaven and earth and spent all the gold in Ghana and South Africa to get Bay from behind bars.

But how is Bay to know this backward language of love? If Aint Kit were talking to me like this I don't think I'd see it either.

I'm a backseat driver, and they know the roads of Mimosa far better than I do.

Aint Kit pulls Aunt Silence's car out onto the street. I wipe my wet eyes with the back of my hand.

"Maggie," Aint Kit barks, "reach in my pocketbook and get Bay a tissue before she mess up Lee-Bet's carseat with all her shit." I do as I am told, and Bay takes the Kleenex, quiets down, and blows her nose.

The rest of the ride is silent. When we get to Old Letha Road and turn onto its twisting limb, I wish my dead grandmother would come out into the light of day and tell me the word she told my mother, her daughter, which my mother couldn't quite catch in the commotion of grief and reunion with her mother dead and living at the foot of her bed.

I blink the moisture from my eyes, clear my throat, and look out the window. This is no splendid Eden; it is a quiet, pretty family yard and grounds with trees around a smallish house. Aint Kit slides the car into the makeshift drive, and the wheels roll over the strip of a million little rocks. She snuggles the fender next to a big tree. The car quits its slight sway. And we just sit. Till Bay swings open the car door, stomps over the rocks and weedy grass and into the open back door. Aint Kit looks after her.

"I should have dropped that basket with her in it in the river. Drowned her like a little ole stray cat.

"Left her up side a mountain like one of them Chinese girl babies. I know what I mean!" Aint Kit glares at me and everything. "Hmpph," she says harshly. "I know what I mean."

Then we get out the car and move the rest of the evil humor of the day to the house. Aunt Silence isn't home.

Bay stands over the stove shoving cold biscuits into her mouth. When Aint Kit and I come in, she runs into the shabby bathroom annex and heaves out flour and lard and saliva and whatever else she's got in her into the toilet bowl.

"Bay wants her mama!" I say to no one else like I'm talking to those stone-cold biscuits Aint Kit left on the stove after breakfast.

"Bay wants her mama." Aint Kit repeats what I said, adding an incredulous and fed up tone. "Well, I want mine."

Then Aint Kit slams out the back door. She hollers back to the house, "Bay, don't you take your incarcerated self away from this house. Magdalena, I'm going to see my mama." She doesn't ask me or Bay if we want to go with her to the country to visit my only living grandparent.

When I go in the bedroom Bay is lying across the bed with a cold, damp towel over her eyes. She can't see me, but I know she knows I'm there. She wiggles her fingers at me, and I go sit beside her. We stay that way—she stretched out with one arm dangling in the air, me sitting with my legs lax and face propped in my hand.

"Tell me about yo school, Maggie," Bay directs me, like a conductor orchestrating a happy flute in a grim symphony. So I tell her about Eden, about Leona, Essie, William, Steve, and everybody I know in FBO, about the two Homecomings and schoolwork and art. Talking softly to Bay is like describing the dainty details of a dream to an insomniac. Bay laughs at something from Eden and her laugh is still weighted with the heaviness of tears, but she laughs anyway to be close as my mouth to the antics of rich White kids and lucky Black kids without a real care in the world. Such careless lives are carefree to Bay, and she will not let me stop telling her about Eden.

Aint Kit brings home those hot tamales that Littleson and I used to love—red grease running and sliding from the spicy, hot meat mixture through the cornmeal wrap onto the thin wax paper in which each tamale is rolled like a spice baby in a receiving blanket. We used to wait at the door, Littleson and me, for Aunt Silence to bring the brown paper bag with more spots on it than a Dalmatian. Spots testifying to the messy, delicious greasiness of the treat inside. Littleson and I ran to her to beg just one bite of a heavenly treat that was hot as hell.

Bay and I do not run to meet Aint Kit, even though the smell of hot tamales insinuates its way into the bedroom and disturbs our peace. We don't move, either one of us; we just lie on that big bed in the little room and look at the ceiling. Aint Kit makes a lot of noise in the kitchen, but we won't go to her, and she won't come in to us.

We are still in separate rooms when Aunt Silence arrives with Grandmama Patsy Grace, who Aint Kit hadn't gone to see.

I remember how it was when it was Littleson and me in this house. We peeked from behind doors till someone told us to come forth into the hubbub. There was always a hubbub when some important family member came in. A sweet commotion. People fluttered and brushed against one another. Embraces boomed and echoed through the house. That is the way it is now—embraces and echoes. Bay and I come out of the room in time to see Aint Kit run to her mother's arms like a little kid. So Bay and me can't get there first. I think Aint Kit wants her story told first—to gain the audience's sympathy. She is angry with me because my sympathy for Bay has for the moment superseded my gratitude to her. After all, Aint Kit has paid my way to Mimosa. I'm here to preen and bleed for her. But the last thing you can buy is compassion. I have that for Aint Kit, but she hasn't bought it from me. She thinks she has.

Coming into the low-ceilinged living room punctuated with the sound of Aint Kit's voice, I promise myself never to accept any other gift from her. Because there's no telling what she may think she's bought. I own this heart. I know it. And I give it away.

I can hear a sonic boom when Bay lets Aunt Silence hug her. Grandmama Patsy, who is past eighty, just looks at Bay and says, "I s'pose you satisfied." Bay begins to cry afresh. And Grandmama tells her to come sit with her and rest her mind.

"Bay, when you goin to learn to hold them horses?' Grand-mama asks her, soft but strict.

"Talk to her, Mama!" Aint Kit yells fiercely from the kitchen, where she's gone to put hot tamales on a platter, like this show of concern and support for Bay was her idea all along.

"Grandmama Patsy, I don't want y'all to be ashamed of me. I don't bother nobody. I put on my best dress and was just trying to have a good time. I did my head nice. I plucked my eyebrows and did my makeup real nice. And they just come bothering me."

"Your mama said you didn't start it," Grandmama tells Bay.

"You did?" Bay looks up at Aint Kit who's setting down the tamales on the side table. Bay is so grateful.

Aint Kit looks awkward then, so afraid, like somebody is about to identify her in a police lineup.

"Yo mama Gussie said it, Bay," Aunt Silence says gently, easing the awkward disappointment in Aint Kit's love and reminding Bay by the sweet tone of her voice that she was always loved. "You sure are lucky. Your mama Kit come flying down here to bail you out of jail and your mama Gussie got them people to drop the charges against you. They some of her distant relatives and she did some crying and talking for you."

Aint Kit loves to find excuses to have me come over her house to observe what she owns. One time she asked me to untangle her expensive jewelry. It was all a jumble in her music-box jewelry case that played "Them There Eyes" when you first opened it. Aint Kit told me to untangle the strands of pearls from the gold strings, disconnect the rhinestone broach from the diamond ring, unhook the silver necklace from the sapphire earring, the ruby ring from the center of the knot in the necklaces, and find her three wedding bands she'd thrown in there the night before.

For one so attentive to money and things, her jewelry box was a shambles. I had to make things right without breaking anything; make my gestures as delicate as a neurosurgeon's inside somebody's open head, and make no noise besides, because Aint Kit swore she had a headache. "Them There Eyes" frolicked on brightly, but the needle-sharp notes of the jewelry box didn't disturb her. She couldn't stand to hear her jewelry in that dreadful tangle. The lovely dazzle pieces threatening to break.

This room right now with Aint Kit standing erect and demolished with her back to us, Aunt Silence leaning and looking reassuringly at a happily perplexed Bay, and Grandmama Patsy closing her eyes to it all is like a music box, jumbled up with strands, beginningless and endless, cameos and lockets and rings of feeling. I cannot untangle this. I am barely seventeen. I put my hands in my skirt pockets, where they twitch nervously.

Aint Kit is ignoring me. And Bay had made herself scarce as "a decent man," so Aint Kit said when she couldn't find her.

She was stirring a simmering pot of grits and beginning a lie about the time she waited outside the bathroom door for her second husband to step out the tub and come out that door naked except for the towel she brought home from the hospital wrapped around his hips and self.

Now Aint Kit's telling her mother, Grandmama Patsy, how she squatted like an African Indian with the grits pot steaming into her face making her skin sweat-shiny and pores wide open like she was giving herself a facial instead of preparing to do bodily harm to her second husband. She was going to dash that pot of grits on his bare back as soon as he came through the door.

She'd come home from work and it was the same old thing. He just didn't know how to take care of nice things. He left his mark on her lovable things. Deep rings on the tub, beer stains on the coffee table, shoe polish on the towels with Great Lakes City Hospital etched in the corners, and splashes of urine on the toilet bowl because the man just couldn't aim. Lipstick on his boxer shorts propelled her to the stove and her cooking pot and the white and red box of slow-cooking hominy grits.

"Kit, you ain't tell me you scalded any of them mens," Grand-mama blows across the top of black, scalding coffee. She likes her coffee strong and honest with no cream or sugar. She despises any lie, thus this coolness blowing off her when she listens to Kit sometimes.

It's the coolness of her mother's interruption that causes Aint Kit to fumble and flounder in her tale telling. "I didn't actually pour them grits on him, you know. He stayed in the bathroom so long I got tired of squatting and waiting so I just slid the pot in the doorway and left it there. I went on to bed. And it musta been an hour later, I heard him hollering. He put his big foot in that pot. Chile, he had a hot foot. He was hopping around on that one black foot holding that white grits foot in the air. Then he ran up in the bathroom, standing on the good foot, stuck the grits foot in the commode. Later on, he come up in the bedroom and asked me how the pot got left there. I tole him I was fixin him some breakfast. Some grits to go with that fish he come in here smelling like."

Kit is lying and no one is looking at her.

Aunt Silence is like her name. And Grandmama Patsy turns her mouth down and blows into her coffee cup. I watch a bird just outside the dining room window. Aint Kit is so embarrassingly pitiful, all lonely in her lie, sitting at the table with nobody looking at her, I cannot keep myself from asking, "His foot was okay, wasn't it?"

Relieved, she recognizes me as her ally again, rescuer of her face. "The grits weren't so hot by the time he walked in 'em. The pot was sitting there a long time."

"Ummmmhp," Grandmama Patsy says.

Aunt Silence asks me to come with her to the voter registration center. Because I've been kind to her, Aint Kit tells me to go on. I have purchased a brief freedom by my allegiance to her; she thinks that. Aint Kit and Grandmama Patsy have to locate Bay. "I still got bail money on that girl"—Aint Kit says that's the only reason she wants to find the woman she's called her daughter for more than twenty years.

"Imagine that—a grandmama who's a well-known ghost!"

Aunt Silence chuckles when I exclaim this. "What'll I tell my friends at school?" I am thinking of their faces: Leona's and Essie's, awed and a trifle envious. I am thinking of others who don't respect people or things too much out of the ordinary, who'll look at me warily. I am thinking of the professors who'd hoot at the superstition of Blackpeople. Negroes to them.

"Don't spread it around," Aunt Silence cautions me. "Everybody don't need to know."

A caution from Aunt Silence, who is always praise and affirmation, is a rebuke to me, and I lapse into a silence that mimics her legendary one. Mimosa whizzes by in a blur of earth and buildings. Everything looks like dust and sun and greenery. A nip is in the air.

208

"I guess telling you not to draw attention to yourself won't do no good. Like telling a flood to stop at that doorstep." Her voice is rumination. "I was different too. Kit told you her version of my story. Your mama probably did too. I lost my head. I'm sorry, sugar. I lost my mind over a man. Mostly because I was carrying around in my head a tower of babble, everybody scrutinizing my business, and talking to me. All them voices clamoring so loud I couldn't hear my own." She looks out the window while humming a little like her brother who is my father. She doesn't say ah-ya-ya. More like uh-ho. Then she says, "Two advices to you. Don't care about small talk and keep some secrets until you want to let people in. Trust your own judgment. Trust your conscience. It's there."

"That's kinda sneaky," I protest.

"That's wise, darlin'," Aunt Silence says. She stops the car in front of a busy, old building with a welcome mat of grass around it and a swinging sign that says MT. TABOR CHURCH.

"You got important things to do, Magdalena. I saw that in you when you were justa little-bitty girl. Shoots, I saw that even crazy as I was when I came home from the hospital and you were just born. You were born distinct, pretty, and old."

We giggle over being different. Aunt Silence stops first. Her tone is determined when she says, "Different ain't so bad, when you're doing the right thing. Shoots, lots of time doing the right thing is downright odd." She brushes my hair softly. "Listen to me, sugar, I sell insurance. It's all a risk." She gives my hair a final stroke. "I like your natural."

We cross the mat of grass and walk into Mt. Tabor Church. It's not a big place. The voter registration project is in the foyer. There's a blown-up snapshot of Fannie Lou Hamer and some other women and men on one wall, Reverend Doctor Martin Luther King Jr. on another wall, and John F. Kennedy on another.

There's a stairway to the choir loft, where yet another hero photo might be. Two doors as one open to the church proper. Those doors are wide open and wide sunlight pours through the windows and dances on the pulpit.

People looked up and smiled when Aunt Silence came in with me. Now she introduces me. And tells me the names of people and what they do. Aunt Silence shows me a map of the county into which they go fearlessly in search of Blackpeople too long ignored, or too threatened, or too obstructed and denied by old law and brute power to speak up through a voting machine. Their aim is to make the new law mean more than ink and ceremonial ink pens for President Lyndon B. Johnson.

Aunt Silence and I sit in the back of the church. She tells me the dream. I watch the sunlight and grow sad as something inside me pulls away from her a little. I am a student at Eden and we are going in a new way. I know that. And I feel like an ingrate too. Not nearly grateful enough for what was given me from the work-bruised hands of others. I look down at my hands, folded in my lap, loosely, waiting for their task.

She talks about poor Blackpeople using the vote to gain political power over their lives. She herself has gained some power over her life just by working for the vote for others, working for power in the hands of the people over their own lives.

"I'm a new woman, Maggie," she says. "We can be a new people."

She dreams on aloud. She has memorized the Bill of Rights like a newly naturalized citizen. But she is different from those who come in ships and planes and believe all the promises are true. Aunt Silence believes they can be made true. I tell her about the new Americans. She says their love is a bride's love; hers is a widow's. The widows of old washed the consumptive body, preparing it to be born again. She believes this.

She tells me of the disgraceful infant mortality rate among our people, the illiteracy, the shameless disregard of public institutions and public services heaped on us who are poor and Black who built this state and this nation. She tells me about the land stolen. And even as she recounts the crimes, she forgives the past and refuses its burden of impossibility and says we can make things happen right.

But I do not forgive.

At Eden we are in the mood for holding grudges. I am not sure I want to make things right in Aunt Silence's way. I cannot look at the beauty of this woman who is my father's sister and my mother's dearest friend. People who believe with such selfless purity are radiant to me. I cannot stand the light blazing off her, coming through the milk-smooth chocolate of her skin, threading easily through her silver hair.

I don't know what to say.

Soon Aunt Silence stops talking. She cocks her head at me quizzically and pats my hand. We are the same color, and her hand on mine is nice. "We all have our part in the service," she says.

Then we just sit there in the back of the church, looking straight ahead intently, like somebody's sermonizing or somebody's singing in the front. Some angel's bathing in that pool of sunlight. After a while, Aunt Silence says we should do nothing but be happy Grace women today. That's what she tells her coworkers we are about to do as we leave Mt. Tabor behind us.

We ride aimlessly but ritualistically up and down the country roads between Mimosa and Letha. Aunt Silence slows beside the gates of the graveyard where my two grandfathers rest angrily, I know, because they died so young. Malachi Grace, everybody called Gracie, felled by a stroke at forty-nine. Abraham Dancer whose heart caved in at thirty-five. The gates are closed and we cannot enter. We keep on going past the manicured expanse of the White cemetery further along the same road. Two traditional burial places: Mt. Zion Resting Place of Colored and the Right-Hand-Side Cemetery for Whites. "Even in death," Aunt Silence says just like she said when she watched James Chaney being buried without Michael Schwerner and Andrew Goodman, with whom he had been murdered.

It is like riding through history, wandering so down and up these roads. I enjoy especially the twists and bends on Old Letha Road. Way out in the country, when I'm just looking out the window and don't say anything for a while, Aunt Silence says, "Looking for somebody?"

I just smile shyly and do not deny it.

Hesitantly, she offers, "Do you want to see——" at the same time I ask her, "Show me the spot where it happened." Then, obediently, and silently, she drives me to that narrow strip of road where my grandmama and eleven other girls and women died, and one Whiteboy died, and the culprit went crazy behind the show of blood and mayhem.

Trees come up close to the road in that spot, which is unusual it seems to me. But Aunt Silence doesn't mention anything about anything out of the ordinary. It's all mysterious. Young trees, slender and flexible as the girls of Eden, pose like happy girls waiting to be painted.

This is a lovely spot. Hard to know so much blood has been swallowed up by this sweet earth. "My mother's mother's blood ran here," I remind myself in my head. Then I wait for an answer. Then I look around me. I promise this stretch of road, these trees, that sun, the rather stark cotton field fenced in the distance, "I will paint you."

The only sound is the sound of Aunt Silence and me breathing. We are quiet, Aunt Silence and I, and do not want to move a muscle. We are quieter than we were in church. I cannot count the minutes we linger here.

When the sun moves down a little and the cool of evening is foreshadowed, Aunt Silence says, "Let's leave." And we do.

And just what would I have done if I'd met a ghost? Shaken her hand?

Bay's tears have all dried up by the time we get home. Aint Kit, having run out of abusive words, is just beginning her tears. Bay has been to see her mother, Gussie, to thank her for getting her cousin to drop the charges. Then Bay stayed and visited with her Gussie way across town without telling Aint Kit. Aint Kit got a freelance cab to take her and Grandmama Patsy back to the country. She wanted to arrive in style. Then Kit searched high and low for Bay, who'd just appeared an hour ago. Aint Kit has been slinging words for an hour. Now Bay is sitting with a little smile on her face, too tired I guess to pretend she wasn't still happy about her real mama saving her.

Kit spread her fury around, sparing only me, for now.

She moves in on Aunt Silence and her Black work. "Doing all that Black work, getting these niggers and peckerwoods so stirred up yo own mama Patsy Grace can't stay in her own house. It's too damned dangerous for your own mama to stay in her own house. Now you dragging Magdalena in on this stuff too. Next thing I know I'll be taking Magdalena home in a box with her brains blown out."

I just love this part. Me with scrambled brains.

"And what would Sam and Ca'line say about you then? It's bad enough, this girl's"—pointing to me—"grandmother is a ghost before her time. Do she," pointing to me, "have to be one too?"

The telephone rings. Aunt Silence, who hasn't batted an eye through Kit's monologue, answers the phone and doesn't answer Kit's question. She calls me to the phone.

Essie's on the line. She has news.

I'd been asked to be on the decorating committee for Black Homecoming, so I did wonderful roses of red, black, and green for someone tall to hang. Long-faced Leona and Essie said, "Lucky you," when I grabbed my medium-sized suitcase and overnight case from the set Mama and Madaddy gave me for high school graduation and headed for the front door of Wyndam-Allyn. They were sorry to see me go. Stray streamers came unglued from their designs on the doors, slithered on the floor like serpents, and reached out for me. Now Essie is reaching out for me. She has tracked me down all the way to Mimosa, Mississippi. She called the Grace house and got the number from my mother.

"This is going to cost you," I tell her. But Essie doesn't care and I don't either, because now I don't have to keep listening to Aint Kit's infected mouth. Ever conscious of company, even over a long-distance telephone line, she's quieted down and whispers her terrible scenarios to Aunt Silence, who's sitting on the couch staring at her, shaking her head.

Essie babbles on about love and Eden and what I'm not missing. Her voice sounds fresh, like a brook, and it does too babble. About Homecoming. Black Homecoming. William taking her to Black Homecoming in spite of the trouble he is in. The screwiness of love. Sex. A Blackgirl crowned Homecoming Queen of Eden University campuswide. Imagine that. Just when we make our own party, they let one of us in on theirs. More about William and William and William.

Finally, Essie says she'll be glad when I come back. I answer, "I'll be glad to see you too." I'm not sure about Eden.

Nothing much is happening when I get off the phone. It's raining outside. Inside the air is thick as wool. It itches like wool too.

I sit down in the midst of conflict and talk about Eden's first Black Homecoming Queen. I sound to myself like Susie Coed. But Silence, Kit, and Bay look so pleased when I talk this college talk, I cannot cheat them.

A Blackgirl crowned queen by Whitepeople. This is progress. This is vindication. This is a drop of honey in the bitterest brew. Who am I to complain about the indignities of Eden to women who lived by signs that said COLORED and WHITE, who as grown women were called "gal" and forced to call young Whiteboys "mister"? They whispered stories of whole families that moved north in the deep of night to avoid the common law of Whitemen. These women who had until recently no vote, no voice, no visible strength in the wider world love me. They love too this Blackgirl crowned queen, tipping in high-heeled slippers across a serene campus. Once my grandmothers walked barefoot or in run-over shoes to a one-room schoolhouse. Once we all walked in run-over shoes to school.

When the room is permeated with this sweetness, I am lulled. I leave them smiling and climb into Grandmama Patsy's high bed. It is raining harder and the air inside has opened a little—like a seam. It is so dark in this low-ceilinged room—I stretch out my hand and wish the ghost of my mother's mother would come to me now and make sense of everything between Mimosa and Eden and beyond for me now.

But the ghost of Mahalia Dancer does not glide through the rain that crushes the dust to mud along Old Letha Road, does not come up the back steps and come in through the back door or the front. Does not pat Bay on the cheek approvingly and sing the lies out of Aint Kit's mouth, does not sit down with Aunt Silence and chat awhile.

The spirit of Mahalia Dancer does not come to the Grace house on Chinaman's Store this night, no matter how heartfeltly I yearn for her. The dark gives up nothing to me. So I close my eyes and go to sleep. Tonight I want to dream of my grandmother and the rescue of life surviving life and death. Perhaps she will appear in a dream in Eden again and ease the disquiet I feel when Eden crosses my mind. I almost wake, but I don't.

It is the mortal hands of Aunt Silence that crowd the hand-sewn quilt around me in the middle of the rain-filled night.

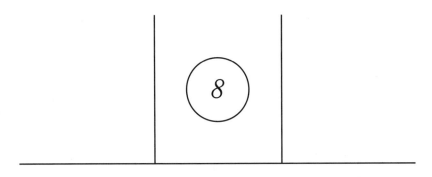

Essie

Essie Witherspoon was a shy and fragile girl when I first met her. We had grown up in neighborhoods not far from each other. We knew the same bakeries by their smells that rode through our streets on the wings of the Hawk, the one movie house on the boulevard where Sunday shows were twenty-five cents and the projectionist ran ads for the latest Brigitte Bardot movie during the kiddie shows, the same Laundromats, grocery stores, churches, rib joints, and taverns. The same vacant lots. We came upon the centralizing church steeple from different sides, distances, and angles.

Essie knew Jeannie, my childhood friend who had one child at fifteen and another at seventeen. When Essie and I found each other it was as if we had found a new corner of home.

Essie is a tiny-boned girl with the biggest Afro I have ever seen. It stands richly around her head like the cap of a tropical tree. Each night she braids it from the center of her head and sends the twisted plaits down around her face like tamed snakes

217

caught in a dance to a charmer's flute. But Essie is the charmed one. The one who is enchanted.

The night after Black Homecoming Essie was watching William and William was watching her while he danced with Rhonda who he's suddenly back with. Rhonda was watching Essie too. She printed her body on William's and held him. Her breasts stabbing him in the ribs. Abruptly, Essie moved to another angle of the room and got too close to the four-foot-high speakers, so that the noise was making her nearly insensible. She watched the two of them, but she didn't see. She only saw herself, miserable and rejected, an ache inside her female organs, a girl's sorrow. And she saw at that moment in which William slow dragged Rhonda across the floor, the turning points of her life. The points so sharp they pinned Essie in them forever.

"Honey, I like ta died!" Essie was saying into the phone to NeeNee, her best and only friend, when Fredonia's slap unpropped her hand from her imaginary hip and uncrossed her little legs.

"That's for actin grown," Fredonia said. "You ain't no woman." Fredonia scalded herself out of Essie with her eyes; she scolded her own cameo set in the girl's face. Then Fredonia turned back to her steaming stove-top works and to her company. Blinking her Liz-Taylor-as-Cleopatra mascaraed eyes (thick, wide black bands outlined the eyes and wound around the side of the head) and sighing, ruffling the coppery waves atop her head with her free and still-stinging hand, she made motions in a pot of chili beans, more concerned with conversation and company than food or child.

Essie's eyes were burning and she rolled them at Fredonia's spine and rounded rump. Fredonia was mouthing some delightful outrage.

"So I told that *Black* nigger, I told him, 'Honey, I am not a player—I do not play.'"

"That's right, girl," her company said.

"I'm a woman."

"That's right."

"I'm a woman." Hand on hip, face thrust forward, outlined eyes wide for emphasis.

"You a woman. Ya gotta tell these niggers. That's right." Lorraine sipped Schlitz at the kitchen table.

Fredonia banged the stove with her soup spoon. A flurry of flecks of hot-pot liquor popped onto her arm. She cursed and reached for her towel, which she kept in a corner like a prize-fighter. She caught Essie's eyes on her.

"Don't you look at me that way."

"What way?"

"The way you lookin at me now."

"I ain't even lookin at you."

"Don't cut your eyes at me, you little whore."

"Fredonia!" Lorraine incredulous. "Cool down, girl. Don't call the child no whore. Next thing you know she'll be in the bushes."

"She probably already been there . . ."

"You was . . ." from under Essie's breath.

"I was what? Little bitch. I shoulda left yo skinny ass with yo grandmama."

"I wish you hadda . . ." Essie mumbled.

"What?"

"I ain't say nothing."

"You a lying little heifer too."

"Girl, cool down. This heat got you goin," Lorraine interceded again. Fredonia was successfully diverted.

"Girl, this ignorant city ain't shit. You ever felt fall weather like this? Just as hot and sticky." Fredonia was gay with a topic for crisp new talk. She wanted to laugh. She needed to laugh. She wanted to shake her butt. She was still young. Her daughter, Essie, was only ten. And Fredonia was tired of Woody, her present husband.

Fredonia and her men did not get along long. Suddenly, she did not fall back against her pillow satisfied; suddenly, she saw him as stingy. One day she realized that he smacked when he ate, "sound like a greasy hog."

He was possessive at parties. Talkless after loving. Knocking her against the walls when whiskey rode his mind. Knocking her down and knocking her up.

She had been married three times. No divorces. Just civilized Mississippi separations and remarriages. She couldn't live with fault. When she packed Essie from Big Mama's and told Big Mama about Woodrow Witherspoon and her secure family feeling, how she wanted to make a home for him and her children, how they had applied for living in the high-rises and they were on the waiting list, how she had at last found a quiet man without fault, Big Mama had simply said, "I hope your glass house is shock proof, Fredonia."

As it happened, Woodrow Witherspoon had feet of clay. In a manner of speaking. He never washed his feet. Fredonia, in time, found his silence sullen and his dependability boring. Again, she was dissatisfied. Again, her laughter turned to tin. And her eyes restlessly ferreted out an object upon which to heap her ridicule, because her own life terrified her.

"Lorraine, Lorraine, it's gone rain enough for Noah." She flicked the flimsy curtain at the lonely living room window. She was in the high-rises now, but they were not the penthouses she'd imagined. She called the Homes the "pen house" apartments. "Oh, it's gone rain on the unrighteous can't treat a woman right. Drive all them rats inside!"

Lorraine laughed, "I'ma make like I don't know you talkin about Woody."

"Who a Woody? Or rather, *what* a Woody? I don't know no goddamn Woody." Her voice had grown slightly ragged. "Woody. Sound like a dummy name to me. And he say 'bout much as Charlie McCarthy. Damn dummy." She punched holes in a beer can. Sucked. Pulled her blouse at the throat for air-conditioning. Her voice was slurred as she got ready for bedroom confidences. Lorraine slid forward in the rickety kitchen chair that squealed under her thick body's weight.

"You know what he did last night?" Fredonia asked Lorraine.

"Naw, girl."

"Come crawlin upside me greasy as bacon and smellin like between Miss Lacey's legs—what you doin here? Didn't I tell you to go somewhere?"

Essie wilted under her mother's fresh attack. There wasn't far enough to go inside the small apartment.

"What you lookin up in my mouth for? Don't *look* in *my* mouth. Countin cavities. You ain't no dental assistant."

"I ain't say I was."

"You get outta here. Always got something smart to say to me, when I'm yo mama and you ain't mine. And I got ass kickin on my mind. Got a husband don't know he a husband and a child don't know she a child."

"Freddie, leave the child alone," Lorraine petitioned, pity stricken for the stricken Essie. "I needs me some cigarettes."

"I got some Lucky Strike right here. You send her for somethin' send her after some day-old bread. She get it today, it be a day old when you get it, girl. Bitch slow as constipation." Fredonia tickled her own self then. "And look like it too. Face just as tight and evil. Turd-faced child talk like Woody. And he ain't her daddy. Don't say nothing; just grunt for somebody to fix his plate or bring him the paper, which he can't read anyway. Or else he askin me some simple-ass question like where I been." She shoved a quarter into Essie's hand, then crushed the hand into a fist. She pushed a vague admonition against Essie's temple with one of her own fists.

"Watch where you're going," she said.

Essie staggered out the door, propelled by the force of her mother's love.

The park trees, premeditated as murder in the first degree. Across the street, the buildings gray with red windows, yellow with gray windows, white with red, brownstone aged to grayness, crayoned clumsily as a first grader's art assignment, "My House," against the sky.

The wind was witch's breath, driving away the heavy, unnatural autumn heat. Like devil's teeth the chips of rain stung her young skin.

Essie.

She tracked through the thin strip of boulevard between the two bread factories where the smell of baking loaves hung from the trees like leavened leaves. Her sneakers crushed a trail of grass and leaves. Rain thrashing aslant along her back. Essie was running to beat the rain and her mama's wrath.

"Where do the moon go when it rain?" Questions permeated her mind like new smells. Her wide nostrils were flared in curiosity. Tantalized. Knowledge was a rich gumbo. She craved as children crave: earnestly and openly. She would question Fredonia, her questions like the sound of brash young metals, high and fast, incessantly beating against wooden love and tinsel nerve. "Do the moon be there when it rain and we don't see? Like

I be there and my mama don't see me." Fredonia would wonder in annoyance where all Essie's curiosities came from; what curio junk shop her mind traded in. This child's peculiar ways mocked her in half-hidden mirrors of gawky-gawking years. Fredonia would wonder where Essie came from, but she knew.

For some reason the moon roomed noisily in Essie's head tonight, like a clock frozen on a lonely orbit of missing hands. She was still sullen and aching from Fredonia's slap and more from Fredonia's corded tongue, but mostly she ached for the absence of tenderness.

She knew there was no hope. She would be skin soaked and hair nappy by the time she made it home. But keep the bread dry no matter what. Yet even if she kept the bread dry, Fredonia would curse her kinky hair. (Who can love a knotted head? At best, one wants to straighten it.) It would be all her fault. It would all be her fault.

She daydreamed. A dream less complicated than hair; a tender-headed dream. She may as well slow walk through dream. She thought, *She blame me all the time anyway.*

Lightning made an acid streak across the sky and thunder ruled the world. All the while Essie was looking near blind through rain, searching for the moon.

Children in two-floored houses were huddled in hallways as she passed. Sooner or later some one of them would risk the rain, run out into it, defy it in the ritual dance. They would make a chanting ring as the others joined the bravest one. "Rain, rain, go away. Come again some other day." Trying to make an appointment with misery because they knew it must come. And thinking a postponement was the best that they could do.

Essie was humming softly to herself, "Rain, rain go away." Her feet squeaking in sopping wet sneakers kept up a neat rhythm section. "Rain, rain . . ."

Woody would hoist LaVette high upon his big shoulders. He opened his clamped silence to coo to her, to woo her, and wonder at her honey roundness and minute hands. He watched her like Time, the clock of his best days.

LaVette basked in an aura of royalty. Her name was "French"; Woody rolled it upon his tongue as lovingly as he rolled his whiskey. LaVette was his second, Northern comfort. His first was Southern. He wasn't unkind to Essie; he provided for her and even spoke to her every now and then. He simply did not love her. She did not belong to him.

Silk. His rap was smooth as silk. Silk. Silk. Silk. When he was fine and a figure of shine and flamboyance. When he was fine . . .

The neighborhood made myths about how he got his limp; his twisted walk, some woman said, was caused by a twisted, shriveling syphilitic spine. His kiss was unclean, they said, his saliva crystallized and rotted the flesh of young girls. This was the legend, the reigning rumor, that Lorraine and Fredonia and the other bid-whist players exchanged through cigarette-cramped mouths. The boys on the balconies of the Homes, the boys on the corner, said that he had been shot. The sawed-off nose of a hand rifle had opened, blasted through nerve, cartilage. His leg was dead.

One leg hung like a leather strap; he whipped it forward twisting from the middle in order to walk. Doctors at County, who threw their hands up at bringing him back to his full capacity, dispensed prescriptions to dope the resident, residual pain. The medicine brought brief relief. The medicine made his brain powerful and his pelvis deliciously silent. So silent that he listened for the minor stirrings of it and responded with his imagination, because that was all he had to hold in his hands. His dreams were hard dreams of power.

No way to call this home. Trembling with wetness Essie anticipated her home block. The gray upright matchboxes were set in more barren concrete. Shivering and disoriented by the rain for a moment she couldn't choose the building where Fredonia and Woody's mailbox was set in a row of broken locks and stolen news. Cement seemed the same; her world a room of mirrors repeating the same stone mistake, row upon row. Choosing at last she found her familiar way, back, back to the lukewarm supper of chili, saltines, and Kool-Aid. It was chilly now. The weather had changed without warning.

In fading curiosity Essie looked over her left shoulder. The moon was nowhere. Entering the stone-cold hallway a dank urine odor opened her nostrils. She knew that she was back, but she could not call this all the way home. Home was Big Mama, arms that wrapped around her.

Shivering, she climbed the stairs.

Silk was on the sixth-floor balcony cooling his sweaty body. He liked the new cool that swept over him. There was always this burning on him. Sometimes he thought he would look down and see his body smoking. But he was cold by the time his eyes caught sight of the rest of himself. He was looking over the railing at the muddy rain river forming around the building. The contractors had never gotten the land level around the Homes. Rain or snow was always collecting in the uneven places. In wintertime great big patches of ice froze so that women tiptoed across the ice to make it home safely.

He watched Essie rush, rain sleek and cloth slapping her breast bulbs and buttocks. He watched her huddling forth with her filled jacket cradling dry bread in her arms. Her face escaped him; her expression was a blur to him. But the set of her, wet and dejected, he grasped. The vulnerability, the unawareness, called to him.

Silk twisted away from the rail, went into the dark and fuming stairwell. He knew that Essie Witherspoon lived on five. He knew she was straggling up the stinking isolation of the concrete steps and walls. The rain and dark and want of food had driven the inmates to their cells. Essie was the last.

Silk had been studying her. The way the little nubs punched out through summer T-shirts. The way she handled LaVette like a grown woman, feeding her summer sherbet Push-Ups and wiping her mouth with her own saliva. Her saliva. Essie covered her sister with the comfort of her own pliable body on the cement playground where the jungle gym grew like a wide, steel tree.

Three flights up she was feeling her body, conscious of discomfit. Her panties sopping and dripping. Her gym shoes making ugly sound tracks up the stairs. Cloth itchy and tight on her chest and arms and legs. She could not see; the closed landing door shut out the little light.

Outside the fourth-floor landing he was breathing and dreaming his hard dreams that were perfectly blank. And when he heard her on the stairwell, running now on the landing, he threw open the door. Comically, it slapped her face. She stumbled. He opened his arms for her and she stepped into a hard, twisted road of flesh. With one of his arms Silk hugged her arms to her frame. He locked her mouth and yanked her down. Her gym shoes made a wet rail where he dragged her. He propped their two bodies against the huge steel door. No one could enter again. No one could get out.

At this time Essie's mind was as empty as his, except for a wild tangle of fear. A bramble of terror. Clawing for freedom against the smelly dank, the sour taste of hand across her mouth and her nose, clawing for breath. He was listening to his body as eminent domain. Massive strength.

Some leaves of bread were loose from the loaf and spilling across the landing. And there was a breaking between Essie's legs.

✦

Mrs. Levergate, who lived on four, had come to Fredonia's door. Her face was wet. Her printed housecoat spotted but not spoiled, for the bloodstains fit into the pattern. Cletus was a lean young man standing always in the shadow of his mother's love. Nineteen.

Mrs. Levergate was talking slow and quiet to Fredonia. Fredonia in front of a curious Lorraine. Fredonia looking through the door, over Mrs. Levergate's shoulder. Cletus in the shadows. Essie a dirty crumpled bundle of damp in Cletus's arms. Essie was clumsy in Cletus's arms. He was embarrassed; his mother's blanket did not cover well; Essie was naked from the waist down. Her eyes were wide open as if invisible fingers jacked the eyelids up. She looked into Fredonia's dazed face. Matter-of-factly she said, "Somebody. Somebody mash the bread, Mama." She thought that was why Fredonia, weeping way in her throat, tore her from Cletus's good arms and rough rocked her in curses.

Before a barnyard of high steel and stone the women were chickens whose eggs had been stolen, whose eggs cracked, clotted from cold in spite of their steady warmth. Battered old hens, they had seen the young yolks and whites of the children's broken eyes discarded and still throbbing yolky and milky mingling with wine and urine and blood and menstrual discharge from some discarded woman's discarded napkin wiping anybody else's cracked concrete.

And their faces too cracked with wise laughter and worry and knowing talk. Their clucking cluttering the air, climbing the project floor by floor it grew so furious.

Two policemen cut them with the arcs of their nightsticks. The blue men made a path for themselves. And the women made a wake for the path with their words. "They betta be careful a them po-lease. I tell you the time my cousin Ola Mae daughter wenta one a them activity after school and her and her little girl friends they was 'bout 'leven years old? Well they was comin home about seven o'clock at night and it was just barely dark comin from school and these two Negro po-leasemens crawl up 'long side them walkin down the sidewalk, ask them they mama knowed where they was at. And quite natchelly Ola Mae daughter and her friends they scared and they shame say Naw. They was getting ready for they whippin as soon as they hit the doe. And these two Negro po-leasemens say, 'Git in the squad car.' And quite natchelly them three little girls gone and do what they tell 'em to. Girl well do you know them two lowdown dirty dogs took them chil'ren up in one of them deserted parking lots down on Berry Street and raped them in the bushes? Now that don't make no kind of sense girl and then drop them on a corner near 'bouts they school and tell 'em they better not be stayin out at no nighttime and they better not see 'em no more or somethin' might happen to 'em."

"Honey, you can't trust none a these dogs."

"Somebody oughta go with them ain't no tellin if they get to the hospital. One of these mens needta go. Where that little girl daddy at?" The speaker thrust her gaze toward her own husband accusingly. He was standing in the shadows around the assaulted mailboxes. The corners of his wide mouth folded down. Shaking his head from side to side meditatively and spitting out the sour taste of his thoughts along with the chips of his chewed-up tooth-pick that poked out of the corner of his bent mouth.

The moon was pouring a moving light that rinsed their raggedy faces. A torn strip of cloud tore the center of the moon's face making puzzles of the light. A woman kept on talking, so loud she must have been chastising the moon that saw it all and said nothing.

"Uhmmmp, uhmp, uhmp. I wish I could git in a snake's head. All this free stuff trottin around here begging and these whores steady traffickin and they wanna do something like that to a child. I wish I could get in a snake's head. I'd do me some brain surgery. They oughta put his ass under the jail then open up the sewers and flood him out and let him float on away with the rats. I mean it. I sure do mean it. It wouldn't be none too good for him. I wish I knowed what make folks do stuff like that. Messin up that child like that."

Fredonia was carrying Essie in her arms through a crowd of musk and whispering. Essie was floating under a raging moon. A circle of them. Some women were saying, "That little girl." The police were taking her. There was something she had done. She was dizzy with the sound of sirens that raked their way down the flooded street and up the wet boulevard. There was a blue stain across her eyes. She folded her painted face into Fredonia's breast while Fredonia was talking, unfolding cloth from her purse.

Saying, "Essie, step in these panties, baby. Move yo legs. They would be torn. This would be the torn pair." A new shame flooded Fredonia: her child had been raped and her underwear was raggedy.

The police car smelled of leather and grit. The odor slipped into their bodies from the seats, from the men in their blues. And they were marked. They were in the back of a police car, so they stank. They were riding in a police car and no one could be innocent.

"What I do?" Essie whispered. "What I do, Mama?"

Fredonia started to cry. Shushing Essie. They were riding all the way to County. Essie adrift in an aura of humid leather and law, but for Fredonia's arms and aromas she would have drowned.

This jagged night everything was a puzzle jamming together. Fredonia's arms were holding her. Binding them together. LaVette she'd left with Mrs. Levergate. And if Essie was going to jail, Fredonia was going too. Fredonia was loving her. Loving her. Fredonia's fingers with their bright red nails shut Essie's trembling lips. Her hands smelled sweet and spicy with chili seasoning that would be so hot it would burn Woody's insides. Essie was cupped and she closed herself in the aromas of seasoned hands and colognes and Jergens lotion and husky beer breath. All of these smells circled her now.

She kept heaving the torn feeling out of her head. Bramble branches of pain pushed through her. Fredonia would be angry soon—blood had soiled Essie's panties even as she'd put them on her. The Whitepeople at the hospital and the jail would see and say that she was dirty. Essie shook with sighs; her teeth rattled. She looked out the glass of the police car. They were at the hospital entrance alongside an ambulance unloading a stretcher. In the red glare of the white ambulance she saw the moon. It was watching her, the face unwinking. Solemn. Clear and clean after the rain and cloud. Startling. Secretive.

All she'd ever wanted was to be loved; to be held and cradled. Her hair felt like a brick on her head. She felt an overwhelming compassion for herself. She wanted to hug herself right on the hem of the dance floor where William danced with Rhonda. Her need was so visible to herself, she thought that everybody could see it. All the brothers who reached over her to dance with somebody else. Especially she thought William was acquainted with the bruised child who looked around the corner in her eyes. Hadn't he danced with her the night before?

The thought of his knowing made Essie grit her teeth and walk through the middle of the dance floor. Her head held high and tilted back so far she seemed to look down her nose at the music, the dancers, the entire set. So her need seemed displayed arrogance. Once I overheard some dark dudes put the word out that Essie Witherspoon "is a hincty broad. Looking down her Miss-Sidity nose at everybody and her stuck-up ass come from the projects. She a refugee from the Homes."

I wished that they could walk in her skin. I wished they knew her like I think I do.

She tells me all about everything when I come home from Mimosa. How after we talked William had gone back to Rhonda. She tells me what Rhonda and Lydia Rushing, the White Home-coming Queen, said. Rhonda and her bosom buddies think I am useless and Essie less than that. Rhonda knew William has a yen for Essie so Rhonda is extra sweet to Essie in a very condescend-ing way. "I am woman; you are child," is the way she plays it in front of William and everybody else.

"Essie and Maggie didn't know how to deal with the univer-sity police." That is what Rhonda told Lydia Rushing, Essie says. "Things got out of hand." So it was our fault that William was arrested after he hit that Whiteboy?

"Too far, too fast, too soon," Lydia agreed, Essie says. "Maggie, can you believe they blamed me?" I can. Not to mention blaming me. So it was our fault that William got arrested for hitting that Whiteboy? Rhonda and Lydia are superior beings: upperclassmen. Been around the world and back again. They have regular sex with their boyfriends. How adult can you get? It seems Rhonda told William she is late. They can't break up after all. And William is in so much trouble he needs her and her support and her daddy's connections. Essie can't stop talking, and when she makes herself quit she grinds her teeth so hard her jaws pop.

I almost tell Essie about my grandmother the ghost. But now isn't the right time. The things of Eden, especially William, are more real to her than anything in this whole wide world.

Essie has gone home this weekend and Leona and I do nothing after a set in one of the halls. We've come back disgusted and worn out. I count the limbs of a tree by the window. There are seven-times-seven limbs on that tree that stands naked in the paralyzing winter. The snow is no longer new and it's a nuisance, though Leona and I found a long stretch of unbroken snow to plant our footprints in on the way back to the dorm from the dance. I am uneasy with my life and that is all I can call this feeling. Uneasy. Nothing too elaborate, beyond a deep desire to know Sarah Mahalia is with me. My grandmother and all the others. And why would they want to be here in Eden going to silly parties with us and watching Oakland get too drunk and try to take off her clothes because she said she was nineteen and no man had ever loved her? Leona blamed Oakland's tears on the music, which was so romantic it struck notes inside her that had never been touched before. I don't know, because it was the same music we've always listened to. So why now does it stir up so much want and throw us into such bad moods?

I just know if I saw my grandmother now as I look out the window, she would be standing beside the tree with seven-times-seven limbs, and the word that worries me, the one she spoke to my mother, would be coming out of her mouth into the cold as a cloud, and it would turn into a stone, magic in midair, defying gravity, and I would rush down from this room for it and put it in my pocket, and save it to read it later like the Rosetta stone that provided a key to languages unknown and known. And that stone would provide me with an answer to my life, which I swear right now is spoken in an unknown tongue nobody up here in Eden understands, including me.

Essie is back with a bang of the door. She's tear streaked, hair awry, and face bloated from crying. Her voice sounds hoarse when she says our names. That's from screaming at Fredonia. Until they flew at each other and didn't have to scream but boxed instead. Woody Witherspoon pulled them apart. They were tangled up like warring moths. Essie stripping the bright wings from her mama, smearing the sheer paints from the woman who'd been all made up for a party. Fredonia wants Essie to come home to babysit on weekends.

And when Essie had gotten home, having had time to think and brood on the long El ride to the Homes, she had had enough. And more than enough when Fredonia stayed out till three with a mysterious new boyfriend. Woody had come home at two drunk and crying, "Where is my Fredonia?" Then he told Essie his tale of woe, the one he'd told her thirty times before. How he turned over his money to Fredonia, brought the things he got hot from a man on the job. The hair dryer. The toaster oven. The radio. The TV. So why wouldn't Fredonia let him come back home?

He loved all his babies from LaVette on down. All four of them. The ones Essie had come home from college to babysit.

Woody had fallen asleep on the couch with his mouth open in the middle of a sentence.

Then, as if sensing his stupor, Fredonia had arrived, glassy eyed, with a paper carnation in her Afro wig she bought from the Korean hair store. A $19.99 special on hair that didn't look as good as her own underneath it.

Essie had told Fredonia about her hair, how cheap and bad it looked. As if hair were the reason she was mad. Fredonia had lit a cigarette and let the smoke roll back into her eyes for a minute or two, then she had lunged at Essie to give her a good whipping, pushing the kitchen table into the living room, bumping into the stove, turning on the eyes by accident, rattling the refrigerator until it bounced.

Finally, Woody had awoken, after all the other children had gotten up and run screaming through the house like ambulances going to pick up themselves. He had pulled them apart, shouting, "Essie! Essie, have you lost your mind?"

He never asked Fredonia anything. He already knew. The wig was burning on the lit stove eye. Fredonia was bleeding from the mouth, threatening murder and humiliation, how she would tell all of Essie's Black Power friends up at the school that Essie mistreated her own mama.

This story is too much for Leona and me. I'm so embarrassed for Essie I can't look at her. Not like the few people who were on the El with her this time of morning. People on the El, Essie says, were scared of her. She was bloody and hateful. Me. I am ashamed. Her life is another thing that doesn't make sense. And the tortuous confusion of it is burning her up. She is thin, thinner than when we first met. Love and resentment each taking a pound of flesh a day.

Leona, sitting on Essie's bed by the window, looks out the window. Essie sits stiffly at her desk, touching each one of her books and ink pens and notebooks, as if each tiny thing were an anchor of some kind without which she would have to shoot some terrible rapids. I'm sitting in the middle of the floor, and the room has no secrets.

Leona starts telling Essie about the party she missed. She only talks about the good times, how good the music had sounded, and how everybody danced, moving across the dance floor like free spirits. Leona took out the part about Oakland taking off her clothes and the Black Greeks from the other campus who dropped by to drool at the women in FBO and sing about women's sexual parts and the joy they had brought for them. She left that out so Essie would think we'd had a good time, that somebody here was having a good time.

"I missed it." Essie peels some dried blood from around her nose. She holds a pencil so tight I can hear it start to crack. Then Essie loosens up and sighs a little, "Was William there?" is the thing she asks.

Simba, the artist we met at Great Zimbabwe, loved a captive audience while he worked at his easel in his apartment in the City. He was Mr. Entertainment. Every action had a flourish. He wielded his paintbrush like a conductor. I guess we girls were his musicians. Or his instruments. For a little while, he'd been an actor. But he gave up acting because the writers got too much credit. And the words that came out of his big mouth he wanted to be his own. He hated words anyway. He said that image was the thing that broke people's hearts and made them whole at the same time. To look, really look, at one of his paintings was to look into the eye of God. That's what Simba said. His talk, much as I hated him, pumped me up. I loved words too, but pictures I craved, and I ached when there was nothing for me to dream in. That's why I'd come with Essie and Leona, even though I hadn't been wholeheartedly invited. I asked him questions. Sometimes he'd answer. Sometimes he'd look at me, not wanting to disclose the things I wanted to know.

"If I tell you that, then you'll know my magic," he balked. Then he talked about things I already knew. After a while I stopped asking questions and just listened and watched.

"At-ti-tude," Simba announced. "The sisters got at-ti-tude. They got big beautiful space inside, and they own the territory. In they badness." He praised them excessively. Then he cut them down to size. "But a lot of that space ain't opened up yet. Take a man to do that for a woman. I'm going to call this bad number—this is—*The Virgin Queens.*"

At the same time Leona opened her mouth to denounce that title, he told her to shut up because she was ruining the picture. I was looking over his shoulder. It was beautiful. I knew Essie and Leona, and I knew them in this painting but there was more. How had he done it? By exaggerating the eyes, and heightening the cheekbones, and tilting the mouths so that they were wise. The focal area is the eyes, eye level, two pairs of eyes, one bold, one wounded.

Again, it was Leona who broke the rules. "It still isn't too late to put Maggie in the picture," she said, and implored at the same time.

"Painting," Simba said. "I am painting. Not picturing. You see any cameras? Cameras steal the soul. Paintings amplify the soul. Dig it."

He looked at me for the longest he'd looked that day. "I can put Maggie in this. She needs to be somebody's mama. Sisters like you born pregnant." He swept over me with his eyes like he'd checked my résumé at the end of my life already.

"What does that mean?" I wanted to know, mad and hurt at the same time.

He was back to painting, as if he didn't need to look at me anymore in this life. "So many of you brown rounds just alike. You must make yourselves." I'm not particularly round, a size 9. Just not tiny or tall and thin.

I should have left then, but I didn't want to lose any more face in front of my friends. They were looking like guilty twins who have just won a trip around the world, and they have to leave somebody behind. The excitement of the trip was in their eyes, and the guilty complicity with Simba, who just plain didn't like me. And I'm standing in his apartment. So I stayed in the background the rest of the day and didn't go back with them on their other trips to his studio while he completed *The Virgin Queens.* That day I spent the rest of my time in the seven mirrors that were positioned opposite the bay window. I wanted to get myself just right. Black eyebrows like wings. Cheekbones rising like steep hills. Eyes unguessed, recondite. My two friends were The Virgin Queens and I was a face in waiting.

Waiting. Leona and I sit in one of the parlors of Wyndam-Allyn, the particularly picturesque room with couches with legs like bowlegged baby legs, pink- and brown-striped satiny couch upholstery, and tableside lamps with fringes on the shades like grass skirts that do a rapid hula when you bump up against the tables. The hula so frantic and out of place we're scared to cause it—something might fall and break. We sit primly in the rose-tinted glow of the lamps; that soft glow pushes against the powerful darkness you could almost open the window and touch.

The setting is very turn of the century. We've been waiting just that long for Essie to come home and be just a queen. William's queen. One by one we've waited on the girls in the dorm for this. Waited to hear the story of love consummate and superb, having taken place in dorm rooms, hotels, cars, and the late-night living rooms of sleeping parents.

It's Essie's turn. And this is the day we never would have thought would have come to pass. But Rhonda helped true love along.

"Poor Essie," Rhonda, William's fiancée, sighed when she heard that Essie was typing William's poli-sci paper in one of the vacant upper rooms of Blood Island. Leona told me later how she stopped reading long enough to listen to Rhonda go from room to room on the Island, commenting like one of the Traveling Mercies on Essie's devotion to William. It was Saturday afternoon today and there was hustle and bustle in every corner of Blood Island as we cleaned up after the Friday night after set and got ready to watch a film on Malcolm X in the basement.

Rhonda was in the *BloodLines* office, chattering above the rattle of paper and the crank of the duplicating machine, while the staff tried to get out the monthly mimeo sponsored by FBO. I was doing my cartoon series for this month. It was a caricature of the visiting Greek boys who came here like Neanderthals in search of mates. Everybody says I'm on the case, even the brothers who hate it when I don't draw them like the warriors and kings they are. I have one character I created just for William, a girl named HOBM, Hard on Black Men. That's me. And Leona. And Yvonne. And company. HOBM was just talking about the visiting Greeks who had come in with clubs and stuff to get some women. She was saying something tart like "Beware of Greeks bearing gifts."

Here comes Rhonda, hunting for somebody to talk to.

"How you doin, Miss Lady?" she drawled amiably, the first time she's spoken to me in a civil tone in two months, since she found out Essie likes William. Actually, most of the time Rhonda makes like she doesn't see me. I am thinking of what she and Lydia Rushing said about Essie and me when William first got into trouble. He's still in trouble. I've heard Rhonda still blames Essie and me.

I fiddled with the pens in my jar, taking the time to glance up at her for half a second. Her eyes looked eager. "I'm okay. Just working on my column."

"You and your roommates are so serious. Leona, Essie, and you. Especially Miss Essie. But she's not just serious about the struggle like you and Leona. She's serious about everything." Rhonda sounded amazed and admiring. My drawing hand slowed as I waited for the punch line.

"Essie's a sweet person," I said, more emphatically than I'd intended.

"I know," Rhonda agreed real quickly. "It's kind of sweet the way she's so serious about William. Acting like he's Martin Luther King or Malcolm X or somebody like that. She follows him everywhere and gets all nervous when he says something to her. It's so endearing. But it's sad too. I feel a little sorry for her."

"You don't have to." My mouth felt swollen like somebody'd hit me in it.

"But she's not getting anything at all out of all that work that she does," Rhonda persisted mercilessly. "I think I'll find her a boyfriend. You know somebody she's got her eye on?" Rhonda looked me in the eyes. If we'd been in sixth and eighth grade instead of college, she'd have given me something real for my mouth to be swollen about, and then told me to give that to Essie for a boyfriend.

"You should ask Essie that," I advised her. Then I started running my pen around the page so earnestly she must have thought I'd been seized by artistic inspiration, so she moseyed on away.

I looked up just as she left, just in time to observe Leona come and stand in the doorway. "I heard every word that cow said," Leona said. She was almost as angry as she gets with White teachers who forget her name or her presence.

A little time after this, William found out about what Rhonda was going around saying. I didn't tell. Neither did Leona. But anything that happens on Blood Island has a way of getting found out. Like the time Leona and Steve were studying upstairs in the library alone and Steve told Leona he'd row across a river just for one kiss from her. Leona, who's always got something smart to say, didn't say anything behind that rap. She just kept her mouth closed and kissed him back. Before that sweet little kiss was cool on their lips, Steve and Leona were coming down the stairs and brothers were lined up singing, "Row, row, row your boat," at the foot of the stairs.

Now there were only two people in that library, and unless walls and books can talk, and hear, who overheard that little piece of drama? Leona and Steve avoided each other after that. Talking furniture broke up that romance before it began. Just like talking furniture was working on William and Rhonda.

William hauled Rhonda into the room where Essie sat typing his twenty-page research paper. He asked Essie to please leave so that he could talk to Rhonda alone.

When the yelling started, Leona and I and the *BloodLines* staff could hear it all the way down the hall. The walls conducted the noise, vibrated with it.

"Who the hell do you think you are, Rhonda?" William shouted. Rhonda sounded confused, so subdued we couldn't hear exactly what she said. We just heard William because he said, "Listen to me. And listen to me good. You don't go around here embarrassing me like this. Acting superior to somebody. Essie never hurt you. It was me."

We could hear Rhonda's denial then. "I wasn't acting superior to her. I was just saying—"

Leona and I came into the hall so we could hear what Rhonda was just saying and see what Essie was doing in the middle of the commotion.

She was slim as a dandelion standing there all alone. She was counting the typewritten pages of William's paper on Tanzanian Ujamaa for Postcolonial Systems class. Essie's shoulders hunched together every time William or Rhonda hollered her name. Her back looked like an accordion somebody on the *Lawrence Welk Show* was playing too hard, slamming the two ends together, and an embarrassing sound coming out. Essie's sound, if she'd made one, would've sounded like that.

"Essie," I whispered down the hall to where she stood on one foot like a disabled flamingo, riffling those pages so fast they blurred and broke out of her hands and flew around the hall, sailing.

She dropped to her knees and scrambled for them while Leona and I came to help her retrieve her work and whisper underneath the shouting that was still coming from behind the closed door. Essie was crying now. A tear sliding down her nose, holding, then splashing onto the typewritten page two.

"You gonna mess up all your hard work," Leona consoled her with an admonishment. Essie ducked her head to wipe her nose on the sleeve of her blouse. While Essie traveled down the hall on her knees, picking up paper and crying softly, Rhonda bawled freely, loud enough to be heard on the first floor—through the front door, on the porch, Hamla told us when she came upstairs with her coat on, looking worried and scared that somebody had been assassinated and she hadn't heard the news.

Now Rhonda was screaming, "You not taking this right, William." Rhonda's voice had almost congealed with the mucus in her throat. "I didn't mean to hurt anybody."

"I don't care what you say you meant." William was talking through his teeth. He stepped into the hall and slammed the door on Rhonda's hiccuping and breast clutching.

"Essie," he said, passing over Leona and me. Essie acted like she didn't hear, just kept collating papers.

"Leave it!" William shouted. Essie jumped to her feet and dropped the papers again. William scooped them up and rattled them around in his big hands till the pages were lined up. "Get your coat," he said, and Essie did.

That was the last we saw of her. Following in William's footsteps. Not even waving good-bye to us, as they turned on the landing and were snatched up by the sunlight that came through the door when William opened it. They'd bumped into Hamla, who was standing in the hall with her mouth open.

It was three-thirty in the afternoon then. It is three-thirty in the morning now.

Leona and I are camped out in the dainty parlor, curled up like cats on the baby-legged couches, because we want to be the first to see Essie Witherspoon come through the pathway of trees on William's arm. We want to be the first to know what it was like. First, after William, that is. If he even knew.

Is it truly the ecstasy the songs have led us to believe? Promises scattered like stars in the sky above a college town. A paradise for which all-male singing groups pledge acts of heroism and legerdemain, and of which all-female singing groups cry fidelity, rapture, and suspense. "Oh, it's in his kiss." "Maybe." "My baby loves me," and, "It's like an itching in my heart." Or is it more than all the honey-throated singers can convey in words or sequins or synchronized stage steps that make our tongues hang out of our mouths? Essie knows.

It is the appearance of two shadows on the path under the streetlamp in the middle of the enclosed area between the dorms, one shadow elongated as a tree, one less so, that sends Leona and me tripping and bumping into things on our way out of the parlor. We leave the lights on, casting rosy glows, and the grass skirts of the lamps shivering in passionate welcome and farewell.

We duck like new espionage recruits behind the lobby counter, where everything is dark. When the front door opens it lets in a wreath of light from the bulb above the doorway and Essie in the middle of the wreath. Then she turns in the gentle illumination and William roughly pulls her back out the door. His hands all over her behind. His kiss so serious, his tongue working so, I think he must be teaching Essie another language. I'm blushing. I didn't mean to see all of this, but it is so thrilling. Leona and I go back down under the counter till we think the kiss is over, but when we come back up, it's still going on.

"Handle it, William!" Leona exhorts and praises too softly for him to hear, but loud enough to send me into giggles I smother with my hand.

Then the door we've left ajar so she doesn't have to ring the bell clicks and signals the end of the endless kiss. Essie walks up the steps, pausing with each step. When we come out from behind the cover of the counter we catch her touching her mouth. Her lips look plump.

"Don't say nothing. Just let me look at you." Leona leaps over the counter and lands in front of Essie. My legs are not as long, so I don't come over as stylishly as Leona.

"Do I look different to you?" Essie smiles.

"Should you?" I ask her back. I don't mention how her mouth has gotten fatter and her eyes quieter. They'd say it's my imagination. Maggie and her imagination. Leona and I keep looking at Essie for whom Simba must now think of a new title.

Essie doesn't exactly look at us; she looks around us. Not wanting I imagine to lay her eyes on anything just yet that's not William. She grins, and that's for us. Some of it. But, the truth is, Essie can't stop smiling. Like the Cheshire cat, the little good-bye of years may wash away her body, but that luminous smile will remain. A body unto itself. An arc. This is encouraging.

Later, after Leona has nodded off, Essie gives me details. Essie has gone ahead into new territory and come back to tell me of a strange and wonderful land of love. Even as she describes it, it remains a mystery to me. William took her to his room. His roommate was out of sight and out of mind. "I hope I didn't scare you when I fired on that Whiteboy," William said.

"You were something else," Essie said she said.

"'You're something else, Essie,' he said. 'You're a goddess. Men should pay homage to you.' Then he kissed me. And he kissed me again. And he started unbuttoning my blouse and pulling it out and unbuttoning my jeans, and pulling them down and pulling his down. He got up when his pants were off and he was in his shorts. He put a chair under the doorknob. I wasn't thinking. I just wanted him to come back and finish what he started. He came back and took it out."

"Was it bigger than a ketchup bottle?" Leona asks drily from the other side of the room. She turns over in the top bunk, throwing back the covers and leaning on her elbow. She's been feigning sleep.

"It wasn't *that* big." Essie giggles a little. "He turned around to put on a rubber." She pauses. I don't want to ask what happened next, but Leona does.

"Then what did he do?" Leona asks like she is keeping some kind of score for performance.

"He kissed me some more. Open mouthed, with his tongue." Essie smiles. "He held my breasts. Then . . . he put it in. And we danced. I love to dance with William."

I'm still on how big it is. I don't even use tampons.

"Maggie, it was—oh! He said, 'You're my girl, Essie. You are mine. I won't let anybody hurt you ever, girl.'"

I am so happy I am speechless. I am so happy for Essie who is officially a woman. The shadows don't matter. What happened to her before.

"I gave it up on prom night. I almost did a couple of times before. We did the do all summer long," Leona confesses, fully awake and blasé. She goes on to share details of her first time in the backseat of a Cadillac. It is interesting imagining her long legs finding space in a cramped place. Her feet almost out the window. I am listening, but I can tell Essie's only half listening. She's in the land where only true lovers may go. I want to go there one day soon.

Just when I am sure that Essie's adventure is the ceremony of our lives, and everyone is talking about their new love, and Rhonda's crying fits are the talk of the town, another brother named Russell Garner is beat up by a gang of six Whiteboys each dressed in a twin bedsheet that doesn't cover him completely.

Russell was alone at the observatory on the lake watching the lights in the midnight sky through a high-powered telescope when they fell on him. Campus security describes Russell's black eye and torn lip and cracked ribs as "an unfortunate prank." On the Island, we don't see it that way. We get very serious about sheets, especially when Whitepeople are wearing them and it is not Halloween.

The grad students are in session on Blood Island. William and Steve Rainey are defendants. Or is it Eden University? They've worn out the junior KKK. The topic changes. "So, blood, you think it's acceptable for there to be only one Black full professor in the whole of this esteemed university? No Black associate professors or assistant."

"That's not what I said," William responded antagonistically.

"Turner's going back at the end of the year. He's going to retire in London. He's got family there. You know how those Pan-Africanists are. Maybe he'll lecture overseas." The grad student leans back on the sofa, lights a Kool, and puts his feet up.

With books in hand I fast walk across the room, hoping to be invisible. I reach the long table against the wall and take a seat.

"We have to make our presence here at Eden felt. Did you know the maids and janitors are planning a strike? We have to support them."

"Shit, maybe *we* should strike," another grad student says.

"Yeah, and get all Fs," William mumbles almost under his breath. His hearing has been postponed three times. He keeps on studying. He has straight As.

Even the tough grad students have to laugh. They get mostly As too.

"They'd love to be rid of us. They're looking for a way around the government now. Ten years from now there will be no more Negroes in Eden." They guffaw again.

Then Steve speaks for the first and only time, taking up the charge, "We have to make our presence felt *now*."

"Yeah, that's the imperative," Mr. Kool agrees. Then blows smoke rings like he's biding his time and lassoing a promise.

Yvonne Christmas comes in and her transistor radio is blaring Aretha Franklin as loud as it will go. "*Respect.*" Yvonne Christmas is hair, breasts, big hips in jeans like a Yoruba sculpture. "*R-E-S-P-E-C-T.*" The male grad students look at her lazily, as if they don't dare trust themselves to look at her with wide-open eyes. Then she starts talking about Vietnam and the casualties so far this year. The world outside Eden presses in. It reminds me of that song about a girl, her boyfriend, a letter, and soldiers, so many soldier boys in Vietnam. Maybe I am mixing songs. I only remember a part of it. There's so much to remember.

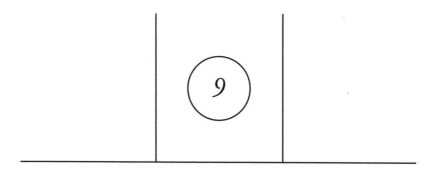

Spring 1968

Wyndam-Allyn is the oldest women's dorm on campus. It's three stories covered in ivy that houses a multitude of insects. The invasion of spiders, beetles, and wasps heralds the arrival of spring in Eden, even before the calendar does.

One day Essie kills a spider that wove a web from Leona's bunk to mine. I warn her that according to my mother, who was born between Mimosa and Letha, Mississippi, and who knows some things, spiders are a sign of good luck. They aren't like roaches that could turn you off of any creature that crawls. I don't tell Essie she is going to pay for the murder of a good spider, because Essie's paying for enough already. Her period is late.

I'm sitting, looking out the bay window of Blood Island. It is two or three in the morning, but the porch light and streetlight combine against the darkness, and if I didn't know what time it is I'd think it was daybreak. I am singing "A Change Is Gonna Come," a song Sam Cooke left behind before a woman who was Black killed him. His sorrowful death spread out across newspapers while Blackgirls lined up to cry for a voice they would have died for. We couldn't weep away his song. A song about being born by the river in a little tent; I was born by a river in a small house on Chinaman's Store.

That Mimosa summer after Eddie died, Lazarus, grief stricken and brave, loved to climb trees and look out over the road to see whatever came or was coming. I loved to sing Sam Cooke songs that caressed my back when I sat on the front porch. The songs floated through the screen door from the radio nestled in a doily on the thin-limbed side table in the living room.

Our friend had died, someone had killed him, and we were alive and sweating under a blistering Mississippi sun. Under a full Mississippi moon our grandmother Sarah Mahalia Dancer was liable to come stepping through the sweetish mist the insecticide truck left in its wake in the evening coolness. Littleson, who was Lazarus, was determined to see her first, to greet any ghost who came calling. I'd pull in the thick cloud of mosquito spray and inhale the voice of the singer that made a halo around me, light spreading through the screen, as I sat and pushed back the thought of ghosts, new and old, and chose the yearning and the delicious thread of something else in the air.

I had just started having periods that year, so the blood always surprised me, even when it wet my panties and turned sticky, then began to soak through my shorts. That's the way it did one night when I sat with Sam Cooke's living voice hanging over my head and my brother hanging in the darkness in a dark tree. Everybody dark. I sat on the steps until blood stained the steps; and the heavy wetness woke me up from that song, that voice. Grandmama Patsy fussed and scrubbed the spot with cold water and bleach when I went inside at last to do the cleaning women must do. No ghosts came that night.

Now I can feel the hard, troubled core of my heart dissolving inside of me as I sing the part about it being too hard living but being afraid to die because "I don't know what's up there beyond the sky." Memory has been playing a trick on me, making things perfect. "A Change Is Gonna Come" hadn't even been sung or thought of, that Mimosa summer. It is from some later season, when I'd grown more accustomed to regular blood. The song fits now at winter's end, where Blood Island is quiet as blood, properly contained, going back and forth from the heart, faithful and unobtrusive.

I look out onto Carson Street and the backside of the big auditorium where the Annual Spring Revue is held. I don't know what I expect to see. But I know it's something. Something.

"Is it that bad, Maggie?" Steve Rainey asks from behind me. He has caught some of my sad song. The party is over and just about everyone else is gone.

The party was in the basement. I was dancing the funky Broadway, hunching my shoulders, buckling my knees from side to side while swinging my loose arms in the opposite direction from my knees, and fanning my hands in the same direction as my knees, when I looked up and saw Leona and Essie going up the steps, leaving me to dance with Daniel Moody. I'd thought they'd come back for me. That was hours ago. Hours since Daniel Moody had gone with Oakland, and left me with the broken face and the halfway-broken heart.

The heat is going down as the rest of the bloods set out in search of after sets, or beds, or councils of love analyzing the significance of who was dancing with who and who disappeared with whom. The cold-blooded councils all female and all male in separate dorms. When we're all together on Blood Island, Eden is warm. Now the door opens and closes and the warm goes with each leaving.

"I don't know," I finally answer Steve Rainey. He searches my face like a traveler meditates on a map. If Leona is who he wants, I don't tell him she *been* gone. He'll have to ask. I'm not in a volunteering frame of mind. Volunteering got Emmett King, a boy on our block, sent to Vietnam. It also got Essie's period late.

I go on humming and looking out the window. Like I did when I was three and new to the North and the world.

"It's getting cold," I observe as I crawl into my coat, then clutch it around me.

"Spring's almost here," Steve promises, like he ordered it just for me, but the store is late delivering. He's like this all the time. I wish Leona liked him.

We sit while cold takes the last traces of heat. I still don't want to have to face the Hawk outside or the evil weather inside the dorms, where arguments are breaking out in the dining hall regularly. "What's FBO stand for?" some Whiteboys from the men's dorms mutter among themselves, just loud enough for some of us to overhear, just low enough so we can't get a witness. "Foul Body Odor, FBO," they answer among themselves. And we call them funky hunkies, albino mutants, under our breath, or somebody will scream it. Soon we'll all run out of breath and just get ugly.

We get on one another's nerves in the smallest ways, like an old married couple that hates each other but lives in the same house while the divorce goes through. When winter snow turns to prespring rain, we can smell the damp rainy smell on one another and hate the difference in the human smells.

Hair, coiled or wispy, loitering near the drains in the sinks of the communal bathrooms, we rinse down with vigor and disgust, hating the difference. When we catch the strains of the other's music pouring out of different stereos, we plug our ears and howl like dogs forecasting death. We just rub one another the wrong way, even when we bump into one another in the halls. We bare teeth and snarl at the difference.

Too many differences do me in, so I'm sitting past midnight on Blood Island. Just me and Steve Rainey and a beautiful, wondrous moon like the pregnant belly of a ghost, just stunning. Someone will start the rumor that we were dancing horizontally on the floor all night long. Doing it. But after the rumor is passed from mouth to mouth, going in and out without a thought, like breath, it will quiet down. "Steve and Maggie are friends," someone else will say. "They were probably talking about Leona. You know Leona's got Steve's nose wide open. And Maggie's in love with Sam Cooke this week. She got a thang for ghosts." That's what they'll say. Then somebody else will laugh. Because we laugh at differences.

"Can I kiss you?" Steve asks out of the cold that's turning blue then gray with light.

"What?" I say, not sure I've heard him right. His face is serious, and he looks at me intently. He licks his lips lightly, like he's nervous and remembering the taste of something sweet and good. The gesture isn't lascivious. I can feel myself tremble as we drift toward each other.

The heaviest thing about the kiss is his breath on my face. When it is over, soon, very soon, because it is only the brushing of lips, we look away. I am nervous now. That little kiss was so unexpected. It is my second one. The first was prom night. Thus it was expected.

"Thanks, Maggie," Steve says.

I don't say anything or look at him much, not even when we leave Blood Island together and he walks me back to the dorm. In front of Wyndam-Allyn he kisses me again, right upside the forehead. Again, a light kiss, more spirit than flesh.

In the room, Leona and Essie are still awake. They ask me what happened to me, and I ask them what happened to them.

"Well, excuse me, Miss Grace," Leona drawls.

Essie just says her period came while she was dancing with William. So she and Leona came home to celebrate the relief of the bloody visitation. She sounds all knowing as she talks about late periods and pregnancy fears. Like she and William have been married and sleeping in a double bed for years, instead of that one night in his single dorm bed. I don't have much conversation, and after a while they leave me alone and keep on talking about sex. Tonight Leona showed Essie how to insert a tampon. She can manage one now.

I watch Leona out of the corner of my eye and try not to feel guilty because Steve Rainey kissed me. She doesn't like him, she says over and over again. But I am a traitor and I know it.

The nights of pseudospring are heavy dark just before rain; the moon and the stars are indiscreet and loud as Blackfolks talking street. The air is heavy, and the wind comforts you when you run, cradles you in a walk. All the fires in your mind are blown to near stillness by the wind; the voices we pass between us this night are wind noises, are minor soothings. It is this night that Essie and I find out about silences, about knowing nothing to say. Nothing.

William walks between us. Won't leave us alone. Won't leave Essie alone since she is his second fiddle and he'll play her again when he gets ready. But he makes his solicitude seem impersonal, so he talks about how Blackwomen got no business walking this campus alone. "That's what's the matter with Blackwomen now. They're always alone. Always doin for themselves." Don't we know we need protection? Don't we know we're queens? William's making us uncomfortable talking that trash. Leona would say, "Talking that shit." She's cussing fluently by now. Even in Swahili.

We think he is high. But there's no whiskey mouth. No reefer eyes. No shades on at night. Not high. But cool. Rapping some Blackness on us. We, Essie and I, have been told enough about protection. Don't know we supposed to be protected. Last month Delta Z insulted a Blackwoman. From the frat house windows they called her all kinds of Black bitches. Even worse, K-Phi almost molested a sister in some bushes. The university made the culprits send the sister a dozen red roses of apology. The roses had thorns that added to the scratches the frat boys put on her arms and legs when they were trying to pull her down. Before she found the power to kick them where their ugly babies come from.

William walks between us this night, being all warrior. Being warrior worth six feet one and 140 pounds with additional brass knuckles weight included.

After a while, we are just walking when a Whiteboy who looks like a man comes up in the middle of the path. He's Sigma Chi strong. A wide load of two hundred pounds of cold, hard muscle that makes two of William, and he's striding slow in the middle of the walk.

Through the short night distance, William and his eyes spear; everything is stark and still in abstract war.

Sigma Chi's shoulders bar the walk. He's double William's weight.

Essie and I shiver and our blood kind of stumbles.

By reflex, we tend to part into the wintry patches of grass. William grabs and holds us to our right of way. "Don't move," he commands. "Don't give this Whiteboy one inch." Why does William always meet trouble with Essie and me? Are we magnets for conflicts? Are we trouble like my cousin? Are they out to get us?

So we meet like two armies at a belligerent intersection. This Whiteboyman in his might and William in his trim pride that stalks and poises to pounce.

On the edge of the walk, the wind is dabbling, flirting a damp against the sparse leaves and bushes. This university is a beautiful fairyland and all the young things growing in its plan.

William and Sigma Chi meet in a delicate, deliberate collision. Sigma Chi steps away and William holds the earth.

"Man, you gonna walk over us?" William asks softly. The question as soft as his hand movement fitting into his brass knuckles in his pocket.

Whiteboy arrogant. "You people think you own the sidewalk?" Neither answers the other's question.

Essie and I silent in a fumbling dread. William, would you want us to help you? And what if, just if, when you losing, would you rather we watch your shame from the throne of glass you making, breaking at our feet? You beat the other one, but can you take on every one of them?

We stand there in a tableau with a tableau inside, me and Essie, the two men. I think of shuffling raging bulls or wildebeests, you know? Horns locked and tracking in each other's dust, never really movin: William in his protecting pride and the Whiteboy shielded in Whiteness, equipped with the power of William and Essie and me.

A sparse new rain starts speckling our faces. Somebody shifts: Sigma Chi. I sense something now. It is all dry in my nostrils. I smell the dread of the brother and the enemy. They are afraid they will have to draw blood. They are each afraid to be the one to lose. We are in a tableau with terrible masks to save some face.

The rain in its wind is a free agent. Breaks the mood. Sigma Chi, shrugging, hisses and walks away. There is a tightness in his ass when he walks.

William stands firm in his face. Then turns fast, abruptly, into the moist darkness without looking into our eyes.

Essie and I are the ones left. Struck. Dumb.

Perhaps this night is the corner in time we turn and meet a new place. Everything has seemed possible before, now it's drastic. William's hearing is two days later. He and the first Whiteboy, the drunk one he beat so bad.

There is no jury of his peers; if there were, it would be composed of twelve members of For Bloods Only, sitting over to the side in the now-empty seats. The judge, big and florid, like a manufacturer of Biggifying Pills that I dreamed about but couldn't remember exactly how this time, is behind his bench and a bailiff stands to his left side between him and the jury box. A court recorder is typing soundlessly away at a seat behind a little table with a little machine on it.

Essie, Leona, and I take our seats behind William's family and Rhonda. They wouldn't let us come inside while the judge was talking to the White defendant, Bruce Faulkner. Now, as we enter, the defendant is standing behind a table. He is looking appropriately sorry. He stands and crosses his hands in front of his privates. He receives a slap on the wrists.

"I have read the depositions from Magdalena Grace and Essie Witherspoon and I have read your statement. There are some inconsistencies. However, the arresting officers' version of events are in concurrence with yours, Mr. Faulkner. The court finds you not guilty of all charges. Be a bit more cautious when you are out and about on campus. Eden is not a garden." He actually chuckles.

My mouth is open; so are Essie's and Leona's. I raise my hand, trying to get the judge's attention. The judge looks at me sternly. "The court does not recognize you, young lady. Let us move on."

The bailiff says William's name and the docket number. William's attorney starts to speak. He is a Black attorney, a graduate of Eden University School of Law, the best in the City. He is the one who kept getting postponements in the hopes that the officers would not show up for the hearing or Bruce Faulkner would recant his story that he was walking along minding his own business when William jumped him.

"Did you land the first blow, Mr. Satterfield?" the judge is speaking directly to William. But he's not even looking at him. He's looking at something on his bench. Like William is so much paper to him.

William looks at his attorney who nudges him to answer. "Yes," William says simply.

"Yes?" the judge says sharply.

"Yes, your honor."

"That is assault and you are guilty, young man, but the court has received a number of character witnesses on your behalf and your academic record at the university is stellar. I find you guilty of disorderly conduct. Three years probation and two hundred hours of community service. The court is in a generous mood." All this in a tone that is a combination of censorious and casual.

Tears are easing down Essie's face. Leona hands her a handkerchief. My hands are clenched fists. William turns around and looks at his mother, whose beige face is tight. She hugs him then turns around and hugs Rhonda on her other side. William looks straight into Essie's watery eyes. He shrugs dejectedly. She rises and leans forward. William's mother takes his arm and turns him to the judge. She glares at Essie. The judge bangs his gavel. "Court is still in session."

He goes on, "The court strongly admonishes anyone that lying on a deposition is against the law. Don't perjure yourselves for anyone."

"We didn't lie," I snarl under my breath.

He is toying with us. Court is dismissed. He bangs his gavel the last time.

"We did well," William's attorney says. Rhonda's father is an alderman in the City. He called in some favors.

Why did they name kangaroo courts after kangaroos? "Boing! Boing! Boing!" I write around the kangaroos in the courtroom scene that represents William's trial as I visualize it for my cartoon in *BloodLines.*

"Very funny," Steve Rainey mumbles when I hand him a copy of the newsletter. "So funny I forgot to laugh. I for-got to laugh."

William's hearing is the turning of a corner. Maybe there's an escalator around this corner. The tension here (like they say about the War) escalates. The talks FBO's engaged in with the university to make the space more hospitable to us break down. There's a mood, not whimsical, but deeply profound in Black students across the country, who find ourselves disgruntled with begging and outsideness. We want Black studies that apply to our lives. That lend us breadth and depth to tackle our Black condition. That's what we call it. The Black condition. Comparable to pregnancy. Expecting something.

The *Eden Daily,* in an editorial, describes Black studies as Chitterlings 101 and Collard Greens 203. A poster of Buckwheat, the colored one of the *Little Rascals* from the thirties with wild ribbonlike rags tied around his myriad plaits, grins down from walls around campus. A bubble coming out of Buckwheat's mouth says, WHERE YOU STUDY BARBECUE? The caricature stabbed a tender place inside each of us in FBO. The frustration of being so misunderstood, so maligned, set our teeth on edge, locked our jaws in a rage that froze our faces and set our Afros on higher ends. Leona, whose father had made a small fortune off mambo sauce, took even more passionate affront than any of us in For Bloods Only. "Whoever did that needs to be chastised severely," he said. We all have an idea of which fraternity did it.

Any jokes about barbecue are for Leona a form of signifying. And Leona doesn't signify for play. She's ready to fight if somebody says "Yo mama" or "Yo daddy." So all around us is the immediate slur, as if the *Eden Daily* had just said "Yo whole generation." There's nothing left to do, except fight. We walk around with our hands in fists, because we've been pummeled enough just for being. We're the whole generation that was water hosed down, bitten by dogs, beaten with nightsticks, spat on, strung up, shot down, and called ugly and stupid just enough to make everything that is inside us stand up. Even if it hasn't happened to one of us personally, the happening finds us and subtracts from us, each.

We are all touched by the knowledge that we are each available in some way to subtraction. And we know the higher math of the jokes in the *Eden Daily*. We know the new arithmetic behind the scorn of Eden.

Someone threw a beer bottle out of the fraternity house window. The one with the Confederate flag. From inside came a Rebel yell, or what was supposed to be a Rebel yell. Trixia said it sounded like Tarzan on drugs. Trixia and one of the brothers were walking by, heading north. A shard of glass cut Trixia's calf. Now she is on Blood Island with blood in her eye. She is dabbing with a tissue her bleeding leg.

"They could have hit me upside the head with that beer bottle. That glass could have popped up in my eye and put my eye out. These Whitefolks getting wild. I'm from the South. I know." Trixia looks like she's been crying real tears.

"They don't know the Civil Rights Act was passed and we have a right to be here. They don't know we have a right to be here without any laws passed to make it so." That is what comes to me.

"It's time we set things right," Steve Rainey says quietly.

Trixia says, "William Satterfield gave one of them an ass whipping and look where it got him." She once spit in somebody's face.

"We have to draw the line," Steve says. And that's all he says. The room falls silent. At least I don't hear anything else about it.

A week or so later someone slips a note under the door of the *Eden Daily*. "Black Ghosts Whip Rebels—A New Day in Eden," while Steve Rainey sleeps at the side of my bed. We've been talking throughout the night, whispering, while Leona snoozes. Essie is afraid that someone will check our room and find him there. But no one does. He came in around midnight. I was on the desk and buzzed him in. We slipped to my room. He was breathing hard, dressed all in black, except for blue jeans. He had a black cap on. He wouldn't tell me where he had been or what he had been doing. I knew.

The *Eden Daily* publishes the note and it is a new day in Eden all right.

The Rebels had been routed. The twenty fraternity brothers trounced by seven or so Black Ghosts moving swiftly and muscularly in the darkness. (I could see them like Jacob Lawrence paintings come alive.) The Ghosts had taken out the lights, then taken out the Rebels. The Ghosts moved like an ill wind, but they were good. They didn't dance above anybody's heads like tongues of fire; they knocked heads together. They said not a word; they just spoke with fists.

In the end after the assault on the frat house was over and midnight was striking, the swift Black Ghosts flew. The Rebels, still dazed, called campus police. They weren't so dazed that they didn't know their attackers had been Black, and they weren't so dumb they didn't know why or what had earned the ass whipping. Still they identified the attackers as Black, even if they couldn't identify them by individual face (they all looked alike) or name, and they said the raid had been unprovoked.

The university tried to send William home to East Orange, New Jersey, but too many witnesses (he had been at a dorm meeting of all residents, mostly White students) could account for his whereabouts. The administration called in all brothers; threatened them with expulsion. No one broke because only a few beyond the holy ghosts knew who had done it. I knew and Essie and Leona knew because we guessed.

The university put *all* the Black male students on probation. They are subject to a twelve o'clock curfew and must sign in and out of their dormitories with destinations notes. Where they used to be able to go to Tech or the library at certain times overnight, now they need a pass. It is like slavery. And if Blackmen are in slavery, Blackwomen are too. It's what Professor I. B. K. Turner would call a dialectics. You talk about one, so you're talking about the other. Or as Bay would say, "Simple as that."

"Bloods on lockdown. Bloods on lockdown. Bloods locked up!" Mr. Kool comes striding through the door of Gorée. He is a grad student and does not have to submit to the university's edict. If they had even thought him culpable, he'd be in jail.

That's what he says as he settles into his usual seat and takes out one of his trademark cigarettes. He takes a drag. "One day you niggahs *will* go crazy and the shit will hit the fan." He exhales. "Hit the fan." What a picture that is—shit hitting the fan.

One evening when the boy with the dirty blond hair at the library security-check counter tells Essie she doesn't look like her own face on her ID card and she must not be a student registered at Eden and can't take out and must put back the six books she needs to write her paper, Essie snaps, "Some days your mama doesn't look like your mama, on those days does she have to put you back?"

The boy behind the security-check counter says, "You could use some etiquette lessons, Miss Witherspoon." He reads her name off her ID card. The one he says she can't use.

"You could use a pair of eyes," Essie escalates and accelerates as she gathers up her books to get out.

The dirty blond boy grabs Essie's wrists, yelling, "I didn't say you could go," while Essie yells back, "Get your hands off me," and I'm screaming, "Get your hands off her," and people are staring and some boys who could be littermates to the dirty blond boy hustle over to stop Essie and me from breaking the arm he's stretched out for Essie. We're both of us girls slamming on his hand and arm with our books. I can hear my own voice and Essie's going, "Let go. Let GO."

He lets Essie go. And he lets me go past the counter without checking my books. Essie and I are still rolling our eyes at him, and he's mouthing obscene curses and stuff at us, when one of the librarians rushes down the stone steps toward him, and his friends with golden Greek letters across their purple sweaters walk toward him while they look at Essie and me like they'd like to smash us till our insides are smeared on their soles.

Essie speaks up about things now. I'm not sure if it's because the experience of William's love has been a kind of medicine that sealed a split inside of her, or if it's been an explosive that opened a rumbling inside of her until her true self shot out like a geyser. Maybe Essie's metamorphosis is strictly because of her William; nowadays a woman will change anything for a man. Some girls give up straightening their hair because their men insist on Afros. (And some girls don't get Afros because their men will only have straightened hair.) More than likely, however, it's the fever of the time that has made Essie mad. I don't know. What I do know is that being with William has given Essie faith in a future with him. She believes he has chosen her.

Sometimes when we sprawl around our room and jabber about desire and all the he-said, she-said, who-kissed-John stuff, I can feel another self, inside me and removed from me. My girl troubles are trivial to her. She is sad and wise on one face; the other face is wise and joyous, relieved of all these petty fibrillations of the heart. But she is relieved because she has traveled through this room of teen and postteen tears. She has been here before and gone on even as I am being here. She watches over me. Perhaps I have known about her most of my life. Without knowing her name. Being a colored Catholic was easy. In the first-grade classroom of Our Lady of Perpetual Help, I scooted over to one side of my seat to make room for my guardian angel that watched over me, protected me, and guided me. I gave her no name then, but now I know if I permitted myself to focus on her airy presence, if I stare into some high ceiling inside myself like an infant enchanted by light, I would say her name. Wouldn't it be Magdalena Grace?

Instead, I turn inside to the girl sitting Indian style on the lower bunk bed playing a game of divination with two other girls.

Essie says, "Leona, you'll marry first because men like you so much." Leona protests and demurs, but she looks halfway pleased by Essie's prognostication. Each of us wants to be assured by the others that she is desirable and will not be alone, at least not because no one has chosen her.

Essie continues, "I'll be second because William won't marry me before everything's settled and that'll take a while. And, Maggie, you'll be last because you don't really need anybody."

Girlish expectancy falls flat to the bottom of my belly.

Yet Leona has different numbers. "Maggie will be first because she's always mothering somebody. And every man is looking for his mama to wash his socks and fix his chicken and gravy."

"Me?" I'm giddy, because to be talked about is so flattering and embarrassing. "I'm nobody's mother, honey." I'm light headed.

"Yes, you are," Leona says emphatically, turning her mouth down strongly and nodding her head in rapid affirmation of her good judgment. She is sitting in the middle of the floor; now she stretches her arms back and leans on them like a pinup girl, or an empress in royal recline, or a goddess worn out from designing fates. "You're used to taking care of people. All those baby sisters you got."

It is true. For every peanut-butter-and-jelly sandwich of my own, I've made one or two for others. Yet I am the selfish one. I've always taken the bathroom in the house for my personal space. Sitting on the toilet, drawing imaginary flowers and fairies and legendary saints or practicing a speech for student council, while one or two of my younger sisters did an emergency dance before the bathroom door, clutching between the legs and hopping on one foot then the other, I was not all considerate maternity. My older sister, Pearl, reminds me often of those gross thefts of privacy at the expense of others. "Oh, the pools of pee caused by selfish me." I'll roll my eyes when Pearl scrapes memory for my past offenses.

Leona says Essie will be the second to wed because she needs someone so much. To which Essie blanches like Leona's come carrying a bowl of steaming expellant to wash her entrails out with. And Leona says that she'll be last because she doesn't give a care. I remind her of one of our first conversations, when she said she wanted a career in case her husband left her. She says, "Not having one till never or later makes it less complicated. I just know I don't want to be bothered with a man underfoot. He'd probably be underfoot too. They're all so short."

Not only has Essie determined that William's future is her future, she's also taken his present for her own. His fire is her fire. Her William is more furious than ever because Eden U. won't listen to the needs of Black students, because I. B. K. Turner hasn't been asked to stay another year at Eden and act as head of a Black studies department, because a Whiteboy fronted him off in front of Essie and me, because a sister was humiliated by name-calling drunks, because junior members of an impromptu KKK beat up Russell Garner, who doesn't get in anybody's way but the Milky Way, because Malcolm X was assassinated three years ago, and King is talking against Vietnam and saying the struggle for American imperialism is part and parcel with the struggle of oppressed colored people in America proper, and Whitepeople like King less and less and now he's come up north and stayed in the rat-infested West Side apartment to highlight the horror up north and found a hate so deep it stunned him and sent him back south. William burns from his mouth to his heart to his groin because his brother Philip, always more a Boy Scout than William, is dead in a country called Vietnam. William is angry because his mother is angry because one son is dead and another has fallen from grace or been pushed from grace. William cannot stop being angry, and neither can William's Essie.

Leona wonders how the new outspoken Essie will fare at home. Fredonia, Essie's lunatic mama (as Leona and I call her behind Essie's back—we describe her to Essie as one in want of psychiatric help), has demanded that Essie come home again over the weekend to babysit. This after the bloody fight they had last time Essie went home.

When Essie told her crazy mama she couldn't babysit for her, her mama went off on her over the phone. "If you're not in this rat-trap by Friday eight P.M. I'm gonna have Woody drive me up there and drag you by your nappy hair on home here to me. Then you can move back in here and help me with these kids sometimes. You ain't got no business living up there with them sidity peckerwoods and jigaboos. You ain't got to live up there to go to school up there, I can tell you that right now."

Essie told us that she had to cancel a date with William. She had an emergency at home. (Leona said, "Yeh, her mama is an emergency.")

Essie was looking lonely and intense, putting herself into her studies. Everything depends on her becoming a doctor. She handles calculus and more chemistry than that between her and William. She goes to study sessions with Black and White students. On a tiny frame, she pulls her own weight. She pulls her own weight.

It is the middle of the night and our buzzer is ringing insistently. Leona yawns and mumbles, "It can't be Essie," because she knows Essie took her key card (a plastic card we second-semester freshmen get so we can come in after two in the morning). It is after two.

We put coats on over our nightclothes and stumble toward the lobby. Past the blind light of the lobby that hurts our sleep-sensitive eyes, we see police, Mrs. Sorenson, and Essie, screaming and tear streaked, in the little parlor. The same one Leona and I waited up for her in that night a few weeks ago, before we were issued our cards.

Essie, her mouth pulled grotesquely wide and her hair wobbling from side to side, is hiccuping out her story to the three policemen who look like dark blue machines with legs and close-clipped hair covered by blue hats. Their big presences crash through the Victorian time frame of the parlor where Mrs. Sorenson in a white, high-necked robe with frills around the collar curves her long-sleeved arm around Essie's shaking shoulders. The lace of Mrs. Sorenson's wrist brushes Essie's cheek.

"This is an outrage!" Mrs. Sorenson bites out. Looking from Essie to the policemen, then back again.

We see all this fast because we rush right away to comfort Essie who is in trouble. Mrs. Sorenson stands up and Leona and I take up where she's left off—soothing and touching Essie who is in trouble. Not angry, disappointed trouble as when she's had a brawl with her crazy mama. Not pissed off, defiant trouble as when she read the checkout boy in the library. Not confused, empathetic trouble as when we didn't know what to do to help old William go against Sigma Chi. By no means, not the injured pride, bruised heart trouble as when William was with Rhonda. This is real trouble. Palpable and terrible.

When she lifts her face—nose swollen and clogged and her eyes reduced and reddened—I see what I'd never seen before. This is terror, vomit-inducing and bowel-throttling, because there's nothing you can do.

"They tried to rape me, Maggie."

She looks at me.

"Who?" Leona screams.

"Those two Whitemen."

Mrs. Sorenson is laying into the policemen about inadequate protection for Eden's female students. We don't even hate her then. She is on Essie's side. When the policemen try to say Essie shouldn't have been out so late alone, Sorenson won't hear it. Essie had been in a study group. No one walked her back to the dorm because the White students believed the campus was safe. (Especially since the brothers were on curfew.) Mrs. Sorenson says, "This campus should be safe at any time." This from the woman who would ground you for being ten minutes late for dorm closing in our first semester. At that moment she is in a wild, parental rage induced by fear that something has almost happened to one of her charges. She says something "loathsome and obscene" would have happened. She is magnificent.

Mrs. Sorenson chips away at the policemen so thoroughly they stumble brokenly out of the parlor like little boys or broken windup toys. Their uniforms holding them up, they go off to do their duty. My mind is a mess. "Policeman, policeman, do you duty, cause here come the girl with the African booty." That jumps up and down in my head, detached, in comic blasphemy against the real shivering of Essie in my arms. I hold her tighter, keeping us both from breaking open.

"What happened?" Leona asks Essie.

"I was walking home—to here—and they hollered out the car window at me, 'Hey, mama.' And I waved my hand like this." She twists her hand in a dismissive sign called "forget you," a polite "fuck you." "And I kept on going. They got out of the car and jumped in front of me. Up in my face. They looked like poor White trash. Greasy long hair and nasty clothes. Stinking. The short one put his face two inches from mine. And he said, he said . . ." Essie swallows real hard, panting to catch her breath. "He said, 'You ugly black bitch. Suck my dick.'

"I tried to walk around them, but they grabbed me. That one did. There were some girls still in the car and they didn't even say nothin'. When he spun me around I could see them in the car window. They ain't say shit though. And they was girls too. And oughta know how I felt with this man breathing in my eyes, telling me to suck his dick. He pushed me and I fell down. I started screaming and they jumped in the car and sped away like some bank robbers."

Essie's story hit campus like a mortar bomb my brother Lazarus who was Littleson then would tell me about. Those were imaginary bombs we played with. This is psychic. Essie went home for a day. Even Fredonia was looking good to her now. Fredonia was honey and not her usual vinegar. William called after Essie'd gone. I was on the switchboard, but he didn't recognize my voice till I called him by name. Then it was "How you doin, Maggie?" but real distracted like he had his mind on business.

"Do you know about the meeting, Magdalena?"

"What meeting?" I say so loud my mouthpiece jiggles a little.

"Keep it quiet, sister. It's on the Island. Tell," he pauses, "Essie and Leona. Nine o'clock. Now get me Trixia so I can tell her. Oh, and keep on pushin," he adds.

"You too," I say and buzz Trixia's room once.

"If we cannot protect our women, we are not Blackmen. It's . . . as . . . simple . . . as . . . that." This is a voice that sounds like William's, only older, more tired. I hear it as we come up the stairs to the upper room of Blood Island.

The room is packed with us in all hues in a somber mood. So many faces. Leona leads the way through the throng; I follow. A reluctant, wounded-looking Essie brings up the rear. All eyes are on her.

Trixia breaks the sudden silence. "I don't feel safe on this campus. I feel like I am up for grabs." She's a little theatrical, but there is more than a grain of truth in her voice.

"It's time that we move the struggle to another level," Mr. Kool says. He is without his cigarette in a tight space, but he is still cool.

"The Central Committee has met," William announces, "and we propose that we take over this motherfucker."

I feel a thrill in my bones at the very idea.

"Anybody who does not want to be a part of this better leave now."

One brother and two sisters thread their ways slowly toward the stairwell. "I didn't come up here to get put out," one sister throws over her shoulder.

I didn't either. The thrill turns to a chill, a cold thought. "Mama and Madaddy didn't send me to Eden to get put out." I look around me at the faces of FBO members as close together as the books that line the built-in bookshelves on the wall. *White Man, Listen!; Why We Can't Wait; The Autobiography of Malcolm X; Jubilee; The Souls of Black Folk; Selected Writings and Speeches of Marcus Garvey; A Raisin in the Sun;* and more: the titles speak to me. I see the faces of Aunt Silence, Aint Kit, especially Grandmama Patsy, and I don't want to throw their dream away, but I want to keep it too. I want them to be proud of me because I am a Grace woman and I walk with my head held high. I think of my other grandmother.

"All right now," Mr. Kool says. "The shit has hit the fan."

"It most certainly has," Cletus the Elder says in a dangerous kind of way.

Then Christmas says, "The Central Committee has laid out the plan. The only thing that is required is fidelity to the plan and to each other."

"Is that all?" Leona snorts.

"Lydia, you work in the Finance Building in the afternoon. You have the first task. Stay in the office after hours, after everyone has gone on the appointed day, and turn off the alarm. Then let the first wave in."

"I can do that. How will you know when to come in? I don't want to turn on the lights, do I?"

"Wave a handkerchief at the bathroom window."

"Keep your eyes open," Lydia purrs. "I'll be fluttering my hankie like a Southern belle." Everybody cracks up.

"The first wave, led by Steve Rainey, will enter at eight-twenty P.M. with weapons and usher out the cleaning staff that arrives at eight. It will be a peaceful transition that should take three to five minutes. Right after the housekeepers exit, the second wave, led by Patrixia, will enter through all available doors to make the entrance speedy. The third and final wave will be composed of the rear guard, people like Magdalena Grace, who will be our timekeeper from her post at the switchboard of Wyndam-Allyn. Yes, Maggie. That's you. Close your mouth." Everybody looks at me blushing and they laugh.

"After Maggie is in, we seal the building."

"What's Maggie's job?" Trixia asks, sounding like a jealous little girl.

"She'll contact each dorm captain. Here is the list." She hands it to me. "And she'll give the word to leave the dorm through windows and side entrances unobserved, quietly. There are cars assigned, bringing supplies. Maggie will give the signal. Our Lieutenant Uhura will say, '*Uhuru*' Swahili for 'freedom,' to each dorm captain and the dorm captains will pass the message to the brothers and sisters in each dorm. All right? If something goes awry, the Central Committee will contact Lieutenant Uhura, who will call each dorm captain and say, '*Tutaonana*' meaning 'See you later.'"

272

We don't like the second version. Leona begins to chant, "*Uhuru. Uhuru. Uhuru.*" And soon others follow, then everyone. It is a rhythmic wave sweeping through us, above and around us.

"You Negroes are crazy!" Yvonne throws up her hands.

"Be cool. Be cool," Cletus presses his hand down in front of him as if to press down our enthusiasm. "Yvonne isn't finished giving instructions."

"Thank you," Christmas continues. "You will each receive instructions from your wave captains. And your dorm captains will tell you how you each are to exit your dorms. Until then let's be compliant with this repressive probation and keep curfew and carry passes like good slaves. Keep on pushin, y'all."

Keep on pushin . . . Recently, I've fallen into a series of troubling, troublesome dreams from which I awake with racing heart and hysterical hair and eyes. At night I begin to anticipate these dreams in the way we Grace kids looked forward to *Shock Theatre* on Saturday nights. The host, Marvin, with the Coke-bottle-bottom glasses, a cross between Peter Lorre and Mr. Magoo. Marvin could also be the White twin of Russell Garner. He is famous on Blood Island, not only for being beaten up by the sheet crew. He is infamous for his one-hour-only visit to the Island in which he announced that love is all a chemical reaction. All feeling, said he, is composed of chemicals, and people might just as well be test tubes. Now I wonder what test tube shook him up. The boy is just goofy and tantalized and terrified by the chemical dream of life. I am too as I prepare for bed, sliding the Sears nightgown Mama gave me for Christmas over my head.

I love these dreams as I love the interesting fire in myself. Dreams are the violent mystery, the excitement of a Blackgirl-woman. At Eden I have grown more blasé as I refine my cynical air. I slip into the glittering costume of profanity. I cuss like a lime-mouthed sailor. Leona witnesses the evolution. She says it all began with *shit* first thing in the morning. The word forms with an impressive force that my lips curl back to sizzle out. I have been audience to the most artistic blue language all my life—rarely inside that house on Arbor Avenue, but all around it. It embossed the street. Zigzagging out of the mouths of men who worked on cars and chased buses. It flew in figure eights from women just up from the South who sat on stoops eating chunks of Argo starch out of blue and white boxes. It flew from the mouths of boys and girls coming home from high school with small, greasy brown bags of potato chips broken up and drenched in hot sauce in their hands. Later, the ice babies perfected the art, worked it into language acts that were battalions of contempt.

As the days of Eden have gone along I've progressed from that first *shit* in the morning to words that spiral with razors on their ends. These words were the costume I wore. Deep inside I felt nothing I could put my finger on. Nothing I could draw or trace. Until I began to dream furiously and luminously. After the planning meeting at Blood Island I dream more intensely.

First, the dream of Leona, Essie, and me walking in the most lush Technicolor garden. We sing and pick pretty flowers, flowers that turn to birds that tremble and fly away from us. Then I dream of my grandmother Sarah Mahalia Lincoln Dancer, smiling, then fire, then screams.

Second, the dream of standing on top of the administration building with the glass dome. I stretch out my arms and think I will fly. Then the most awful feeling of ineptitude as I flap my wings but do not move.

It is the third dream that is more than a fragment. It is a full-fledged scenario of chaos, taxing and wondrous to be inside. I can feel myself lifting in bed to observe it more keenly. It is like being inside Picasso's *Guernica* or a wonderful collage of printed papers, *Train Whistle Blues: I* by Romare Bearden, I recently discovered, and it blew me away. So many Black faces and significant shapes. It is that kind of dream. You want to be careful with every detail, juxtaposed, leaping out, pushing out against one another.

I am at the switchboard. Dressed only in my flannel Sears nightgown. The red flowers on the flannel like a spray of eyes watching me. A multitude of eyes. Madaddy gave me a watch with a slim black wristband. I'm wearing that too, in case someone calls and asks me the correct time. It is the middle of the dream in the middle of the night. I know this. Martha and the Vandellas are singing, "Calling out around the world / Are you ready for a brand-new beat? / Summer's here and the time is right for dancing in the street."

I see Aunt Silence and she puts her finger to her lips, shushing me, as if I might spill a secret, then I am still connected to Aunt Leah-Bethel and answering another line at the same time. "What's happening?" I only say once, not twice like Steve Rainey, when a voice from my childhood answers. It is Eddie who is dead. "Maggie, when you gonna learn to fight? You fight like a doggone girl. Girl, you the worstest fighter on Arbor. When you gonna learn to fight? When you gonna let me learn you? Huh, Maggie, huh, Maggie, huh?"

"Eddie, you dead."

"Old stupid girl. I'm talking to you ain't I?"

In the dream I answer him. *"Can you see me?"*

"Clear as day. Fight, girl. Fight."

He won't talk anymore. Puts somebody else on the line to mess with me. The dream deepens into chaos. The wires are spun around my hands like the vines that grow around Wyndam-Allyn. When they're creeping across my chest and I can barely breathe, much less call out, comes a voice gentle and confident, deep as the river that runs not too far from Mimosa, where I was born. "When this world ends, a new one begins." Then that voice slips away and I am scrambling through the wires trying to come up with it again and I get only fragments as the dream disintegrates. Malcolm X says, "Even pigeons come home to roost." And I think I hear pigeons sounding like their voices are trapped and beating against a wall in their throats and bouncing back and back. The pigeons are in cages dying, fumbling. Someone says, "Send your brother to Vietnam. Kill two birds with one stone." Pigeons.

Now that voice, resonant and buoyant and sweet. "When this world ends a new one begins." And Martha and the Vandellas, "All we need is music, sweet music, there will be music everywhere."

Now I am sitting in a classroom while still at the switchboard and the professor is looking at me. "Miss Race, why weren't you in class last week?"

I snap awake. It's 7:15. A slow evening, as the new campus revue has opened at the auditorium. And I have traded places with Maureen. Sorenson's still out as we knew she would be. No one has called to say the word *Tutaonana*. I have calls to make. I begin to call each dorm. To leave the signal. I simply say the word *Uhuru*. I can see them in my head. Black students pouring out of their dorms carrying blankets and supplies. Stealthily. At last Wyndam-Allyn. I call Trixia, who is dorm captain. They wave to me as they sneak past the outside window, hurrying. Leona, quick as lightning, brings my stuff, and I leave the desk and follow them. Our noses black in the darkening air. Our backs straight as ironing boards. We walk. Then we run. The Finance Building is open to us, opened by Lydia Rushing, who has hidden in the women's washroom since 4:45 in the afternoon, who has spontaneously sprouted an Afro. We are taking over. We are taking this damn building.

I enter into an open lobby space with a bank of six teller windows to the right. I walk to the back with my pillow, blanket, purse, and shopping bag of supplies: Kotex, apples, bananas, toothbrush, toothpaste, lotion, washcloth, soap, deodorant, clean underwear (three sets). In the back is a large office space made larger by moving the desks up against the walls. Three windows look out onto a side street. Past this large room are the mail room on one side and a small kitchen on another. At the end of the hall is an employee lounge with four round tables and four or five chairs at each table. There are two sofas and three vending machines in the lounge.

On the second floor of the Finance Building that we have taken over are office rooms and conference rooms. People have spread out throughout the building, a brother at every window and door. Essie has placed her bag in a room upstairs to reserve us a space for privacy and Leona has placed her bag in the common room on the first floor where the action is so that we can be in on the action when the deal goes down. The Central Committee meets in the employee lounge.

The Central Committee is escorting the cleaning staff, a Blackwoman in her forties, her hair in a French roll and gold defining her eyetooth, medium weight, and a Blackman in his sixties, drawn up and salt-and-pepper hair, both of them saying, "Just because we talking about a strike, you don't have to." "Don't mess up your good thing now." I am settling in the common room when Steve Rainey tells the woman, "You do what you have to do. We're doing what we have to do."

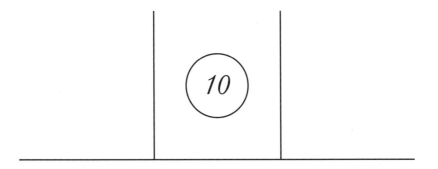

This Is Dedicated to the One I Love

Russell Garner wears glasses, which isn't unusual. Since we are the smart kids from our "inner city" public or private high schools, given as a rule to reading in the dark, reading fine print, and squinting into microscopes and at movie screens, many of us wear glasses at some time or another. But Russell's glasses—not the lightweight wire rims that are the utilitarian, spare fashion—are platforms of glass encased in plastic frames heavy as mahogany. They reflect his eyes out at us, huge, grotesque, and awesome. He is in love with stars, and Leona says with those goddamn glasses he can see clear across outer space, penetrating deeper than light. We don't know whether he is nearsighted or far, we just know he has no vision. He is all big head and glasses, like a boy epistemology student I fell in love with once at a high school dance.

Steve says Russell looks like Tweety Pie, the big-headed, big-eyed canary who is always being chased by a salacious cartoon cat named Sylvester who sprays spittle when he talks.

"I thought I thaw a puddy tat," the tweetering Tweety Pie exclaims. And Steve mimics Russell in that voice.

"You did thee a puddy tat. You did. A big, bad cat. He's a Black Panther." William and Steve divvy up the lisped lines of Sylvester and their own responses.

Sometimes they call Russell "the Martian" because he is a student of stars. Russell is the only Black student in the astronomy department ever. He majors in astrophysics. He is one of five undergraduates, Black, in the Eden University McAffrey Institute of Technology. There are seven or more continental African graduate students in Tech. Leona says they come to Eden to remember how to build bridges and roads, and skyscrapers that glisten in the African sun and lock the African heat inside the windows that do not open. They learn how to build airplanes that swing and throb through the sky like bees without wings.

Leona repeats what I. B. K. Turner says his teacher, a stoop-shouldered Mason with a basement apartment full of books and papyri in ancient languages, told him. "The Africans will come here to remember the technical mysteries they brought up the Nile with them to Egypt, which was then the crown of Africa." Because Professor Turner won't be here long (he's just visiting), Leona wants to remember all that he tells us. So she repeats it. I listen as if I hadn't heard it before in class.

Leona is one of the five Black undergraduates in Tech. She studies physics with Steve Rainey and Russell Garner. "Russell is sweet," she says by way of his defense against blood censure. Steve says he's sure Russell is sweet as any big-headed bird who doesn't know what he sees. I align with the underdog (in this case underbird) and say Tweety Pie always defeats the cat. Steve says nothing. It is Steve who chides Russell most scornfully. This is a puzzle, for between William and Steve, of all the brothers, Steve is the one with the empathetic heart.

Now some chord of sympathy is pulling me to Russell Garner, who's sitting in a corner behind his big glasses. I open my mouth and start talking: "Professor I. B. K. Turner says there are West Africans who live in cliffs, who are kind to dogs because they owe them this debt for finding water during a terrible drought, who can see stars no one else can see with even a high-powered telescope. They can see these stars with their naked eyes. Do you know them?" I feel gangly trying to talk to Russell so I start off in a rush. Russell looks up from his book. Looks at me as if he's trying to remember what planet he saw me on last.

"I never heard of them," the Martian says with no regret.

"Oh." I shift from foot to foot, tasting foot in my mouth. I feel that dumb talking to him. Then he begins to tell me about the birth of the universe. The Big Bang. It sounds revolutionary, so I listen with interest. Russell bobs a little when he talks. He bobs on about the birth of the universe of matter, which was born as the temperature of everything dropped ten to the eighteenth power degrees. "In that moment"—he bobs like a lively electron—"at the moment of the great coming together, energy turned cold and slowed to matter."

I sip my canned tomato soup out of a Styrofoam cup, shiver, and ponder the cosmic cold. Russell's raw-boned features have stretched into animation. His eyes on fire do not warm me. Steve saunters by and drops his olive army jacket over my shoulders. He is not in love with me, in spite of that kiss. There have been no other kisses between us. Steve doesn't want anything from me. He is kind.

Russell watches me shrugging into the warm corners of Steve's coat. There are stars in his eyes. In those big glasses he can see a planet light years away tremble and die, and he must grieve until those eyes turn small as peanuts. He is different, but now I know why Steve can't stand him.

"Why must you always take your intelligence so far from home?" I ask him.

"Who are you to tell me where to live?" He chuckles and the glasses lift a little above his eyes until I can see how really small they are, then the glasses slip down onto the bridge of his nose. "I have as much right to the universe as any man. Because my configuration of atoms combined into molecular structures that produce a deeper skin shade is no rational reason I should be deprived of full intellectual inquiry. We're all an orderly amalgam of atoms. Why don't mine add up to the right to be curious about something other than the color of my skin which is as much a chemical accident or whatever as any man's skin color is purely physical phenomenon."

I can feel cold air go in and out my open mouth. All I can get out is "Why are you here?"

He waits awhile. Air rushes between us emptily. I know what he says next is a lie.

"I was curious." He clears his throat, pushes his glasses more securely onto his nose.

"That's not a good enough reason to kidnap a building, Russell. Why are you here if you don't believe in it?"

He smiles vacantly and looks around the room through those glasses, looking the way an old man looks who has retired and come back to see how the people who still work there are getting on without him.

The Martian throws back his big, close-cropped head and laughs, adjusts his out-of-style horn-rimmed glasses. "In some ways I'm in wild pursuit of comets which only leave tails in the sky, and those too disappear soon. And then it is all forgotten, maybe talked about every now and then, in the next hundred years or so." He glances around him again, laying his looming eyes on Yvonne Christmas, Cletus the Elder, William, Steve,

Leona, Essie, Johnnie Mae, Rhonda, Broadway Bill—then back to me. His gaze is full of fascinated pity.

I had come bearing sympathy for the outcast. "Curiosity killed the cat, Russell, and birds ain't above being killed by it either. That's why what happened to you happened to you where it happened to you." Those doggone stars he loves so much got him beat up on the lake.

"Excuse me," Russell says and all the while the phrase turns backward, like he hadn't asked to be excused but was dismissing me and everything that had happened to him on the earth of Eden.

"Kiss my comet tail, Russell." I aim for his eye, hoping he does what he does. Flinch away, afraid of getting hit—again. I swish away and Russell pushes up his glasses and looks after me curiously searching for whatever he searches for.

We sit around with open books in our laps, but the books have no allure and life is a siren.

Yvonne Christmas sails out of the employee lounge cum Heart Headquarters like a cruise ship hung in a painting, beautiful and bright with lights. "I want it on the record that I was against the guns. We don't need them to reach an agreement," she says coldly to the space over her shoulder and the closing door. So Yvonne Christmas is in charge of lunch preparation now. Good sisters assist. Christmas is telling us like it was in the days of the Freedom Riders and the marches and sit-ins before. Yesterday seems a thousand years before, a great slab of ice separating ages.

"How does it feel to have a water hose turned on you?" Essie has imagined this.

"Not like water. Hits you like a ton of bricks. I was holding hands with a brother who was picked up by a jet of water and slammed against a tree. Hurt his spine." Christmas is shaking her head and spreading Peter Pan peanut butter on brown Muslim bread. I spoon strawberry or grape jelly onto other slices. Leona puts the sandwiches together.

"What did you feel inside?" Essie is relentless, her hand steadily stirring raspberry Kool-Aid and sugar in the big plastic container. Her eyes do not leave Christmas. They keep asking.

Yvonne breaks Essie's probe with a quiet command. "Add crushed pineapples and O. J. to that." Yet Leona and I want to know what it feels like too, so Leona opens the pineapples and I pour O. J. into the Kool-Aid. Essie goes back to staring at Yvonne Christmas, who begins to cut beautiful red apples into wedges like cutting apples is the most intricate task, a delicate surgery requiring vast skill and imagination. Yvonne doesn't look at us. She talks, instead, to the tabletop, as if it can understand such stoicism better than me. And we become quiet as wood, knowing then she can tell it.

"I peed on myself when the dog came at me. It was not pleasant, little sisters, to soil yourself. It was humiliating. That's what it was. Humiliating. It's like a rough baptism when the water hits you and everybody else, but you keep on coming even if your feet are running away. Your spirit keeps on coming. And we did." She looks up then from the table slick with apples' juice, scattered seeds. "Remind me to show you my dog-bite scar."

Broadway Bill has turned on the music and the Supremes have come in with us, all plaintive, happy alive, pleading, "Baby, baby, baby, don't leave me . . . Baby, baby, where did our love go? And all your promises. Don't you want me no mo . . ." Then the music goes a little dusty with the Shirelles' "Dedicated to the One I Love":

Life can never be
Exactly like we want it to be
I can be satisfied
Knowing you love me
There's one thing I want you to do
Especially for me
And it's something that everybody needs.
Each night before you go to bed, my baby,
Whisper a little prayer for me, my baby,
And tell all the stars above
This is dedicated to the one I love.

I wonder who I will love and dedicate my prayers to.

The phone rings and Broadway cuts the music down. Steve Rainey answers; everybody in the room watches as his face screws up.

"Who is it, Little Stevie?" Of course, that's Christmas because she calls Steve Little Stevie as in Wonder. "If it ain't someone with some power we can negotiate with, hang up," she tells him.

Steve acts like he doesn't hear her. He makes his voice deeper, meaner, more mannish. "It's just some White fraternity boys with miniature dicks talking about they got guns for niggers." This part is loud for the benefit of us in the room and the callers on the other end of the line. What follows is mouthed directly and quietly into the receiver. "You come in here with those guns and we'll blow you right back outta here with cannons. You like bleeding?"

"Cut it short, Rainey," Cletus snaps, and Steve does what Cletus means. He hangs up.

We all sit and look at one another for a while. Air sits in my chest. I can't see anybody breathing. Then it's as if somebody has said, "That's it," because Cletus, William, Steve, and some other brothers go into the little room to the side and come out with the meanest guns I've ever seen.

Thus far my experience with guns has been minimal. My daddy brought a German Luger home from the War with him. It's got a long snout like a Doberman pinscher, like Calypso, the albino terror, painted a steely black. The sight of the gun made our hearts turn to stone and our eyes jack open like full moons with dark centers. My daddy's gun was the announcement of celebration. On New Year's Eve he stood on a kitchen chair and reached way to the back of the top closet shelf and brought it out. He'd sit on the side of his bed, not the same side he sat on to play his harmonica, whistling and cleaning the souvenir gun. Loading it with bullets. Counting as he loaded.

The gun had more chambers than a heart. He filled each one with a bullet that looked silver to us. Littleson said he was killing werewolves. And Mama said shooting up in the air like that, the bullets had to come down somewhere sometime and probably hit somebody. My daddy whistled some more and went out the door to the back porch. We watched in the doorway, letting the cold air in, breathing seeable cold, as one year went to sleep and another one got up. Madaddy would stand with his legs apart and, whistling uneasily now through his teeth, lift his right arm over the balcony. Standing in the same spot my mama stood in to call us home to dinner. Shadows would fall back and down from around his arm, and his sleeve would penetrate the cold and the blackness of midnight. He aimed over the porch railing. Then he'd stop his whistling and squeeze the trigger. Fire sneezed out of the snout of the Doberman pinscher gun, a greedy snort. And my daddy would take up his whistling again after waking up the new year and killing the old one.

When the brothers bring in the long rifles and the short guns, I know for sure we are watching the birth of a new time. And some season is about to die.

Steve parts the window blinds on one side; William parts them on the other.

"Who's out there?"

"University police."

"What they doing?"

"Nothing."

"Are they coming in on us or are they gonna talk?" Leona asks what everybody wants to know. That's her way. It has been twenty-three hours since the takeover, and we are well into our roles.

"Are they going to meet our demands?" Oakland whines. Whining's her way or bluffing. Whining with men. Bluffing with women.

"If we stand firm," Steve reassures her, just like her whining asked for.

"I think it's time for culture," William announces from the window. Still looking outside out of the corner of his eye.

I am on the Culture Committee, and I know the program is ready. Camille called Hamla will come out from the little room where the guns were, where she has changed into her other-worldly poet's regalia. She assumes another persona. Somber faced under a severe *gelée*, in jeans and print dashikilike top, she reads love poems to her Blackman, which is most amazing because everybody knows Camille called Hamla doesn't have a man. (A whole lot of us don't.) She has poems though. And brothers who at a dance or casual encounter wouldn't look at her pretty brownness twice fall in love with the poem reader. They

287

yearn for her voice to wrap around themselves. Her voice is pretty and warm, soft but loud enough to touch each corner of the room.

> *In the twilight*
> *I follow you as you stand*
> *With the long spear*
> *In your hand.*
> *My heart is open*
> *To you and Africa.*
> *I follow in the footsteps*
> *Of both of you,*
> *Trusting where you lead.*

Camille is Hamla now. As Camille she is everyday sister. Nothing spectacular, the brothers would say, putting her in or on just above the beast category. That's the way I've heard they separate the sisters and classify us for further exploration. I'm a beast to most, but for two or three votes. I am a darker shade of brown. I'm like Hamla—she writes about her wonderful warrior; I draw mine over and over again. Thinking once I have his face just right he will appear.

Now Hamla weaves a transformation spell. And we sisters look again at the brothers—hair and wrinkled army surplus jackets—standing sentry, and plotting strategy at the blackboard. Now they are our African warriors.

> *In the night*
> *We lie down in the grasses*
> *Of our ancientness*
> *And sleep the sleep*
> *Of the peace of victory.*

I mark your weight on my thighs
And I hoard your seed
In me.
Tomorrow I will blossom Black and
So Beautiful.
Black man
In the night whispering victory.

Hamla smiles shyly while applause cracks all around like a crop of thunder. William looks out the window; car lights come through near his shoulder. The people outside want to know what the noise is about.

William waves his hand and we all get quiet, torn between the poem and the light from outside. Now every heart is beating for love and anxiety. Adrenaline is high and every mood is urgent. Now this love Hamla read-sings about is the only thing we have, besides the guns no one really wants to use.

Four brothers who have dubbed themselves "The Prognosticators" sing the Impressions' "Keep on Pushing" with only finger-snapping guiding the a capella song.

Now look a look (Look a look)
A look a yonder
A what's that I see?
A great big stone wall
Stands there ahead of me . . .
Keep on pushing.

So we sit here and try to be revived while the brothers parade around with ugly guns. We push against fear, against the university police outside, against the Eden fathers who haven't yet asked us why we're holding their building hostage, against our parents who will say, "I didn't send you to no college to raise a ruckus and act a fool and get expelled." Most of all we push against our self-serving dreams of being the ones who are singled out and rewarded for keeping quiet and stomaching the abuse that has come with privilege.

Barrington Childress puts his lips to his horn and we groan mercy inside. He isn't like the indigo-garbed musicians of Great Zimbabwe. No indeed. The eagerness and defeat in his face as he strains to play provokes pity and shame. Yet he keens and pitches, jumping up and down like a man in the middle of mass murder. He spins around, then he looks like a boy in the middle of a tantrum, and his horn sounds like a noisy child who hasn't been raised right. He's not John Coltrane or Pharaoh Sanders, who plays so fiercely his irises roll up into his brain while we watch the whites of his eyes.

Leona and I won't look at each other; we look at Essie who sits with her legs twisted in a lotus position and her mouth twisted in a grin.

After the tantrum is over we all sing "Lift Every Voice and Sing" ("The Negro National Anthem"). We women place our right palms over our hearts and pour everything in us into the song. The men hold tightly to the weapons. The music is one glistening stream of sound, mellifluous and tangled. We sing as loud as we can so the men outside with more guns will hear us and think we are too beautiful to shoot. As if such sound could stop the downward thrust of the billy club. Or make the walls of Eden come tumbling down.

Essie, Leona, and I grab our pillows and some Kool-Aid. We take to the stairs and the small upper office rooms. As soon as the door clicks, we start in on nothing, trying to be normal. Leona looks out the window. Essie chooses Barrington to chew on.

That's easy. He can't play a horn, but he can play women. We act like this is the most important conversation in the world.

"Childress is such a dog," Essie sneers prissily.

"William ain't?" edgy Leona goes in with a needle.

"William doesn't try to rip off anybody."

"He doesn't have to try. He does."

"William doesn't talk to everybody the way Barrington does."

"Give him time. He'll get around to it," Quick Stick Leona says, arching her eyebrow. She sips her drink now. And I suffer for Essie who looks thin as a thread now. Her voice sounds all wispy when she says, "So you want William to be with Rhonda?"

Leona looks stubborn because I guess she can feel my eyes on her, telling her to stop. "He's back with her, isn't he?"

It's true. Now that we are in the building, Rhonda and William are back together. I don't know how it happened. I can't look at Essie.

When I do, I look out of the corner of my eye. All the air is out of her body and her eyes glint like threads spinning.

Nobody is saying anything when Trixia bursts in without knocking. She looks at each of our faces, lifts a hand in a half-hearted greeting, then she backs out with a dopey grin on her face. Repelled by the tight texture of the air in our little conference room.

"My mama told me familiarity breeds contempt. Trixia is pretty familiar," I declare to declare war on somebody outside the three of us. I don't care about Trixia's nosiness. I don't care. I'm just tired of waiting. Waiting on everything. I've run out of fingers and toes to count the hours on. Next I go to the hairs on my head. I could come out of this building bald. The siege is not like *The Battle of Algiers*. "I just don't like him playing with your feelings like this," Leona tells Essie. Leona's still got that stubborn look on her face, but now it's not so hard. As if protecting Essie's vulnerability were the way she could protect her own. She picks up Essie's Kool-Aid cup and drops it in her own. I'm at the window now, looking out at the campus security cars lined up like a phalanx of dragons. I'm the first to see the TV truck pull up.

Hamla is singsonging her much requested "Black Man–Woman Poem."

> *Musical key, you unlock the universe*
> *Until I sing your song.*
> *Pharaoh, you have chosen me to sit*
> *Beside you as Black Queen and we rule*
> *Each other's hearts.*

"Oh, wow!" Leona exclaims as we swagger down the steps. "Oh, wow" is hip to say. It is past boredom, past surprise, past hurt, and past longing. It is super cool, not like "right on" which is too much in the middle of things. So passionate it's embarrassing. And the White kids are saying it now.

"Right on!" Rhonda shouts back at the poet.

"Oh, wow!" Essie echoes Leona.

I am last in the line of three women on the stairs. I stand here awhile surveying the large common room. The scene looks like this: two women with *gelées* on their heads bend to clean a coffee urn; three men and one woman like two prints of Hale Woodruff's *Card Players,* cubed countenances and insouciant grace of figure, play an animated game of bid whist; two pre-med students at a blackboard mull a chemistry equation; four men sit at a table counting bullets; one woman sits crocheting a red, black, and green floppy hat for her boyfriend; Hamla sits on a stool staccato chanting her Black love poems while Royal Thomas beats the drum poised between his thighs and Zipporah Handy blows extended kisses into a flute. It is sweet, the blending of flute, drum, and voice. Voices flow through the building and I tilt my head to listen to the activities in upper rooms and backrooms. In small rooms men are cleaning and recleaning guns while caressing thoughts of firing them and trembling a little inside. Women and men squint and frown into huge textbooks while their minds wander across blank, white pages of possibilities. Marvin Gaye and Tammi Terrell swear above their heads, "Ain't nothing like the real thing, baby," back and forth, the male voice and female voice in a unison that diverges, then swells together again.

In another room, women prepare soup and sandwiches in a makeshift kitchen area. And in yet another the Heart—the Central Committee of FBO—goes over the university's options and possible responses.

From a far upper room the smell of marijuana drifts down; then the smell shifts into incense. I listen deep and deep and a sighing grunt and whimper escape from a last, unmarked room. Everything, now, crowds into my eyes, clamors and careens. I know if I could listen harder I could hear every heart beating in quick steps.

It's hard to remember how we got here. And I guess we all came by different routes anyway, so even if I can follow memory like scattered bread crumbs back to a kind of beginning that would only be one road. Maybe too all the roads begin at some like place where each of us was betrayed, sent out from our dream of paradise or Eden with a few bread crumbs in our hands.

Russell Garner, even if he won't admit it, sat looking up to his little bit of basically black sky, tracking his stars on the lakefront, when his point of view changed. After that night he moved a little closer to the rest of us. Sat in a corner of Blood Island one winter afternoon, watching the race of snowflakes to the ground. Still some evenings I've seen him stealing loving glances at the sky, in the middle of FBO meetings. And I know he sits with new fear and even newer bravery on the observatory steps in the thick cold of night. Now, when he haunts the windows of our ransomed building, I'm not sure if he is just checking out police cars or stealing a glimpse at his heart's desire.

Lydia Rushing is Eden's first Black Homecoming Queen. Not the queen of Black Homecoming, but queen of them all. Her golden, heart-shaped, freckled face shimmering from the front page of the *Eden Daily* and the two "major" newspapers of the City, and the Black daily newspaper that usually headlines murders too insignificantly colored to be news to anyone but the also insignificantly colored. (Eddie's death made page three: BOY BEATING VICTIM DIES OF LINGERING INJURIES.) Lydia Rushing's smiling face could be cut down to locket size and carried around as my brother Lazarus does.

The last morning in Mimosa when I sat with Grandmama Patsy, Aunt Silence, Aint Kit, and Cousin Bay around the dining room table, it was chatter about Lydia Rushing's victory that held the disappointments down. My relatives could set the cut flowers of their dreams in the waters of Lydia Rushing, and the pretty blooms lived throughout the morning.

But Lydia is only Lydia to herself. And her story is the one that drives her. Her crowning and the applause, warm and congratulatory on that cold evening, the hand shaking of the officials, the bouquet of roses fat and red like healthy hearts on slim, stiff green veins, the crackle of her silvery white dress as the cold hit the material, the wet seeping through her open-toed Cinderella pumps as she stomped through the new rain, rain crystals on her eyelashes, her hands and feet wet cold, her flowers smothered in frost, on the way back to the dorm, unescorted after the coronation.

How could I ever tell the women of Mimosa, Mississippi, that part of the story? They wouldn't be surprised. And their lack of surprise would be a measure of their hurt. And then I would hurt more and suck on the dry misery of the defeat like the last bread crumbs in Lydia Rushing's journey to this building. It sits in my throat. Lydia Rushing has a successful modeling career now, in spite of the reality of that evening. But what will the designers and stores that use her image say when she appears with her bouquet of red hair? What will they say when it is clear she has participated in the taking of the Finance Building?

Maybe Essie's way is the definitive path. After all it was her story that propelled us here.

Maybe Essie's way is the definitive one—a road populated with grotesques, monsters, half men. We can point to her landmark and follow the furies that sprout there for us.

My way, as usual, was the dreamy one. The night after the attack on Essie, before the meeting where we planned the takeover, the leaders called an emergency meeting of FBO. It began as they all begin. With "The Negro National Anthem," written by James Weldon Johnson more than half a century ago. "Lift every voice and sing till earth and heaven ring," we sang that night under tumbling, uncombed Afros, as if the words had been burned in our throats, in our hearts, upon our birth in Eden.

That night—caught up in the swelling heart of trouble, chaotic and huge—lifted us to the edge of weeping. "The Negro National Anthem," which we rename "The Black National Anthem," was ragged that night, the way we sang it shot with panic and compulsion. Not like and yet so like that time I sat with Silence in a small church and watched angels bathing in the pool of sunlight under the pulpit of that church that was also the center of the voter registration drive: something rides the air. I could not then in that old, rugged church believe in Aunt Silence's unrequited love of the place she dreamed as America. I could believe in only us that night on Blood Island as we sat on the edges of our seats. Like notes that have just jumped out of the singer Nina Simone's raging, dark, and opulent throat—young, gifted, and Black. And angry.

Professor I. B. K. Turner said nothing is new under the sun, including the way we felt, and the way we'd gathered. He didn't say much more when Yvonne Christmas, who was facilitator of the meeting, called on him to speak. He said that this meeting was an indignation meeting. African people are good for indignation meetings. Because we love to be indignant, and there's so much to get indignant about. Such writhing takes the weight off; we don't have to do anything about the situation. Except talk. It is marvelous theater.

He delivered his comments in a mild lilt that maddened us all. We got more indignant. Hating the way he made us feel and not understanding why we felt so small, and so gauche and gawky in our fury.

I. B. K. Turner has that effect on us. He is our history. Along with Leo Hansberry and Chancellor Williams, Turner is a pioneer in African history. We think Eden is sorry they borrowed him for this year from a Negro university in the Northeast where he is hidden away in the dusty library. He is more than history; he's mission. He tells us to forget his titles and names. Remember his initials stand for "I Be Krazy Too." He tells us this silly joke one day, then he giggles like a six-year-old. He is sunny when we are cynical. Because he's not made peace with the world, but with himself. He is an old-time renegade. A gentle man who loves to stay at home with a good book, loves to while away the hours decoding hieroglyphics, reconstructing the transformation of

Egyptian ideographs to Yoruba words, marveling at the continuous way of culture to live inside people. But he has spent, he says, a third of this life in meetings.

When we visited him at his home, his wife of fifty-five years scolded him. He had forgotten to comb his hair. He had a head full of hair, silvered and willful. He slid his glasses from his nose to his hairline, touched his hairline, and forgot about hair because he'd found some book he'd been meaning to call to our attention. George Padmore's *Pan-Africanism or Communism* or W. E. B. Du Bois's *The Souls of Black Folk,* or David Walker's *Appeal,* or Linda Brent's *Incidents in the Life of a Slave Girl.* He poured me a cup of tea and stirred in sugar cubes and heavy milk, in the British style. The cup was dainty, its rim gold. The gold was cool against my lips. He watched me sip. I spilled nothing, and this seemed to please him. Then he addressed me most seriously. "I will tell you about languages now because painting is a kind of language. How language bends the mind and seduces the heart. Magdalena, four hundred Africans were taken from the Gold Coast, two hundred died en route. Two hundred slaves arrived at Annapolis. How many Africans remained?"

I knew his traps by then, so I said, "Four hundred Africans taken. Two hundred Africans died en route. Two hundred Africans arrive."

Pleased laughter animated him. His glasses leapt off his forehead, clattered to the floor. He looked at the twenty or so students without them. Squinting keenly I think he saw our brain cells struggling to keep up with his.

"Think of it then," he exhorted, stretching his arm out, then snatching it back. Jumping a little in place. "How long does it take to transform an African into a Negro thing? By what process does this occur? What are the implications of this transformation for us here and now? Is there an antidote? How do words guide our perceptions? Is the idea of slavery more palatable when it happens to Negro slaves and not to African people? Is this language the guardian of reality? Or is it courier to the lie? Is there an antidote?" He laughed that day, delighted with his questions.

That day the lesson was language, pejorative and mercenary. The night of the meeting we realized after he'd left us to spoil in our hot tempers that the best words could turn back on you and rot you if you didn't live them. We decided to do something.

I think that's really how we got here.

Yet I know that in some way I arrived by dream. After the meeting, we went back to our dorms and met some more. All the Black students in each dorm all gathered in one room in each dormitory. Talking way into the night. The Whitegirls fell strangely quiet around us, seeing or sensing some new lucid sparks leaping out of our nappy heads and our snappy eyes. In the halls or bathrooms they crept along the walls because they knew we were looking for somebody to look at us cross-eyed.

Once we'd shouted all the talk out of our heads, we stumbled to our rooms and our beds. My body was tense and sore; my head pounded with plans. Things were out of my hands as usual; I could not shoo them from under my eyelids. Last month some junior Weathermen whom Eden officials hadn't caught yet burned down the ROTC building. Guns and rifles were missing. Half of the campus population got up in the middle of the night, threw coats over their shoulders, and went and danced in the meadow before the bonfire. I could still see the colors of fire on my eyelids. In the bottom bunk, in the room with Essie and Leona, I lay insomniac and flickering, flickering in the bones, like that fire. Until, worn out with my own self, at last blackness washed over me.

I dreamed of my grandmother, Mahalia Dancer, a dark woman with a good head on her shoulders when she wanted one. I think I dreamed her. I think she smoothed my brow and blew calm into my ear. She whispered, but I do not know what she said.

That is how I got here. I came by dream.

✦

Nothing happens during the night. We are still here; the police are still there, and Sherman has a tape recorder and he is going around the room collecting our reasons for being here. "This is dramatic stuff," he declares while he presses PLAY and RECORD simultaneously. "It's imperative that we record our revolution."

"What're you going to do with these tapes, Sherman?" Christmas asks.

"Hey, beautiful sister, I'm in this for the masses."

Christmas cuts through jive obfuscation. "Who're you selling them to?"

"Hey, just hold it now, Christmas. You got to get some understanding, my most beautiful Black sister. Money is not your enemy. Money is your friend."

"You act like money is yo mammy," Christmas says so drily everybody laughs.

"Money is his mama," Cletus chuckles. "They mint Negroes like Sherman in the United States Treasury." Cletus says this in that easygoing way men have of talking bad about one another.

"You can say whatever you want about me. Cause I know you had to come get me to be treasurer of this little chicken-butt organization. Cause I respect the cash. I give it to you straight, don't I?"

"What you going to be when the revolution comes, Sherman, a mortician?" another brother asks.

"Whatever's fair," Sherman shrugs.

Christmas is looking at him coolly. "If you cut a deal with the wire services, Sherman, that money goes to the organization."

"Listen," he touches his tape recorder. "This is mine. The tapes are mine. The mike is mine. And the labor is mine. The goddamn questions are mine—"

"And the risk is ours collectively—so you can't—"

"Woman, don't tell me I can't—"

"Hold it down," Cletus snaps. "You see what even the promise of money is doing?"

"You'd better tell Mr. Bloodsucker leeches went out of style centuries ago," Christmas is snarling.

"Aw, you're just mad cause none of you thought of it." Sherman sounds dopey now. Like a little snot-nosed kid who knows he's done a bad thing.

"Let's talk about this like family members. Civilized." Cletus sounds so reasonable, even though everybody should know family members aren't civilized with one another. That's why they invented company manners and hospitality, so as not to subject others to the barbarism of intimacy.

Christmas wraps her arms in front of herself. "He's a step-brother to me. And money is his mammy and she ain't never done right by me, except to exploit."

Sherman looks tired and annoyed. "Why don't you go make yourself useful, Yvonne. Rustle the warriors up some sweet soul food so the brothers can make some decisions."

"Hey, hey, hey, hey, now"—Cletus jumps in, cutting Sherman off. Laying a hand on Yvonne to stop her launch toward Sherman.

After quiet negotiations, during which a major percentage of Sherman's fee from the news media is assigned to FBO, just as Christmas wanted, Sherman runs the tape and we each tell the stories that brought us to this building. I don't tell him about my grandmother, Sarah Mahalia Dancer. Somebody like Sherman would try to catch her to put her head on the *Ed Sullivan Show* and her body on the *Original Amateur Hour*, or all of her on *One Step Beyond*. I am reticent, yet ever listening, and I absorb more details of the disillusioning journey that ends and begins in this building.

"My name is Leona Cassandra Pryor. I am the only daughter of August and Valerie Stillson Pryor. My brothers are August the Second, and Weldon Pryor, Gus, and Donnie. My father is a restaurateur. A barbecue king. He always believed in being the best that he could be. He makes the best mambo sauce in the City. He's always excelled. But oddly enough my father had to sue to buy the house we live in. It was in a Caucasian neighborhood then. We won the suit; now the neighborhood is all Black. We're magicians, right? We can change streets from White to Black.

"I've always been interested in housing. Perhaps the housing difficulties of my family and my community added purpose to my natural inclination to love structures. I am a student of architectural design. That's what brought me to Eden University.

"Okay. How did I get in this building?

"I know I have earned my place in this university. I just want the administration and my fellow students, the Caucasian ones, and the people in this racist town to stop acting like they have to put up with the Whiteman's burden, namely me. I'm fed up with genteel White supremacists acting like I'm a bad joke they have to put up with. I'm tired of being ignored in classrooms. Getting a B instead of a well-deserved A. Tired of professors acting surprised when I talk in complete sentences. I'm tired of being a token, and knowing that there's the distinct possibility that after we have passed through this place, the doors will close again on the thousands of intelligent and talented Black youngsters in the City searching for a way into this American dream, which is at best a phantasm that our ancestors made substance out of their sweat, tears, blood, and confiscated labor.

"So. I'm sitting in this building until the fathers and mothers of Eden University will talk to us about opening up this environment and assuring us that there is truly a permanent place for Afro-Americans in this university structure. And until they do, I won't move."

✦

Katherine Pearl is home from her school in the City. She has gotten through on the Finance Building line after Eden University called the house for Madaddy to tell him, my legal guardian, I was a part of a student takeover and there could be serious consequences. It was before two o'clock when he left for work, so they got him as he was going out the door with his lunch pail in his hand. The Dinty Moore beef stew in a thermos in the lunch pail. My father shook his pail a little in annoyance to be delayed. Pearl has handed him the phone. My father sounds mean and angry. "Well," he says, waiting for me to explain my self-destructive actions.

"Some Whitemen tried to rape Essie," I choke out.

"They better not have," he says, relenting a little.

"They don't treat us right," I tell my daddy. "They treat us like niggers." I say that word that we are not allowed to say, the one we can get a whipping for saying. He knows what I mean. That puts him on our side.

"Don't let nobody treat you like no nigger," my father says. "Do I have to come and get you?" he asks stiffly. There is fear

302

and reluctance in his tone. He's not ready to give up the dream, the source of his brag: a daughter who is a student at Eden University, one of the great universities.

"They say you might lose one of your scholarships," he says.

"Which one?" I ask in spite of myself.

"Er, ah, that little one you got last," he sighs.

"The Breton?"

"Awww, yah, yah," he expels the sounds.

It's the smallest sum but the most prestige. Or so the university said in the letter bestowing it.

Katherine Pearl comes on the line. "You're breaking Mama and Madaddy's heart. You know that, don't you?"

"Why don't you go back to school?" I snap and hang up the phone.

The next call is from Essie's mother. A shaken Essie answers the phone with trepidation, after Rhonda who is in charge of the parent line calls her ever so sweetly to the phone. I can hear Fredonia Witherspoon yelling from where I am standing six feet away from Essie. "If your ass get expelled from that school you going to be babysitting for the rest of yo life. I promise you that." Click. Essie's eyes are huge like one of the sad-eyed urchins in a painting by a streetside artist. Fredonia, the artist. Rhonda looks pleasantly sympathetic. William is, after all, to paraphrase the Supremes, back in her arms again.

More mothers and fathers call, distraught, frustrated, furious. They have fewer demands than we do. They want to know why. They want to know how long. They want to know if we have lost our collective minds. Johnnie Mae gets off the phone with her mother. She has to leave the building now. No ifs, ands, or buts. NOW! She packs up her gold-edged overnight case and slips out of the hostage building through the side door. She puts her hands up like a criminal surrendering to the campus police. They let her go.

It is raining and I stand on the toilet to see outside, watching the downpour slant down to the lawns of Eden. The orderly grasses bend heavy with defeat.

Someone in a hurry taps on the bathroom door and I come out, tucking my top into the band of my jeans as if I had biological business in the solitude of that room instead of my labors of the heart. From where I stand I can see the room we are holding hostage: the men at the window, backs pressed to the wall like gangsters who won't surrender in old movies from the Depression, rifles hanging on their arms, pressed to their sides; cadres of women sitting cross-legged on the carpeted floor, rolling bandages for the wounds of a war that so far is only waiting, Leona and Essie rapidly typing and reproducing the demands that the Central Committee, the Heart, has drawn up in its sessions that seemed endless. The tick-tick of the typewriter scoring the Motown sound on the radio—the sound of young America. All the voices are Black.

I lean on the doorframe, sagging. All energy gone from me. Heavy apprehension pushing me from my focus. The low background of the rain amplifies into a swoosh that sends Essie's typewriter's tick-tick, Leona's mimeograph rumble, the Motown sound to the industrious rustle of ants on a mountainside. Insignificant.

"Hey, y'all," I holler to the room at large. My voice coming to my ears wide and light. Sagging on the doorjamb, I lean into the eyes that look at me. "How many ways can this story end?" A bold question for me. The rain is loud now.

Oakland, as Florence Nightingale, spins bandages into a fat ball. "It could be like the movies."

"Oh, shit." Leona groans at the mention of Hollywood, but one thing about us—we adore democracy.

"Let her finish," Roberto, who is not Latin, says, and Leona makes an acquiescent face. Grudgingly.

"Like in the movies," Oakland develops her scenario. "They throw in the canisters of tear gas and wait for the desperadoes to come staggering out, choking and stumbling. Then they gun every last one of us down."

We don't like that ending, so she changes it.

"Or they come through the fog of gas for us with their gas masks on. Anyway, the shit hit the fan and we splattered."

"They could just drop a bomb," Essie drops and keeps on typing.

"They're saving them for Southeast Asia," Yvonne Christmas now. "Not because they love us better than they love yellow people, but they love this building and their records. One day, however, they will invent a perfect bomb. It will annihilate people. Poof! And leave the real estate intact." We all laugh at the very idea.

Yvonne takes off her reading glasses. She breathes on them and wipes them on her sleeve, reminding me of one of the nuns of my childhood. "In my scenario," she continues, "they institute a blockade and nothing goes in or comes out of here."

"That's cool. We like to be to ourselves." Larry Clarkesdale from Harlem at the window.

Yvonne puts her glasses back on. Now she looks like a nineteenth-century schoolmarm from the North who has jour-neyed south to teach in freedman's schools. Her wire-rimmed glasses, her thick chestnut hair stretched back into a bun secured with a hundred wide-legged pins, a book open on her lap—I'm going to get her in pen and ink.

"They turn off the water and wait us out. They think that thirst or toilet stink will send us out. They don't know we brought our own water to drink and little store-bought washcloths to wipe across the funk." Yvonne's gaze is steady as Harriet Tubman's when she pulled that gun on that man and told him, "You keep on going or die." "We do have pots to pee in and do other stuff too. We empty them out of the window, if necessary." Everybody cracks up. I see turds sailing out the window. Gross.

"They turn out the lights and wait for us to get tired of fumbling in darkness. We don't curse the darkness; we have candles. They turn off the heat, we have blankets and pillows and thermal underwear. Their blockade, if they choose one, would last for weeks until we ran out of food and water. And then we'd turn this into a hunger strike and stay on until we fell out dehydrated and comatose one by one. That's how committed we are. That's how serious. This isn't child's play like they're telling one another it is. This is serious as a heart attack. We understand protracted struggle." She looks at each of us who will meet her blazing eyes. And her deadly glance is martial music superseding the girlish implorations of the Supremes on the box. We could come out of here on stretchers. For real.

God bless Leona who has the devil in her. She supplies the scenario of the last outrageous ending for our siege.

"They could put our parents on over the loudspeakers."

Everybody hoots, but Leona isn't finished. "And my mama will come on the airwaves and say she gone beat my butt if I don't come out of this building this very minute. And my daddy come on over the bullhorn (just like he needs one) and he says, 'Don't make me come in there after you.' Like I'm asking him to. Then they call in Johnnie Mae's mama and we'll all go running out of here like somebody stuck a lit firecracker up our behinds."

We are deep into laughter now, and I am more buoyant than I've been for days. I swing in the doorway, going and coming at once.

Serious Essie doesn't look up from her type tapping, though she smiles at the pages as if everything in this room pleases her. Finally, she says very matter-of-factly, "They could ask what we want and we could meet with the president and the deans and read our demands, then dialogue, and come to an agreement and sign a treaty of some kind."

"I hope some kind ain't the Indian kind." Roberto again.

"No. I mean a real victory treaty," Essie says confidently. She has everyone's ear because we know she was the last reason we are all here. The attack on her was the thing that made the hands fly off the clock and sent us into a new time.

"We could have everything we want," she says. "Black studies. Our own Black experience and its significant place in American history and culture explored and studied by us and others. Serious recruitment by the admissions office in so-called inner-city high schools, committed and community-oriented Black faculty like Dr. Turner, necessary financial aid for Black students, and respect and protection for Blackwomen on this campus."

Now all the brothers look embarrassed because she's said something they can't do and they believe they should be able to.

I know that what Essie said is everything we asked for in the document she and Leona are typing, but something rises in me and will not be still. I start talking. "I believe in what Essie said. I think we all do, deep down inside, or we wouldn't be here, but I think we want more." I don't know what I'm thinking until I say it so I stumble along, the words finding me. "Not every Black faculty member we get will be a Professor Turner. He teaches us how to think for ourselves. He gives us the example of a lived life. A life lived in a community, people believing in something, dreaming. Not cut off by the walls of the university. We want a place, a world, where nobody is treated like a *nigger*. Where Blackpeople are respected. Where Blackwomen are truly known as beautiful and treated beautifully. We want to be surrounded by beauty and what we need. We want what's ours, reparations for what we worked for and were never paid for. We want our forty acres and our mule. And we want the Indians, the ones left, to get their land back."

"Like a birthday present," someone interjects. Titters.

I don't stop. "If we keep on we could get equal opportunity and the redistribution of wealth with account of labor. We could call a halt to this war and war research and U.S. support of White supremacist governments in South Africa, Rhodesia, Angola, and Mozambique." I start to slow down as I realize so many eyes are on me, studying me. "We want to change the earth and the way things are for all people. Something good and decent for everyone." I didn't know I had it in me. I am breathing hard, nervous now that I have revealed too much of myself. I want more than a picket fence. I want more than Eden and that makes me sad in this moment. I just stand there, listening to myself breathe, looking at the mystified faces looking at me.

"Sister, you believe these Whitefolks going to get up off all that?" Roberto asks; there is real concern in his voice, not sure about the state of my mind. Before Roberto can get his question out good, Steve Rainey whirls on him like a crazy man. His jacket flaring open, so I catch a glimpse of a cartridge belt. "Goddamnit, that's why we're here, Roberto."

"For all that?" Roberto's mouth is open in surprise at the curious audacity of Steve and me. "Gee, I didn't know," Roberto says sarcastically. Sarcasm makes Steve madder and me sadder at the weight of all the injustices passed down to us.

"People don't always get what they ask for, Steve," I say in as noncommittal a tone as I can manage. I'm standing in the center of the doorway now. He's at the window where he's been glaring out.

308

"I'm so hip," he says in a language not like his usual. "They get what they take."

The air cracks like a blanket full of electricity we snapped between us. I let it lie. Because Steve is a mad dreamer and I want us all to be just like him. A little. But the fury flaring out of him has been directed at me for once. I guess my face looks like Steve Rainey just hit me. Hurt and stunned I guess I am, so Steve Rainey comes over to me, himself again, and puts a hug around me. When he releases me from the warm enclosure of his khaki-covered muscles, I slap him upside the head.

Steve lies down between Leona and me, and we are safe, while Essie shivers at my other side, longing for William who is lying in Rhonda's arms. Rhonda's breasts are pendulous, and Essie and I whisper about them.

"I don't know, Essie. It could be birth control pills or it could be—you know." We're afraid of birth control pills, the clots that float to the brain, the water gain, the freedom that the tiny pills buy. I watch Essie's eyes lock again on William reposed in Rhonda's pregnant or pill-bloated embrace. Essie sighs noisily and Steve sits up and looks across me at her. He doesn't say anything. Just looks and lies back down, fitting himself against Leona's back. Lying on his stomach, he flings one arm across Leona and the other across me, reaching until his fingertips touch Essie's arm. We three lie there blinking and silent, while Leona sleeps quietly as a tree on a windless, wingless night. Outside it is still raining.

I will remember this moment. The half light of silhouettes created by the light from the hall. I will remember the stirring and the pieces of whisper that rise from the bedclothes we took from the dormitories. All the blankets a gray green with beige Eden stamped on them. We stretch across the common room like palettes of wounded soldiers on stretchers. The swishing and rumpling of hair as we turn and toss on our makeshift beds interrupts the quiet, feeds it. The anonymous voices in the washroom where man and woman have gone to kiss and touch each other.

He says like someone trying to keep a secret, muffled, "Please."

She says pleadingly, "No, it's against the rules." Then she coos apologetically but seductively and promises him something sometime after the Revolution.

I relax against Steve's shoulder. He is trustworthy and kind, like Lazarus, my brother, whom I slept beside as a child before I knew about the red valley that separates women and men. Steve's shoulders, like Lazarus's, are wide as a bridge.

We are in the news. It is the third day of our siege and we gather around the radio and the black-and-white TV, neither much bigger than a bread box on the tabletop. If we weren't in this building we'd think they were talking about some other building, some other Black students. According to the news there are half as many of us here and our demands are double. We have asked, according to the news, for courses in soul food preparation, Brer Rabbit philosophy seminars, and James Brown as a significant literary giant. Somebody must believe the TV and radio; they keep reporting the same lies.

Yvonne reassures us. "Any news is good news," she says. "At least we're a matter of public record."

Nothing else in the news interests us much. Not the movement of the War, not the strike in Memphis, not the presidential campaign. To us, none of this is important. But believing this doesn't make it any easier being it.

Larry climbs through the back window with two shopping bags from Bee and Birdie's. He had been watching the campus police and knew when they snoozed or looked the other way. He slipped in and out of the building like the Holy Ghost that he was. Yvonne Christmas says that is so undisciplined to send out for eats during a state of siege. But since you got the hamburgers and the fries and the chicken wings we might as well eat. He says, "If I'm going to jeopardize my future as an attorney and be disowned by my daddy, I can at least have a full belly." We all, including Christmas, begin to eat, swallowing the lumps of our futures in our throats. She and Cletus the Elder Levergate have fellowships and future teaching positions at stake. The graduate students have made a choice, an adult decision. As usual, Essie, Leona, Hamla, and I begin to ask Christmas things. About her days with the Freedom Riders. Her days working voter registration in Mississippi.

"Maggie's from Mississippi," Essie volunteers.

"Who ain't?" Hamla says, a little jealously. She's been getting a lot of attention for her poems, and it feels so good she wants to keep it.

"I ain't from Mississippi," Leona says emphatically. "I was born right up under the wing of the Hawk."

"Me too," Essie says. Full of regret.

"I was born in Alligator, Mississippi," Hamla says wryly. Woman laughter, sweet and light. Alligator, Mississippi, is too funny.

"I swear," Hamla declares.

"Where in Mississippi were you born, Magdalena?" Yvonne Christmas asks me. She has not forgotten me who finds herself now shy in her presence.

"Mimosa," I clear the frog from my throat. "Mimosa. It's right in the Del—"

"The Delta," Yvonne finishes, "I know where it is. I worked voter registration down there, Freedom Summer. Beautiful people down there."

I tell her about my Aunt Leah-Bethel then. But she already knows her and has worked alongside her. I don't tell her we call Aunt Leah-Bethel "Silence." I am nervous with happiness. I dabble a french fry in a pool of ketchup like a thin paintbrush in a pot of paint. Yvonne glows on about my auntie.

"Uh-huh. I see it. You look like her. Got her color."

I beam.

"Miz Leah-Bethel is something else, girl. When those crazy rednecks fire bombed the house the first time, she went out on the porch with a shotgun. And blasted away. She fired that bad boy and the force knocked her back up in the house just barely out the line of fire when those crazies were shooting at her from the car. Of course, they came back later to finish the job, but she wasn't home."

"I heard about that," I say. Not saying too much more, because right now I don't want to get into the other part of my family. The legendary Mahalia. Part of me wonders, wants to know if Yvonne has heard of her too. Instead of asking I move to something safe. "Aunt Leah-Bethel makes beautiful quilts and doilies. She sends them to my mother."

"I know she's good with her hands. Passed it on to you, huh. I'll be," Yvonne exclaims. Yvonne sounds older now, like one of Mama's church friends. "That's so excellent, just excellent."

"She took up making stuff when she got sick after her low-down husband left her," I chatter on like a little girl with the grown folk's news.

"Sometimes you have to get sick in order to get well," Yvonne says. She looks up as Cletus the Elder comes into our little room. Her eyes looking up at him are soft. They make me want to cry and love somebody—like an old record by the Chantells, or Martha and the Vandellas singing "My Baby Loves Me."

Elder doesn't say anything to any of us. He doesn't say much to mere freshwomen anyway. Suddenly he squats and pokes into my pile of fries. Then he swirls one fat as a thumb in a pool of ketchup. Ketchup gets all over his wedding band. He looks at Yvonne and takes ten nibbles to eat one french fry. I look away and down, not meeting Essie's or Leona's or Hamla's eyes. I wipe my greasy fingers on my funky jeans and clear the persistent frog from my throat again.

I think my Aunt Silence would like Cletus the Elder Levergate. But my grandmamas, Patsy, or Mahalia, who is dead, would not approve of these transgressions of the flesh. Or would they?

I've been thinking of Aunt Silence and my grandmother Sarah Mahalia Dancer all day long off and on. I've been thinking of my two granddaddies in the colored graveyard near Mimosa and Letha. I know this time of year the crepe myrtle tree just outside my grandmother's (now Silence's) house is in a full pink flowering. My mind keeps going back to that spot in the road where my grandmother gave up the ghost and became ghost, beheaded and ambulatory. My mind keeps rushing back to that spot as if I had an appointment there.

Now Essie sits like an obedient daughter between Yvonne Christmas's legs, while Yvonne's fingers fly swiftly between the three strands that make up each of Essie's many bedtime braids. It is dusk and time for putting hair up. Yvonne says she likes to fool with hair. Hair. Hair. Hair. The race is obsessed with hair. "We worry more about hair than freedom," Yvonne says. She says if worse comes to worst she will go to cosmetology school and learn hair so she can open a salon in her kitchen. "I'd never be out of work," she jokes. "If we opened enough hair salons, we'd have full employment. We'd be slaves to hair. Lord, look down upon the heads of your children worried about the fur on their heads."

"She can talk," Hamla mumbles. "She's got a full head of hair. Ain't nobody ever reached over her to dance with a sister with a ton of hair on her head and can't dance."

Yvonne acts just like she doesn't hear. Maybe she doesn't hear because she's swung her neck sharply to look at the TV just as a special report breaks into the regularly scheduled program. She leaves Essie's hair half braided and half free.

The television man says Dr. Martin Luther King Jr. has been shot in Memphis. More details later. Then the news comes on the radio.

Suddenly, we're not the center of our universe anymore. There is a current that sweeps us all up at once, and nobody has to tell us to come to the television set. We're all around it. A crowd of us. The sound of the radio coming over our shoulders. Now television and radio saying the same thing. The Reverend Doctor Martin Luther King Jr. has been killed in Memphis, Tennessee. Shot in the neck.

The phone is ringing and no one answers it. It rings and rings. Is it ringing? Where does one scream begin and another one end? Who is sobbing and who is shrieking in tongues?

Blurry eyed I can see Yvonne Christmas, my hero, in a grief as terrible as the grief of Miss Rose, Eddie's mother, when they rolled her son's dead body across her path and shut his face away from her forever. It was Miss Rose who was the first woman I ever witnessed turn into a bird; incalculable sorrow crafted in her wings. It is Yvonne Christmas I see turn into a snake, cut in two with pain, writhing this way then that, no part of her body related to another in the jigsaw of despair. But the snake makes awful, testifying sound as if she had climbed out of the loins of each of our horrors.

"I'm tired of this," the snake says. Yvonne says this. She whom I have never seen daunted. "I am so tired of this . . . I am tired of Whitepeople. I'm tired of marching and sittin in here. Why we have to march to be treated right, like human beings? Father, would you tell me would you tell me please? I'm tired of prayin in, sittin in, cryin in. I'm tired of indignation meetings and church and Jesus would you save. He dead. He must be. They killed him. God, you hear me?" The cry twists out of her, scales on it, mucky with misery. Then some profound rage jerks her body.

"God, I'm talking to you! You dead or deaf! You the motherfucker. You the first motherfucker. Why you let them kill that man? Why you let them?"

The blasphemy in her question punches me in my chest. Knocks me breathless. I am crying like a child, so full of tears I can't catch my breath. I reach out my hand to Yvonne, but she is too far away from me. Separated by the veil of tears. She is rocking, a snake half lifted, and rocking.

"Aw, Yvonne," someone murmurs, condolences thick in the voice. I do not recognize it. "Aw, Yvonne," someone says.

The voice I know is Sherman. "Don't get hysterical," he says.

She's woken up some from the awesome grief-trance. "Forget you, Sherman. History has already forgotten you are here. Martin Luther King is dead. He died at seven-oh-five. Ain't you dead too? We are all dead, don't you know? They have finally done it and I want to bust out of this little building shooting. Do you hear me? Shooting. So just for-get you, Sherman. You don't exist."

"I'm hurtin. Everybody's hurt," Sherman says. I believe him.

Yvonne is all up in his face now. "Let's go kill somebody. I am ready to take some crackers off this earth, cause they do too good a job taking Blackmen and Blackwomen and anybody with a heart who ever had a feeling for justice and decency." She almost chokes on justice. She keeps on saying it then. Until it is a low chant. Then a soundless mumbling. And she is a silent, jangling snake, hung in the air. Then Cletus comes from the other room and places himself around her. Her new crying shoots out around him like water shooting wild around a stone. Like the water arcs bigly around a wooden plank in a fire hydrant on a murderously hot day. Relieving us of some of the heat. Her sorrow is ours.

Her arms flail around Cletus and he holds them to her and pushes her into the john away from every crying eye crying with her because some crazy Whiteman or a committee has finally killed Martin Luther King Jr.

I close the door to the restroom, lean against the wood, then slither down to the floor because I have no strength in my legs. No strength in Yvonne. No strength in anybody. No strength anywhere. Leona has Essie, who is rocking and crying under her half-and-half hair, and Rhonda has her hands on William, stroking his extravagant hair while he buries his face in her heavy breasts. Everybody is up for grabs. I'm still sitting on the floor, leaning my back into the sound of Christmas's crying and Elder's attempt at consolation for what is beyond consoling. His soothing sounds are meant as much for himself as for her.

Sherman, who is trying to observe so that he won't have to confront his own feeling, turns up the television and we watch the details of the assassination. Images reach out for us from the screen. Stricken faces. Faces.

The mountaintop speech. "I've been to the mountaintop and I want to tell you this evening that we as a people will get to the Promised Land." Then the wave from the balcony of the Lorraine Hotel.

Then we watch Memphis weep and New York and Los Angeles and Chicago. Crowds crying.

Transfixed, we watch the screen. "We oughta be there," Leona says wistfully, like a traveler a long way from home. "We oughta be home. With our people. I wanna go home."

Someplace in the crying, William has come to. Now he seems heavier to me. His face fatter, older. His voice is thick as earth, gravelly. "We stay here," he says. "They want us to come out now, crying like children. They want us to forget about it and walk away." The look he sends around the room dares anyone to budge. "Our task is right here in this building. And if we don't go out with a treaty, we go out fighting. And if they come up in here on us . . . Anybody can't live with that, better go now." We all fall quieter around this proposition. We expect this ultimatum from William.

"Maybe we should go now and be home supporting our families. William, you're not from around here." Leona says.

It's Steve who shocks us all now as he, without shirt or shoes, but with gun belt slung around his torso, leaps onto an accountant's desk, scattering ledgers and writing utensils. His bare feet toe-grip the smooth mahogany finish of the desktop. He inhales great gulps of air; his chest cavity expands and his abdomen hollows out. Light skates off his glistening torso. Sweat breaks out on the foreheads of those of us brave enough to really look at him.

We wait for Steve to scream a half-comic vengeance cry, but no high-voltage scream comes out. Instead, a whisper, hoarse and rubbing rough the air.

"Death before dishonor." He stares each of us in the face, one by silent one. His gaze sends a shiver through the room.

"What exactly does he mean by dishonor?" I whisper just seconds before Leona hollers. "You better talk what you know!" Leona doesn't appreciate standing in line for death. We've just witnessed death's mighty work. And the genuine fear in Leona's voice, the muted quiver in her command, the comic truth, are enough to shake us all loose from the cold premonition that stares at us out of Steve's eyes. We all begin to talk loudly and quickly. Steve continues to stand on the desktop like a prophet marooned at a dizzying height, until William slaps him on the thigh and tells him to get down from there.

Christmas is out of the restroom now, having wept out all of her rage in the private place with Cletus the Elder. Her eyes are downcast, not in her amazingly direct gaze. She is still stunned and ashamed by her own violence and wild fury directed at God who didn't pull the trigger but allowed it to happen. "You will have to forgive me my outburst. The worst has happened and it's no real surprise. We need to be strong and do some serious meeting. We have things to talk about." This is the voice of Christmas, who is almost herself again, only everything about her is drier— voice, hair, eyes. Everything about her body is dry. Cletus the Elder comes just behind her, looking like a vengeful spirit that has slipped into this world from the next and wants only blood.

We wash our faces and hands, comb out hair, pour drinks of Coke or water to clear the path from our throats; we compose our faces and sit down to meet. We have to decide what to do: all walk out and away from Eden forever; all withdraw until our demands be met; all leave now and go to town and burn and loot and shoot Whitepeople down (those guns are no longer for decoration or idle threat); all stay and wear armbands and surrender to the university authorities; all stay and return to our dorms and return to our classes and smile and study and act as if nothing has happened and wait for the Whitepeople to grieve; leave and get some weapons and work with the Republic of New Africa, the Panthers, EARTH, or some underground so underground we can't say the name, work to overthrow a racist system that tore the wings off an angel and shot the song right out of his throat.

"If they killed King what they gonna do to us?" Hamla asks.

"That's not the right question," Cletus says.

"Well, what is?" Lydia Rushing asks.

"They killed King—what we gonna do to them?"

"Oh, sure," Russell Garner says with a sarcasm I didn't know he had. "We have enough firepower to annihilate half of the Whites in America. Let's get serious. We have to look at this situation intelligently."

"That lets your looking out, Russell," Lydia says. Russell is the closest thing to a Whiteperson here.

"It's no need to get personal. We have to love one another, brothers and sisters. That's what we're about, isn't it? Loving one another," Cletus urges us like he is a candidate for the ministry.

After a while the meeting is an awesome collage. Tensions rise further. Even Essie and Leona go at it. "Why should we leave now when we just got here?" Essie asks. Her future is blank without Eden. The gestures of each member seem bigger as she or he rises to address the group, the tempers that go off like flares on a dark highway, the TV voice bleeding into our own, the telephone ringing, ringing. The voices of our parents, administration, other Black students calling from campuses around the country, urging us on, urging. The phone keeps ringing because we will not shut it off. More talk. More soft weeping. More fear and greater hurt. There is news of fire. News of broken glass. News of running feet and Molotov cocktails. News of sniper fire. All of that news in our voices. Must we stay or must we go?

It is late when Leona's daddy arrives with his attendants carrying the buckets of shrimp, chicken wings, buffalo, spaghetti, corn muffins, mustard greens, potato salad, coleslaw, tossed salad, and tin plates of sweet potato pies, caramel cakes, and the cute little

Coca-Cola in the teeny bottles that keep the taste contained and just right like it is in Mimosa, Mississippi. We gather around the window when the brakes screech and the footsteps fall noisily, different from the stealthy trod of security police and Eden town policemen. University security detains Mr. Pryor and we eavesdrop. Mr. Pryor is not alone. Besides the three assistants, he has lawyers with him. We hear "pattern of harassment"; we hear "self-defense"; we hear "peaceful protest." ("Not exactly," Cletus laughs at the window.)

We can make out these scattered words: *fool, baby, starve.* Then whole indignant, dignified sentences: "You'd better get out of my way. I'm not about to let my baby girl starve. I have lost one business tonight. They come and boint me out just like I had hurt somebody. I wrote SOUL BROTHER all over my window, but people were too mad and hurt to read. The devil has been roamin the earth this evening. Now you mean to tell me, you think I'm not going to see my baby girl. I've lost dreams tonight. I'm a dangerous man."

With this last he inclines his head like a bull about to gouge a picador. The university policeman talks to an administrator on the car radio, then he instructs Leona's daddy to talk us out of the building. He steps back and Leona's daddy comes on through with the BoneYard entrées and sides, and the love that has not abandoned us. His two assistants jump out of the van and help him carry things to the door. Inside, the sentry opens the door wide enough so they can carry in the food and drinks.

Leona walks to him. From the look on his face, piteous and anguished, we know she is the only person in the room for him, but no one could feel left out of his look. This is the look, a search for injury or neglect, a frantic love in his eyes, which includes us all. He tries to smile. "I thought I was gone have to come up here with my belt."

Leona's twisting her hands in front of her chest like a little-bitty girl. I remind myself that this is my friend, fearless, tough, together, don't take no stuff.

"I was worried about you, baby girl. Wasn't sure you was doing the right thing or acting stupid, going along with the crowd." He steps toward his daughter who is taller than he. I'd always thought he was exceptionally tall, but he is only medium height.

"Dr. King was murdered tonight in Memphis. I guess you heard that."

"We know, Daddy."

His voice turns gruff and thick like coffee grinding. "What's the right way? I don't know anymore. I was not too hip on your being up here in this—"

"You told me."

"Maybe this is the time they talk about in the Bible. And a little child shall lead them. I just wanted to make sure you was all right. Your mama was worried about you. Call her."

"Okay. I'll try again." They are close enough to hug, but they don't.

Mr. Pryor spins his hat in his big hand. "How long you going to be in this building?"

He asks the room this.

"We don't know yet," I say, suddenly brave enough to speak to him, who is too much like Sam Grace.

This reply tortures him. He nods his head quickly, three times, struggling resignation in each nod. Acceptance of the possibilities. "At least it's safe in here." He takes a long, long look at Leona, who looks back at him. The room wills her to speak, "Thank you, Daddy."

He beckons to his assistants, who sweep past efficient as the Muslims he taught them to emulate in their instant, unobtrusive service.

"Look out for yourself." He is halfway out the door. The grinds of his voice lingering behind them.

"You too, Daddy," Leona yells, but she is in his heavy embrace before her voice reaches him. She flings her slim arms about his thick neck, squeezes, and lets go. The brothers at the door tell them it is time to let go. They slam the door, securing us in the building.

Leona's crying, and we can hear her father walking away from us. But we do not hear his engine start up. Not at all this long, mourning night.

I go to the library to study. Choose the seat where window looks at more greenery. Perhaps to strengthen me. I go to read a book that has no words. I am driven to sleep. I wake in a dream: the ugliness seeps through my dark skin into my bones. And I am twisted in the shape of a beast. In my dream I am some thing, someone obscene. In the shape of my self I go to the librarian, who is the colored lady I smile at and speak to. I ask her why she does not expel the White rock group singing and clapping into the silence of my study. For I must read and know the word-less books of Whitemen that they might smear me with their feces and with ash upon my forehead anoint me. It is the mark of the beast. The brown-skinned lady says it is important that they practice. I smile and say, "Oh." I do not say, "If they were Black there would be no music here." This is the mountain in my mind. Then there is a mountain with a pool of blood at its crest. I return to my seat by the window. I open a book. I look up. Into the face of the Whiteman across from me. Over the features of my face he sees the features of a wolf. I see inside his sight. I am angry. I am no beast. He shakes his head, "No." The Whiteman next to me looks up and sees me. Something hot is in the blood in my head. I rise and feel my face change into a piece of snarling metal. And I squat and stalk like a beast. I am no longer woman. I am man. Then beast. The dogs of their masters encircle me. One hates me, as dog despises wolf. I will kill him. I am beast. The Whitefaces turn to me in wonder without fear. I will kill them. And in that moment that my flesh has lost its woman-look I wonder what rising rounded moon of evil has made me a beast. I wonder and disbelieve the transformation of my beauty. My consentless transformation. A heavy sorrow turns within me. I wake in the day trembling in the smell of fresh fear. I doubt that I am human but the window shows me. The Whiteman across from me stares his disapproval. I have offended him.

Before this siege, coming out of the library one evening I caught William and Steve Rainey transfixed in whispers. They were sitting on the rim of the fountain behind the library. The sound of water rushed over their words. Their messages occult. They startled me. Two men in blue jeans and khaki. William lithe and long, his Afro shaved down; Steve stockier and stubborn jawed, with sheepish eyes and a mouth that turns down from turning down. Behind their backs white water fell then rose over the fountain rim to spray their hands. William shoved his wet fists into his pockets. Steve started brushing the surface of the water. This is the bowl of water we wish in, pitching pennies and dropping dimes for luck. I waved to him but they didn't take their eyes from each other or the wishing water. I headed back to the dorm without their noticing me. It was late in the dinner hour and no one was about. No other footsteps interrupted or augmented my own.

I was alone just as I am now as I lie thinking about sleep. Steve had lain down beside me but at some time he got up, maybe to watch TV and cities' nightmares. I can't remember when I fell asleep again, but I must have because I am dreaming or dreaming I am dreaming. What happened is our worst nightmare. The nightmare in Memphis spreading to other cities. I am dreaming in a dream so tangible the images float off the screen, exaggerated and sensible as African sculpture, a place where real joins surreal and is alive in body and spirit. This is the story William tells later that I dream in glimpses now, fractured and terrible:

They were running like Black Ghosts, a part of the wind, across campus, having left the car behind on a side street near Eden Road's intersection with the City. There were no campus police cars about because they were all around the Finance Building, which William and Steve had sneaked out of. The Black Ghosts arrived at Old Science, panting from the sprinting. William cuts the wire and Steve breaks the window and drops a sack inside Old Science, where I used to wash beakers and test tubes and witnessed the test subject pigeons in their cages. The moon is a cartoon moon; its light stretches their shadows as Steve lifts himself and falls inside. The wind is high and would snatch the words from their mouths. They say little. William stands watch. He beats his hands together. He blows into them. He stuffs his hands into his pockets and sends out balloons blown up with curses from his mouth. William says later he senses something is wrong. Steve is inside too long.

Steve screams and I can hear the scream in my dream. A bright flicker inside a window of Old Science. The gasoline and his hands go up. Steve backs over something in the darkness. Moving away from the blaze that is him. With his flame hand he picks up the can. Gibberish comes from his mouth. Agony language. He half gallops, tripping over things in the invisibility, clumsy agony fumbling against impartial air. Then William with the full moon behind him is calling his name. And William is beating down flames, smothering him, and hauling him out of the building. Someone is yelling behind them. A security guard slow on his feet. The entire night is swamp. And they are running.

It was an accident. Not like the one that took the life of my grandmother Sarah Mahalia Lincoln Dancer. The life she didn't know was taken so she walks Old Letha Road looking for it or something else. It was an accident—not spilled milk but spilled gasoline. His hands on fire before his eyes. The anguish.

One of the window watchers sends up a shout. They had been hanging around windows like pigeons, pacing back and forth. The shout breaks my dream. I wake up and know it wasn't a dream. Isn't. The first floor is ascramble with activity, muffled cries. "Oh, God, Steve." It's Christmas murmuring. Moans; that could only be Steve. He is smoking. His gloved hands smoking. Hurry. Something tells me. Hurry. He's burning. I fly down the stairs.

They're beating the smoke out of William's clothes. They did it. They actually did it. Sisters in head rags are rolling bandages like young revolutionary Nightingales. Their eyes are brimming with fear. They look like horses in a burning barn. They move skittishly.

"Something went wrong, Maggie. If this makes you sick, go back to bed," Hamla snaps me up. She's smoking a cigarette. Something I didn't know she did. You'd have thought she'd have put out the fire. No matter how small. But each puff is courage.

Christmas is holding Steve Rainey up. Her back to the wall. His eyes don't focus. He's moaning. "Shoot me," he hollers from his gut. "Death is better." I go to him. He can hardly stay in my arms he's jerking so. Everything is happening double time. Rhonda and some others want to put something on his wounds.

"We can't tell," Rhonda says. "He'll go to jail."

Essie is pre-med. Cletus the Elder looks to her before he heads to the phone. He asks for the fire department, emergency, burn unit.

Rhonda says, "He'll go to jail."

William is sitting in a corner weeping softly. "It's so fucked up," he says wonderingly.

"He needs morphine," Essie says.

"You mean like heroin," Leona says.

"I mean like morphine to ease his pain."

Down the street they come. Fire department ambulances. Police cars. Police to join the sleepy campus police that had blocked us in. They're coming with their Biggifying Pills that have puffed them up, and their guns that make them invincible, omnipotent. They're coming with their Belittling Pills like big bees that sting us inside. Shrink us down to Negro children.

Steve is still moaning as the troop of attendants sling him on the stretcher. "Good thing you didn't put anything on that burn. He's got a chance," the paramedic says to Cletus.

"Go on," Steve screams. He means for us to do what we have to do. His eyes roll around in his head from pain.

The police jostle us. Growl at us. "Move it out of here," they command. "The whole world's gone crazy." Their voices are biggified, hollow like the giant's in "Jack and the Beanstalk."

"Don't you college kids have anything better to do? You oughta count your blessings."

"They oughta throw the bunch of you out of here."

"Is this what ya come up here for? To burn up buildings. You coulda stayed home and done that."

"We're on our way," Christmas yells as we start packing up our stuff in the half light of morning. Cletus has just gotten off the phone with the administration. We will sign a treaty. There was one casualty. That casualty was too much. The university has found the men who attacked Essie. It was not Eden students. They were not connected to Eden, just traveling through from the City. They had told a Whiteguy in a bar about it. They'd

326

been dazzled by the beauty and affluence of the place, seen the "Negro girl" as a part of it all, felt small and locked out and they'd struck out. The university was exonerated. As for Steve and his accomplice, if he indeed had one, they would be dealt with. Everyone is tired. We will sign a treaty assuming that our demands have been met.

"Let's act like we got some home training," Yvonne Christmas says, as she and the grad students bring out the brooms, the mops, and pails and cleaning supplies that the housekeeping workers left behind. We begin to clean the building. Leona and Essie and Trixia take the lounge, where all the work of the Heart had been done. I get down on my hands and knees in the washroom, where much of the crying and letting go had been done. I scrub the tile and let tears fall onto the floor and I wash the floor with my tears.

Much later when that Finance Building is so clean it almost breathes, when I am waiting to use the telephone, I slip into a catnap that does not break with reality. Everything is a college collage painting full of edges like Romare Bearden's.

El-Hajj Malik El-Shabazz sits in a field of flowers. I go to meet him as he waits for me. I am not alone, going to meet Malcolm. A flock of us float toward Malcolm. How heavy our hair is. I can feel it, weighty and exuberant. A roar rises out of us. He says, "Pick the flowers now," and we pick them, bending like cotton pickers, fingers swift to ply the bright blossoms from the stalks and gather them up. Malcolm says, "Look," and we turn to see a man standing in the mist atop a mountain. "Will he come down with the commandments?" I say out loud in the dream. And Malcolm says, "You already know them." Steve Rainey is with me and he begins to eat the flowers and his mouth runs blood. And Leona falls to her knees and cradles a bouquet that turns into a long rifle. I hear crying and I know that it is Essie. I am at my easel and I begin to paint the flowers, painting furiously, working because the flowers dissolve into pools and lakes of blood and blue tears.

Voices all around me: Yvonne, Cletus, William, Russell denying, Hamla, Trixia, Rhonda, Oakland, Johnnie Mae, Sherman lying, Roberto who is not Latin, Larry, Lydia Rushing, Lazarus, Katherine Pearl, Mr. Pryor, Sam Grace, Caroline, Aunt Silence, Aint Kit, Grandmama Patsy, Bay, Eddie who is dead, Sam Jr., Honeybabe, her husband C.C., Anne Perpetua, Frances, Ernestine, Shirley, Charlotte who came to live with us, Essie's mother Fredonia, Hamla's cousin Berry, and the EARTH men, and Great Zimbabwe, and Miss Memphis, and Uncle Blackstrap, and I. B. K. Turner, and all the voices, all the voices, and a man standing on top of the mountain, turning to a tree, turning to a stone, turning.

I know I'm awake when I hear Yvonne Christmas's voice as clear as springwater rising above the commotion, "King was a man. We were his children, but we are Malcolm X's children too. Someone else will rise out of our collective Freedom Dream, out of our Heart that is broken now. Some other ones will rise. We're a Movement, brothers and sisters. Let's get going."

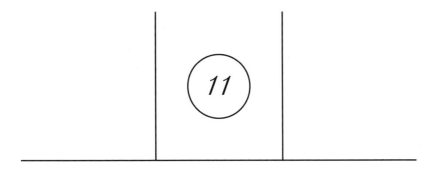

Curfew Time

Aint Kit swear she bought one of them early watermelons from a traveling man going down her alley.

"I don't know why I had such a taste for watermelon. It's April too and the sugar don't be in most of 'em yet. They taste like water, but once in a while you can get a miracle. That's what I was thinking." Pearl is telling me this, what Aint Kit said on the phone to Mama while Pearl eavesdropped because she could tell from Mama's face this was too good to miss. She sounds just like Aint Kit when she's telling how she prophesied after the fact. Her voice weighted down with foreboding. Her pauses nine months pregnant.

"You know you don't see that many of them watermelon trucks round here. That is most unusual. So when I heard my big dogs bark I knew they wasn't hungry cause I'd just cooked them up a coupla them T-bone steaks I keep in my freezer." ("You know them dogs was starving to death," Pearl interjects into her mimicry. "She keeps them hungry so they'll be as mean as she is.")

"They was barking and howling something turrible. So I went on into the backyard and the garbage cans in the alley was running over. And here come this truck loaded down with melons drawin up the alley. My mouth started watering for one of them early watermelons. So the man stopped when I said, 'Gimme one of them melons.' He give it to me real cheap. I should have *known* something. He was justa smiling. All I could see was the gold all over his teeth. Look like a street in Heaven. He had his hat pulled down over his eyes so I could just barely see a little glint. Oooh, and he was black and uglyyyyyyyyyy. Ooooh. He was ugly. Look like somebody beat him when he come out the womb then shoved him back up in there and mixed him with the afterbirth." ("You ever notice how Aint Kit loves to call people ugly?" Pearl asked me.)

"Anyway, I figure anybody that ugly got to be lucky. How much bad luck can a person have? So I picked that watermelon up like a baby. He ask me if I want a plug but I told him naw." ("Now I know this is made up," I tell Pearl. "When you ever know Aint Kit to miss getting something free much less pass up trying something out without parting with that money she keeps in her bra. Next to her heart." Pearl laughs so hard she almost can't get back into the Aint Kit voice. She clears the giggles and hoots from her voice.)

"Now I had knocked on the melon to see if it sounded good and it sounded deep and wide inside and it was heavy. But I carried it in my arms, the big dogs was lapping at my knees, and the ugly man got back up in the truck and drove on down the alley. I thought it was strange the way he come down the alley directly to my house real slow and he drove off real fast like he was making a getaway. Dust was jumping back off the truck wheels; it couldn't hold on. He was flying down that alley. I went on inside. My mouth wasn't nothing but water by now. I set that watermelon on the kitchen sink. I put some newspaper down first cause I didn't want to make no mess and draw no ants." ("Ants my behind. Aint Kit knows she means roaches. Just like she's never seen them. They're older than she is," Pearl says.)

"Then I got my big butcher knife so I could cut it clean. I remember thinking when I was holding that knife in my hand that that melon was round like somebody's head. Then I say, 'Kit what's done got into you. You just as crazy.' So I positioned my knife on the middle and pressed down quick and pulled at the same time. It just fell open in two equal parts and oooooh, oooooh, my heart split open and jumped in my eyes. Inside the heart of that melon wasn't nothing but worms. Worms just jumping and crawling. They was black and ugly and wiggling. I hollaaaaahed. Oooh. Oooh. Oooh. Then I said, 'Kit, what is this? What is this?' I shoved both of them pieces of worm something into the sink and I turnt on the water real hard. I was flushing worm. Justa flushing worms. Trying not to lay my hands on that slimy mess. They wiggled on down the drain. Like devils sliding into hell. Umph. Umph. Umph. Oooh!

"I was shaking I was so scared. I had to go lay down and catch my breath. So I climbed on upstairs and got in the bed. But my mind kept holding them old ugly worms. Every time I close my eyes I see worms. So I turned on the TV. And do you know—her pause is bursting, laboring toward delivery—and do you know the first thing I saw on the TV was the Reverent Doctor Martin Luther King shot in the throat in Memphis. I was shocked. It knocked me unconscious like that time my husband was in the ring and he got KO'd. I was too paralyzed to move. It come on they said he was dead. The Reverent Doctor Martin Luther King Jr. dead in Memphis. Oooh-wee Jesus. Some dirty, dirty, dirty assassinating peckerwood done kilt that man. I said, 'Oooh Kit now you know what them worms was telling you.' I was too hurt to walk so I crawled out of bed like a baby, and crawled back down the stairs and called you Ca'line, cause I didn't know if y'all TV was working or if everybody was waiting by the phone to hear about Magdalena up in that building. Ca'line we got to go up there and get that baby cause these murdering hunkies don't care who they kill."

Pearl tells it all. Then she says, "You know what all that worm melon rigmarole was about, don't you? Mama's been talking for weeks about a dream she had. It was a baby girl on a mountaintop and the baby girl was naked and had eyes like black pearls. She was beautiful. She climbed to the top and she tipped over the precipice. When she was falling she turned into a bird. Mama said she thought it was a dove but it was black with lustrous wings. It fell down but it flew up. Then it opened its wings and they covered the sky. She told Aint Kit about her funny dream. So Aint Kit had to make up an omen fast. You know how jealous she is. She says she saved the rinds so everybody can see. She gone put them in a jar." It's my turn to go "oooh" at the thought of the sight of wormy rind sealed in a jar.

Pearl says, "I don't know why she has to try to dramatize all this stuff. King was assassinated. That's bad enough. We don't need no extra movie. I'm glad you all got out of that building in one piece."

"I'll be home in two hours," I tell Katherine Pearl.

"It's kind of rough, Maggie."

"I'm coming."

"Girl, why don't you stay in school?"

"You home. I'm coming home. I don't want to be up here with all these Whitepeople right now. They running around here crying crocodile tears. I'm leaving now."

"Wait a minute." Pearl moves away from the phone. I hear voices. Pearl is back. "Lazarus'll be there in forty-five minutes to pick you up. Just bring everybody with them guns. We might need them." I think Pearl's joking, but I can tell she's afraid she's not. The brothers came out the building armed with rifles and cartridges that they turned over to the university, whose property the weapons were. That was part of the treaty. (The brothers who had them kept their own guns. That was not in the treaty.) Yvonne said armed struggle has to be organized and planned; spontaneity is good for music but bad for war. Her voice was dry as toast and her mouth was pinched when she said it.

"Essie's coming too."

When we got home Arbor Avenue was quiet. No birds flew overhead. And no children were outside playing or running errands. Pearl went back to school, after making sure everything was all right and leaving me in stitches with her rendition of Aint Kit the prophet. Pearl is a senior at a college for women run by nuns. Her school is on the edge of the City, in the opposite direction from Eden. The neighborhood is all White, Eastern European and Irish. And you have to be ready to fight to go out for a late-night snack around there.

Essie sleeps in Pearl's space in the bed we slept in when we were small. Ernie and Shir inherited the bunk beds. The house is smaller now, and to make room for us when we return we have to fit into the spaces we filled when we were way younger. This is inconvenient, but it is safe the way the house fits around us now.

Essie's feet are cold as she slides under the covers beside me. Her hands brush against me briefly as she pulls up her covers. Her hands are cold. Her voice quick and thick when she tells me no one was home at her mama's. That's why Leona had to leave us behind when she drove off with her daddy. Essie was stranded. She let the phone ring thirty times. Then she hung up, dialed again, and let it ring fifteen.

"Where could they be?" she wonders.

I ignore the question; instead I tell her about the time I spent Christmas holiday, the day after Christmas until New Year's, at Aint Kit's house that was on the West Side then. When I got home Littleson had scalped my brand-new blonde Christmas doll with his brand-new Christmas tomahawk. How I'd cried and Aint Kit had cussed to see me cry so and all that good merchandise ruined.

"You got any love objects at home?" I ask Essie.

"Just my brothers and sisters. I took everything else to school with me." Essie smiles halfheartedly. "My mama wears my clothes. So I have to hide what I like."

I don't say anything. Because you're not supposed to talk about other people's mamas. At least not to them.

Essie reads my mind.

"Fredonia's not really bad, Maggie," Essie allows. "She just had me when she was real young. Sixteen. And she thinks I made her miss stuff. She wants to be young and have young love and young parties and you know." The covers shift when Essie shrugs. "She needs me."

Essie gets out of bed to call home again. I just lie there listening to police sirens and midnight voices full of panic and desperation outside my window. The City has imposed a strict curfew.

Tanks go by rumbling like huge, prehistoric monsters. Soldiers, some of them dark as me, all of them young, lean and pose on jeeps and the backs of trucks. They try to look comfortable with the weapons that are even younger than they are. The trucks that ride them are larger than the one my grandmother, Mahalia, rode in to her red death and alleged resurrection.

Littleson and I used to wave at the soldiers, the stray jeep full, as they glided toward the old armory not far from the lake. We'd thought that armory was closed down, open only to rats with tails long as bayonets. But it must be busy now with battalions of troops coming in. I don't wave at the young Black private with hair cut so close the kink is abolished, resting his hands on his rifle. I snarl at him and the tanks and the jeeps and the big-ole obscene bazooka not like the bubble-gum bazooka. Not a thing for children.

There is no more rain. The street's wiped clean of water. The world, once round, is now slit and dry like an eye wiped harshly of tears, like a resistant child's eyes, a child still angry and ashamed to have been caught crying in public, even though the death of royalty warrants weeping.

On the boulevard the shops are closed and boarded up. Frightened shop owners and managers have scrawled SOUL BROTHER in hurried letters across the boards and the remaining windows. Like Israelites painting their doorways with blood against some promised plague. I can still smell the smoke, even though the fire and the riot are quiet. Outbreaks were minimal on these streets; on the West Side whole blocks burned. We watched the burning on TV like survivors watching snapshots and close-ups from the War. Censure, delight, contrary pride, vengeance, and weird foreboding as we watched the goings-on.

Miss Rose said, "They need to go burn some Whitepeople's houses down. Insteada burning our own."

"Whitepeople own the businesses," Lazarus said.

"Not all of 'em." Madaddy eyed the TV, his face lit up. "What that girl name, Maggie? Your friend—Leona. They burned down her daddy's chicken place and it was doing good business. Was nice."

We watched the young men, sleek with exertion, clothes coming off from running, running with clothes and bottles and meat slabs and TVs and radios in their hands. We listened to the report of guns coming across the TV screen. Way 'cross town.

The bakery thrift shop is boarded up now. The big bay windows that usually say BREAD and DONUTS and CRUNCH CAKE shielded in plywood. Broken loaves litter the sidewalk; sheets of bread, white and doughy as Wonder, lie on the curb and in the street. Pigeons—discreet, obsequious, and industrious—peck at the gluey slabs. They coo. The noon sun sharpens everything. The April wind is spurious. I am cold and don't know why. But the sun heats my face. I squint at the soldiers, and the pigeons and boarded-up buildings and the littered loaves. I cannot think of why I am on the street on the way to the store. To buy what? When what I want right now right now cannot be found and fondled over like mixed-quality produce, or scorned like old meat in the butcher's case, or swallowed fast like the stuff the brothers tore through the streets with, newly seized from the busted-in and busted-up liquor store on the corner.

Everything is so shabby now. Violated and battered. The air no longer sweet with the smell of baking bread from the three bakeries, but bitter with the remembrance of fire, the taste of smoke. Another group of soldiers and machinery goes by. Pigeons scatter and rise from the street. One is too slow and is knocked against the side of a tank, felled, then run over by the tank. The boy soldiers lean over the edge of the truck. A sandy-haired one, looking at the bird, says, "That's one dead pigeon."

They think that's so funny.

"So's yo mama," I want to say. Say something to the booted boys in khaki sent to keep people who've lost everything in neat, polite lines of mourning. Sedate. Safe for someone else's democracy. (The mayor says, "Shoot to kill." The mayor says he wants law and order. The soldiers came.) I can't remember now. When was Arbor or the streets around it safe? When was there law? What is the last order?

When did anything make sense?

One August the whole street took to the pigeons. Mothers stoned them from back-porch railings; their sons were Davids armed with slingshots or BB guns. Whatever. Their missiles landed between birds' eyes so that the stricken birds toppled over like edible bowling pins. Then they were feathers turned motley between fingers, bellies gutted of an awful miscellanea: berries, organs, common seeds. Limbs were severed, and feathers and some feet discarded, but most amazingly to us children—drumsticks, like chicken or turkey only diminutive, just right. "Oh, I want a little-biddy baby bird leg!"

That year, I don't remember which one, I think was extra lean. Our neighbors lived bountifully on the edges of hunger. They flew in the face of it while it gnawed their insides into blues that blasted up and down the block.

Some, like Caroline, my mother, spoke out against the slaughter of the birds. They gave a thousand reasons for not doing what their ancient instincts understood to be "just not right." They said that those birds had been born free and had raised themselves. They had not been bred to die. My mother said that pigeons were filthy, even the beige and silver-gray ones that people tried to say were so much better than the ordinary browns. My mama said no fowl was dirty as the pigeon. Pigeons walked anywhere. They were full of diseases. Whoever ate them ate disease.

Mama said, "That kind of fowl ain't fair game. Eating a pigeon is no different from eating your next-door neighbor. Cannibalism. That's what it is. Sheer and simple." The freedom of pigeons, beyond borders, or their hygiene she did not trust.

Charlotte, the neighbor girl who had run away from home to our home, had eaten pigeons and potato salad. That is why what happened to her happened. She told us about eating pigeons, how good they tasted. "Taste even better, if you hungry," she said, as she picked her big, pearly teeth with a toothpick and scratched her scalp under that blonde wig she wore. Charlotte walked with a swagger born from her wide legs, like a cowboy without any courage or experience, drunk with the whiskey of pain. She was tall and thin and walked runways on weekends at church fashion shows, fashion shows sponsored by beauty colleges. She dreamed of making a glamorous living as a model. Something a Negro girl did not do.

She acted strange all the weeks she lived with us, jumpy and accusatory. She accused Littleson and Junior of stealing her panties. The house was in an uproar. "This is the thanks I get," Honeybabe said, "for bringing her here." I thought it was pigeon eating that made Charlotte so sad and crazy and not just her crazy daddy. It turned out she was pregnant and her daddy was crazier than anyone knew and tried to give her away to drunk pigeon-eating friends. She was a nice girl then, pretty, faded yellow, who wanted to be a model and liked pretty things. She didn't want to be given away like a little pigeon to be devoured by greasy-mouthed men so she ran away to our house.

Cousin Bay (who was visiting, having run away from Aint Kit for the weekend and come running over to our house where the door and my mother's arms were always open until my father shut them—door and arms—after Charlotte, and sent Bay back to his sister's house) licked her fingers daintily, crumbling up the oily brown bag red and wet with hot sauce and gritty with potato chip filings. "Pigeon meat too tender to be a nigger. On the other hand, dark meat do be juicy and pigeons most time look pretty dark on the outside. Mama Kit cooked one once; it kept cooing and doing outside her bedroom window, so she caught him with a butterfly net like the one she said they used on Aunt Leah-Bethel when they come to carry her to the crazy house."

"Kit knows better than that. She got two freezers full of meat. She don't need to be huntin nobody's pigeons," Mama sniffled over the raw onions she was cutting up to go on top of the black-eyed peas.

Miss Rose took the sniffle for a sniff of superiority or contempt. She sat up in the kitchen chair and talked all hot and huffy to Mama. "Caroline, you got a husband with two jobs. I'm a woman alone. If you got hongry enough you'd eat pigeons and feed your kids pigeons too."

Mama didn't say anything, but I could tell she was mad and stubborn. She stirred the big pot of black-eyed peas, then bent down with a towel in her hand to pull the black iron skillet of corn bread from the oven. The heat from the oven reddened her already-red face.

Mama would fix a different kind of bean or soup Monday through Thursday. Saturday she'd cook greens, sweet potatoes, fried chicken or pork chops. And Sundays chicken baked or fried, pot roast, or steak in gravy, mashed potatoes or macaroni and cheese, peas or green beans with the potatoes cooked in them. The meatless Fridays of our rigidly abstinent Catholicism, she fried fish or salmon croquettes, which were really mackerel, or baked tuna casserole, or fixed fish sticks and meatless spaghetti. There was no place on her menu for pigeons.

Beans (pinto; thick, starchy butter beans; red beans, always with rice; and navy beans, before Uncle Blackstrap became a Black Muslim and made navy bean soup every day and stunk up the house trying to digest it) filled our hunger pains and stretched our palates to distinguish the subtle difference in taste and texture, the sundry and succulent moods of beans. Mama the bean connoisseur would not touch Uncle Blackstrap's Muslim bean pie.

She would not touch that bean pie, packaged perfectly in an aluminum pie pan and wrapped in clearest plastic sold in the

Muslim bakery further south from our house. Nor would she that summer eat those pigeons or allow us to. Eating pigeons was beneath my mother's idea of human dignity. My daddy agreed with her. No one should have to eat behind what walked in dog dung, ate garbage, and pecked in sewer drains. That's what Madaddy said when he came home from work that midnight after Mama's clash with Miss Rose. He sat at the dining room table with a Chinese-food carton full of nicely spicy breaded and deep-fried shrimp from the fish place not far from the concrete ravine where the post office stood. "A pigeon—" my daddy told my mama loud enough for me to make out in the dark curiosity of the bedroom where I still slept with Littleson because nothing yet could convince us we were not twins, and not even sex could separate us—"Them pigeons ain't nothin' but filth, I'm telling you. Not secondhand but second body garbage" (pronounced *gah-bij* like something so slimy the word must be scowled and spit out of the mouth).

That's what my daddy said the night after the pigeon fest was over. But before that, in the afternoon, in my mother's kitchen, my mother let the corn-bread skillet slip out of her hand and bang onto the stove eye. So it made a lot of noise, and Miss Rose who had been slumped a little in her chair, satisfied that she'd got that business with Mama about haves and have-nots off her chest, sat up and took notice when Mama gave the final reason why those pigeons shouldn't be messed with.

She warned that those pigeons were the property of the United States government and whoever devoured them was eating against the law. But the women who ate earth shipped up in boxes from the South, who ate Argo starch out of blue and white boxes, removed the tags that claimed the tender meat for a federal government that lived a million moon miles away. A white face. Efficiently, they removed the tags, and the one or two capsules strapped to the inner legs of the birds they gave to their sons and my brother Littleson. The capsules looked like silver bullets, closed tight with something inside.

The women and men cooked the birds outside. Flat flags and balloons of smoke rose from the open pit in the largest yard on the block. They ate the barbecued meat and sucked the bones, then threw the clean bones into little heaps that the ants fell on later. The hills of bones stayed until the garbage man came and swept the remains up into the truck. All the days that the bird bones lay on the ground, few pigeons flew by and none landed in our yards. Perhaps they smelled their futures in the dead fireplaces.

A few days after that, federal men wearing hats and trench coats in the August heat came to investigate the death of the pigeons. The lady next door looked up from her box of starch and pointed them down to the big building with the big yard where Mr. Rucker happened to live with about four hundred other people, families in rooms as small as sugar cubes.

Mr. Rucker was working on his car in the street in the front of the big building. He wiped his hands and looked at the federal men who'd just asked him a question.

"What pigeons?" Mr. Rucker said. And he had turned the meat over on the grill.

The federal men didn't flash a smile; they flashed imperial-looking badges. Like junk costumery off of Flash Gordon. The federal men told Mr. Rucker that the pigeons had been the property of the United States government. He and all his neighbors could be imprisoned for destroying them.

Mr. Rucker said again, "What pigeons?" He aimed his rancid breath at the Whitemen and the Whitemen stepped back. Then they left walking inside the heat of those coats.

Two days later Mr. Rucker was back in front of the building working on that car. His face was in the belly of the car. A police car pulled up. A policeman yelled out the half-raised window. He told Mr. Rucker to move his "broken-down heap" out of the street. Mr. Rucker didn't show his face. One policeman got out of the car. He hitched up his gun and billy club when he hitched up his pants so the pants would grab his crotch.

The policeman tapped Mr. Rucker on the shoulder. He drew his head out of the bowels of the car, a "What now?" look on his face. The officer stood before him with his hand on his holster like John Wayne. He said, "I said move this shit out of the street."

Mr. Rucker said, "Shit."

Children are nature's all-seeing journalists. There we stood observing at the closest range. We weren't sure if Mr. Rucker said *shit* out of defiance or if he was simply repeating the policeman's name for his raggedy car.

The Whiteman took his word as challenge. He hauled Mr. Rucker by the back of his neckline. He threw him against the side of the car. Frisked him roughly. Then the policeman yanked his handcuffs out of his belt and he swung Mr. Rucker around so he could cuff him.

When Mr. Rucker saw the shackles he began to fight. He lashed out at the policeman, his oily knuckles leaving streaks on the Whiteman's white face.

Amazed, the officer in the car radioed "officer needs assistance." Then he jumped out of the car into the fray.

We journalists became war correspondents witnessing the carnage and recording news briefs in our memories.

The second officer had his nightstick knocking Mr. Rucker in the head, while Mr. Rucker screamed, "Naw, naw," through the blood in his mouth. His mouth was full of blood like he'd taken a big swallow of a thick berry drink. "Goddamn you, bastard," he said, and blood with teeth in it trickled out of his mouth.

The two policemen wrestled him to the ground, heaving his hands behind his neck. The two men said in one voice, "Don't be cussin in front of these kids, motherfucker. Stop this bullshit."

Mr. Rucker kept resurrecting himself halfway. Each time he tried they called him nigger. Like they were using *nigger* to push him into the earth.

Nigger was everywhere, even in the sound of the siren on the paddy wagon that pulled up.

More sad cursing through blood in the mouth. The knots on Mr. Rucker's head seemed to rise under his kinky hair. Blood was in his eye.

I had begun to whimper. And Littleson said, "Quit it! Quit it! You better stop!" But the policemen didn't listen.

They tossed Mr. Rucker like he was a bushel of rotten potatoes into the wagon. He rolled on the floor, insensible, but still rising up. The only thing he could lift was his head. So his head was resisting arrest.

The policemen turned to the cluster of cringing faces—wide, consuming eyes, potential mouths, and nostrils that could flare out. One policeman said, "You, kids, get away from here. Move 'em out. Go home."

Then they drove away and left us in a thick silence.

On the way home, Littleson and I met a pigeon strolling along the curb. Littleson threw a pebble at the bird and hit him on his side just as he raised his wings and took to the air.

Grown people blamed the pigeons too. They said the law had reached its hand from Washington, D.C., and the FBI had fingered Mr. Rucker as trouble and sent the local authorities to smash him under their thumb.

Caroline said she had known that the eating of pigeon flesh would bring nothing good to any of us after our bellies were filled then half empty again. Even those of us who had not eaten but had witnessed would fall under the luck. I believed what I was told and what I had seen. Pools of pigeons at the bases of statues downtown parted without blinking for the Whitepeople who walked right on through. The pigeons could elevate themselves to the highest skyscraper and then swim downward into sewers without blinking those red eyes. The pigeons could make blood berry fill a man's mouth and molehills of misery rise around his head like a crown of thorns.

Over the years I have offered them sacrifices, tossing torn bits of bread down across the curb. But none of my offerings are enough.

After Essie was raped by Silk, she used to cry for her mama to move them away from the Homes. When the elevator wasn't working, she'd have to face those stairs, again standing in the door to the cavern that led up to pain beyond pain, a pressed-down feeling that surged up in her. She would wander nervous and agitated by the mailboxes and wait for a group of children to come galloping in from school or play; she would wait for women loaded down with brown paper sacks of groceries, the smell of slightly tainted meat walking ahead of the laughing and complaining women. Behind the women Essie would climb the dark stairwell. Men, single or in groups, she would not follow. Their shadows, the deep rumble of their voices that shook the air behind them in air quakes, the smell of them, was too much like Silk, a net she couldn't work her way out of.

Silk, the crippled boy who raped Essie and two other girls, served a seven-year sentence for burglarizing an apartment near the lake. The woman who lived there, asleep behind those black sleep blinders, woke up to two Blackboys picking through her jewel box with the spinning ballerina on top spinning to music from *Swan Lake*. The music of the jewel box and the muffled protests of the woman as Silk and his buddy shoved her, outraged and frightened, into the closet, made up Silk's swan song. His friend left Silk behind and Silk was caught less than a block away from the apartment with a lunch bag full of costume jewelry. The woman who slept behind blinders kept her precious stones in a safety vault in a downtown bank. So Silk went to jail for stealing fake ice, glass and paste, and sticking a White-looking woman in a closet that was big as a living room; he didn't go for what he did to Essie or the two other girls. One girl named Phyllis. The other's name no one would say.

For the time that Silk was in jail, Essie was afraid. All those years mothering Fredonia's babies, rushing to the cry before it became a cry out of one of those sweet, tiny mouths, wiping eyes and behinds and noses and mouths; all those years of studying and doing homework; all those years of fixing dinner and cleaning up on Saturday morning and taking the clothes to the Laundromat three blocks away instead of the one in the building because it was too lonely and quiet a place; all those years of looking through the glossy magazines and dreaming, dreaming over the shiny pages of *Seventeen* and laughing over "Boy, was my face red!" in "Calling All Girls"; all those years of reading books borrowed from the library and given to her by teachers who told her they saw the intelligence doing somersaults behind her eyes, intelligence to be trained and fed right, by teachers who recognized the wounded beauty of her spirit and believed and made her believe that logic was the surest salve for anything, including the fear; all those years, Essie was afraid.

But her mama, Fredonia, wouldn't move them away.

"She couldn't move us away," Essie says, now that we are freshmen at Eden and in FBO and Black and conscious and home during the riots and King is dead. "Of course, Fredonia wouldn't ever tell me she wouldn't move because she couldn't. There was no place to go but a hole in some landlord's wall with mice and roaches running in and out of it, cold water, no heat, and sleeping in your overcoat and watching TV in the kitchen with all the stove eyes turned on and pots of water steaming trying to carry some heat. My mama wouldn't ever admit she didn't have a choice, her and Woody when he was there, she rather make like I was being silly for being scared all the time."

I don't say anything about Essie's mother. I don't think anything either because we're on our way to see her because nobody answers the phone at Essie's home. Essie called and called while I went to the store and crossed the street against tanks. She didn't see them, and refused to imagine them because her mind was on her family. We talk in spurts on our walk to the Homes. Mostly, I think about what I see.

Buildings, not even ten years old yet, but rapidly aged like insubstantial beauties dependent on silicon and dye gone awry, more pale than beige but dirtied to a gray; for miles they rise. Each one sixteen floors of dirty beige-gray. They remind me of one of my least-favorite monster movies: *Cronus.* You know, where the aliens come and first what they've left is a spacecraft, then the saucer drops legs and grows a top like a house, and it starts to walk, pulling and feeding off all the sources of energy humans have to offer. I don't remember how the Whitepeople in the movie saved themselves from Cronus. And I don't know how we can survive here. The talk of TV and the squall and squawk of radio and the yell of babies jump out the windows onto our heads as we walk toward Essie's place in all of this. Discarded dolls, chicken bones, and potato chip bags spill out of too-full garbage bins. The garbage bins are waterlogged and smoke-scarred like somebody tried to start a fire in them.

That's what happened. A boy about nine, open faced and excited, who reminds me of Lazarus when he was Littleson, tells us how and who set the trash on fire and when and how the firemen put out the flame. Watching his smart, good face, with his eyes so alive, bed feathers still in his hair like he was caught in the middle of considering being a bird, buttons gone from his plaid shirt and a hole in the knee of his lint-fuzzy but clean corduroy pants—watching him I wonder why the firemen put out the fire. He says his name is Pete. For Pete's sake, for Essie's sake, this whole sixteen-floor building should go up in smoke.

The brothers at EARTH were right, I'm thinking.

One time Mama tried to show me how to garden, a little patch of earth just beyond the back steps she called a victory garden where she grew whatever would grow. "You have to be careful you don't place certain seeds too close together, and when the greens come up you have to thin them or they'll fight and choke each other. Everything grabs for sunshine. Everything wants some space."

There are so many mailboxes lined up on the wall I can't count them. The names blur. Or my eyes. "What can come out of this place? People all mashed down on top of each other."

Essie, furrowing her brow and nibbling her bottom lip nervously, presses the button for the elevator.

Nothing happens.

Twenty minutes pass.

"Broke," Essie explains with a shade of embarrassment and something else in her voice. Just like this whole impossible building belongs to her or she belongs to it and its deficiencies are her failures. Essie sucks air through her front teeth disgustedly. I'm not sure a broken elevator is bad news after all. Anybody could get in that little box with us. The box could get stuck. Then where would we be? And with whom?

When Essie leads me to the thick metal door of the stairwell, so thick Superman couldn't see through it, and she opens the door to the worst and most whiskey-drenched night I've ever seen or smelled in the middle of the day, I wish for the elevator. Each stair step is a possible assault. Each step echoes Essie's rape. I know this.

The bulb is out. We feel our way up. I crack some stupid joke about the blind leading the blind from behind.

"By the behind," Essie throws over her shoulder, as she puts my hand on her hip. "Hold on," she orders. There isn't much to hold on to but I do. All the way to the tenth floor, where Essie's family stays now.

Two little boys carrying a kite are the only people on the tier. The kite is white, star shaped, and clumsy in their hands. They carry it between them.

"Hey, Bertram, you seen my mother?" Essie gasps. She's still breathing hard from feeling and fumbling up the ten flights in a panic.

The little boy named Bertram shakes his head. He hasn't seen anybody in Essie's family.

"The TV is on," the little boy says. "I heard it when we went by the doe. Somebody in there." The little boy points down to the last apartment facing us on that tier.

Bertram has his own business on his mind. "You see this kite?" he asks Essie. "We gonna take it outside and burn it up. Naw. We can burn it up right here and let it fly all the way to the boulevard where it can fall on them soldiers and burn them up."

"Yeah. Burn 'em up," the other little boy agrees.

"Kites are supposed to be happy," I say more to myself than to the two determined boys.

They ignore my cue. "When I get big I'm gone drive a airplane and I'm gone drop it on them soldiers and set them on fire."

"Why don't you save your pretty kite for a nice day?" I say while I watch Essie move to the door at the end of the tier and watch her knock.

The little boy named Bertram is tempted by my suggestion but only for a second. He is more determined than ever to set the kite on fire and drop it on Whitepeople down below. Even though, right now, there are no Whitepeople down below, they are in his scenario.

"The problem is," I say, "if you set it on fire and throw it over the balcony it's not going to fly far and more than likely it's going to blow back in on somebody on the seventh floor."

"We gonna burn them up too," the other little boy says.

At the end of the tier, the door to Essie's home opens and a thin little girl stands on one foot like a skinny-legged bird. She's got a pleated skirt that looks like an old-fashioned cheerleader's outfit and she's twirling a baton.

Essie hollers my name and I tear myself away from the junior bombardier-arsonists and go where my friend has gone.

"So this is where Essie Witherspoon comes from!" a tiny part of me takes time to marvel as I lay eyes on the bare-walled flat, bare except for a flurry of photos rising from the top of and all behind the TV. The TV top like an altar. There are school photos of the children and party photos of Fredonia and Woodrow Witherspoon and a man Essie calls Mr. Nobody who lived with Miss Fredonia for a time when she and Mr. Woody were broken up. Even though they're divorced now, they're still joined and Essie says her mother tells Mr. Woody the picture stays there as a reminder that he has been replaced. "They waitin in the wings," Essie says her mama says just before the argument begins or ends.

"Maggie, this is my little sister Moneeka. That's a cross between Monica and Monique from Fredonia's French-fried phase. Moneeka, this my friend Maggie. She my roommate at college."

"You go to college too?" the little girl with the baton oohs.

"Where is everybody?" Essie asks.

"They went to jail," Moneeka tosses over her shoulder as she tosses the baton toward the awful concrete ceiling and waits for it to fall into her hands like marvelous good luck she knows is on its way.

"Put that stick down and tell me what happened, Moneeka Fay Witherspoon!" Essie shrieks and snaps at the same time.

The baton slaps into Moneeka's palm. "Ernest got arrested for stealing a ham. And Mama and Daddy Woody went to get him out of jail. Everybody else went over to Auntie Fay's house to stay except for me. I wasn't here when they left so I got left. I was at practice. We going to be in the parade."

"Yeah. Yeh. Yeh," Essie hushes and hurries her at the same time.

"What police station Fredonia them go to?"

"Essie, you know." Moneeka sounds exasperated, and Essie looks at me like if I weren't here she'd have that little girl by her hair and that baton upside her head.

"Martin Luther King dead," Moneeka says. Her voice sounds too old for a nine-year-old girl in a cheerleading outfit, twirling a baton. Her eyes open wide in conspiratorial surprise.

"Just like we didn't know, Moneeka," Essie says.

"When we be in the parade in August we gone be real good for Reverend Doctor Martin Luther King Jr. and for everybody."

Moneeka is so earnest and sweet with her promise a lump jumps in my throat. And I stare around the room while Essie uses the phone. She calls over to her Aunt Fay's. The rest of the children are there.

"No. I wasn't up in that building, ma'am. It was some of the other Black students." Essie looks me dead in the eyes while she's whispering this reassuring lie over the phone to her Aunt Fay. Looking at me while she's doing it is like crossing her fingers, negating the sin.

Moneeka puts her hand on her hip like a little old sassy woman. "Oooh, Essie. You told Auntie Fay a big old story," she says when Essie hangs up the receiver. The door to the apartment opens and a woman in a shiny red wig comes in with a hot chip on her shoulder. She starts with Essie.

"What lie you been tellin?" Fredonia Witherspoon greets her daughter instead of saying hello. "One in jail for stealing, another one want to be a liar. A liar and a thief."

A big hulk of a man comes in the door behind her and she points to him. "Rich man. Poor man. Beggar man. Thief. Doctor. Lawyer. Indian chief. All that shit to choose from and here come a liar, a thief, and a po' man in one household."

So this is the legendary Fredonia. Legend enough to wear a Blackgama mink coat, like one of those women in the magazines that say, "What becomes a legend most." "Money," we say when we turn to that page. Fredonia does not have money. She takes off her well-worn imitation leather jacket and throws it over the back of a kitchen chair. Then she sits down.

She's out of her run-over heels and rubbing the balls of her feet. She squints at Essie. She squints at me. "Light me a cigarette, uh, Moneeka. And don't wet it all up."

Moneeka drops her baton into a chair and gets a cigarette from Fredonia's big purse and lights it at the stove eye. The big man who must be Woody touches Essie on the shoulder, he nods at me, then he goes through a bedroom door and into a deep masculine silence.

Fredonia has her cigarette now. It's dangling out the side of her mouth as she continues to rub her feet.

"Fredonia," Essie starts. "You know I told you about my roommate Magdalena Grace. This is she. She lives not too far from here. We didn't ever see each other before we got to that university though."

Miss Fredonia looks at me. "How are you?" she says. It's not a question. But it's not a flat statement either, because she's not out and out rude. Just in a real bad mood, which from what Essie tells me she been in for the last eighteen years. She's thirty-five years old.

The first time I remember seeing or knowing my mother Caroline she was thirty-five. Young and laughing and pregnant with somebody. I must have been five or six and I was standing up under her elbow while she sat at the kitchen table snapping green beans. The sunlight sprawled all over everything, picking up the freckles in my mama's face, the red highlights still hiding in the black and new gray of her hair. Even the sun was in love with Caroline. I could not be close enough to her.

"Maggie," my mama smiled at me, "how would you like to have a baby sister or brother?" I jumped up and down, shaking the arm that went up and down like a lever when she snapped the green beans. My mama was thirty-five then and she was beginningless, creatrix, matrix who pulled babies out of the ethers of her laughter and kissed a wound to quiet.

Fredonia Witherspoon is thirty-five and she is hard faced, harsh mouthed, panic eyed, and hiding under a wig. An old young woman, jealous as a demon of her daughter's youth, growling like a gargoyle at the gates of Essie's tomorrows.

"You thought I wasn't going to say nothing to you about you being all up in that building, didn't you? You thought I was finished with what all I have to say," the gargoyle growls suddenly, shooting a quick stream of cigarette smoke out of her mouth behind the question. "I ain't forget nothing. I guess if that buzzard hadna kilt King and scared the Whitepeople to death thinking what the niggers going to do, you still be up in that building with them other fools."

"I guess so," Essie says.

"You look intelligent." Miss Fredonia glares at me now as if to say my looks have deceived her.

"If you all want to imprison yourselves you all can bring your black asses down here to these projects and try to live. Take over this shit talking about taking over somebody's building." She's out of the chair and tapping her foot. "That's got to be the stupidest thing I ever heard of." She shakes her head and dips it at the same time, like she's got Parkinson's disease, an aggressive case.

"As a matter of fact, Madame Essie and Maggie, I'm busting loose out of this prison tonight. I am going outside and find me something to laugh about for a change. Do you hear me? I'm laughing. Huh!" She is at the door to a well-stuffed hall closet, pulling out dresses that don't look bad. Dramatic and different. Essie's told me Fredonia is a wonderful seamstress, even if Essie can't sew a lick. Essie's grandmother was always after Fredonia to try to do something for herself with "the gift of her hands." Fredonia makes dresses to party in.

Bathwater is running and I am sitting in the room they call the living room. Let's just say it's a communal existing room. I search for knickknacks of Essie. There she is in a small photo on top of the TV. A little golden girl with two long braids that dive past her shoulder and a nostalgic grin at that age. Nostalgia for something that should have been. This concrete room makes me feel heavy inside. Mrs. Witherspoon is keeping up a steady monologue from the bathroom. About the mayor commanding the police to shoot to kill any looters. About Ernest over her sister's house because she didn't want him back in this building for a while. At least not till curfew was over. About the curfew for everybody under eighteen.

"You better have a good reason to be out or the police will arrest your ass. They lockin up Negroes wholesale," Mrs. Fredonia Witherspoon yells from the bathroom. "Essie, you and your friend can stay here with Moneeka till I get back. Maggie might wanna spend the night. If it's curfew time by the time I get back. Woody, you going to take me on that run?"

Woody mumbles something and all I hear is that old record about curfew time in my head. A song about a boy being out late at night and his mama telling him he'd lost his mind. Breaking curfew is illegal. Like now. Everybody is illegal.

Mama and Madaddy will have a fit if I'm out after curfew over in the Homes while riots keep breaking out and the National Guard goes cruising down the boulevard like the Germans moving into France. Madaddy has held off some because Essie was at our house and so much was going on in the world. Staying out after curfew would be just the thing to set him and Mama off. A real chance to give me the grief they don't know what else to do with.

Nervously I sit in the existing room of Essie's project apartment. Listening to the justly infamous Fredonia Witherspoon screaming through the bubbles in her bath about Moneeka twirling that gotdamn baton in the house and breaking that furniture she's still paying Austin Brothers for. You know the ones. "Austin loves me. Austin loves me. Austin Brothers. Oh, they love me so." "Especially when you paying them incredible interest on that sorry-looking merchandise," Lazarus would say every time that commercial came on.

"Essie, may I use your phone to call home for a minute?" I ask. Wordlessly she brings it to me. I can tell by the screwed shutness of her mouth if she opened it she would cry like a baby. Embarrassed beyond words by her mother. By the simple ugliness of the apartment. The cold furies racing between her and Fredonia embarrass me, as bad as when I'm in the company of Aint Kit and Bay. Moneeka sits hunched in a plastic-wrapped chair, gazing at the television set. People on TV are crying. There is a special on called "Assassination America: Killers of the Dream." They show clips from the assassinations of John F. Kennedy. They mention Medgar Evers. And throw in Malcolm X. Then they end on Dr. King. By this time Fredonia, in bra and half slip, is in the room rubbing deodorant in a fuzzy armpit.

She says, "I wonder who they going to blow away next? These folks ain't playing out there."

She watches me as I dial the number to home. "Essie said I could call home, Mrs. Witherspoon. I hope it's okay."

"Just so long as you ain't from Albuquerque, New Mexico, or somewhere." She's rubbing under the other fuzzy armpit now, heading for the closed door behind which is the stone-quiet Woody.

Anne Perpetua answers the phone and she says Mama's at a memorial mass for Martin Luther King and Madaddy's still at work. "You better get here, Maggie," she orders with the complete authority some little kids think they have before school and stuff knocks that autonomy out of them. "You know you can't be out after no curfew. The mayor going to shoot to kill you."

355

"Tell Mama I'm waiting on a ride," I lie. "Back to school," I lie some more.

"You better not take no building again, Maggie. Madaddy say you gone get it."

"Okay. Okay," I say. Then I hang up.

Anne Perpetua has a nose for news and a mouth for judgment, full of what I better not do. People are always telling her what she better not do. She gives orders in self-defense. To protect her personal authority against a constant barrage of commandments.

Everybody has something "to serve and protect," even if it's just protection against the fact, like posting a sentry at a hurt or a fear. Guarding a wound against scab-picking eyes.

Now I know what Essie tries to hide from some of the most bourgie members in FBO, the ones who talk coolest and stand and walk like jazz musicians past high on music or drugs. Hand and head movements in a kind of syncopated slow motion. Their collegiate vocabularies sequined with *dig, dig up, man, jim, listen here, like hey,* and *shit* (the pronunciation squandered over three syllables, three octaves). The children of the middle class are the most militantly poor. They do a lot of what Miss Rose used to call po' mouthing. Now Miss Rose would shake her head to see the offspring of the new and old Black middle class assuming the dress and elegant musical slouch of the least of our brethren.

Essie is the child of those whose costumes they jump into. But she'd never admit it to too many people. We all know these class games are pretend and the worst thing she could be on campus is who she is.

Essie (I can see this now as she moves around the would-be living room tidying up, then putting empty Budweiser cans in the grocery bags turned garbage bags in the too-tiny kitchen that is not really separate from the so-called living room) must hide these rented stone rooms. Or be assigned here forever by herself.

I can't see a thing out of the big window. It is as if someone has taken black paint and painted impenetrable night over the view. The lights are out on what is called the balcony but is a tier. And the balcony resonates with the heavy patter of gym-shoed children running like swift imps. Names they call one another punctuate the blackened night air. This is a night that has no beginning. This is a night that has no end.

It's all so unnameably sad I begin to shake. I want to do something, something more than sit in the classrooms of Eden in touch with the prolific foliage. I want to do something more than sit in FBO meetings and squabble and plot. I want to do more than break glass and come away with a piecemeal wardrobe, a few pounds of meat, or bottles of Canadian Mist, like the brothers I've seen on TV. I want to do something more than break the lock on the TV repair shop and come out with a black-and-white color set, the picture tubes thick with ghosts. More than a brief Molotov cocktail in the window of a patrol car or jeep, though that would feel good and make a short, hot light.

Given the choices I do not have, I would take all my art supplies—the pure powders of raw pigment, indigo, manganese, umbra, and cobalt blue and cobalt light green—and fling them out over all this gray space. And then say like Reverend Persons in Star of Bethlehem Missionary Baptist Church, "Spring forth! Spring forth!" There would be sweet creation in living color.

But I'm living in Essie's almost living room and Essie is doing everything domestic but sitting. Moneeka has gone to sleep with her baton beside her like a burglar stick. It is her protection and her promise. She's hung her head over the side of the bed, so as not to disturb the new coiffure she's experimented with. Copied from *Seventeen*. The blonde hair in the magazine center parted to

357

hang to the shoulders around a blue-eyed, pink carnation face. Moneeka, like her half-translated, half-made-up name, is too original to accept the unreasonable facsimile of the magazine beauty. But she, just as I and all the others like us, doesn't know this, so she hangs her head out of the bed.

The door to her cell-like bedroom is open and I can see her now. Quiet as a flower. The bedclothes rising and falling with her ever expensive breath as she breathes.

Essie and I are watching TV with the sound turned down real low. The movie is *The Beginning of the End* or *The End of the Beginning* or something. It is about giant grasshoppers coming up from downstate Illinois and attacking Chicago. They climb up skyscrapers and block traffic on Michigan Avenue. Essie says if a giant anything crawled up the side of one of these projects it would be a giant roach. We sit in the dark snickering and listening to the chirp, chirp of the movie-enlarged insects. Outside, there is more to fear.

They try everything on the grasshoppers. Soldiers, just like the ones I saw today on the boulevard come in to contain the bugs with flamethrowers and grenades. They consider using an atomic bomb.

"You think they'd drop a bomb like that on us?" Essie asks.

"Naw, that would really be biting off your nose to spite your face." But I'm not really sure about it. If I were the Vietcong I'd look out. The generals in the monster movies are always in a hurry to dump a bomb on somebody. Just like the blonde women in tight skirts are always turning their ankles in high heels, then lying down screaming waiting for the monster to jump on them.

We are jumpy, Essie and I, and too afraid to try to sleep. Except for the sleep we slept at the Grace house, we've been insomniac or somnambulant ever since we went into the building. Almost afraid to blink, we might miss something.

"Let's call Leona," I suggest. It's late but Leona has her own phone and we know she must be up watching the end of the movie. The scientists have discovered that the grasshoppers may be lured by sound. So they hook up some loud mating music to a high building and trick the bugs into the Chicago River.

"Did you see that?" Leona hollers into the receiver. "You know them bugs wasn't nothing but supposed to be us. Falling for that old loud music!"

When the movie ends, after the man and woman kiss, Leona tells us about her father's store. Things are worse than he thought at first. Nothing can be reclaimed from the wreckage.

"He's real upset," Leona says. "He's mad too, but he's more hurt than anything. He does a lot of good for the community. He really does, but you know." In Pryor Province, a block-long stretch of the City on both sides of the block, is a Laundromat, the original BoneYard restaurant, a funeral home, and a barber college. Or there was a restaurant and Laundromat.

Today Leona went down with her father to his restaurant; they swept up ashes and glass. Waded through a pool of mambo sauce thick as blood. "Remember when that fool threw that mambo sauce on that boy, Hamla's cousin, at Roscoe's?" Leona says.

"I wonder if they burned Roscoe's," Essie says. Her face next to mine on the phone.

Leona says Roscoe was posted at the barbecue house door just like Governor Wallace at the schoolhouse door. He was heavily armed. That's real funny to us. We make fun of everybody because everybody's hurting and we don't know what side we're on. When we can color everything black and white, it's easy.

It's past midnight and Leona is too tired to laugh anymore. She says her father will give us a ride back to school tomorrow, which is today after the sun comes back.

Next, I call home. My father's at work, and my mother's angry with me.

"I'll talk to you when you get home, young lady," she says quietly.

"I can't get home. It's curfew time."

"Why did you stay over in those projects until curfew time, Magdalena?" Unlike my father, my mother knows my name and it doesn't sound so nice now.

I don't answer her question. My mouth is full of tears. Why'd I wait so late to call? I can't think of the lie I told Anne Perpetua earlier.

Mama is short. "Let me see if I can get Honeybabe or Junior or somebody to come get you. You be ready when they get there."

"Bye," we both say like we're sick of talking to each other. Essie doesn't look at me anymore after she looks at me once. I am misery personified, gone my cocky humor and peer-group savoir faire. I blink to empty my eyes. I sit and feel my nose fill up, evicted into childhood by my mother.

Essie looks at TV with no sound.

"What's that smell?" she sniffs.

"I don't smell anything." I try to sound normal, but I sound like I have a cold and a case of hurt feelings.

"It smells like smoke." Essie's got an edge. She's out of her seat. "Something's burning!" she exclaims as she rushes for the door. She yanks it open. Great dragons of smoke gobble up the doorway.

"We have to get out of here!" I'm screaming.

"Moneeka!" Essie shrieks.

"Moneeka!" I shriek. "Maybe we should go out the back."

"Ain't no back door," Moneeka says calmly, wide awake and in the front doorway, smoke billowing around her. Moneeka sweeps the path in front of us with her baton. We ease into the smoke and head for the stairwell.

We're all standing on the ground looking stupid, looking up to where we just came from ten floors up on the building that is not on fire. At least the entire floor wasn't on fire. One apartment was. Bertram and his friend started the fire with that doggone kite. They were testing it out by setting it on fire in the house.

"You know what?" Moneeka shivers a little in the April night air. Her feet are bare. "I'ma kick Bertram's butt with this baton." She brandishes it like a nightstick. "I sure am," she repeats.

Police cars are parked helter-skelter like roaches over honey. The blue lights twirling faster than frantic roach antennae. Static voices blaring from their car radios. If roaches could talk they'd sound like that when they take over a kitchen at night, until you turn the lights out, then they know how to disappear. These police are ready for action. The first smell of smoke is an eleven alarm and they are ready to contain people. Luckily, the fire truck came at first call. And no snipers ambushed them. When I was a little girl I loved firemen best and waved to them as they flew by—heroic and bravura brave, a bunch of red-faced men in deep blue slickers, holding on for dear life to the keening truck. Now I wish firemen harm least of all. Swiftly, they stomped out the flames in the apartment three doors down from Essie's.

The police have Bertram and his buddy and they manhandle the boys. Throwing them this way and that. Until Bertram's mama, I think, yanks him away from them.

"He didn't know what he was doin," she cries. "He didn't know." And to the boy whose eyes have grown to make room for the terror she says, "You didn't know, baby."

"It was an accident," she says. Then panic makes her wise. Her voice is firm and cold when she speaks to the police officer, "I left the iron on. It was my fault. It was an accident."

"Why'd you go through this business of he didn't know? Is the boy culpable or what, lady?" the exasperated policeman asks.

"You got some place to stay tonight?" The neighbor woman touches the mother's shoulder. "Y'all can move in with me. We can double up."

"Now that's a real fire hazard," a policeman scowls. "All you people bunched up like rabbits. Jesus Christ."

Now comes Fredonia, Woody-less, home. She is glum, panic eyed, as she beats a path through the crowd, searching the faces of the children loitering amid the vestiges of the excitement. I can see her, but I don't tell Essie. I watch Fredonia as she spins once, then twice, in the blue twirling of the police car siren lights. It is the dance of the lost she does, half turning this way, then that; she looks like what she is, a mother looking for her lost daughters, fearful that they have been damaged, but she is a daughter too, damaged and young, and her turning is the searching of the lost trying to choose which way to go, trying to find her way home.

When her lost glance falls at last upon Moneeka and Essie she lets out a cry—at once jubilant that what deaths she has feared have not come to pass and regretful about everything. Moneeka and Essie look shyly back at her.

Moneeka says, "Mama, we not burnt up. We smelled the smoke."

It is Moneeka Fredonia snatches into her thin embrace. Essie whose shoulder she grazes with her right hand. I don't want to intrude on this, so I don't follow them as they go back upstairs to sleep in a smoke that lingers and tempts the eyes to tear. I am not Fredonia's daughter. And I will not go with them, even though Essie sends me urgent hand signals to come. I shake my head.

"I'll see you tomorrow," Essie mouths. Then she goes dutifully and a trifle carelessly into the stairwell after her prodigal mother and precocious sister.

More people have already started to move back into the building when Mama and Honeybabe arrive. Honeybabe, driving her little black Volkswagen bug, pulls up beside a police car.

"You can't park that car there, lady," a fireman says. Everybody's in charge.

"I'm meeting somebody," Honeybabe throws a shawl over her shoulders. Mama sits in the little round-headed car. The blue from the police car's light splashes across her face. I walk toward the car a little sheepishly. It's the middle of the night and my mother is displeased with me.

After the Africans Honeybabe and Charlotte used to date graduated and went back to their newly independent nations or went to Texas to make money-mammy with their home-government-paid-for-degrees, after Charlotte was well on her way to giving birth to her baby instead of a modeling career and went to stay with her aunt who sold God from door to door in a magazine that yelled at people to quit sleeping, Honeybabe got together with Cornelius Chestnutt, her eighth-grade sweetheart. They married in spite of his last name and occupation. He was a career soldier with the United States Army.

Honeybabe went with him to serve his country in Germany and France. She saw Paris and Berlin, which Madaddy loved to remember from his days and nights in the Occupation Forces after World War II. Honeybabe was a good army wife who went everywhere her husband went; just like the little lamb Mary had. She didn't go to Vietnam though. He is there now. And she's here waiting. And saving money. They will open a record shop or maybe a hardware store when C.C. (our name for Cornelius) retires at thirty-eight, after twenty years in the service. "Nuts and bolts and music that's all the people need," Honeybabe said C.C. wrote home in a letter.

"Wait'll he find out they have burned down the record shops and the hardware stores. Wonder what he'll say then," Honeybabe said this morning. I think C.C. will leave music alone and go with the steady supply of household and garden needs. He chose a career based on the steady supply of war, didn't he?

We all like C.C., but his business in Vietnam is the cause of a lot of throat clearing around the dinner table. Lazarus, like Stokely Carmichael, has said, "Hell no, we won't go." And C.C. wrote to Honeybabe that he was really hurt by Lazarus's statement that a Blackman in Vietnam is a dead fool. C.C. told Honeybabe he was fighting for the only country he knew. When Honeybabe told Lazarus what her husband said, Lazarus said C.C. ought to try fighting for his life. Everybody is a little hurt and disenchanted with relatives over the whole mess. Mama even thought out loud one time that the service would make a man out of Lazarus, whom she calls Littleson sometimes.

"A dead man," I said, sounding a lot like Lazarus.

We gave up discussing the War and trying to eat at the same table on Sundays too.

Honeybabe's marriage to the army man has given her confidence. She's seen so much of the world she acts like she owns it. It is she who stops Mama from making me cry right here on the street. When Mama opens her mouth, Honeybabe says, "Get on Maggie's case later, Mama. Let's see what's going on with all these police cars." Honey has always been nosy.

Mama doesn't say anything. Just sends waves of disapproval my way. We walk over to the last of the crowd that lingers around Bertram and his mother.

"Wait a minute," Honeybabe mumbles to herself. People move out of her way.

Honeybabe peers with her head going to one side and ducked down at the same time into the darkness that is not all that dark because of the police lights. She retosses her beige shawl over her shoulder and squints.

"Well, I'll be," she croons in that soft amazed tone of our father. "Look, Mama, Maggie, that *is* her." Just like we've argued her down that somebody isn't who she said she is.

"Who?" Mama asks.

"Charlotte. Charlotte Rucker!" The name exclaimed so exultantly Honeybabe both answers Mama's question and causes Charlotte Rucker to turn around so that they can see each other eye to eye.

It is Charlotte. Why hadn't I seen it before, all the time she was negotiating her son's freedom with the policemen? All that while when she'd been lying about who started the fire. Why hadn't I seen the beauty that was once hers in the face of the boy so excited about kites? Looking like Charlotte when she'd been excited about being pretty once.

It hurts to know that there's no real reason why I should have recognized Charlotte Rucker. It is not simply time that has been unkind to her and stripped her yellow skin of its vitality, robbed her brownish hair of its natural luster, and burned it out so around the edges that it looks as bad as that bad blonde wig she used to wear, a replica of the watermelon man's horse's mane. She is still thin, her body bony and her face gaunt. But Twiggy is the rage now, a model no wider than a coin turned sideways, with eyeliner thicker than her thighs. Still Charlotte is too old and too Afro-American. And her thinness is thinner than her frame. From her eyes thin light looks back at Honeybabe, who swoops Charlotte into a well-rounded embrace.

It is not simply time that has been unkind to Charlotte, and it's clear by her brittle reserve that it will take more than the appearance of three females from the promise days of her young and arrogant beauty to bring back the self-adoring bloom that made other people adore her.

She grabs her son by the shoulders and shows him to us. She smiles rather sillily, a smile not unlike her smiles at her private joke in the days when she sat on our couch for hours and did and said nothing but smile and get on our immature and condemnatory nerves.

"This is Bertram, my son," she says. Her voice too hospitable and gay in a fake way. "I made the mistake of telling him go fly a kite."

The joke is lost on Mama and Honeybabe. Honeybabe jumps right in. "Did I hear you right? Do you need a place to stay? Come stay with me, so I won't be lonesome while my man's at war." Honeybabe is gracious enough to make it seem like she's making the invitation because she is in need. "Girl, we got a million things to catch up on."

Charlotte says, "I can show you everything that's happened to me right here." She bumps both Bertram's shoulders with the palms of her hands.

"He's so handsome and intelligent acting," Mama praises. "Isn't he, Maggie?"

"Uh-huh," I say, trying to get back into my mother's good graces.

Bertram and I just look at each other. I don't say a word about the kite, the fire, or killing soldiers. Especially not killing soldiers, in front of Honeybabe. She's sensitive about that. Bertram grins at me—a flash-fire grin charmingly designed to keep me quiet. It is enough.

I'll let him be a little boy again, and maybe his mother will be Charlotte again, instead of this hank of hunger, a silly grin, and hair that looks worse than a wig.

Charlotte's apartment is as big as the living room of our house on Arbor Avenue. For the concrete walls, she had made collages out of magazine ads featuring the top models of the day. A half collage devoted to Naomi Sims. A whole one devoted to Twiggy. Both cardboard treasures trampled on by firemen, then water-logged until the photos pucker on the cardboard, run, and tear.

Charlotte rummages through the wet ashes and scorched ends of clothing and memorabilia; we take what can be saved in egg-shaped hobo bundles. Each of us, Mama, Honeybabe, and me, looks hurt in the face by the fire that has taken everything away. We trek down the stairs with the soggy bundles. We stuff the front trunk of the Volkswagen. Then we stuff ourselves into the miniature car.

By now, too tired to talk, we sit in silence. Each one of us dazed in front of the maps of our own heartbreaks and prayed-for healings. Mama severs the silence with a gentle inanity about it being best to move at night, that way the burglars won't be able to see what you have in your new apartment. Everybody smiles real hard.

After we've pulled away, I must look back. But it's not me who is turned into a pillar of salt. It's each and every one of those buildings. Pillars and pillars of salt. Salt blocks framing the ice babies. A locked ocean of longing and entrapment.

There are no mountains here. The only height achieved through the climbing of dirty stairs.

Bertram is asleep in his mother's arms. I sit next to them in the back, so it's easy for me to see that Charlotte can barely hold herself together, much less the boy. How she trembles, as if each pulse were a low-grade earthquake! Easy for me to see but hard to look at.

A Grace Note

Eden is still Eden, yet apprehensive and guarded when Leona, Essie, and I get back the next day. Strange, I feel as if I have been gone a thousand years, as if a bridge of centuries separates what happened in the Finance Building from a night in the Homes. I don't have much to say to anyone, not even Essie and Leona. I am removed, like a dreamer in sleep.

Because King is dead, White students give us space. The way neighbors offer gifts of memorials and condolences, then avoid the family in grief. Because of the takeover our Blackness has an element of danger. They back away from us. We own the sidewalks. Maureen, with whom I once traded hours at the front desk, she who once shared confidences with me, mumbles greetings and rushes away from me as if her parents have been right all along about Blackness. It is full of terrors.

Even if it is fleeting, for a time Eden is new even as I sleepwalk and we have the power to walk around naming things, including ourselves. We are Black and no one had better ever call us Negro again. We are Blacker than we ever thought we would be. The music of it is heavy in the air like an exotic perfume born in the dark skin. It comes out of us and aromatizes the space.

We should be exuberant because the university has met our demands for Black studies, promised to increase Black faculty and add more Black students. There will be no reprisals against the students who participated in the takeover. But as I walk the campus to classes and look at all the Whiteness around me in sour contrast to the Homes and my neighborhood, where businesses have been burned out and charred wood left in their wake, I don't believe wholeheartedly in the treaty anymore. Treaties have been broken.

One morning I go to the mailboxes and there is a letter for me. It is from the university. I finger the embossed stationery. I have lost the Breton Scholarship. The family that sponsors the award rejected me as a future candidate. I have offended them in some way. I can imagine how. In a place deep inside I rather knew they would take back this prize. Yet they cannot take back my easel. That's what I mumble to myself, "You can't have my easel."

Campuses across the country erupt. Black students, still reeling from the murder in Memphis, seize the moment and take over buildings and make demands in the new way. At Eden we were the forerunners and we offer them encouragement and advice, but something inside some of us says, "Wait and see." There is still Steve Rainey twisting in our eyes, burned hands and pain-tight eyes.

On Blood Island we celebrate the victory in a meeting and ask the unspoken question about Steve Rainey. The upper room is crowded, but not as crowded as before the takeover. People have to catch up on their studies. They are in the library or their dorms, heads deep in the cracks of books. Trying to make the grade. And we are here in the upper room trying to make sense of what happened with Steve Rainey, our casualty. Trixia's voice is strident, "I just want to know if Steve is still in the hospital or is he in jail. What hospital is he in? Can we get some information here?"

"I'm sorry, sister, I can't help you with that," is all Cletus the Elder will say.

"For those of you who want to see a copy of the agreement it is in the common room. It's signed and there for each of you to examine." Christmas offers us something. She has lost an offer of a teaching position. And Lydia Rushing has lost a modeling contract. Her Afro was too big and intimidating for the customer.

In the closed space with not so many people present, Mr. Kool smokes a Kool and gloats. "It was a heavy thing we did," he says. "Very, very heavy."

It was so heavy I can still feel the weight of it. I sleepwalk through the rest of the semester, wishing I were home. It's a wonder Mrs. Sorenson didn't fire me for participating in the takeover. She could not have known my full part in it. Yet she looks at me sternly when I report for work, as if she knows my part in past events. But how could she? She's not so big to me anymore. She who used to give out Biggifying and Belittling Pills in my dreams.

Steve Rainey worries me. I know he is in trouble. It's not like in that happy-ending forties movie when the man is in trouble and a whole lot of people are praying for him, sending up earnest, heartfelt prayers: "Lord, please, help George Bailey." A whole town praying. Only a few of us even mention Steve Rainey after the blowup in the upper room. Perhaps we fear guilt by association. This doesn't stop Leona, Essie, and me from asking, even though Trixia has turned her attention elsewhere. We are loyal, after all. And he is our friend. Which is more than we can say for

William, who is closemouthed and jumpy like a gangster on the lam in a thirties movie. Only worse, because his pain is real and we cannot hate him completely for letting Steve take the blame. But maybe he knows where Steve Rainey is. When we three come into Blood Island and William happens to be there we don't ask him anything. He averts his eyes, especially from Essie. His eyes look weary, as if his nights have been sleepless.

On the way back from Western Civ one morning I make a detour that surprises me. I walk instinctively, without thought, behind the library, past the wishing well, and toward the restless blue-gray lake. I find myself in front of Old Science, which is where I must have been going. Men on scaffolds are painting the nineteenth-century clapboard, two-story house a dazzling white like a sheet. There is no trace of the burning that happened there, that Steve and William did, although no one says they did it, especially not William, who was the agreed-upon silent partner, and Steve's part we hear is only supported by circumstantial evidence. A can of gasoline obtained for a car that ran out of gas while bringing supplies to students in the Finance Building. That's the story.

Old Science has been restored, sacrosanct. In its subbasement scientists still research pigeons and animals. The desecrated skeletons of poor Blackmen and Blackwomen still line the halls and the organs of the poverty-stricken soak in formaldehyde. The memory of tears measured and analyzed hangs in the air. In its rooms scientists enjoy the benefits of government contracts to conduct war research—biological warfare. "Was it worth it, Steve?" I whisper to the wind rising off the lake. My body burns then turns cold as I stand on the walk in front of the old and innocent-looking building. Then I turn and walk fast to Wyndam-Allyn, without looking back, fearful I'll see Steve Rainey at a window of Old Science in my troubled mind's eye.

As spring deepens, the beauty of the grounds does not woo me awake, the breeding grounds of my discontent. The new leaves propagate on the trees, the birds return in variegated, colored feathers and song, and spiders, artistic and discreet, go about their intelligent business in the ivy-covered walls of Wyndam-Allyn and the other stone dorm buildings in the court-yards and thoroughfares of Eden. None of this nudges me to a full wakefulness.

In the time that the pigeons blanketed the sky, my father looked up at them one day as they swept the way between us and heaven. He told me that those pigeons were special because they had been educated. "They served a purpose, Maggie Lena," he told me, calling me out of my name, in his special historical name for me. I already knew the pigeons were homing pigeons, deliv-ering messages across enemy lines, like a pigeon express. "They did more than that," my father said. "They were trained to sit in the bombardier section and line up the hairline sights to drop the bombs. They were educated. Intelligent." Then my father looked at me. His look telling me my mission. Now I do not *feel* special. I do not *feel* educated. And look what happened to those special pigeons.

As I lie unsleeping in the bottom bunk, I am thinking of a painting by Jacob Lawrence, of all the paintings I have seen by Jacob Lawrence, of how the Blackpeople speak on canvas— eloquent, so powerful, muscular, they defy the two dimensions of canvas. I want to capture us in my own way. I have to educate myself. How? I lie on my bottom bunk, making churches with my fingers.

I have heard of something wonderful, a mural on the raw side of an abandoned building in an area slated for urban renewal that never comes. The mural is bright and big with images of *our* heroes: Muhammad Ali (once Cassius Clay); Aretha Franklin, whose voice has colors; historical saints like W. E. B. Du Bois and Marcus Garvey, who wouldn't have stood to be in a room together, together on the wall; a band of musicians in action. More than twenty artists had come together and worked under the watchful, restored eyes of a community gathered around the scaffold. They had received threats, these artists, who called themselves revolutionary, but on they had painted, giving the people's beauty back to them.

Honeybabe sent me a clipping about it from the major White newspaper. She thought I might be interested. I am. My dreams, when I actually sleep, are murals. My life is in my hands, invisible before me. My life is a question like the name of a distant cousin on the tip of my tongue. I think of home as I first knew it.

At first I was a stranger to the house and the house to me. Maybe I was a little girl still used to the deep dark of Mississippi nights with no streetlights, the smell of growing things and the everywhere earth, the open doors and absolute freedom of dancing on dirt outside that house where I was born down south. Anyway, in the North, I was up in the middle of the night, singing, looking out the window into the darkness of time, singing. I remember kneeling on the windowsill like a communicant. Singing. But I don't remember the song.

I roamed the house at night after everybody else had gone to bed. I would not stay down, nestled between two sisters in a full-sized bed with chewing gum stuck between the carvings on the headboard. I'd pull off the wad still dented in places from my sister's teeth and smooth from contact with the wood and put it in my own mouth, while my bossy older sisters slept. (In the morning the gum would be stuck in my plaits and the wild growth of tight hair that wouldn't stay in plaits. Gummy. On my face where I slobbered it out when I, at last, climbed into bed to sleep.)

They called me the Midnight Rambler. Not even Lazarus who was Littleson then, a brother only eighteen months older than me, could get me to fall asleep when he did. He tried. Mama tried everything—lullabies in her sweet, lilting voice, stories that stirred my imagination so I only slept to dream them.

Later, alone, I wandered through the darkness, happily, till my father came home from work just before midnight. When he came, my father picked me up and kissed me. Then he said, "Go to bed." And I would go. Running, while he said my name (what he thought had to be my name) over and over, chuckling to himself, "Maggie Lena, Maggie Lena."

But one night after Madaddy was home, when I was two or three years old and it was two or three in the morning, I got back up and wandered through the house of sleepers. I turned knobs and made music begin. I climbed onto the dining room table and dipped into the sugar bowl, silently supping each icy-sweet granule. I watched the haloes of streetlights through the windows and did not know I wanted paper and paint to reimagine what I saw outside and inside the window. I sat in my mother's rocking chair and conversed with a figure who sat in my father's recliner with her feet up on the footstool. She told me she was tired of walking.

"What you doin?" I asked at two in the morning, at two or three years of age.

"Been calling for my people."

"Where yo people?"

"'Cross Atlantic River. 'Cross cotton. 'Cross all them people crying. Yours is too."

"What they doin? Playin with the fishes?" I heard the river part.

We talked a longer time about things I can't remember. I asked her her name, but she didn't answer. My oldest brother, Sam Jr., did. He stood squinting through the sleep in his eyes.

"Who you talking to, Maggie?"

I, I am told, did not answer. I pointed instead to the chair where the woman with the red scarf tied at her throat sat with her feet up.

"Ain't nobody in that chair," Sam Jr. mumbled as he bent to pick me up. He carried me to my mother and father's room. Mama called him in before he knocked.

"June, you got Maggie?"

"She was sitting up in your chair, Mama, talking to somebody. Only wasn't nobody there." My mother reached out for me. She wore a blue cotton nightgown and her hair was all around her head. She was probably pregnant again. Her stomach all round.

"Who you talkin to, baby?" she whispered. Her breath was like rosemary. Her face was very near mine. It was enchanting like the moon from the window; there was a halo around her, like a picture in one of Sam Jr. and Honeybabe's religion books.

I remember that I whispered back to my mother, because whispering seemed good. "The lady," I answered in a hushed voice that was louder than my normal one.

"What lady?" Mama asked in the same way she would ask Ernestine which bottle she had drunk from when she found her standing on a chair in front of the medicine cabinet.

I yawned and looked at my feet.

"She feet hurt."

"Oh," my mother said, a question and a worry in her tone. "Sam, you go on back to bed."

I kept talking. "Her had on a scarf." Pronounced *scarpf.*

"She did?" Mama was moving her baby belly aside to make room for me.

"It was red." I knew colors and loved knowing them.

"It was?"

"Uh-huh. Her had a red scarpf tied around her neck."

376

"Go to sleep. You were just dreaming a picture, baby."

"Unh-uhhhhhhh!"

"Yes, you were. I'll give you a piece of paper and some Crayola so you can show me tomorrow. Now open your mouth so Mama can see if you got some gum." Satisfied, she whispered. "Go to sleep."

I fumble through finals. I am always thinking in this wake sleep—about Steve Rainey, about Essie, about Leona, about my grandmothers, one living, the other dead. (I wonder what my grandmother Sarah Mahalia Lincoln Dancer would say to me now. What did she say then standing at the foot of my mother's bed or walking down Old Letha Road?) I am thinking about my aunts, one a liar, the other a visionary who works for a better country than this one is now, who works for a dream, about my family, the Graces. Already Eden has begun to recede in reality and the house on Arbor Avenue looms large and welcoming, lucid with color and its nourishments spicy on the tongue. Excitement, like a spirit, surges up in me, hurrying me away from Eden. It is similar to but different from what I felt the day I waited so anxiously to be here in Eden, to begin. I am the traveler who has stayed in a foreign land too long, who is anxious to be home.

On the last day I am packing suitcases and boxes and I catch myself in a sun-startled moment studying my hands, the beautiful, brown strength of them, wondering what I must do with the gift of these hands—draw cartoons as I did for *BloodLines*, sketch or paint at my easel, find other artists to paint murals with, or simply sew glittering dresses to wear on a Saturday night like Fredonia, Essie's desperate mother. I think of her now. Turning every which way in the street that night, and I turn in the room looking to gather pieces of myself. I understand her better. "No more jokes about her," I say to that full-length mirror that hangs on the inside of the door to the closet. "She never had what you have. And if you didn't have it you could invent it."

Blackpeople invent things people need like ironing boards and traffic lights, shoemaking machines. Whitepeople invent the "peculiar institution," Jim Crow, and rocket ships messing up the weather. I think and laugh a little at the Black axiom that sounds like something someone old would say. I am old and I am young. I have been to Eden and back. I am still seventeen and this is still the longest year of my life, longer than the one when I spent the summer in Mimosa and discovered a portion of the mystery of the Graces and the Dancers.

In the dream I had the night before, I knew I was sleeping in my single dorm bed, but I was flying like music just above my head, wrapped in Garvey's colors of red, black, and green. I was Black and joyous. I was flying a few feet above my tender, sleeping body. I marveled in my sleep. I am going home.

The chess game that lasted all school year long is over. Cletus the Elder is the victor over Mr. Kool. Cletus, relaxed and laughing over his victory at the chessboard, was approachable yesterday, so the three of us approached him as he was on his way up the stairs from the basement of Blood Island.

"Congratulations," Leona said, buttering him up.

"We knew you would win," Essie added. She was sincere.

"So did I, Essie," Cletus the Elder said with no arrogance. He was putting arrogant Mr. Kool in check. Then Cletus the Elder looked at Essie, really looked. And we were shocked that he remembered her name in such a particular way. Did he remember too when he carried her when she was a little girl, torn and dazed? He smiled at Essie and she lit up like a little lightning bug, a firefly, enjoying this brief, special recognition. Then he smiled more soberly at me and looked directly at me who hadn't said a word but must have been looking like I was going to ask him something.

"Don't ask me where Rainey is. He doesn't want you to know. Hold tight." Then he picked up his briefcase and headed toward the door, taking the stairs two at a time.

Last night we had a final set on Blood Island, dancing in the basement. They pulled up the Ping-Pong table to make more room to dance to James Brown's "Cold Sweat." They put on "Twine Time" and we called it "Freedom Time." We danced till we sweat, happy to stay out past midnight, relieved that the brothers do not have to carry passes. We promised to memorialize the time we took over the Finance Building by having a Bloods Go Crazy weekend every year. Instead of chanting "Bloods on lockdown. Bloods on lockdown. Bloods locked up," we chanted, "Bloods go crazy. Bloods go crazy. Bloods go free."

I sipped virgin punch and considered Steve Rainey. I guess I looked pensive. Leona and Essie said, "Girl, what's wrong with you? School is out!" Essie's fake happy because she doesn't have to see William and Rhonda together for at least an entire summer. Her eyes are as big as forty-fives, Smokey Robinson's "The Tracks of My Tears," or the Chantells, "Maybe"—"*you'll come back to me.*" "Nothing," I said, "nothing is wrong with me," and smiled like I'm so relieved and glad it's over.

After the dream last night, I awakened happier than I'd been in Eden in a long time. I know that I am leaving. I'd rather not come back.

Now Leona and Essie, getting a ride with Leona's father, have gone on ahead of me. I can see them from our window. They turn and wave, "Bye, Maggie. Talk to you later. Bye, Maggie." I wave back, watching them go down the lane. There is not a pigeon in sight, only the dainty birds of Eden and their dim songs. There were no tearful good-byes from Essie, Leona, or me. We have plans for the summer. Essie and I will work at any job we can find. Leona will go west with her mother, a long vacation. I wish that I could travel by slow, luxurious train and paint the landscape in pastels, setting up my easel at any stop along the way.

I am last to leave because I am working the switchboard, calling all girls to come and rejoin their families or be off into the world. Now the front desk is empty and no one buzzes my younger sisters in as they walk through the open lobby doors and burst like bossy boss ladies into my room to get me.

"Come on, Maggie," Ernestine commands.

"Maggie, Madaddy's waiting. He double-parked," Shirley says.

"Yeah. Yeah. Yeah," I answer, annoyed and happy to see them.

Then my father appears like a genie in a Sunday suit uncorked from a jar. His arms crossed in front of him. "I got a park. Oh-ho-ho. What we got here?" He accepts my kiss on his cheek as he leans down to pick up the heaviest luggage. *I am a Grace and I am leaving this place. Magdalena Grace is leaving Eden.* My sisters grab the rest of my belongings. *Belongings.* I think. *I don't belong here. I belong with them. I am a Grace and I am leaving this place. I am a Grace.* I pick up my heavy easel, my only new acquisition from Eden, and I follow my father and my sisters home.

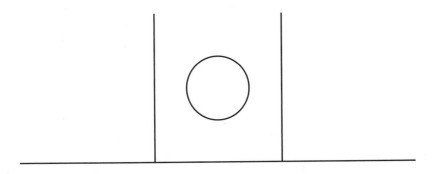

Epiloque

June 1968

Dear Aunt Silence,

I know I am not yet fully grown but all my bones are crumbling like dry stalks of once-living things into a senseless blood. I take my arms and wrap them against me. From my mouth I breathe the scent of wilted flowers. All around me there is a sense of withering. All around me children are dying from the murder of dreams and dreamers.

People I have grown taller with have been cut down. The music of their dust once ran riffs against the cold street corners, shot light across the shattered glass sparkling in the alleyways. All around me pieces of their souls are splattered through the sky. The smell of decayed meats gathers in my garments.

I hear myself talking on the telephone and all the whys in my friends' voices. The answers I think are tangled in the wires with the echoes of all the dreamers who are now my ancestors and I am shaking my head.

I am always opening my mouth and closing it. The taste of my tongue is wineless and tear salted. I could call God a murderer. He would not care. Nothing cares. Aunt Silence, explain. I cannot understand. Cannot tolerate all this dying. All this violence. Shutting doors, shutting dreams and dreamers so abruptly.

What should I do? How do I face the muffled murder in our marrow? The cool thin icing of my brother's blood? What can I call a weapon but my love?

In faith,
Maggie

CREDITS

ABOUT THE AUTHOR

Angela Jackson was born in Greenville, Mississippi, raised on Chicago's South Side, and educated at Northwestern University and the University of Chicago. Her *Dark Legs and Silk Kisses: The Beatitudes of the Spinners*, winner of the 1993 Friends of Literature/Chicago Sun-Times Book of the Year Award in Poetry and the 1994 Carl Sandburg Award for Poetry, and her selected poems, *And All These Roads Be Luminous*, are both published by TriQuarterly Books/Northwestern University Press.